GUNS OF THE VIGILANTES

GUNS OF THE VIGILANTES

WILLIAM W. JOHNSTONE

AND J.A. JOHNSTONE

PINNACLE BOOKS
Kensington Publishing Corp.
www.kensingtonbooks.com

PINNACLE BOOKS are published by

Kensington Publishing Corp.
900 Third Avenue
New York, NY 10022

PUBLISHER'S NOTE: Following the death of William W. Johnstone, the Johnstone family is working with a carefully selected writer to organize and complete Mr. Johnstone's outlines and many unfinished manuscripts to create additional novels in all of his series like The Last Gunfighter, Mountain Man, and Eagles, among others. This novel was inspired by Mr. Johnstone's superb storytelling.

All Kensington titles, imprints, and distributed lines are available at special quantity discounts for bulk purchases for sales promotion, premiums, fund-raising, and educational or institutional use.

Special book excerpts or customized printings can also be created to fit specific needs. For details, write or phone the office of the Kensington Sales Manager: Kensington Publishing Corp., 900 Third Avenue, New York, NY 10022. Attn. Sales Department. Phone: 1-800-221-2647.

PINNACLE BOOKS, the Pinnacle logo, and the WWJ steer head logo Reg. U.S. Pat. & TM Off.

First Printing: August 2021

ISBN-13: 978-0-7860-5117-5
ISBN-13: 978-0-7860-4760-4 (eBook)

10 9 8 7 6 5 4 3 2

Printed in the United States of America

On a bright, clear West Texas morning in the late summer of 1888, when across the prairie blue mistflowers were in bloom and lark buntings sang, lawman and vigilante Dan Caine shot beautiful Susan Stanton right between the eyes.

The killing haunted historians for generations and even London's *Strand Magazine,* of Sherlock Holmes fame, was intrigued enough to publish an article about the incident under the headline, *The Medusa Mystery,* so-called since to look into the woman's face meant death.

But there was no mystery about Susan Stanton's demise. She was said to be a temptress, a witch, the most beautiful and dangerous woman on the frontier, fast with a gun and a demon with a knife, and the tale of her downfall begins, as it inevitably must, with a bloody massacre . . .

In all his born days, old tinpan Fish Lee had never seen the like . . . the entire Calthrop family massacred . . . and it was white men that had done it.

Fish looked around him, wide-eyed, everything sharply delineated by the glaring sun.

Big, laughing Tom Calthrop had been shot several times.

Nancy, his plump, pretty wife, died of knife wounds and unspeakable abuse. Their ten-year-old twins Grace and Rose and sons Jacob, fifteen, and Esau, thirteen, had been shot and Grace, possessed of long, flowing yellow hair, had been scalped. There was no sign of sixteen-year-old Jenny Calthrop, and Fish reckoned she'd been taken.

The family dog, a friendly mutt named Ranger, lay dead in the front yard and only Sadie, the cat, had escaped the slaughter, but now mewing in piteous distress, the little animal twined and untwined itself around Fish's boots like a calico snake.

All the bodies, sprawled in grotesque death poses, lay in the main room of the cabin.

The dusty, white-bearded prospector picked up the cat and held her close in one arm as he looked around him again. Part of the cabin had been scorched by a fire that had burned for a while and then gone out, and the smell of smoke still hung in the air. There was blood everywhere and amidst it all the six Calthrops lay like marble statues. It was a wonder to Fish how still were the dead . . . perfectly unmoving, their open eyes staring into infinity. The china clock on the mantel tick . . . tick . . . ticked . . . dropping small sounds into the cabin with clockwork dedication as though nothing untoward had happened.

The walls closing in on him, Fish Lee pulled down Mrs. Calthrop's skirt so that others would not see her nakedness as he had and then stepped out of the cabin. He lingered on the shady porch for a few moments and then walked into the hot, West Texas sun. The calico cat wanted down and ran back inside, tail up, where the people she loved would no longer make a fuss over her.

Fish lit his pipe and then took a pint bottle of whiskey from his burro's backpack. The little animal turned her head and stared an accusation at him.

"I know, Sophie," he said. "But this is strictly medicinal. I seen things this day that no Christian man should ever see." Around him were the tracks of horses and high-heeled boots, most of them clustered near the well, and Fish figured six or seven horses and riders, though he didn't have enough Injun in him to make an accurate count. Tom Calthrop's bay riding mare still stood in the corral in back of the ranch house, so horse theft was not the raiders' motive. But the cabin had been ransacked, so they'd been after something. But what? Cash money probably . . . what little the family had. Fish took a swig of rye and then another and pondered that answer. He shook his head. Yeah, it was most likely money, but damned if he knew. Going back two decades, Fish Lee visited the Calthrops once or twice a year and was always given a friendly welcome and dinner and a bed for the night. He knew that in recent years with cattle prices low, Tom barely scraped by as a rancher, and money was always tight. He bred good Herefords, but they were few in number because he could no longer buy additional stock and hire punchers to work them. The boys helped and did what they could, but neither of them were really interested in ranching. Fish remembered Nancy telling him, "Jacob and Esau are readers, and readers aren't much help come roundup." At the time, she'd smiled, but he'd seen bittersweet concern in her eyes.

Damn, that had been only a six-month ago. And now the Calthrops were all dead and the young boys being readers and not riders no longer amounted to a hill of beans.

Fish Lee was short and wiry, dressed in worn-out colorless clothes that he'd had for a long time. His battered top hat looked as though someone had stepped on it, a pair of goggles on the brim for protection against blowing sand. He had a shovel in his pack but didn't have the strength to bury six people. He had a Bible but couldn't read the verses, and he had a Henry rifle but no enemy in sight. In other words, as he stood in afternoon sunlight beside his uncaring burro he felt as useless as tits on a boar hog.

"Sophie, we'll head for Thunder Creek and let the law into what's happened here," he said. "Sheriff Chance Hurd will know what to do." He read doubt in the burro's dark eyes and said, "He will. You'll see."

After one last, lingering look at the cabin where shadows angled across the porch where the ollas hung, Fish shook his head and said, "Oh dear Lord in Heaven, what a terrible business."

He then led Sophie west toward town, walking through the bright light of day under the flawless blue arch of the Texas sky.

CHAPTER ONE

"I send you out to investigate a murder and you bring me back a cat," Sheriff Chance Hurd said.

"With all the rats we get in here, we need a cat," Deputy Sheriff Dan Caine said.

"Rodent or human?"

"Both, but mainly rodent. I saw one in the cell the other day that if you whittled down to middlin' size would still be as big as a hound dog."

"Well, I guess the cat is kinda cute at that," Hurd said, eyeing the calico that sat on his desk and studied him with fixed, glowing attention. The lawman sighed. "You feed it. Now, put the Kiowa back in his cell and make your report. The coffee is on the bile."

"We'll need the Kiowa when we go after Jenny Calthrop and the men who murdered her family," Caine said.

"The Indian is a drunk," Hurd said.

"Drunk or sober, he can follow a cold trail best I ever seen," Caine said.

"Dan, we ain't following no trails, cold or otherwise," Hurd said. He was a big man with a comfortably round belly and heavy bags under expressive, and cold blue eyes that gave him a basilisk stare. He pointed a thick forefinger at his deputy. "We're city. The Calthrop spread is Concho County and always was."

Hurd's chair scraped across the jailhouse's rough pine floor as he rose and stepped to the stove. He took a couple of cups down from a shelf and poured steaming coffee into both. He handed one to Caine. "Fish says seven riders."

"He thinks there were that many. He isn't sure," Caine said. "I saw the tracks, and I'm not sure either."

"What did the Kiowa say?"

"He says seven, maybe eight."

"Too many," Hurd said.

"The Kiowa says that judging by her tracks, one of them was a woman, but I'm not sure of that either. But I read a dodger that said Clay Kyle runs with a woman," Caine said.

"Black-Eyed Susan. Yeah, I know," Hurd said. "She's named for the prairie wildflower, or so they say. And she kills like a teased rattlesnake. I heard that too. But it wasn't Clay Kyle done this crime. Get that out of your head. It's too far west for him."

"No matter. The sooner we form a posse the better," Caine said. "So why the hell are we sitting here drinking coffee?"

"Like I said, we're not going after them killers," Hurd snapped. "And, like I already told you, it ain't Clay Kyle an' them, because he never, and I say never, rides west of the Brazos. Everybody knows that."

"That's not what old Fish Lee thinks," Dan said. "Fish gets around, he talks to people, some of them lawmen and Rangers. He says there's stories about a crazy man by the name of Loco Garrett who scalps women with long, blonde hair. He makes a pastime of it, you might say, and there's a ten-thousand-dollar price on his head, dead or alive. Grace Calthrop was scalped . . . and Garrett runs with Clay Kyle."

"There's plenty of big windies told about Clay Kyle and

his boys," Hurd said. "Don't believe all you hear." The sheriff studied Dan Caine for a few moments and then said, "The county sheriff is living up Paint Rock way and I already sent him a wire. It's his responsibility. Me and you, we got enough to contend with when the punchers come in on Friday nights." He smiled. "Fright night, I call it."

"Lucas Ward is nearly seventy years old," Caine said. "He delivers warrants during the day and at night pulls padlocks on locked store doors. He's not about to ride out after seven killers on a chase that could last weeks."

"And that's exactly why we're staying put," Hurd said. "If you and me was away from Main Street for weeks, Thunder Creek would become a wide-open town, and wide-open towns attract outlaws, gunmen, gamblers, fancy women, and all kinds of rannies on the make. The damned burg would fall into lawlessness and come apart at the seams."

The sheriff's statement was so absurd, so palpably false, that Caine smiled, his teeth white under his sweeping dragoon moustache. "Chance, look out the window, what do you see?"

"A town," Hurd said. He was an inch taller than Caine's lanky six feet, a heavy, joyless man with rough-cut black hair, long sideburns that flanked a spade-shaped beard, and a nose that had been broken several times, a relic of his wild, outlaw youth. He dressed like a respectable law clerk in a charcoal gray ditto suit and a wing collared shirt and blue tie. But he had none of a clerk's sallowness, his weathered face being as dark and coppery as that of a Cheyenne dog soldier. On those few social occasions when he had to deal with out-of-town rowdies, he wore twin Colts carried in crossed gunbelts. It was not an affectation, but the mark of a shootist, a man to be reckoned with.

"Look at Main Street," Caine said, turning in his chair to

glance out the fly-specked window. "Three fair-sized frame houses, built in a rickety hodgepodge style, but painted white and shaded by wild oaks. The houses are surrounded by outbuildings and behind them two dozen tarpaper shacks that could fold up and blow away in a good wind. There's Doan's General Store that doubles as a saloon. Ma Lester's Guest House and Restaurant for Respectable Christian Gentlemen, and Mike Sweet's blacksmith shop with its steam hammer that he claims is the eighth wonder of the world. What else? Oh yeah, a rotting church with a spire and a cross on top but no preacher, a livery barn and corral, and a windmill with iron blades bitten into by rust. And all of this overlooking a scrubby, gravelly street throwing off clouds of dust that gets into everything. Oh, I forgot the Patterson stage that brings the mail. It visits once a month . . . if we're lucky."

Caine swung back and stared at Hurd. "After the law rides out of town, do you really think all those gunmen, outlaws, gamblers, and fancy women of yours are going to beat their feet in the direction of Thunder Creek, population ninety-seven? Hell, Chance, even the town's name is a lie. It seldom thunders here, there ain't even a creek, and half the folks are as poor as lizard-eating cats."

"Poor but proud. There's enough money out there to pay your twenty-a-month," Hurd said.

"That's three months in arrears," Caine said. He waited to let that sink in, and then said, "Did I tell you about Nancy Calthrop's wedding ring?"

Hurd rose, poured himself more coffee, and sat again. "No, you didn't."

"She was very proud of it. Showed it to me one time. She said it was a rose color made from a nugget of Black Hills gold that Tom bought from a Sioux Indian one time and inside the band it said "*forever*."

"I'm glad she liked it . . . it being a wedding ring that was rose gold and said forever and all," Hurd said.

"Somebody cut off Nancy's finger to get that ring, and I bet right now he's wearing it," Caine said.

"Why are you telling me this?" Hurd said.

"Because I want to go after the feller who's wearing that ring and hang him," Caine said. "And I want the animal that scalped Grace Calthrop. And I want to rescue her sister Jenny. And, Chance. I want you to authorize a posse and I want you to do it right now. Time is a-wasting."

Chance Hurd sat in silence and studied the younger man. Caine was in his early thirties. He was a good-looking man with jet black hair and eyebrows that were slightly too heavy for his lean face. He had a wide, expressive mouth and good teeth, and women, respectable and otherwise, liked him just fine. Dan Caine looked a man right in the eye, holding nothing back, and most times he had a stillness about him, a calm, but of the uncertain sort that had the brooding potential to suddenly burst into a moment of hellfire action. He seldom talked about himself, but Hurd knew that the young man had served three years in Huntsville for an attempted train robbery. He'd spent the first four months of his sentence in the penitentiary's infirmary for a bullet wound to the chest he'd taken during the hold-up. At some point during that time, probably in the spring of 1880 according to most historians, he was befriended by John Wesley Hardin. Prison life had tempered Hardin's wild ways and Wes convinced the young Caine to quit the outlaw trail and live by the law. Released early in the summer of 1882, Dan Caine drifted for a couple of years, doing whatever work he could find. He arrived in Montana in January 1884, the year the citizenry, irritated by the amount of crime in the Territory, appointed hundreds of vigilantes to enforce the law. Hard-eyed hemp posses dutifully strung up thirty-five cattle and horse thieves and an even dozen of just plain nuisances. Dan didn't think Montana a good place to loiter, and in the fall of 1885, owning only his horse, saddle, rifle, Colt revolver, and the clothes he stood up in, he rode into Thunder Creek, missing his last six meals. Chance Hurd liked the tough, confident look of the young man and gave him a job as a twenty-a-month deputy sheriff. Caine made no secret of his past, but, having ridden the owlhoot trail himself a time or three, Hurd was willing to let bygones be bygones. That was three years ago, and now it looked as though their association was about to come to an end.

"Dan, you're willing to go this alone, I can tell," Hurd said. "Why?"

"Because I liked the Calthrops," Caine said. "They were good people, kind, generous people, full of laughter and of life and the living of it. They didn't deserve to be slaughtered the way they were and their oldest daughter taken. Now they lie in cold graves, all of them, and their killers run free, warm in the sunshine."

"How the hell are you going to find a posse in Thunder Creek?" Hurd said. "You think about that?"

"Holt Peters and Frank Halder helped me bury the dead," Caine said. "They're willing to ride after the killers."

Hurd made a strange, exasperated sound in his throat, then, "Peters is an orphan stock boy at the general store and Halder is a momma's brat who wears spectacles because he can't see worth a damn. As far as I know, neither of them have shot a gun in their lives." The sheriff smiled. "That's two. Go on . . ."

"Fish Lee says he'll go if he can find a horse," Caine said.

"An old man with the rheumatisms who's half crazy with the gold fever," Hurd said. "That's three. Go on . . ."

Caine glanced at the railroad clock on the wall. "It's gone two-thirty. Clint Cooley will be getting out of bed soon. He owes me a favor or two."

"A washed-up gambler who drinks too much and is trying to outrun a losing streak," Hurd said. "He's in Thunder Creek because his back is to the wall, and he has nowhere else to run. Maybe that's four, maybe it's not. Go on . . ."

"Cooley is good with a gun," Caine said. "That's a point in his favor."

"Sure, because he carries them fancy foreign revolvers; we heard that he's been in a dozen shooting scrapes and killed five men," Hurd said. "Only problem with that is that nobody can say where and when the killings happened. Me, I don't think he's gunned anybody. He just ain't the type."

Caine didn't push it. Cooley was a man with his own dark secrets, and he'd never heard of him boast of killings. Wild talk always grew around lonely, unforthcoming men and meant nothing. This much Dan Caine did know . . . the ivory-handled, .44 caliber British Bulldog revolvers the gambler carried in a twin shoulder holster were worn from use. But how and when he'd used the pistols was a matter for speculation, as Hurd had just noted.

"The Kiowa makes five," Caine said. "Yeah, I know he's a drunk, and we believe he's the one who killed Lem Jones behind the saloon that time, but he's a tracker."

"I never could pin that shooting on the Kiowa," Hurd said. "It doesn't take much evidence to hang an Indian, but it was like good ol' Lem was shot by a damned ghost. No tracks, nothing."

Caine smiled. "Now he is dead, he's good ol' Lem. When he was alive, he was a mean, sorry, wife-beating excuse for a man. He needed killing and hell, I sometimes took the notion to gun him myself."

The sheriff sighed. "Lem cheated at cards and he was hell on blacks and Indians. Hated them both." Then, "All right, round up your posse, Dan, but leave your badge right there on the desk. You ain't going after them killers as a deputy sheriff of Thunder Creek."

"Why?"

"Because what you're doing is not authorized. Now put the badge on the desk like I said."

Caine removed the nickel silver shield from his dark blue shirtfront and laid it in front of Hurd. "Now what am I?" he said.

"Now what are you? As of this moment, Dan, you're no longer a lawman but a vigilante . . . and until a few minutes ago I'd have thought that as likely as hearing the word love in a Wichita whorehouse. A man can sure be wrong about some things, huh?"

Caine stepped across the floor to a shelf that held a number of Texas law books, three novels by Mr. Dickens, an unthumbed Bible, and two quarto volumes of *Webster's Dictionary of the English Language,* the late property of a preacher who'd taken over the church and died a week later of apoplexy.

Caine flicked his way through the pages until he reached V, flicked some more, and then said, "Vigilante. It says what I am right here."

"Read it."

"'A member of a self-appointed group of citizens who undertake law enforcement in their community without legal authority,'" Caine said. He paused and then said, "This part is important because it explains why folks like me do what we do. It says here, 'without legal authority'"—then louder—"'typically because the legal agencies are thought to be inadequate.'"

Hurd nodded. "Now you know what you are and what I am." He picked up the badge, opened his desk drawer, dropped it inside, and then slammed the drawer shut. "Good luck, Mr. Caine," he said. "And thanks for the cat."

CHAPTER TWO

"Damn you, Caine! You make a habit of waking a man at the crack of dawn?" Clint Cooley yelled from behind the closed door of his cabin.

"It's almost three in the afternoon, Clint," Dan Caine said.

"Like I said, the crack of dawn," Cooley said. "I should come out there and shoot you down like a mad dog . . . like a . . . a rabid wolf."

"I need you, Clint," Caine said. "Big doings coming down."

"Then why the hell do you need me, lawman? Speak, thou apparition."

"Tom Calthrop is dead, murdered, him and his whole family, and young Jenny's been took," Caine said. "And as of a few minutes ago I'm no longer a lawman."

A long pause and Cooley said, "How do you know about the Calthrops?"

"Because I buried them today," Caine said.

A bolt slammed open and a tall, well-built man, dressed only in his underwear, stood framed in the doorway. "I knew Tom Calthrop, and I liked him," Cooley said. "What do you want from me, Dan?"

"Ride with me. Help me find his killers."

"What about Hurd?"

"He won't leave Thunder Creek."

"He's afraid of his damned shadow. He has the back-bone of a maggot."

Caine let that pass without comment and said, "Ten minutes, Clint. Don't wear your fancy dressed-up-for-the-poker-tables-in-New-Orleans duds. It could be a rough trail."

The gambler eyed Caine from scuffed boots to battered hat, taking in his canvas pants, blue shirt, army suspenders, and the washed-out red bandana tied loosely around his neck, a blue Colt in its holster worn high, horseman style.

"Dan Caine, when I want sartorial advice from you, and that will be never, I'll ask for it," Cooley said. "Now bring me a cup of coffee, will you?" He glanced at the blue sky and shook his head. "My God . . . the crack of dawn."

"Not for the Calthrops," Caine said.

"No," Cooley said, his handsome face suddenly serious. "Not for the Calthrops."

Dan Caine walked from Cooley's shack in the direction of the general store, smiled, and touched his hat to the local belle, Estella Sweet, the blacksmith's daughter. She was seventeen years old that year, a slender, elegant girl with wavy blonde hair that fell over her shoulders in a golden cascade. Some said, out of her father's hearing, that it was high time she was wedded and bedded, but Estella showed no inclination to partake of holy matrimony or of mattress time either. It should be mentioned here, because historians of the more sensational kind always draw attention to it, that the girl had prodigiously large breasts. But she bore them proudly, her scarlet, front-laced corset jutting aggressively ahead of her like the figurehead on a man o' war.

Under the corset Estella wore a light gray shirt in a railroad stripe, and a front-bustled skirt of the same color fell to the top of her high-heeled ankle boots. She wore a flat-brimmed, high-crowned hat, and her blue eyes were protected from the sun by a pair of round dark glasses with a brass frame. Around her neck, poised above her cleavage, hung a small silver pocket watch with a white face and black Roman numerals.

For the cowboys who came into town on Friday nights Estella was one of the sights to see. But it was very much lookee but no touchee, because blacksmith Mike Sweet was a powerfully strong man, hard, dangerous, and profane, very protective of his pretty daughter, and with no great liking for the cattlemen who provided 90 percent of his livelihood.

With an outstretched hand, Estella stopped Dan and said, "Holt Peters over to the general store told me about the Calthrops. Dan, who could've done such a terrible thing?"

"I don't know, Estella," Caine said, seeing a distorted version of himself in the girl's dark glasses. "It might have been a man called Clay Kyle and his boys, but that's far from sure. I aim to find out."

"You and Sheriff Hurd are going after them . . . the killers I mean," the girl said.

"I'm going after them," Dan said. "Sheriff Hurd doesn't want to leave the town without a lawman. Don't worry, I'll bring Jenny Calthrop back safe and sound."

"Jenny's been my friend since, well, forever . . . since we were both children," Estella said. She smiled. "And I never minded it a bit when folks said she was the prettiest girl in Concho County."

Dan grinned and said, "When it comes down to who's the prettiest gal between you and Jenny, I'd say it's a tie. You're both as pretty as a field of bluebonnets."

Estella's uncertain smile slowly faded. "Find her, Dan. Bring her home."

Dan said, "Clint Cooley, Holt Peters, and Frank Halder have all volunteered to join my posse. And maybe old Fish Lee if he can rustle up a horse. Oh, and the Kiowa."

Estella frowned as though she was about to say something, changed her mind, and said, "Then do be careful, Dan. And make sure Frank Halder remembers to wear his spectacles. He forgets them all the time."

Dan Caine's answer to that was a smile and a nod, but Estella Sweet wasn't quite done with him. "You could always get some cowboys to join you," she said. "The ranchers hereabouts set store by Tom Calthrop."

"I thought about it, but the fall gather is coming up, and the ranchers want their punchers to stick close to the home range. Besides, I don't have time. We're pulling out now while there's still a few hours of daylight. The Kiowa can track in the dark, but he's not keen on it."

"Then good luck, Dan," the girl said. She laid a slim hand on Dan's shoulder. "I think you're going to need it."

Holt Peters, an orphaned boy around sixteen years of age, and Frank Halder, short, fat, and myopic, were in Doan's General Store when Dan Caine stepped inside.

"Howdy, Dan," said Pete Doan, a middle-aged man with sunken cheeks, hollow temples, and gray eyes tired out from constant pain. "Sheriff Hurd raising his posse to run down those killers?"

"Not Hurd, just me," Dan said. He answered the question on Doan's face. "Somebody has to stay in town and look after things."

"Is that so?" the storekeeper said, not liking what he'd

just heard. "I'm the mayor of this burg, and I say there isn't much to look after in Thunder Creek."

"Sheriff Hurd doesn't see it that way," Dan said. Then, "Holt and Frank, you listen up. I'm no longer a deputy, so this posse isn't legal. Sheriff Hurd says I'm a vigilante, and I guess that applies to anybody who rides with me."

"I'll stick, Mr. Caine," said Holt Peters, a tall, good-looking boy, a blue-eyed towhead who'd outgrown all his duds and was wearing Pete Doan's threadbare castoffs.

"Me too," Halder said, blinking behind his spectacles like a plump owl. He was a year older than Peters and a head shorter.

Doan looked skeptically at Dan. "Who else have you got?"

"So far, Clint Cooley and the Kiowa."

"That's it?"

"So far."

"What do you mean, so far? Where are you going to get anybody else?"

Dan Caine smiled. "How about you, Pete?"

Doan took the question in stride. "I've got a cancer growing inside me, and I haven't sat a horse in twenty years. All I'd do is slow you up."

"Pity. I'd sure like to have along a man who fought Apaches back when."

"When I was a Ranger, I fit the Comanche, not Apaches," Doan said. "It was a long time ago and something I wouldn't want to do ever again."

Dan nodded. "I can understand that."

"I reckon you'll understand it better if you catch up to the killers who massacred the Calthrop family," Doan said. "A sight of my bad experiences were written in blood and lead." His eyes opened and closed several times as though blinking away remembered images, then he said, "I've loaned each of these two . . . vigilantes . . . a .32-20 Winchester and a box of shells each. The rifles are old, but they still shoot. What else do you need? Supplies? You'll need supplies."

"Yeah, I do, but I'm a little short of the ready at the moment," Dan said. "I'll need to talk to you about that."

Doan, a normally sour man, managed a thin smile. "Coffee, cornmeal, dried apples, bacon, and a pan to fry it in. Tobacco? You got tobacco?"

"Truth is, I'm kinda low on the makings," Dan said.

"And tobacco. I'll sack up the stuff, and you can pay me when you get back," Doan said. "Bring back Jenny Calthrop, and you don't have to pay anything at all."

"And a cup of coffee for Clint Cooley," Dan said. "Add it to my bill, Pete."

"Coffee is on the house," Doan said. "The pot's on the stove."

CHAPTER THREE

Sheriff Chance Hurd stood at his office window and smiled as he watched the little drama playing out in the street that unraveled part of Dan Caine's plan.

It seemed that the widow Halder did not want her son to be a vigilante.

The woman, tall, gray-haired, and plump with long and strong arms, dragged young Frank from the saddle of the family nag and took hold of the reins of the horse in one hand, her son's ear in the other. Even behind glass panes and at a distance, Hurd heard her yell at Caine, "Be damned to you! I lost one son to war; I won't lose another to outlaws."

The widow stomped away toward her shack, leading the horse. Her tormented son bent his head, favoring the ear clamped in his parent's strong thumb and forefinger, and stumbled along, yelping, "Ow! Ow! Ow!" at every step.

Hurd saw Clint Cooley open his mouth and say something, but couldn't hear what he said, but the gambler didn't look happy.

"Caine, what the hell?" Cooley said. "Now there's only three of us and the Indian . . . and you can't depend on him in a white man's fight."

Dan Caine drew rein and stared at the gambler. Astride a big American stud with four white stockings and blaze, Cooley rode tall in the saddle, his head held proudly like a bronze Confederate general on a pedestal in a town square. The man had left behind his usual frockcoat, but he'd retained some of his finery, a snow-white shirt with a frilled front . . . washed by the Chinese woman who had drifted into town a year before . . . tan, knee-patch breeches tucked into English riding boots, and a wide-brimmed Panama hat. Cooley's British Bulldog revolvers resided in their shoulder holster and he carried a .44-40 Winchester in a canvas scabbard with leather fittings under his right knee. The gambler rode a three-hundred-dollar horse, and his saddle and bridle were decorated with silver and spoke of the highest quality. Like Dan, he wore an ankle-length canvas duster.

Dan knew that Clint Cooley's luck had deserted him, and he'd fallen on hard times. But in a different time and place it was obvious that he'd rubbed shoulders with sporting gentlemen of breeding, courted sophisticated, elegant women, and enjoyed a way of life far, far removed from the dust and grime and poverty of Thunder Creek.

"Clint, I saw what happened to the Calthrops, and I'll never forget it," Dan said. "I'll follow their murderers to hell if I have to."

Cooley smiled and said to Holt Peters, "What about you, boy? Will you stick all the way to hell and back?"

"I reckon," Peters said. He was tall and skinny, dressed in hand-me-downs, shoes, pants, shirt, and a shapeless hat. He sat Pete Doan's second-best horse, a hammer-headed, mouse-colored mustang with an evil disposition. The animal probably didn't go eight hundred pounds. The boy carried the on-loan .32-20 Winchester across the pommel of a saddle repaired with twine and rawhide, and he had shells for the rifle and a bait of trail grub in a sack. A bedroll was tied behind the cantle and a canteen hung from the saddle horn. All in all, the kid was a little baby-faced and nobody's idea of a fighting man.

"You know you could get your fool head blown off," Cooley said.

"Maybe," Peters said. "But I'll take my chances. Even hell must be better than wearing an apron and stacking cans of beans on shelves all day, every day."

Cooley stared hard at Peters for a long moment, then said, "Yes, I guess it is, kid. I guess it is."

"What about you, Clint?" Dan said. "You know what we're facing. Will you stick it out to the end?"

The gambler shrugged. "I reckon. Even hell is better than trying to buck a stacked deck all night, every night. It wears on a man like a nagging wife."

Dan smiled. "Then let's ride."

"Hold up there!"

The yell came from behind him, and Caine drew rein and turned his horse in that direction. Fish Lee trotted toward him, bouncing in the saddle of a rental buckskin with a rough gait and a mouth like iron. Fish drew rein, something that took considerable sawing on the bit, and said, "Well, what are we? Are we a legally constituted posse or vigilantes like everybody says, including the sheriff?"

"Fish, we're vigilantes," Cooley said. He smiled. "Or what passes for vigilantes in Thunder Creek."

"We're thin on the ground sure enough," Fish said. He looked at Holt Peters. "How you doin' boy?" he said. "I declare, you're growing like a weed."

"I'm just fine, Mr. Lee," the kid said. "I'm glad to get away from the bean cans."

Fish nodded. "Glad to hear it." He shifted his attention to Dan Caine. "Professor Latchford come into town. He told me a message for you, Deputy. It will come as good news maybe."

"Crazy Lazarus? Miss Prunella still with him?" Cooley said.

"Yeah, she is. She hasn't growed any. Still only ankle high to a June bug."

"What's the message, Fish?" Caine said, impatient and only half interested.

"The professor says if he and Miss Prunella can catch a north wind they'll come after you and . . . and what did he say? Oh yeah, they'll give you eth . . . ether . . ."

"Ethereal?" Clint Cooley said.

Fish broke into a wide grin and slapped his thigh. "Yeah, that's the word . . . eth . . . eth . . ." He shook his head. "What you said, gambling man."

Caine frowned, his eyebrows drawing together. "What the hell does ethereal mean?"

"One meaning is delicate and light, but coming from Professor Latchford, it probably means heavenly," Cooley said. "He's full of highfalutin notions like that. Told me he plans to ride his balloon to the moon one day if he can catch a favorable wind."

"Ha!" Fish Lee said. "That's impossible. I bet it would take a six-month at least and he couldn't carry enough supplies for a trip there and back."

"Unless there's apple trees on the moon," Cooley said.

"And pigs for bacon," Fish said.

"The professor ain't playing with a full deck," Caine said, irritated. "The killers we're chasing are down here." He pointed to the sky. "Not up there."

"Well, all I done was give you the message," Fish said. He looked like a man who'd been wronged.

* * *

A rider on a spotted Palouse appeared through the heat shimmer and rode parallel to the vigilantes for a quarter mile before joining Dan Caine and the others. It was almost impossible to read the Kiowa's face, but the man didn't seem impressed by what he saw. Without any kind of greeting the Indian said, "The Apaches are out, Mescalero and Chiricahua."

Dan felt a stab of concern. "How do you know this?" he said.

"After you left, an army sergeant rode into town and read an order from General Crook. The soldier said twenty, maybe thirty young bucks broke out of the San Carlos and that there were no Apaches left in the reservation but women and children and old men. Then he said to Sheriff Hurd, 'The general said that all settlements west of the Colorado must see to their own defenses'"—the Kiowa stopped, recalling the sergeant's words—"'for the foreseeable future.'" And then the sergeant said, 'General Crook says in this trying time we must strive to have faith that everything will work out for the best.' Then the soldier saluted and rode away."

"Hell, when it comes to Apaches, I don't have any kind of faith," Cooley said to Dan. "Do you?"

"Hell no," Dan said. "Twenty or thirty Apaches are an army."

The Kiowa made a sound in his throat, swung his horse around, and rode ahead a hundred yards to take the point.

"Right sociable feller, that Kiowa," Fish Lee said.

Clint Cooley's gaze was fixed on the Indian. "He's a dangerous man," he said. "Maybe one of the most dangerous men in Texas. I'm glad he's with us. He'll help even up the odds."

"If we catch up to Clay Kyle and them, the Kiowa

won't fight," Fish Lee said. "He'll take no part in a white man's war."

The day was still hot, but color had faded from the blue arch of the sky, and the distant horizon had lost its heat shimmer. Around the riders stretched an infinity of grass, rolling country with deep slopes and benches, and here and there sturdy sentinels of wild and post oak, juniper, and mesquite. There was no sound, only the creak of saddle leather and the steady fall of the horses' hooves.

"The Kiowa killed Lem Jones, but it could never be proved," Caine said.

"Yeah, I know," Cooley said. "He beat me to it."

"Killing Jones don't make the Injun a fast gun," Fish Lee said. "I don't want to talk ill of the dead, but Lem Jones was a no-good wife beater who couldn't hold his whiskey. Everybody knew that."

Dan Caine's eyes were on the trail ahead. "Jones wore a gun and he was no bargain," he said.

"Maybe, but he didn't have a gun reputation," Fish said.

"True. But how many men in Thunder Creek do?" Dan said. He turned to Cooley. "None, except maybe you, Clint?"

Cooley shook his head. "I'd say Chance Hurd is a shootist. But not me. I never chased a gun rep. Damn good way to get yourself killed. No matter how fast you are, there's always somebody faster."

Dan feigned deep thought, then said, "Well, now I've studied on it, to my certain knowledge the Kiowa has gunned six men, Jones and five others. And one of those men was Bretton Idle, and that's a natural fact."

"Bretton Idle, the Laredo shootist? Not a chance," Fish said. "Dan, we talkin' about the same Bretton Idle? I mean him that ran with Sam Bass an' them for a spell but dropped out of the gang afore Sam was killed by the law in the summer of '78."

"There's only one Brett Idle," Cooley said. "He was a named gunman in Texas for years. Killed eleven men, they say. The real figure is probably less, but Idle is mighty quick on the draw and shoot, that's for certain."

"Was quick on the draw," Caine said. "The Kiowa killed him, remember. I heard that from a Texas Ranger and the man had no reason to tell me a big windy."

"Was Idle faster than you, Mr. Cooley?" Holt Peters said, his young face alight, a boy fascinated by the glamour of guns and gunmen, asking a boy's question.

"Am I fast?" the gambler said.

"Yes," the boy said. Eager.

"No, I'm not fast. Way back when, I always took my time."

Holt looked disappointed.

"But then . . . I only needed to shoot once," Cooley said.

The boy smiled, his opinion of Cooley restored. "How many men have you killed, Mr. Cooley?"

"Too many," Cooley said. "I think that's why my luck turned bad."

"Ghosts?" Fish Lee said.

The gambler smiled. "No, much worse . . . dreams."

"Bad dreams?" Fish Lee said.

"Yeah. The kind that wake a man in the middle of the night and make him cry out in fear and reach for his gun." Cooley shook his head. "As though he could get rid of a nightmare with a bullet."

"Kiowa coming in, Dan," Fish said suddenly, his eyes reaching into the distance. "And it looks like he's in no hurry." He peered at the rider. "Nope, he ain't flapping his chaps. Must be no sign of Kyle." He smiled. "If it really is Clay Kyle we're following."

CHAPTER FOUR

Sheriff Chance Hurd was a worried man. He should've heard from Clay Kyle by now. What the hell was keeping the man? The Apaches? The savages had never stopped him before.

It was evident that something had gone badly wrong at the Calthrop place, an eventuality that Hurd had not anticipated.

Damn it, Kyle had killed them all, the whole family, except for young Jenny. He had taken her with him, and the why of that was pretty obvious. Hurd reckoned that Clay planned to make the girl his whore for a spell, and then sell what was left of her in Old Mexico. Hell, that was only good business.

Hurd sipped raw-edged bourbon and stared out his office window at the white-painted houses across the street. A ragged coyote trotted between Pete Doan's house and Ma Lester's stick-style boardinghouse, every external vertical or slanted surface and archway decorated with fanciful, hand-carved latticework. It was an overly ornate dwelling, done on the cheap, and Hurd hated it. Every mining boomtown in the West had its row of stick homes, an ostentatious display of nouveau riches that had no place in Thunder Creek.

The coyote vanished and the sheriff sighed and once more pondered the mystery of Clay Kyle. The killing of Tom Calthrop and his family had been unfortunate. Holding one of the children's toes to a fire would've produced the same result . . . the hiding place of the money. Tom didn't trust banks and the rumor was that he'd stashed away more than ten thousand dollars in gold coin. Had Clay found it? And if he had, where was the galloper bringing Hurd's thousand dollar share for the information?

Hurd had questions without answers, and that troubled him.

To make matters worse now Dan Caine had gone off half-cocked with the sorriest collection of vigilantes this side of the Mississippi. If they ran into Clay, he'd shoot them to doll rags and then he and his boys would hightail it back across the Brazos, ten thousand in gold clinking in their saddlebags and Chance Hurd left as penniless as ever.

Damn, life was unfair.

Hurd's wounded stare lifted from his desktop to the window to the street outside.

No! Hell, no! That won't do!

The sheriff jumped to his feet and ran outside. "You get back here, girl!" he yelled, stepping in front of her horse. "And you, Cornelius Massey, where the hell are you going? Get back to your printing press."

Estella Sweet, astride her paint pony, ignored him, as did the skinny, top-hatted little man beside her, mounted on a rangy Missouri mule. Massey was the proprietor and sole employee of the one-sheet *Thunder Creek Gazette,* a man who'd known better times as a big city editor in Boston. But drink had done for him and though he no longer imbibed, the smell of bourbon made saliva jet from the sides of his tongue. Sobriety was a bitch.

Estella Sweet had a bedroll across the back of her saddle

and a .44-40 Henry rifle under her left knee. She was dressed in spurred boots, woolen pants, and shotgun chaps, and, worn over a man's pale blue shirt, a tan colored corset was pulled together by laces and leather straps with brass buckles. At the front of its crown, Estella's wide-brimmed hat had a pair of dust-fighting goggles and she wore her usual dark glasses. Around her slim waist, a gunbelt decorated with conchos supported a long-barreled Colt in a cross-draw holster. The revolver was the same caliber as the Henry. Like Massey, she wore a duster.

To set matters straight, in 1903 it was alleged by the sensationalist rag *The San Angelo Clarion* that Estella Sweet was not a blacksmith's daughter at all, but a corset-wearing whore who, at various times, shacked up with men in Thunder Creek and in later years was involved with the Wild Bunch.

Nothing could be further from the truth.

Estella was the daughter and only child of widowed Mike Sweet, and the blacksmith doted on her. So it should come as no surprise then that he didn't stand in her way when she decided to go after Dan Caine's vigilante posse. Mike Sweet would later say that Thunder Creek was too small and backward to hold a beautiful and adventurous young woman like Estella, and future events would bear this out. Her only contact with the Wild Bunch was the correspondence she kept up with Laura "The Thorny Rose" Bullion, the sometime mistress of the Tall Texan, gang member Ben Kilpatrick. Like Estella, Laura was active in women's prison reform, and the two exchanged letters until Laura's death in 1961.

Sheriff Hurd had spoken to Estella as though she was a child, and she'd ignored the man, but now she drew rein and said, "I won't be coming back until I find Jenny Calthrop, so don't try to stop me, Sheriff."

"Hell, Estella, you're only a kid," Hurd said.

"I'm a woman grown," the girl said. "Don't tell me you haven't noticed. Now step aside and give me the road."

"Massey, talk some sense into her," Hurd said.

"I'm a newspaperman," Massey said. "Since when does anyone ask a newspaperman to talk sense? Never fear, dear boy, I'll look out for Miss Estella."

"Hell, Massey, you ain't even heeled," Hurd said.

"The pen is mightier than the sword, Sheriff," the little man said, flourishing the small notebook and stub of pencil he'd taken from an inside pocket. "Didn't you know that?"

"Mister, this is the West and plenty of pen pushers have been shot by men with guns and maybe ran through with swords, some of them," Hurd said.

"Then I stand corrected," Massey said. "Now, will you give us the road?"

"What the hell am I doing, standing here in a hot sun trying to talk sense into you two?" Hurd said. "Go on, leave, but God help you if you run into Clay Kyle or his like."

"And what will happen to us, Sheriff?" Estella said, her tone scathing, her dislike of Hurd obvious.

"You'll be dead. That's what will happen." Then, a mean little spike in his belly. "Or, Miss Sweet, you'll wish to hell you were."

"Maybe that's what poor Jenny Calthrop is wishing right now," Estella said. She kneed her paint into motion. "I'll take my chances, Sheriff Hurd."

"And that goes for me too," Massey said.

"Then you're a damned fool," Hurd said.

Massey nodded. "I've been told that before."

CHAPTER FIVE

The Kiowa wore the white man's shirt, pants, vest with a brass watchchain, and a U.S. Cavalry campaign hat without insignia. Only his hard-soled, beaded moccasins, crafted from tanned buffalo hide, were Indian. A Colt carried butt-forward in a cavalry holster and a bowie knife completed his outfit. His hair fell loose and straight over his shoulders, and his eyes were wide spaced and expressive. The left cheek of his broad face with its high cheekbones and wide mouth was dreadfully scarred, the result of a saber slash from a cavalry trooper when, in August 1860, his village on the Republican River was attacked by the 1st Cavalry and his family slaughtered. The Kiowa was a ten-year-old boy that year, and ever since then he'd harbored a dislike bordering on hatred for white men. He was not handsome and his usual fierce expression spoke of menace, power, determination, and a barely suppressed instinct for violence. He had a grim, closed-tooth smile . . . a once or twice a year event . . . and eyes as black and hard as obsidian.

White men called the Kiowa "a bad Injun." And they were right. He was bad to the bone . . . and a first-rate fighting man with knife, revolver, or rifle.

Now he answered the question framed in Dan Caine's face . . . and his voice always surprised those who heard him speak for the first time. In perfect, well-modulated English, he said, "The tracks continue to the south and the killers seem to be in no hurry."

"Is it Kyle?" Dan said.

"I have no idea," the Kiowa said. "But judging by the tracks, there could be a woman riding with them."

"Black-Eyed Susan," Caine said.

"Maybe. I don't know," the Kiowa said.

"So what do you suggest?" Dan said.

"It will be dark soon," the Kiowa said. His pleasant voice was not unfriendly, just flat, without emphasis. "Camp here and then take the trail again at first light."

"Suits me," Clint Cooley said. He shifted in the saddle and made a face. "Been a while since I rode any distance."

"Same with me," Fish Lee said. "Most time I walk beside my burro."

"How about you, boy?" Dan said to young Holt Peters.

The youngster would not admit to being saddle sore. "I'm fine," he said.

"Hungry?" Dan said.

"I sure am," Peters said.

"Then we'll camp here for the night." Dan turned to the Kiowa. "Start a fire, and I'll rustle up some grub."

The Indian nodded, his face impassive.

The Kiowa sat a distance apart from the others and when the yellow-haired boy brought him fried salt pork between hunks of sourdough bread, he merely grunted.

The Indian had once known a man with yellow hair like that, an Englishman named Horatio Lindquist who'd looked after him for a while after his parents were murdered up on the Republican. The black sheep of a wealthy family, in 1850 Lindquist traveled from the Port of London to New York in an overcrowded, dysentery-ridden hell ship, killed a man in a drunken brawl in a Five Points tavern, and then fled west in time to take part in the last couple of years of the fur trade. He'd drifted west into California and tried his hand at gold prospecting for a couple of years but never hit paydirt. Drinking heavily, Lindquist drifted east again, killed another man in Bisbee in the Arizona Territory, and then ended up grifting in the settlements along the Republican. It was about then he adopted the Kiowa, taught him English and how to use a gun. That was it, there was little else. Lindquist fed the youngster when he could, beat him when he was drunk . . . until the day the Kiowa was big enough and mean enough to fight back. The Englishman died suddenly of apoplexy in 1872, and the Kiowa buried him, along with any respect or feeling he had for white men.

"Riders coming in," long-sighted Fish Lee said. "White men."

Dan Caine and Clint Cooley, guns in hand, watched two spectral horsemen emerge from the mist-shrouded gloom. Fish Lee and Holt Peters held their rifles. The Kiowa looked intently at the incoming riders but stayed where he was.

"Don't come any closer," Dan said, his voice hard. "I can drill both of you from here, so draw rein and state your intentions."

A voice from the darkness. "Hold your fire, you damned ruffian. It's Cornelius Massey of Thunder Creek town and fair lady come to join your posse."

His voice rising in a hopeful note, Dan said, "Any more of you?"

"Just us, Mr. Caine," Massey said. "You were expecting an army perhaps?"

Dan lowered his Colt, his voice, and his expectations. "Come on in. There's coffee on the fire."

Dan Caine studied Estella Sweet, made even more beautiful by the firelight that rippled in her hair and brought golden highlights to her face. She'd removed her dark glasses and even in the misted, smoky gloom, her eyes were large and lustrous. The duster she wore against the night chill did little to conceal her exquisite body, and Dan thought her the most desirable gal in Texas, if not the whole world. The young man didn't know it then, but very soon he'd meet one lovelier, a woman whose beauty burned like a candle flame . . . a candle flame in a crypt.

"I'm sending you back at first light, Estella," Dan said.

"No, you're not," the girl said. She sipped from her tin cup and made a face. "This isn't Arbuckle. It's some other brand."

"Pete Doan roasts and grinds the beans himself," Dan said.

"He doesn't make a very good job of it," Estella said. She sipped again. "This coffee isn't even made properly. It's swill."

Dan was instantly defensive. A log fell in the fire and crackled sparks as he said, "Nobody ever complained about my coffee before. There's only so much a man can do with beans, water, and a pot."

"Well, I can do much better," Estella said. She sipped from her cup. "But I suppose bad coffee is better than no coffee at all."

"The young lady is right about that," Clint Cooley said.

Still resentful, Dan said, "Well, she's wrong about something."

"And that is?" Estella said.

"You're wrong to think that you're riding on this posse."

Estella frowned. "When I was eight years old and untouched by life's troubles, my grandmother said to me, 'You're going to be happy, my little Estella. But first you must grow strong and proud.' Now I am strong and I know my worth, Dan Caine. So don't you dare try to push me around."

Dan grinned. "Come tomorrow, young lady, I aim to do just that."

"Then come armed, Dan," Estella said, "I will not be laid hands on."

"We'll just have to see about that, won't we?" Dan said, his grin back in place.

Estella drew from her cross-draw holster and fired.

The shattering roar and flare of the Colt precipitated a panicked scramble by Cooley, Massey, and young Holt Peters. All three hit the ground as Cooley cussed and grabbed for his gun. Dan Caine sat frozen in place, stunned, and the Kiowa jumped to his feet and listened into the ringing echoes of the night.

As the others slowly rose to their feet, Dan Caine found his angry voice. "Damn it, lady, I felt the wind of that bullet. You could've killed me."

Estella said, "I thought I saw a big, growly bear creeping up on you, Dan. I was mistaken." She holstered her Colt and touched a forefinger to her lips. "Silly me."

Irritated, Dan said, "Is that all you can say?"

"Dan," Cooley said, "I think the young lady just said a lot more than you think."

"Jenny Calthrop is my friend," Estella said. "I have to find her, and I will not be denied."

Dan Caine was a smart man, and he knew he'd just been taught a lesson. But he wasn't sure exactly what the lesson was. Was it merely that Estella Sweet was fast with a gun?

Hell no, not that. It was more likely that the girl had warned him that she would not be handled or abused. Dan Caine smiled inwardly. He had thought Estella Sweet a kitten . . . but found her a cougar.

Drawing what was left of his self-esteem around him like a threadbare cloak, Dan said, "Well, young lady, you can ride with us, but it's your funeral."

Clint Cooley smiled at Dan's surrender and said, "Estella, angry, aggressive men are loud, but a quiet word and a gun speaks louder."

"I'll remember that," Estella said.

Dan Caine glared at her but said nothing.

CHAPTER SIX

There wasn't much to share among eight riders. Ninety dollars and six cents from the moneybox, Tom Calthrop's silver Waltham pocket watch and gold Masonic fob, Nancy's wedding ring, and cheap necklaces worn by the twins. There were also two Colt revolvers, a Winchester rifle, a Greener shotgun . . . and sixteen-year-old Jenny Calthrop.

"I want the ring," Arch Pitman said. "Ye can share the rest, except for the girl. I say we all have a taste right now and sell what's left of her."

Pitman was a thin man of medium height with a slack mouth and yellow, reptilian eyes. An outlaw of low intelligence, Pitman was nonetheless fast and accurate with a gun, and the rumor was that he'd killed four men. He himself had been stabbed, shot several times, and thrown from a moving train, breaking bones in his back, hip, and right leg. That he'd survived this kind of damage was a testament to his endurance and animalistic courage. Arch Pitman was a hard man to kill.

"What gives you the right to first choice, Pitman?" Clay Kyle said.

"Getting uppity in your old age, Arch?" Susan Stanton said. She stood with her long, booted legs apart, short black skirt, and scarlet tights, and an open, steel gray coat with wide, padded shoulders fell to her ankles. Her thick hair, the color of flame, cascaded in glossy waves from under a man's top hat decorated with a beaded, three-inch-tall band made by a Comanche woman. Two Colts in crossed gunbelts hung on her magnificent hips, and a purple corset pushed up her breasts, between them on a gold chain an oval medallion of Macha, the man slaughterer, the Celtic goddess of war and death. Black-Eyed Susan's face was stunningly beautiful, the way a Greek marble statue of a woman is beautiful, fine featured, and slightly masculine. Flawless skin. An orphan raised by a brothel madame who had no idea she'd created a monster.

Susan Stanton was a stone-cold killer, but Arch Pitman, when the time was right, had plans for her . . . after he'd tamed the cussedness out of her with a horsewhip.

Whining now, the outlaw said, "Clay, I cut the woman's finger off to get that ring. By rights it's mine."

"And you had the first go at her," Susan said. "Isn't that enough?"

"No. I want her ring," Pitman said. "It fits the middle finger of my gun hand real good, and it will bring me luck on the draw." He pointed at Jenny Calthrop. Her pretty face was terrified. "And I want my fair share of that little whore tonight." His grin was ugly. "Help me sleep, like."

Susan looked across the fire at Kyle. A coffeepot smoked on the coals. "Clay?"

"Ah, let Arch have the ring," Kyle said. "It ain't worth much. But nobody touches the girl. In Mexico any brothel will pay big money for a young white woman, especially if she's still intact . . . and they have ways of verifying that."

"She's a virgin, never had a man, ain't that right, honey?" Susan said to Jenny Calthrop.

The girl was scared enough to answer the tall woman

with two guns, the prairie wind blowing open her duster, revealing shapely legs in high black boots.

"Tom Walker stole a kiss from me one time," Jenny said.

"Did he, now?" Susan said. "Is that all Tom Walker did?"

"Yes. He branded a three-month-old calf and then stole his kiss." Her fingers strayed to her face. "Here, on my cheek."

"Lucky he didn't slap his brand on you," Susan said.

The girl said nothing and looked down at herself, tears falling as unbearable grief caught up with her, overcoming, at least for now, her cold fear.

Susan smiled, staring at a girl in a plain brown dress with several snowy white petticoats underneath. She had square-toed, lace-up shoes on her feet, and her fair hair was pulled back in an unraveling bun and tied with a cherry-red ribbon. Jenny Calthrop had large, expressive brown eyes, well-shaped arms and hands, and her small, high breasts barely swelled the front of her dress. She was a pretty girl in a utilitarian sort of way, but unlike Susan Stanton, could lay no claim to beauty.

But in a Tijuana whorehouse, that wouldn't matter.

"Suzie, what do you think?" Kyle said.

"It's pretty obvious that the little slut still has her maidenhead."

"That's good."

"Bad for her," Susan Stanton said. "She won't last a year in a brothel."

"Not my concern, is it?" Kyle said. He turned to the others. "Hear that? Leave the girl alone. When we get to Tijuana and she's sold, you can get your pesos ready and rent her by the hour."

This brought another laugh. But Arch Pitman sat scowling, his lean, hard face pitted and scarred, a grotesque red mask in the firelight.

"Listen up, you damned lowlifes, and listen good," he said. "When we get to Tijuana, I'll kill any man who tries to have the Calthrop girl afore me. I want to be first and for that I'll pay good money."

"Hell, Arch, there's plenty of other whores south of the Rio Bravo," Kyle said. He stared at Jenny. "What's so special about her, huh? Nothing."

"I had the mother and I want the daughter," Pitman said.

Kyle shook his head. "Arch, you're crazy."

"Maybe so, but I want what I want, and I want the girl and I want the lucky ring," Pitman said.

"Arch, you want, want, want," Susan Stanton said. "Maybe I'll keep the ring for myself. Or maybe I'll give it to . . . what's her name? . . . Jenny."

"You heard what Clay told me," Pitman said.

"I want the ring for myself," Susan said. Her dark eyes glittered in the flickering firelight.

"And I said that you heard Clay," Pitman said, his voice, low, level, full of menace. His gun hand was close to his holstered Colt. "Now give the ring to me." Then, to drive home his warning, "I've shot a woman afore. Didn't bother me none."

"I know you have, Arch," Susan said. "Didn't I see you kill the Calthrop woman?"

"Yeah, you did. Kill one, kill another. It's even easier the second time, lady," Pitman said. He was ready, ready for the draw.

Kyle said, "Suzie," using his pet name for her, "give Arch the ring. Give it to him now."

The woman smiled and nodded. "Anything you say. Here, Arch, catch!"

Pitman stood to Susan Stanton's right, between Shadow Beck, the San Antonio gunman, and the breed Doug Avila. The ring spun through the air, glinting in the firelight, and as Pitman reached out to catch it, Susan drew and fired, both Colts hammering. His face a mask of horror and surprise, Pitman took four bullets to the chest. There was no miracle survival this time. Pitman was dead when he hit the ground, and later Kyle covered all four bullet holes with a Queen of Spades playing card and complimented Black-Eyed Susan on her marksmanship. But initially he was irritated. "Why kill him?" he said.

"He called me lady," Susan said, her smoke-trickling Colts hanging at her sides. "I guess he found out that I'm not a lady." She shrugged her beautiful shoulders. "I wanted the ring, Clay. But I don't want it any longer. It's cheap."

"Shadow, find that ring," Kyle said.

Along with Loco Garrett, Shadow Beck had been a member of the welcoming committee that greeted the outlaw when he crossed the Brazos, and Kyle set store by him. "The ring is worth a few dollars, so you keep it," Kyle said.

Beck, a tall, lanky gunman dressed in black broadcloth and a collarless white shirt, scrambled around in the grass for a few moments, found the ring, and then stood and held it aloft. His glance took in the other men around the campfire. "Anybody give me ten dollars for it?"

"Hell, no," a stocky man with a broken nose said. "The damned thing is cursed."

"Five dollars," Beck said. "And it ain't cursed, Charlie."

"Damn right it is," Charlie Bates said.

"Let me see that," the breed Doug Avila said, rising to his feet. He wore a vaquero's finery, high-crowned, flat-brimmed hat, short jacket, thigh-high chaperraras tied to a belt at his waist and worn over split-leg pants, fancy boots, and spurs with rowels as large as teacups. He wore a nickel-plated Colt with a pearl handle that he could shuck from the leather with flashing speed. Nobody messed with Avila or called him a breed to his face, and those who did seldom lived long enough to regret it.

After a few silent moments, Avila said, "Look how the ring glows red in the firelight. It's stained with the blood of dead Sioux and the woman who wore it and that's why it's cursed. I saw Arch Pitman take the ring and now he is dead." He stared at Beck. "Nobody wants your damned ring. It is an accursed thing."

"Hell, then I'll wear it myself," Beck said. He shoved the ring onto the thumb of his left hand. "I ain't scared of curses."

"Or of any man," Susan said. "Isn't that right, Shadow?"

"Hell, yeah," Beck said. "And I don't count on anybody to back my play either."

"Yes, I imagine you don't, Shadow," Susan said. "Tell me something. When did you rape the nice ranch lady who once wore it? Was it after she was dead?"

Shadow Beck, tall and angular, with the long, hard face of a Yankee undertaker and mud-colored eyes, shrugged. "I don't know."

Susan holstered her guns, her face unreadable. "Wear the ring in good health, Shadow," she said.

CHAPTER SEVEN

"Well, I'm for heading for Old Mexico, but I'm open to suggestions," Clay Kyle said to the gunmen squatting around the fire. "Damn his eyes, Chance Hurd gave us bad information on the Calthrop place. Now if we don't salvage something, we crossed the Brazos for nothing." He scowled and nodded in the direction of Pitman's sprawled body. "First . . . Shadow, move that. Drag it into the dark, away from the camp."

"Sure thing, boss," Beck said. He motioned to another man. "Loco, give me a hand here."

Loco Garrett was a vicious killer and hired gun, originally out of the Kentucky hill country. Certifiably insane, it was he who'd scalped Grace Calthrop. Her once beautiful hair decorated the bridle of his horse. He said, "Hell, he ain't heavy."

"He's heavy enough," Kyle said. "Help him."

Garrett cursed under his breath, and he and Beck dragged the corpse into the darkness. They returned with Garrett carrying Pitman's boots, Colt, and gunbelt. "Coyotes out there," he said, resuming his place by the fire. "I didn't see them, but I heard them." He examined the boots closely, grunted, set them beside him, and tossed the gunbelt and holstered Colt to Beck.

"Them hungry coyotes ain't gonna find much meat on Pitman," Kyle said. The men laughed and he waited until they settled down and then said, "All right. Suggestions?"

"Hell, Clay, you're the boss of this outfit. You make the call."

This from a one-eyed man named Morris Bennett, out of Arizona's Mogollon Rim country. He still had his shooting eye and had killed four men, one of them the gun-handy, sometime Indian Scout Jeb Walsh, said to be the meanest and hungriest sidewinder on the frontier. The newspapers at the time claimed that when Walsh worked as a teamster, he got snowed in on the Sierra Nevada's Carson Range spur one winter. Starving, Walsh killed and ate his partner, a man named Roberts or Robertson. After he was rescued, Walsh never denied the murder, but was found not guilty by a Nevada court since he'd eaten all the evidence. Two years later, he and Bennett got into an argument over a woman in a saloon in El Paso that ended with guns drawn. The opinion of all present was that Walsh never cleared leather before Bennett put two bullets into his chest. It was also said that Walsh bled two shades of red that night, his own and the man's he ate, though the *El Paso Herald* reporter who covered the gunfight didn't mention that phenomenon.

Taking Bennett's colorful rep into consideration and the rakish patch over his left eye, Kyle said with a measure of respect, "Y'all heard my man Morris. What do the rest of you say?"

To a chorus of approval, Bennett said, "You make the call, Clay. We're listening."

"Suzie," Kyle said, "what about you?"

"I don't call anyone my boss," the woman said. "But I'll pay heed to what you have to say."

Susan Stanton had just killed a man but it made little impression on her. There was a coldness in the woman, cold as ice, as she stood in the flickering firelight, wild as a Celtic warrior princess. Her red hair streamed in the wind and scarlet strands clung to her face like sword cuts.

Kyle said, "Then all I got to say is this . . . we cross the Rio Bravo into Coahuila and then head into the Sierra del Carmen Mountains where the man they call the Sheik has his hacienda. We'll sell the girl to him. I'm told he'll pay top dollar for a white woman."

"Clay, I hope you have no big ideas," Susan said.

This brought a burst of guffaws from the men, and Kyle said, "None about you, Suzie. I need your gun too badly."

"Sheik . . . hacienda . . . Clay, what the hell are you talking about?" Susan said.

Kyle fell silent, got his thoughts in order, and then said, "All right, listen up, all of you. An old Chinaman doing twenty years for killing a railroad section hand with an iron lining bar told me the Sheik is an Arab and his real name is Bandar al-Salam and he's as rich as Midas. His fort is bursting at the seams with gold. He bathes in a golden tub, dines off of golden dishes, and his two hundred concubines wear shackles of solid gold. And here's where it gets interesting . . . the Sheik is so fat he's lowered on top of his bed partners by a system of golden ropes and pulleys."

"Now I've got a picture in my mind I didn't ever want to see," Susan said, frowning. "Where did this man acquire all that gold? And how do you know that the Chinaman wasn't telling you a big windy?"

"Because the old man was dying, and dying men don't lie," Kyle said. "The Sheik made his fortune from piracy on the South China Sea. I spent six months in Leavenworth listening to the old Chinaman's story. He was a gunner on one of the Sheik's junks, and, a week before he died, he told me that the Sheik was the right-hand man of the Chinese

Supreme High Admiral . . . now let me get his name right."
Kyle reached into his shirt pocket and produced a small
tally book. "I never could figure why, but they let me keep
this in Leavenworth," he said. He leafed through the pages
and said, "Ah, yeah, here it is . . . *Shap-ng-tsai* . . . I wrote
it down. It's a right fancy name for a pirate rogue."

Kyle said that although the Sheik was an Arab, the
Admiral admired the Sheik's ability as a people-killer
and gave him command of twelve armed junks and eight
hundred cutthroats. He captured a dozen British opium
ships and held them for ransom, and hundreds of villages
up and down the coast paid him tribute rather than see their
frail wooden houses flattened by cannon fire.

"And pretty soon Sheik Bandar al-Salam was a rich
man," Kyle said.

Susan Stanton made a face. "For God's sakes, Clay, get
to the point."

"I'm getting to it," Kyle said. "The Chinese government
finally cracked down on piracy and the British, upset about
their opium ships, brought in a fleet of ironclads and sank
every junk they came across, both guilty and innocent."

"And then?" Susan prompted.

"And then Admiral Shap-ng-tsai quit the piracy profession and the grateful government made him an Admiral in
the Chinese army," Kyle said. "But before that Bandar al-
Salam lit a shuck and my Chinaman went with him, so
that's how I know what happened. The Sheik spent three
years in Mexico, moving from place to place; he built his
redoubt in the Sierra del Carmen Mountains and filled it
with gun-savvy hard cases that answer only to him. The
Chinaman went along as a cook."

"Clay, why are you telling us all this?" one-eyed Morris
Bennett said.

"Because the Arab has too much gold and we're going

to relieve him of most of it," Kyle said. He grinned and added nothing else.

But his wild statement drew a cheer that Susan Stanton silenced when she said, "Now that Pitman's dead, there are seven of us."

"Six," Shadow Beck said. "I'm out."

"All right, six," Susan said. "Five men and a woman aim to steal tons of gold from a man who lives in a fortress and is guarded by an army. How difficult can that be?"

Kyle angled a hostile glance at Beck and said, "Shadow, you ain't out. Nobody's out. And, Suzie, you're right. We'd face a bunch of gunmen that outnumbered us at least ten to one. No, we don't brace the Sheik head-on. We take something very precious from him and hold it hostage."

"Like what?" Susan said.

"Like his only misbegotten son, the spawn of the Sheik and one of his concubines," Kyle said. "The Chinaman told me the boy was six years old and that was four years ago, so he'll be ten now."

"So we just walk into the Sheik's castle, grab the kid, and walk out again?" Susan Stanton said. She made a face. "Great plan, Clay."

"A ten-year-old boy is never still," Kyle said. "He'll be all over the place. We hole up somewhere and grab him when we can and then exchange him for gold."

"It's thin, Clay, mighty thin," Doug Avila said. "I reckon you're trying to buck a stacked deck. It's a pity we can't talk to your Chinaman. Why did he leave the Sheik?"

"He told me he saw the man hang six Mexican Rurales who'd gotten too close to his place," Kyle said. "Since the Sheik paid President Portofino Diaz handsomely to look the other way, the murders were never investigated. But the Chinaman had seen enough. He managed to escape the Sheik but a year later killed another Chinese man in a

Dallas alley . . . a knife fight over a black whore. The law didn't care that much, but the judge gave the Chinaman two years in Yuma anyway, just to square things up. The Chinaman was a skinny little cuss, with a story to tell, so when he got out, I befriended him and found him a place to live in Wichita, since I was the deputy marshal of Sedgewick County at the time."

Kyle sat, his head bowed over tobacco and papers, then light flared on his face as he thumbed a match into flame and lit the cigarette. He looked up and said, "Well, who's with me?" he said. "I know it's thin, but if we can grab the kid, we'll all end up rich men . . . and woman. Damn it, boys, it's never been done before. A kidnapping is something the Sheik will never expect and that's why we got a chance to hit him with his guard down."

"Like we hit the Calthrop place," Susan Stanton said.

"Yeah, just that," Kyle said. "Like we hit the Calthrop place."

"They were all dead afore they knew it," Morris Bennett said, his one eye glittering.

"We drew a blank with the Calthrops," Kyle said. "But we won't with the Sheik's brat."

"It ain't much of a chance, but I'll stick," Avila said.

"Me too," Loco Garrett said. "I'm willing to buck the odds. I done it plenty of times afore this."

"Hell, I'll give it a try. I got nothing else to do," Morris Bennett said.

Shadow Beck didn't say a word. He saw Kyle stare at him and nodded. "I'm in."

"Good, then it's settled. We head for Mexico and become rich men," Kyle said.

"Damn right," Loco Garrett said.

* * *

Susan Stanton lay awake, her eyes hidden, curtained by dark fans of lashes. She lay beside a sleeping Jenny Calthrop, so close they shared body heat.

Susan watched Shadow Beck silently saddle his horse and then lead the buckskin into the gloom of the night. He'd walk the animal until he was well clear of the camp and then mount and head for . . . wherever. It didn't much matter. Susan Stanton smiled a knowing smile . . .

Shadow Beck was already a dead man.

CHAPTER EIGHT

The Kiowa could light a fire on top of a snowdrift using icicles for kindling, or so said Clint Cooley. By the time the Indian kicked everyone awake . . . drawing a threat of violence from Fish Lee who could be testy in the morning, the coffee simmered on the fire and strips of salt pork sizzled.

Without a word to anyone, the Kiowa made a sandwich of the salt pork and a slice of sourdough bread and mounted his already-saddled Palouse and rode south, following the Kyle gang's tracks.

"How far ahead of us are they, do you reckon, Deputy Caine?" Holt Peters said.

"A day, maybe less," Dan said. "The Kiowa will let us know."

He looked hard at the youngster, a raw, untested boy. When the chips were down and the ball opened, would he stand his ground and get his work in? Dan had no answer to that question. He had hope, certainly, but harsh reality had a way of banishing that.

Over the rim of his coffee cup, his eyes swept the others, measuring them. He had no doubts about Fish Lee. The old man could be cantankerous at times, but he had sand. Any man who'd stood his ground against Apaches had courage. Clint Cooley had a gun rep but no one knew if it was deserved or not. Had he been in a dozen shooting scrapes and killed five men, or had he killed nobody? Cooley never answered that question, but future events would. Cornelius Massey was a newspaperman and former drunk who favored top hats and frockcoats. He'd killed many a bottle of Old Crow but never a human. He might be a help or a burden. Estella Sweet, now settling her own top hat on her lustrous head, might be stronger and gamer than any of the men.

"Time will tell," Clint Cooley said.

Dan, surprised, said, "About what?"

"About how far ahead of us the killers are," Cooley said. "I had to think about my reply before I had an answer to young Holt's question."

"Time will tell isn't an answer," Fish Lee said.

"I know, but it's all I got," Cooley said.

"Finish here and mount up," Dan Caine said. "I reckon we'll find out soon enough, maybe too soon, how far Clay Kyle and his boys are ahead of us."

The sun was high and a blanket of heat lay on the land when the Kiowa emerged from a distant shimmer and rode toward Dan Caine and the others. For a while, the glimmer elongated man and horse like a skinny Don Quixote on Rocinante and then they slowly settled into the form of the Kiowa and his Palouse, coming on at a canter.

Dan Caine drew rein, and he and the others waited for the man to arrive.

As was his habit, the Kiowa offered no greeting and got right to the point.

"An hour's ride south of here, one man broke away from the others and rode east," he said.

"Hightailing it for the Brazos," Dan said.

"Likely," Clint Cooley said. "A few years back I'd have said a man in a wilderness of grass who makes a sudden left turn is headed for a whorehouse."

"There are no houses of ill-repute in this neck of the woods," Cornelius Massey said. He'd just took a swig from a silver flask and now put it back in a pocket of his frock-coat. He was drinking again. "He's headed for Austin, maybe. Plenty of cathouses and dancehalls in that fair city."

Dan considered that and then said, "Fish, was there once a cathouse near here?"

"Not as I recollect," the old tinpan said. "Too out of the way for whores."

"Clint, how about you?"

"I don't know," Cooley said, frowning. Then, "I heard something from Pete Doan not long after I arrived in Thunder Creek. Maybe it's just a big story because Pete himself didn't think it was true."

"Tell it," Dan said. "But make it short. I don't want to burn any more daylight than I have to."

"Well, the story is that around 1830, an eccentric English millionaire named Glendale or something like that built a tall, Gothic mansion house in the middle of the prairie that he called High Time," Cooley said. "On account of how it had a steam-powered clock in one of its towers that could be seen from miles away."

"Why would Glendale build a tall . . . what's that word?"

"Gothic," Cooley said.

"Then why did he build a Gothic house way out here in the middle of nowhere?" Dan said.

"Because he wanted to," Cooley said. He frowned. "How the hell would I know why a crazy Englishman built a mansion house in the back of beyond? It probably isn't even true."

"I'm sorry, go ahead with your story," Dan said.

"There ain't much more to tell," Cooley said. "Glendale died and the house fell into ruin. Pete Doan said he heard the story from a feller, who heard it from another feller, who heard it from a circuit preacher that the place had been taken over and turned into a whorehouse with a very high-class clientele." He shook his head. "Not for the likes of you, Dan."

"How come I never heard of this place before?" Dan said.

"Because up there in Thunder Creek you lived a sheltered life, Danny boy," Cooley said.

"Have you ever been there?" Dan said.

"No, I haven't," Cooley said. "I've never sat at a card table in that particular gentleman's retreat. As I say, I heard of it from Pete Doan and always reckoned it was a myth."

"Could be that it's a big windy made up by some cowpoke," Dan said. "There are no sporting gents around this neck of the woods."

"Maybe so," Cooley said. "But they could come from a long way off if the whores were pretty enough."

"Hell, in every direction it means at least a week of misery in a stage," Dan said. "All that to lift the skirts of a two-dollar whore? I don't think so."

"Deputy Caine," Cornelius Massey said, "may I remind you that there's a lady present and a callow youth."

Estella Sweet smiled and said, "It's all right, Mr. Massey. I've been around cowboys my entire life, and I've heard much worse."

"And it don't bother me none," Holt Peters said with a grin. "This is interesting."

"You're in the presence of rough-hewn men, Miss Sweet," Massey said. "I apologize on their behalf."

Dan addressed himself to the Kiowa. "We're in the middle of a sea of grass. How did this, whoever he is, piece of trash know where to leave the trail and head east?"

"I think he'd passed this way before and recognized a landmark," the Kiowa said. "There's a boulder chipped away like a stone spearpoint at the side of the trail near where the man turned east. The ones you search for had made camp and the man took his horse and rode away into the night."

"Kiowa, take me to the place where this man left the trail," Dan said. "I think maybe the reckoning begins here."

"We going after him?" Clint Cooley said.

"No, I'm going after him," Dan said. "You and the others shadow Clay Kyle and his killers, but don't engage them. I'll do what has to be done at that cathouse High Time, if it exists, and then catch you up."

"Dan, let me go," Cooley said. "When Kyle signs on a hard case, you can bet the farm that the man's mighty fast on the draw and shoot. I think I know more about that side of the business than you."

"I'm the leader of this posse and it's my responsibility," Dan said. His smile was faint. "I reckon I can get my work in quick enough if I have to."

"How do you know?" Cooley said.

"I'm guessing," Dan said. "I shoot at bean cans."

"So you gun bean cans. Have you ever killed a man?" Cooley said.

"No."

The gambler shook his head. "I'll go in your place."

"No, you won't," Dan said. "I need you right here with the others."

Cooley looked around him at the others. Cornelius Massey, a top-hatted scarecrow on a slat-sided nag and no kind of fighting man. Holt Peters, his fair skin already burned red by the sun, looked what he was, a green boy. Fish Lee, old, skinny, shabby, but tough as whang leather, had far-seeing brown eyes and a well-worn .44-40 Henry rifle that had seen sterling service against Indians and claim jumpers. So long as his health stood up, Fish was a man to ride the river with. Estella Sweet . . . well, she had a pretty face and big tits. As for the Kiowa, he was the best of them . . . and the worst of them.

In all, Cooley decided this was the sorriest vigilante posse that ever hit the trail after a dangerous gang of outlaw gunmen.

"Track them, Clint, but don't engage until I catch up with you again," Dan said. "The Kiowa will leave trail-markers so I can follow you."

"And if you don't come back?" Cooley said, his hand-some face unsmiling.

"I'll leave that up to you, Clint. You can either give up the chase or pursue and engage as you see fit."

"I won't see fit," the gambler said. "That I guar-on-tee."

"Dan, be careful," Estella said, her pretty face con-cerned. "You could be riding into one of those Texas draw fighters the cowboys all talk about."

Cooley smiled. "Don't worry, John Wesley Hardin is in Huntsville."

"I know where Wes is," Dan said, his voice suddenly hard, mouth hard, eyes harder still. "He's wasting away behind bars in a hell prison."

"Hardin isn't the only one," Estella said, her face almost hidden by the wide brim of her hat and her dark glasses. "There's plenty more of them."

"No, my dear, there is not."

This from Cornelius Massey.

"I once interviewed the learned professor Ignatius Overton of San Francisco who'd made a study of a hundred skilled duelists and gunmen," he said. "He discovered that only one man in a thousand has the dexterity, marksmanship, coolness under pressure, capacity for violence, and love of chaos needed to become a gunfighter. Perhaps, Overton said, it could be one in ten thousand. Such shootists are rare and expensive and that's why only rich and powerful men can afford to make use of them."

"You're right about that, Massey. I've known men who got rich selling their guns to the highest bidder," Cooley said.

"Perhaps you were one of them, Mr. Cooley," Massey said, angling his eyes to the gambler's face.

Cooley's expression didn't change. "Perhaps," he said. Then to Dan Caine, "Clay Kyle only rides with the best. If there is a High Time, or even if it's just a hog ranch, I reckon you could face one of them fast guns." Cooley shook his head. "Reconsider, Dan, let me take your place. You were a so-so lawman, but you just ain't cut out for gunfighting."

"I may not be fast on the draw," Dan said. "But I reckon I can outlast Kyle's killer if I need to." He glanced at the deepening blue of the sky. "It's time I was riding."

"Your mind's made up?" Cooley said.

"Yeah, it is, Clint. Every man has to skin his own skunk."

"Good luck, Dan," Estella said. "I'll say a prayer for you."

"Thank you," Dan said. He swung his horse away in the direction taken by Kyle's gunman.

To his back, Cooley yelled, "Surprise him, Dan. A sur-

prised man always blinks and that's when you can shuck
iron and drill him."

"I'll remember that," Dan Caine said, his voice already
sounding distant.

"Dan, good luck," Estella said again, calling out now.

Dan raised a hand, his eyes on the trail ahead of him.

CHAPTER NINE

Without deviation, the tracks Dan Caine followed headed due east like an arrow, pointing the way to . . . he didn't know what or where they might lead. A house, certainly, not a hog farm as Cooley suggested. An old house with a steam clock that could be seen for miles. With his young eyes, Dan scanned the prairie rolling ahead of him, but all he saw was a green sea of grass under an increasingly ominous sky. To the north, thunder rumbled and the air became as sharp as iron and smelled of ozone.

Where was the damn house with the big clock?

The strange thought came to him . . . it was on the dark side of the moon, where Professor Lazarus Latchford and Miss Prunella's balloon had landed to check the time.

Dan shook his head and smiled. The boredom of the endless, wind-rippled prairie was getting to him.

Then two things happened to end his doldrums . . . a blinding flash followed by thunder crashing above his head with a sound like massive rocks tumbling into a sheet iron hopper . . . and in the distance through the chain-mail curtain of the rain, he caught a glimpse of the tiled roof of a house. "Well, I'll be damned," Dan said aloud to nobody but himself. "There really is a whorehouse on the prairie."

Battling a rising wind and a spatter of rain, Dan struggled

into his flapping slicker and rode toward the building . . . a
mansion from a madman's nightmare.

The house named High Time stood tall, grim, and skeletal, partially hidden by a gloomy stand of bony wild oak.
Cold torrents of rain falling from the brim of his hat, Dan
Caine drew rein and studied the place. The house. A relic
of an era long past, it stood three stories tall and looked like
a long-abandoned prison or asylum for the criminally
insane. The main body of the structure formed a rectangle
but added here and there were projecting castle-like towers
with arched windows, a couple of them boarded up, and
cone-shaped roofs. The main rooftop was steeply pitched
and crowned with a forest of gray stone chimneys, several
of them belching black smoke that was immediately
pounded to mist by the rain. The house was covered in dark
tile, torn away in places to expose the wooden framework
underneath.

Withal, High Time was slowly disintegrating but still
retained an air of gentility, of mystery, of hidden fears
and dire omens. Such a place could contain a damsel in
distress . . . or whores in red dresses.

Dan kneed his mount forward again and stopped outside
the main door, a massive oak portal studded with iron nails
in defiant rows, heavy hinges, and a large brass knocker
shaped like a human skull with moonstone eyes. In contrast
to the grim door, each lower window had a window box
with yellow and orange marigolds, and at a distance away
a clothesline strung between two oaks was hung with
female frillies that hung soaked and limp in the rain.

Dan was about to dismount when a man's voice, followed by the unsociable, metallic *chak-chak* of a levering

Winchester, stopped him. Half in, half out of the saddle, Dan thought it prudent to give the man a listen.

"What the hell are you doing here, mister?" the man said.

He stood somewhere behind Dan, not a good place for a rifle-toting, hostile man to be.

Dan Caine swallowed hard and then said, "I'm looking for a place to get out of the rain and maybe a bite to eat."

"What else are you looking for?" the man said. "Speak up now."

"Just a cup of coffee and grub," Dan said, keeping it nonaggressive.

"Are ye looking for sin or redemption?" the man said.

"Neither of those," Dan said, surprised.

As if he hadn't heard, the man said, "Just as well. Ye won't find redemption in there, sonny. But sin, plenty o' that. There's a grand staircase in the house and every step you take of it is a mortal sin that leads to hell. Study on that and your young blood will run cold, cold as ice, cold as the grave . . . and then will come the fire."

Dan figured the ranny behind him was a few bricks shy of a load and decided to level with him. "Did a man ride in here earlier? Look of the outlaw about him?"

He said it, but no one heard him . . . because at that moment lightning flared and thunder roared, obliterating all other sound.

After the thunder grumbled into silence, Dan turned and saw the man for the first time. He was a skinny, bearded old timer wearing a bright yellow oilskin that glistened in the half-light, a plug hat on his head with dark goggles on the brim. A Sharps .50 was rock steady in his gnarled hands and wasn't there for show.

"What did you say, sonny?" the old man said.

"I'm looking for a man that rode in here earlier today,"

Dan said. "He probably has the look of an outlaw about him. I reckon he rode a good horse, sat a saddle no cowboy could afford, and wore his bad attitude like a badge of honor. Maybe he has a plain gold wedding band on one of his fingers."

"Nope, I never seen a feller like that," the old timer said. He raised the Sharps until the muzzle was level with Dan's belly. "Now best you was riding on."

The old man's finger was on the trigger of the rifle and Dan knew an attempt at a draw and shoot was a forlorn hope. The Sharps would blow his lowest shirt button through his backbone before he even started to clear leather. It would be a messy wound, painful as hell, and it would kill him within a few moments . . . if he was lucky.

"Mister, I won't ask you a second time," the old man said. "I never do."

Lightning flashed across the dark sky like the signature of a demented god and shimmered on the wet tiles of the building. Thunder crashed . . . and Dan Caine was aware that his life hung in the balance.

"Artemus! What are you doing with that gent?"

It was a woman's voice, loud and commanding, and it came from somewhere above Dan's head. He turned and saw a heavily made-up woman hanging out an upstairs window, her painted face barely visible in the gloom.

The old man raised his head and shouted over the dragon hiss of the rain, "So far, I ain't shot him, Miss Maguire. I don't trust this ranny. You want I should plug him?"

"Hell, no," the woman said. "You've plugged too many of my clientele as it is. Do what I told you, stoke the furnace, but first take care of the gent's hoss." Then to Dan. "Come to the door, and I'll let you enter. You look harmless and respectable enough to have money in your pocket." She peered closer. "Well, a couple of dollars anyway."

The window slammed shut before Dan could utter a word.

Artemus said, "Stoke the furnace, she says. The damned furnace is on its last legs, like everything else around this dunghill." The man took the dark goggles from his hat brim and settled them over his eyes. "When you look into a furnace you catch a glimpse of hell and your own eternity," he said. "Look long enough and the horror of the sight will burn your damn eyeballs out."

The old timer caught up the reins of Dan's horse. "See you rub him down good," Dan said.

"I know how to take care of a horse, sonny," Artemus said. "I like horses a sight better than people." His face grimaced in a smile. "As you might find out soon enough." He walked the horse a few steps and then stopped and said over his shoulder, "The Apaches are out. Mescalero and Chiricahua bucks holding hands."

The old man's goggles were as black as night, and Dan couldn't see his eyes.

CHAPTER TEN

"Bring yourself in and let me take your hat and coat," the woman at the door said. She held Dan Caine's dripping slicker and hat at arm's length and added, "My name is Misty Maguire and I'm the proprietor of this"—she waved a plump, beringed hand—"haven for sporting gents who appreciate comfortable accommodation, excellent dining, first-rate whiskey and liqueurs . . . and the *raison d'etre* for our existence . . . high-class whores of unsurpassed beauty, intelligence, and cleanliness."

The foyer of the house was illuminated by a huge, crystal chandelier that cast bright light and deep shadows. Dan's senses were immediately assailed by the odors of French perfume, cigar smoke, single-barrel bourbon, and the more subtle smell of dampness and decay and of the dry rot visible around the lower floor windows. But what dwarfed Dan into insignificance was the grand staircase. Its wide and uncarpeted steps rose to a height of sixty feet and added drama to the cathedral-like surrounding. The soaring stairs demonstrated the importance of the upper suites where business of the harlotting kind was conducted and the chaste twins, modesty and chastity, were never invited.

"Step into the drawing room, Mr. . . . ah . . ."

"Caine. Dan Caine."

"Yes, of course. Mr. Caine it is. You'll have a dry sherry once we're settled?"

"I don't know, I've never had a sherry, wet or dry," Dan said:

Misty laughed, the great white pillows of her bosom heaving. She slapped Dan on the shoulder, revealing considerable strength, and giggled, "Mister Caine! You are a scamp. I predict we're going to get along just fine, you and I."

In that, as events would show, Misty Maguire was a false prophet.

Dan stepped into the lamplit drawing room . . . and almost collided with a tall, silver-haired man on his way out. He had intolerant blue eyes and an air of authority and he stopped and studied Dan up and down, lingering for a moment on his holstered Colt. The man looked as though someone held a rotting fish under his nose as he said in an imperious voice, "We dress for dinner."

After the man swept past, Misty Maguire smiled and said, "That was Mr. Harcourt St. John. Take a seat Mr. Caine. Yes, near the fire, that's it. I'll pour you a sherry." Misty brought the drink in a small crystal glass and sat opposite Dan. "Now what was I saying? Ah yes, Mr. St. John. He has shares in several railroads and a dozen steelworks and he's as rich as Midas. He keeps dear Olivia on a yearly basis, but only visits her two or three times in a twelve-month. Like my other kept ladies, Olivia passes the time between his visits knitting, crocheting, and reading her Bible."

Thunder blasted, and the old building trembled as though afraid of the storm. At the same time there was another bang as the door slammed open, immediately putting Dan on edge. His hand dropped closer to his gun, then the sight of two beautiful, no, more than beautiful, women . . . gorgeous, spectacular, dazzling . . . Dan's numbed brain could not come up with the words, but the scented presence of the women quickly soothed his former uneasiness.

At that moment, they were very young and very cross frowning goddesses of a more earthly sort.

"Is it the hot water again, Lucretia?" Misty said.

"Damn right it is," the redhead of the pair said.

"The water like to froze my ass off," the other girl said. She looked to be barely out of her teens, and Dan was acutely aware that her frosty butt was still very much in place.

"Artemus is stoking the furnace, Gwendolyn," Misty said. "You'll have hot water soon. Where are your gentlemen?"

"Dressing for dinner," Lucretia said. She sighed. "Lord Gray feels quite exhausted. He says I wore him out after lunch."

"Coarse, Lucretia, coarse," Misty said, frowning, moving a forefinger with its scarlet-painted nail like a metronome. "We must observe the proprieties at all times."

Like Lucretia, Gwendolyn was dressed in a black corset, laced up the front with red ribbon, crimson tights under a short gauzy skirt and high-heeled black boots that, like the corset, laced in the front and rose to just under the knee. The women's thick hair was piled up on top of their heads in glossy tiaras, but for odd strands that fell in loose ringlets over their faces. Flowers and colorful feathers kept their hair in place, and both had peach-perfect skin, free of any marks from disease or imperfections. Large breasts battled the confines of their boned corsets and rose in creamy mounds above French lace trim. Lest she find herself in harm's way, each carried a single-barreled Colt .41 derringer hidden under her garter.

Dan Caine thought Lucretia and Gwendolyn rare, exotic creatures, and he knew he'd never look at another woman in the same way again. Even Estella Sweet was a pale shadow of these, her fallen sisters, and she could not hope to equal their ravishing beauty. As whores went, these two were the cream of the crop.

"Ladies, return to your gentlemen," Misty said. "You'll have hot water soon and I'll meet you at dinner. Oh, has Mr. Beck settled in?" She looked at Dan and said, "Mr. Beck arrived just before you did." She made a face. "He rents a girl by the night." Then to Lucretia, "Is our dear Violetta with him? I hope she brought some crocheting."

"Not as far as I know," Lucretia said. "Violetta is a slut."

"Now, now, Lucretia, she's as dedicated as we are to the ancient profession. Still, I won't allow her and Mr. Beck to sit at the dinner table tonight. Too low class, you understand. So when you leave here, stop by the kitchen and tell cook to send up a tray for Violetta and her gentleman. What room?"

"Room 32," Lucretia said. She glanced at Dan. "It's the attic room that's right up against the rafters." The woman shook her beautiful head, frowning. "I hate it up there. It's so dark and gloomy."

"And ghostly . . . spooky," Gwendolyn said, shuddering.

"Beggars can't be choosers," Misty said, waving a pudgy, milk white hand, revealing a scattering of liver spots that betrayed her age. "Thirty-two has a nice brass bed and old Queen Vic's picture on the wall. As you know, Violetta was a common whore working the line in Ellsworth when I rescued her. And while I don't consider Mr. Beck a beggar, I most certainly won't allow him or Violetta to sit at table with my gentlemen."

"I should think not." Gwendolyn sniffed. "Beck is a drover of some kind and Violetta Bullen is a tramp."

CHAPTER ELEVEN

Dan Caine watched Lucretia and Gwendolyn leave, his mind busy. It was highly probable that the man called Beck had been with Clay Kyle at the Calthrop massacre and had later decided to visit High Time and his whore. Room 32, third floor. A dark and gloomy landing. It was a good place to take Beck by surprise . . . with his pants down.

Misty Maguire rose to her feet, an obese woman in a green silk dress, feathers in elaborately ringleted blonde hair that was probably a wig. She had a little doll face, china blue eyes that always held a surprised expression, and a little cupid's bow mouth with cherry red lips. (Around 1905, a reporter for *The American Magazine* quipped that the madame's lips were the only cherries to ever set foot in High Time.) Misty's chubby cheekbones were colored with perfect circles of bright crimson rouge, a startling contrast to the rest of her face that was as white as a fish's belly. She was only forty years old that fall, but Texas and her chosen profession had aged her.

Misty waited until a thunderclap shook the house and chimed crystal liquor decanters on a nearby table before she said, "After dinner we'll talk about your needs, Mr. Caine. In the meantime, you may stay here until I return. Help yourself to a drink." The woman smiled. "But first you must observe the grand procession."

"What's that?" Dan said.

"Why, it's the promenade down the stairs followed by a polonaise and then a grand march into the dining room. It's all most elegant and worthy of this house," Misty said. "Each gentleman has his lady on his arm while my footmen play Verdi's Grand March from *Aida* on the piano and violin. I take it you're familiar with that sublime music."

"Oh, yeah, sure," Dan said.

He had no idea what in hell the fat lady was talking about.

"You must stand in the shadows and observe, Mr. Caine. You will see something wonderful that you'll remember for the rest of your life. And just think, one day you may be a part of it. That is, if you have the dinero. Now it's almost time. The dinner gong is about to sound." Then in a conspiratorial whisper, "Come with me. We'll be as quiet as little church mice."

Misty Maguire led Dan to a dark corner in the foyer and pushed him behind a tall potted plant that Dan guessed was some kind of aggressive fern.

"After the procession and the polonaise, you may return to the drawing room," Misty said. "Until then"—she placed a forefinger on her lips—"shh. Be a little mouse, remember."

Room 32, third floor. Dan Caine branded the location on his brain.

Through a curtain of ferns, he watched Misty Maguire climb the staircase. It seemed she was part of the big parade, and Dan smiled to himself. He was aware of the weight of his holstered Colt dragging on the cartridge belt, and once everybody was in the drawing room, he'd head for Mr. Beck in the attic. Dan's face was suddenly grim, hard-boned, merciless. If it turned out that the man had taken a hand in the killing of the Calthrop family . . . it would be better for him if he'd never been born.

But then a warning thought hit him hard . . . like a clenched fist to the gut. He recalled what Clint Cooley had told him. If Beck was one of Clay Kyle's boys, and that seemed increasingly likely, he'd be a named pistol fighter because the outlaw hired no other kind. He'd be fast on the draw and shoot, and Dan had sense enough to doubt that he could match the man's skill with a gun. He could only hope to gain the drop on Beck and get his work in before the gunman giggled and triggered him. And the woman was another complication. Dan sighed, angry at himself. All right, let it go. There was no point in building houses on a bridge he hadn't crossed yet. Then suddenly a piano and a violin played the opening, majestic chords of the *Aida* march and brought Dan back to the here and now.

He peered through the green ferns, then turned away to investigate a scuttling at his feet. Annoyed, he kicked a large rat away from him and went back to his study of the staircase.

As the dramatic music swelled, Dan watched Misty Maguire make her slow, dignified way down the staircase. Her face was expressionless, lost in the moment, but her huge bosom swelled with pride. She had donned a black top hat for the occasion, a yellowed, square clock face with Roman numerals attached to the front of the crown. Dan guessed the old dial was all that was left of High Time's legendary steam clock that could be seen for a hundred miles. If it was, it was surely a disappointment.

Behind Misty, stepping soundlessly, came a procession of the living . . . and the living dead.

Eight white-haired men in black evening clothes, each

had a young woman's gloved hand on his crooked right arm as they came down the stairs in twos. All the men were old, mostly very old, and one of them could have been ninety, a foot shorter than the young thing on his arm. But as a group, the eight men emanated an air of wealth and power, made obvious by thick gold watch chains, diamond rings, and big bellies, the badges of office of the rich and well-fed.

The rat was persistent and again worried Dan's boot. Irritated, he kicked it away . . . and made the fern rock dangerously in its pot. His heart in his mouth, as thunder roared and lightning filled the foyer with dazzling light, he grabbed the teetering fern and held it upright.

But nobody noticed.

The men and women descending the grand staircase were absorbed in the procession . . . wrapped up in each other, bonded by money and desire. The men's faces were solemn, lordly, but the ladies on their arms smiled and bared their teeth. The male half of the promenade was a slow-moving column of somber black and white, but the female side was a silken kaleidoscope of clashing color—magenta, yellow, blue and purple, nodding feathers, fluttering fans, naked shoulders, glittering diamonds, and pushed-up breasts that were white, but not, God forbid, pure white.

As each couple reached the bottom of the stairs, they chose a spot in the foyer and gradually formed a circle, the unsmiling men facing their ladies. Misty Maguire stood to one side, beaming, her face shining with sweat. After a quick glance at the circle, she signaled with her raised hand, and *Aida* came to an abrupt and undignified halt. But after a pause of just a heartbeat, the piano and violin struck up again with Strauss's *Blue Danube* waltz. The couples danced, gracefully moving around the floor in a perfect circle, and the women's vivid dresses flared like the petals of exotic blossoms whirling on the surface of a mill pond.

Dan Caine watched and battled the aggressive rat, now joined by another, as Misty carefully avoided the dancers and crossed the foyer to the dining room. She said something to a gaunt flunky dressed like a head waiter, and the man nodded and opened the dining room doors. Then, couple by couple, the waltzers left the floor and twirled inside. When the last pair, the ninety-year-old and his statuesque partner, entered the room, the doors slammed shut behind them and the music stopped.

Dan aimed one final kick at the aggressive rodents and then stepped into the silent foyer.

CHAPTER TWELVE

Somewhere a door banged, probably the musicians leaving. Dan Caine heard a hum of conversation drift from the dining room, punctuated by female laughter, a whore playing her part. The air smelled of cologne, perfume, and sweat, and the decay of age, as though the house had just witnessed a dance of the dead. Dan quickly covered the distance between himself and the grand staircase and on silent feet climbed to the first floor above the foyer, where several corridors lined with paintings of half-naked women led to bedrooms. Guttering oil lamps placed on spindly tables provided the only light. To Dan's right, at the end of the landing was a narrow stairwell leading to the upper floors. He took the stairs to the second story, arranged like the one below, a series of corridors lined with bedrooms. But there were no pictures of naked women on the walls, fewer oil lamps to cast pools of yellow light and dark shadows. The air smelled of rising damp and mold as though the rooms on this floor hadn't been used in a long time. The walls were covered in dust and spiderwebs and every step Dan took was accompanied by the creak and squeak of protesting floorboards. Like the level below, there was a flight of narrow stairs at the end of the gloomy hallway, and Dan grabbed a lamp and stepped carefully in that direction. But he stopped and smiled when the lamplight revealed writing on the wall, made with either black chalk or charcoal . . .

*Donny Harrow done a whore
on this spot. July 4, 1878.*

Dan's smile widened. That must have been written before Misty Maguire turned respectable.

Room 32 third floor.

Dan's momentary good humor vanished as he climbed the narrow stairs that led to the upper rooms. When he reached the landing, he stood still and looked around, acutely aware that every step of the stairs had screaked. There were three rooms to his left, hastily built with walls of unfinished timber and roofed with sheets of plywood. Dan figured that these were once intended to be servants' quarters but were never finished. Each door had a brass, oval shaped number plate with black numbers . . . 31 . . . 32 . . . 34. An oil lamp burned in 32, adding a yellowish sheen to a casement window that was opaque with the dust of years and laced with cobwebs. Barely visible in the gloom, a series of heavy, triangular-shaped beams held up a roof that soared fifty feet above the third floor. It seemed that the builders had finished three levels of the High Time mansion and then called it a day when the English million-aire died and the money dried up. Now the only living creatures that populated the upper reaches of the house were spiders, bats, a man called Beck . . . and a bargain-priced whore.

Dan Caine pulled his Colt, thinking that he'd followed tracks that led to the mansion, but was the man Beck the

one he was looking for? Was he really a member of Clay
Kyle's murderous gang? Questions without answers. But he
told himself this much . . . he was a vigilante, a breed of
men who were not inclined to give a suspect the benefit of
the doubt. Dan scolded his hesitation and finally listened to
his own advice . . . rightly or wrongly gun them. Better a
hundred innocent men die than one guilty man goes free.
He frowned. Hell, that wasn't the saying. Wasn't it the
other way around? The rhythmic screech of bed springs in
room 32 put the question out of Dan's mind. He'd wait until
the noise ended and Beck was good and exhausted before
bursting into the room and getting the drop. He nodded to
himself. It was a plan, not a brilliant plan, but right then it
was all he had.

The bed continued to rock and Dan waited . . . and
waited. The storm had finally rolled away, leaving only a
rumble of distant thunder barely audible above the cease-
less racket of the brass bed in room 32. Dan Caine shook
his head. Damn, whoever he might be, Beck brought new
meaning to the word cowpoke.

The bed noise reached a crescendo and then abruptly
stopped.

Dan wiped his sweaty gun hand on his pants and took up
his Colt again. He stepped to the room and made a quick decision. A polite knock on the door and a "Howdy Podner"
was out of the question, so . . .

Dan Caine raised his booted right foot and crashed the
door in.

CHAPTER THIRTEEN

Years after these events, dime novels of the more sensational sort did the High Time affair a disservice, especially the New York Boys Adventure Library that in 1897 published a wildly inaccurate tale they entitled *The Deputy's Dilemma or Terror at Murder Mansion*. The novel, which was widely praised, claimed that when Dan Caine kicked in the bedroom door he was met with a "fusillade of fire from the deadly pistols of Solomon (sic) Beck. But dashing Dan Caine triggered his own guns with amazing speed and dexterity and inflicted several hits, forcing Beck to cry out *in extremis,* 'Oh, I am slain!' An innocent housemaid had been dusting the room when the shooting started and Dan said to her, as he holstered his smoking Colts, 'Thus perish all evildoers who believe they can break the law with impunity.' The young maid swooned and Dan caught her ere she fell to the ground. 'You are my hero!' the girl exclaimed. But Dan did not encourage the lass because he'd made a promise to his gray-haired mother that neither a woman's kiss nor demon drink would ever touch his lips. 'I am, dear lady, already wed . . . to the law,' quoth that stout-hearted stalwart."

The reality was very different. Starkly different.

When the door slammed against the bedroom wall and

shattered in a shower of splinters, two things happened. Violetta, the former line whore, shrieked and pulled the bedsheet under her chin, her china blue eyes as round as coins . . . and Shadow Beck smiled and said howdy. Then he said, grinning, "Hell, feller, no need to kick the door down. This gal ain't that hard to get. All she does is scratch an itch."

"Mister, I don't want her, I want you," Dan said. He showed the gun in his hand.

A sheet covered Shadow Beck's lanky body but his big feet stuck out the bottom of the bed. He wore red socks with holes in them.

Beck made a show of using his forefinger to turn his gunbelt on the bedside table so that the butt of the holstered Colt faced him. "What do you want with me?" he said.

"You ride with Clay Kyle and them?" Dan said.

"Who wants to know?" Beck said. He lost his grin.

"Name's Dan Caine."

"Never heard of you."

"Have you heard of the Calthrop family, north of here?"

That struck a nerve. Beck stiffened, revealing his surprise, and said, "No, I've never heard of them, and I ain't never heard of you either. You some kind of law?"

"I was," Dan said. "Now I'm just a concerned citizen." He paused for effect. "What you might call a vigilante."

A taut silence stretched between Dan and Beck, until Violetta cut through it with her sharp tongue. "Well, just you vigilante it the hell out of here, cowboy," she said. "Shadow don't know them people. Anyway, he's been with me the last six months, an' I'll swear that on a stack of Bibles."

"Lady, he just got here," Dan said.

"Says you, Baine, Train, or whatever the hell you call

yourself," Violetta said. "Shadow is going straight and I'm proud to be his kept woman."

"Listen to the little lady," Beck said, smiling. "I've quit the outlaw profession for good, and me and Violetta is getting hitched. So run along, vigilante man, and search for the elephant someplace else."

The woman lifted her hand, allowing the sheet to fall, and wiggled her fingers. "See, Shadow bought the wedding ring already."

Dan was on edge, his belly knotted into a tight ball. Damn, Beck's hand was close to his pistol. Mighty close. Too close. Even with a gun in his face he was relaxed, unafraid, confident in his abilities and of himself. An alarm bell clamored in Dan's head. Hell, Beck was too relaxed, too arrogant. The man was a gun. Had to be. Dan's jaw clenched. Well, there were no other lawmen or kinda lawmen around. There was only Dan Caine . . . and he had to do it.

The ring on the woman's hand was rose gold and showed signs of wear. "Let me see that wedding band," Dan said.

"No," Violetta said, pouting. "You might steal it."

"What does it say inside?" Dan said.

The woman didn't need to look. "It says *forever*. Shadow put it there."

"No, he didn't," Dan said. "The husband of a woman called Nancy Calthrop put it there. Clay Kyle and his boys cut off Nancy's finger to get the ring. And that's not all they did to her."

The woman looked like she'd been slapped. "Shadow, is that true? Tell him it's a lie. Tell him you'd nothing to do with it."

"You shut your trap," Beck said. He was a cornered rat figuring his chances, his gun unhandy on the side table.

"Shadow . . ." Violetta whined.

"Get out of here you damned cheap whore," Beck said. "I've got a man's work to do."

He studied the vigilante and summed him up as just another small-time lawman who carried around a rusty Colt as a badge of office. The outlaw saw Dan's gun shake, just a little, but enough, and Beck figured he could dive out of bed, grab his own pistol, and get his work in while the rube panicked and sprayed lead.

It was a plan, and Shadow Beck tensed.

Whatever else historians say of him, that night Dan Caine was as scared as hell, but he was game. He'd shot bean cans off rocks at ten feet with his Colt and missed more often than he'd hit. But Beck was a bigger target than a bean can and much closer.

Suddenly, in quick succession, two unlikely events happened that swung the standoff in Dan's favor.

The first was that Violetta got violently angry. Sure, she was a whore, but Shadow had called her a cheap whore, words that scalded her brain like hot sauce, words she could not forgive. Those days of working the line still hurt.

The second was more direct. She tore off the wedding ring and threw it at Beck, helped on its way by a stream of vile and vivid curses that must remain unwritten for fear they upset the timid reader.

Violetta didn't know it then, but she'd just signed Shadow Beck's death warrant.

The outlaw instinctively moved to his left to avoid the flying ring, a slight and harmless movement for sure.

But Dan Caine, edgy and alarmed, didn't see it as harmless.

He fired, a hurried, poor shot that burned across the right side of Beck's neck, drawing blood. Beck had skinned his Colt and he raised it to eye level, aiming for Dan's head. It was a practiced motion, very smooth, very quick, a masterly shootist's play.

BAM! BAM! BAM!

Three guns hammered at almost the same instant.

Violetta got her work in a split second ahead of the two men. The Remington .41 caliber derringer she'd retrieved from the pocket of her discarded dress was devastating at close range. A split second before the gunman triggered his weapon, a bullet crashed into the side of his head above the ear. Beck jolted in pain and pulled his shot, and the bullet thudded into the wall a foot from Dan's head. Dan fired only a heartbeat behind Violetta and almost at the same instant as an already dead Beck. His bullet hit the outlaw in the chest . . . but it was Violetta who'd killed him.

Shattering the echoing silence that followed the gunfire, the woman shrieked like a demented Valkyrie, threw herself on Beck's bloody body, and begged him to take her with him to Valhalla. Well, not quite in those words. In 1926, newspaperman Richmond Soames's fictionalized account of the life of Violetta Bullen claimed that she cried out, "Shadow, take me to hell with you!" And added that she hugged the man's bleeding head to her breast and sobbed, "I'm sorry. I rid the ground of your shadow, Shadow." What actually happened was that after hugging Beck she jumped up in alarm, stared down at her naked body, and wailed, "Eew . . . I've got his blood all over me. I think I'm gonna puke."

While Violetta mourned Beck, Dan got on the floor and searched for the wedding ring. Displaying the perversity of inanimate objects, the ring had rolled under the bed and jammed itself against the wall. He got down on all fours, crawled under the bed among the dust, dirt, and dead spiders, and retrieved the ring. Determined not to lose the gold band again, Dan shoved it into his shirt pocket and crawled from under the bed. As Violetta stood at the washstand and frantically used an oversized sponge to wipe scarlet blood from her breasts and belly, Dan Caine began to get to his feet.

He never made it.

Something hard and solid hit the back of his head, and he fell into a well of scarlet-streaked darkness that went on forever . . . and ever . . .

CHAPTER FOURTEEN

Dan Caine woke with a dull headache and a *What the hell happened?* question in his scrambled brain. It took him quite a spell to remember. The events of the night came back to him slowly, piece by piece, like one of those wooden jigsaw puzzles he'd seen kids put together back in Thunder Creek. Then after several minutes of struggle, things started to fall back in place. Yeah, that was it, now he remembered. He and Violetta had killed Shadow Beck . . . and . . . and . . . Dan remembered that he'd dropped Nancy Calthrop's ring into his shirt pocket just before somebody put his lights out. Was it still there? When he tried to lift his hand to make sure that the band was still in his pocket . . . he couldn't. Damn it. He couldn't move any part of himself. His legs were bound together by a heavy chain and his wrists were tied to a horizontal beam a foot above his head.

It seemed that killing Beck didn't set right with somebody, probably Misty Maguire. The outlaw had been one of her regular customers, and in that wilderness of grass such men were hard to find.

Then a ray of hope. Clint Cooley would come searching for him and charge to the rescue. But the thought gave him little comfort and less reassurance. As matters stood, he was a prisoner in the High Time mansion and without a doubt hard times were coming down. No matter how he cut it, things weren't looking so good. There was an excellent chance he could wind up dead.

The morning sun slanted through the timbers of a carelessly boarded, round window. Dan looked around and figured it wasn't a window but the place for the long-gone steam clock. To his right, covered in gray spiderwebs, was a jumble of rusted metal, some sort of wood furnace, a clutter of brass and copper pipes of various sizes and piles of gears and cogs. The black Roman numeral VII was painted on a rectangular ceramic tile that lay on the floor, and like everything else in the room it was coated with dust. A pile of junk and the number that indicated seven o'clock twice a day was all that was left of the fabled clock that could be seen for a hundred miles.

But Dan Caine wasn't about to shed tears over a timepiece. He had to get out of there. And for a solid hour he tried, but the ropes that bound his outstretched arms were cruelly tight and would not budge. He fought to pull himself free until his wrists bled, but his bonds held firm. Finally, breathing hard and so thirsty his mouth was as dry as mummy dust, Dan gave up the useless struggle. His head hung, a man facing a lingering death from crucifixion in a whorehouse.

CHAPTER FIFTEEN

Dan Caine woke with a start. The day was still bright, and dust motes danced in the sunlight that angled through chinks in the boarded window. Dan tried to loosen the rope around his wrists again, but it was a no-go. The bonds were just as tight as before. He looked around him. He was in the place where the steam clock once ticked away seconds, one drop of condensed water at a time. He figured he was even higher in the building than the room occupied by the late Shadow Beck. He seemed to be in a clock tower that faced to the north, judging by the angle of the sun. Towers and turrets were a feature of the mansion, some with pointed roofs as this one had. Unlike the smaller turrets, the tower had a circular shape and was built large enough to accommodate the furnace and workings of a timepiece.

Dan was hungry, thirsty, and hurting. He tried crying out, but the only answer to his croaky cusses and angry yells were mocking echoes. He felt a spiteful pain deep in his gut and angrily vowed to gun all who were responsible for his present wretched circumstances.

Then . . . footsteps . . . slow . . . shuffling . . . ominous . . .

"Who's there?" Dan said. "Show yourself and state your intentions."

"As to who I am, I'm Artemus. As to my intentions, I bring you water."

The old man appeared from the shadows and stepped into the slanting sunlight. A Sharps rifle was slung over his left shoulder by a piece of rope, and he held a bucket of water, the handle of a dipper sticking up above the rim. Artemus, a white-bearded old man with obsidian eyes that gleamed in the light, unslung his Sharps and laid it beside him where it would be handy. He dipped water and held it to Dan's mouth. The water was alkaline and bitter and ran down his chin, but he drank deeply. Artemus took the dipper away and Dan said, "Any grub?"

"No, but you'll get a big breakfast, steak and eggs, before the hanging tomorrow."

"Who's getting hung?"

"You are."

Dan was more angry than scared. "By whose authority?"

Artemus smiled. "By the authority of the lawful court that convened at two o'clock this morning, Lord Gray on the bench as judge, Agatha Brewer, alias Olivia De Laurent, for the defense and Miss Misty Maguire for the prosecution. The jury was made up of six whores who kept dozing off."

"What the hell happened?" Dan said, agitated.

"Well, Prosecutor Brewer told the court that there is no defense for cold-blooded murder and Miss Maguire said, 'There sure as hell isn't.' Lord Bertram Clarence Gray agreed with both the prosecution and the defense, and so did the jury, them that was still awake. Then Lord Gray put a piece of black cloth on his head and sentenced you to hang." Artemus sighed. "It was a quick trial, you understand, not much of a show. Everybody wanted to get to their beds, especially the judge who said he was plum wore out."

Artemus reached out and lifted the Bull Durham sack and papers from Dan's shirt pocket and expertly rolled a cigarette that he held to the prisoner's mouth. "Here, sonny, lick this," he said. Dan did as he was told and Artemus stuck the quirley between his lips and thumb-nailed a lucifer into flame. Dan inhaled deeply, and the tip of the cigarette glowed cherry red in the murk.

"This won't stand," Dan said from behind ringlets of blue smoke. "It's the verdict of a kangaroo court, and I object."

Artemus shook his head. "No one around to hear you object, sonny, well, except for the pretty lady"—he pointed to a dark corner—"over there. But she's been dead for a thousand years and more."

Startled, Dan Caine's eyes probed the shadows. As the sun rose higher in the sky, the clock tower had slowly shaded into gloom, but he made out a pale face in the corner, perfectly still, staring in his direction. "Who the hell is she?" Dan said. Then, "Hey, lady, who are you?" His cigarette bobbed up and down in his mouth.

Artemus said, "She won't answer, sonny. As to what she's doing . . . ah . . . what she's doing is watching you, sonny, the ancient dead keeping vigil over the soon to be dead. As to who she is, well, the French gentleman who brung her here told Miss Maguire that she's the lady Teshet, once a chantress of the temple of the great god Amun Ra at Thebes in Egypt. You know, where the pyramids are. Well, Miss Maguire traded the services of a pair of whores for the Lady Teshet, but it didn't take her long to realize that she'd gotten the worse of that deal. She said the mummy was cursed and made her think of death and Judgment Day. She banished it to the top of the house hoping to sell it one day."

Dan shook his head. "Frenchmen, mummy, I don't know what the hell you're talking about."

"Wait right there and I'll explain it to you, then I have to go stoke the furnace. And get your gallows ready for tomorrow. Don't move now," Artemus said.

"You trying to make a joke, old man?" Dan said.

Dan's question was answered with a cackle, and Artemus crossed the floor into the dark corner. A few moments later, Dan heard the old man say, "Come on, Lady, we're going for a walk." Then a dragging sound, something heavy pushed across the rough timber floor. Then Artemus spoke again, his gravelly voice loud in the silence. "You're heavy, Lady. Any of them French fellers in Egypt ever tell you that?"

Like an apparition, a vaguely human-shaped and richly decorated container about seven feet tall appeared out of the gloom. The case bore the painted likeness of a young woman's face and at three different places it was enveloped in the outspread, protective wings of a strange, buzzard-like creature. Down the front of the case was a column of small pictures and wavy and straight lines that Artemus identified as Ancient Egyptian writing.

"What the hell is that?" Dan said. He spat away the stub of his cigarette. Whatever the box was, he didn't like the look of it.

"You're some kind of ignorant, ain't you, cowboy?" Artemus said. He doffed his top hat and goggles, laid them carefully on the floor, and wiped his sweaty brow with his coat sleeve. "It's a mummy case. The Lady Teshet is a mummy, and she's inside there, all wrapped in bandages, a-waiting for the Day of Resurrection. You never saw the like, huh?"

It suddenly dawned on Dan that he had seen the like. Just after he got out of Huntsville, twenty pounds underweight and fevered, he watched a medicine show in Waco that featured a bandage-wrapped corpse in a painted coffin.

"I seen the like a few years back," Dan said. "I recollect listening to a snake-oil salesman who called himself Professor Leviticus Bookworm. I'll never forget that name. Anyway, he told the crowd that the dead ranny was the mummy of a great Egyptian king who'd lived for a hundred, healthy years by drinking sacred water from the river Nile every single day. The bottle of Nile water cost me my last nickel, and it didn't cure my fever but at the time I thought it made my hair grow thicker." Dan shook his head. "Hell, the mummy didn't look like a king. All wrapped in dirty bandages it was even skinnier than I was. The professor was a cheat and a fraud and so was the mummy." He nodded to the coffin. "Like her."

"You've a good mind, lawman. That is until you make it up," Artemus said. "I guess you think the curse is a fraud too, huh?"

"What curse?" Dan said.

"Want another smoke?" Artemus said. "I'm being nice to you here, trying to stop you studying on the hanging tomorrow."

"Why?" Dan said.

"Because I've took to liking you, sonny. I'm going to hang you, but I like you."

Dan nodded. "That's true blue of you," he said.

Artemus smiled. "Damn right. Sometimes I act like a white man. Smoke?"

"Yeah, smoke."

Dan watched the old man go through the cowboy ritual of building the cigarette with one hand, only a few tiny strands of tobacco dropping on the floor. He licked the paper and then got the thing lit. Dan inhaled deeply, the wished-for nicotine hit carried like a genie on a cloud of blue smoke.

"What curse? That's what you asked, wasn't it, sonny?" Artemus said. "Well, it's right there on the front of the coffin. The Frenchman told Miss Maguire what it says and wrote it down for her. And then she told me. Now listen up, here's what it says . . . *Whosoever disturbs the body of this servant of Amun Ra will meet with violent death. His breast will be pierced by arrows and his body consumed by fire.*"

Artemus smiled and said, "Scary, ain't it? The curse is why Miss Maguire had me bring Lady Teshet up here. She hopes to sell her for fifty dollars someday, but so far, she's had no takers. Men don't come to a whorehouse to buy mummies."

He picked up his hat, settled it on his head, sighed, and said, "Well I got to go and battle the demon furnace. Until I see you again, I'll leave Lady Teshet here to keep you company. But I warn you, she ain't much of a chatterbox."

Pleased with his little joke, Artemus stepped away. Then he stopped, turned, and said, "How do you like your eggs?"

"Huh?" Dan said.

"To go with your steak tomorrow afore you get hung," Artemus said.

"Scrambled," Dan said. "And while you're at it, cook up some for the mummy. She's had nothing to eat for a thousand years."

CHAPTER SIXTEEN

A horned moon nudged aside the stars and the strong prairie wind rippled the grass like the shallows of a dark sea as Estella Sweet stood alone in the gloom and stared into the distance.

Clint Cooley stepped beside her, handed her a cup of coffee, and said, "What do you see out there?"

The girl smiled. "It's dark. I see nothing but moonlight . . . like a pearly mist on the grass."

Cooley said, "You see more than that, young lady. I'm a man and you're a woman and you can see things I can't."

"Do you believe that?"

"Yes, I do."

"Then I'm a cat," Estella said. She tried her coffee. "Good," she said.

"No one knows what a cat sees," Cooley said. "But the Ancient Egyptians worshipped cats because they believed they could see the dead."

"I can't see the dead," Estella said.

"No, but you're seeing something tonight," Cooley said. "Not with your eyes but with what my Irish mother called the second sight. It's a rare gift usually given to women. But it's no gift at all . . . it's a curse."

"What does second sight do?"

"It makes you see a thing that's about to happen or has happened."

"Like a gypsy fortune-teller?"

"Something like that."

Estella looked into the black depths of her coffee cup. "Dan Caine is in terrible danger."

"You see it?" Cooley said.

"No, I don't see it. I feel it." Estella's eyes were troubled when she looked at Cooley. "It hurts . . . a pain in my belly. I think . . . I know . . . that Deputy Caine is going to die." Her gaze searched the gambler's face. "Do you believe me?"

Cooley nodded. "Yes, I believe you. My mother could foretell death."

"Future events are not written in stone," Estella said. "Clint, we can change what is to come. Maybe there's still time to save Dan."

Cooley thought that through and then said, "I'll go after him." He smiled, stretched out his right arm, and pointed with a bladed hand. "Thataway, due east, with two sets of tracks to follow. I'll find him."

"We'll all find him," Estella said. "The Thunder Creek vigilantes must stick together."

Cooley said, "No, you'll stay here with the others. This is my kind of business, Estella. Look at your vigilantes sleeping by the fire, Estella. A half-grown boy, a drunken newspaperman, Fish Lee, game but old, and somewhere out there in the darkness an Indian who doesn't give a damn." He shook his head. "Without Dan Caine there are no vigilantes."

"Then find him, Clint," Estella said. "Bring him back."

"Wait two days," Cooley said. "If Dan and me don't return by then, ride for Thunder Creek and don't look back."

"Where will you be?" the girl said.

"I reckon we'll be nowhere," Cooley said. "We'll be dead."

To Clint Cooley's surprise, as he prepared to ride into the night, the Kiowa grabbed the bridle of his big American stud and said, "I scouted the trail and it's good, well-marked in the long grass. You should reach the big house by morning."

"If such exists," the gambler said.

"It exists. Rich men go there to enjoy fancy women."

"Then it's a cat house."

"Or a hell house." A random gust of prairie wind streamed long black hair across the Kiowa's face that he made no effort to remove. "The young woman who sees the future is right. Deputy Caine may already be dead."

Cooley nodded. "I aim to find out." He touched the brim of his hat. "Much obliged."

"I will look after the others until your return," the Kiowa said. He saw that Cooley was taken aback by that promise and said, "I have no liking for whites, but when I'm paid to do a job, I do it."

"Well, thank—"

The Indian dropped his hand from Cooley's bridle as though it was suddenly red hot. "No! I want no thanks from a white man," he said. "His words are as honest as the smile on the face of a rattlesnake and signify nothing. Go now, gambler. Do what you have to do."

Cooley nodded and kicked his horse into motion. He looked back just once and all of them, Estella Sweet, Fish Lee, Cornelius Massey, and young Holt Peters were on their feet, silently watching him go. In the darkness and the red fire glow Clint Cooley thought they looked like mourners at a funeral . . . his funeral.

CHAPTER SEVENTEEN

They came for Dan Caine at four-thirty in the morning on the day of the hanging.

Artemus, in black broadcloth and his top hat, carried his Sharps Big Fifty, and Dan thought the muzzle looked like the entrance to a railroad tunnel. Artemus, with a man to hang, looked solemn as an undertaker, all his good humor of the previous afternoon gone. With him was Lord Anthony Gray, the hanging judge, a short-barreled Webley .450 police model in his hand. He had cold blue, merciless eyes, the skin of his face so close to the skull he looked as though he wore a Mexican Day of the Dead mask.

Gray stepped to Dan, shoved the muzzle of the Webley against his forehead, and said, "Untie him, Artemus." And then to Dan, "Don't move a muscle, cowboy. Don't even blink or I'll blow your bloody brains out."

"Easy to threaten an unarmed man," Dan said. "Call yourself a lord? You, sir, have the manners of a coward and the speech of a drunken muleskinner."

Gray snarled like an animal, his face twisted in rage. He slammed Dan with the Webley, a backhanded blow that opened a gaping cut on the helpless prisoner's cheekbone and instantly jetted blood that ran down his face in a scarlet stream.

Punch-drunk and dizzy, Dan's head reeled from the savage blow and he tasted blood in his mouth. But between clenched teeth he managed to grit out, "You sorry piece of trash."

Gray raised his revolver again, his face demonic, but Artemus stepped beside him and grabbed his arm. "No, my lord," he said, his voice quiet but formidable. "Let the man go to his death in peace."

Dan thought the Englishman was angry enough to gun Artemus on the spot, but he thought the better of it and said, "Finish untying him, and get this damned thing over with. Use the rope to bind his hands behind his back."

Artemus nodded and whispered to Dan, "No fancy moves, sonny, or I'll shred you into a rag doll with my fifty."

"Studying on it, getting shot to pieces sounds better than hanging," Dan said.

"Any death is better than hanging," Artemus said.

A couple of minutes later, Dan Caine was marched down the stairwell, a revolver muzzle at the back of his neck and a Sharps unkindly prodding into his spine.

A welcoming committee stood outside the house and a few of the whores smiled and applauded. Dan wondered if the warm reception was for him or his executioners. He decided it was not for him when one of the whores broke ranks and tried to brain him with a champagne bottle. She was stopped by Misty Maguire who snatched the bottle away from the young lady and reminded her that this was a solemn occasion and she should mind her manners. She then proceeded to box the ears of the unrepentant whore and sent her back into the house in disgrace.

Dan was uncomfortably aware of the Sharps muzzle

digging into his lower back as he looked around. He didn't like what he saw. In fact, it scared the hell out of him.

Lord Gray took his place among the seven distinguished members of the High Time sporting club who were lined up at the corner of the house to the left of the main door. Like Gray, most were dressed in tweeds, though a couple of the older men wore broadcloth. That all present wore black robes and grotesque face masks "like the KKK in mourning" is a myth made up by a scurrilous turn-of-the-century dime novelist. This man, who called himself Tiny Tim Scratcher, later succumbed to yellow fever in Panama . . . and most folks reckoned that it served him right.

Eleven whores, the kept women of the eight wealthy clients and three spares, were dressed in scarlet corsets and high boots and lined up next to the men. Violetta Bullen had been with Shadow Beck when, as Misty put it, "he was most cruelly murdered." But, being of a lower class of whore, she was not invited to the hanging and was sent to help in the kitchen with the broke-neck breakfast.

As the whores sang "When the Swallows Homeward Fly," ominous black clouds spread across the sky like sheets of curled lead and made gloomy the morning. Dan Caine figured that with better weather and under more convivial circumstances, he might have enjoyed the song.

Misty Maguire, with an eye on the weather and the demands of her rumbling stomach, kept her preamble short, sweet, and to the point. "The condemned will now meet his much-deserved fate. May God have mercy on his soul."

"About bloody time!" Lord Gray yelled. "Now string him up."

Dan felt the Sharps prod harder into his back, and Artemus said, "Get moving." Then in a whisper into his ear, "Die game, sonny."

Dan nodded. "I'll do my best, but I ain't making any promises."

The men and women had been lined up, but now they broke ranks and followed Dan around the side of the house where his horse stood patiently under a projecting beam with a large iron hook holding a simple block and tackle designed to lift heavy beer barrels and flour sacks to the second-floor storeroom. A hemp rope was threaded through the pulley and a hangman's noose dangled three or four feet above the horse's bare back.

Lord Gray took charge. He turned to a pair of pasty-faced, frightened-looking men that Dan figured must be the house musicians and said, "You two, help Artemus lift him on the horse." The men were taken aback, but Gray snapped, "Get it done."

Artemus placed the noose around Dan's neck, he was manhandled onto his mount, and the rope was pulled tight. "Artemus, tie it off," Gray said. "Around the fence post there."

"It's an old post, and it's rotten," the old man said.

"I know," Gray said, "but I examined it. It's strong enough to support Caine's weight for a few minutes while he dances his jig."

A smell of frying bacon drifted from the kitchen window, and plates clattered.

A distinguished looking man with magnificent mutton-chop whiskers sniffed, sniffed again, and then slapped his huge belly with both hands and said, "Hang the scoundrel and let us to breakfast."

Lord Gray took a step back from the horse, raised a riding crop, and looked up at Dan. "Any last words?" he said.

Dan Caine obliged and said, "You go to hell."

But Lord Anthony Gray was no longer interested in what Dan had to say.

His whole, horrified attention was fixed on the arrow sticking out of his throat, its strap iron point embedded under his chin. Gray stumbled toward the others, his arms outstretched, a stunned, terrified *why me?* expression on his face as blood spurted from his dreadful wound.

But now it was every man for himself and Gray was ignored. And so was Dan.

Misty Maguire screamed, "Indians!" and led a charge of whores and beaus toward the house, the men knocking women aside as they stampeded for the door. But a couple of the whores, notably Lucretia and Gwendolyn, showed more sand than the males and cut loose at the circling Apaches with the single-shot derringers they drew from their garters. They made no hits and both were cut down by rifle fire, glossy, golden, gorgeous women destroyed in an instant by lead.

Artemus, who'd fought both Apaches and Comanches in the past, backed toward the door, dropped to one knee, and threw the Sharps to his shoulder. He shot a paint pony that screamed and hit the ground hard in a cloud of dust, and then put a bullet into its staggering rider. The old man rose to his feet and retreated in the direction of the door again, working his rifle, standing wide legged with his face to the enemy, yelling defiance. He killed a second Indian charging with a raised lance and winged a third, forcing him out of the fight. By any measure, Artemus had acquitted himself well, and in future years Apaches who'd been at the High Time fight would remember him as a warrior. But the old timer had taken an arrow to the chest and his left thigh had been smashed by a rifle bullet and he collapsed several yards from the door. Artemus was quickly dispatched by a tomahawk blow to the head that unfortunately in his final moments he saw coming, and the young buck who'd cleaved his skull took his Sharps.

Two Apaches had been killed and one wounded out of a force of thirty, and the rest now came under fire from the house. Most dismounted and settled down to a siege, shooting at anything that moved behind the windows. An older warrior with some gray in his shoulder-length hair stayed mounted and left the fight to explore the side of the house where he'd earlier seen a white man on a horse.

That man was Dan Caine, a rope around his neck and a restive mustang between his legs that tossed its hammer head and tried to make up its mind whether to bolt or not and get away from all the shooting.

The Apache, his name was Taklishim, the Gray One, drew rein, and his black eyes glittered as he studied the white man who was in such big trouble. For a moment, a smile touched Taklishim's lips as he considered shooting his rifle in the air and then watching the man dangle after his horse bolted.

But for an Apache, that was way too easy. Too quick. The rope could snap the fool white man's neck like a twig and kill him instantly. Where was the fun in that?

Given his present circumstances Dan was prepared to be neighborly. "Howdy," he said. Then he instantly regretted it as the mustang responded to his rider's voice and made to walk forward. "Whoa . . . whoa . . ." Dan said. "Damn you hoss, you're gonna kill me."

The Mescalero Apache warrior was one of the most notional creatures on God's green earth. Expect him to do one thing, and he'd be sure to do another, especially if it was a good joke that involved the follies of the white man.

Then it happened.

Dan was horrified as his horse walked right out from under him. He bumped over the animal's hindquarters and dropped into space as the noose clamped tight on his throat, choking, strangling him. Searing lightning bolts flashed behind his eyes and he heard a roaring in his ears like the crash of surf on rocks.

BAAANG!

The slam of a rifle, very close, and the next thing Dan knew he was flat on his back, the rope around his neck suddenly loose, frayed, coiled on his chest like a gray serpent. He raised his head and saw the Apache sitting his pony, staring at him, grinning, smoke trickling from the muzzle of his Winchester. His courage shredded to the bone, Dan could only wait for the Indian to make the next move. He'd parted the rope with a bullet. Would his second part Dan's hair?

For long, pulse-quickening moments two men, mortal enemies, whelps of war gods, were locked in a silence as though the noisy rattle of gunfire so close to them did not exist.

Taklishim, no wild young buck but a seasoned fighting man, waged a war with himself. Dan could see it in his eyes. The Apache had played a good joke on the white man and in doing so had saved his life. Would he now throw that small mercy back in the man's teeth? The Mescalero reached a decision. He swung from his horse, stepped to Dan, and pulled him to his feet by the hair.

Dan broke free and lurched back. "Injun," he said, "stay away from me or I'll kick your ass so hard your squaw will feel it."

The Apache grunted and pulled a Green River hunting knife with a seven-inch blade, a weapon as large as life and twice as real. Dan backed away, fearfully aware of the bound wrists that made him vulnerable.

"Media vuelta!" the Indian said.

"Go to hell," Dan said.

"Turn around," Taklishim said, using English after Spanish had failed. He held his rifle in his left hand pointed at Dan's belly.

"Yeah, give it to me in the back, you damned yellow-bellied coward," Dan said.

The flinty expression on the Apache's face did not change. "Turn around," he said.

Dan had escaped a hanging only to get his throat cut. If he saw any humor in that situation, it's never been recorded. He turned his back on the Apache. A shuffle of hard-soled moccasins on gravel and then a slight tug on the rope around his wrists and the severed bonds fell to his feet.

Dan turned in time to see the Indian jump on his pony. The warrior's red and black streaks of war paint across his wide cheekbones and nose were vivid against his coffee-colored skin. He pointed the rifle at the white man. "When we meet again, this day or some other day, I will kill you."

Dan Caine rubbed his rope-burned wrists and studied the Apache, committing to memory the man's paint, beaded buckskin vest, dark red headband, and leather revolver belt and holster decorated with silver Mexican conchos. A slim scar about three inches long ran down his left cheek.

"I will remember you," Dan said. "You saved my life and I hope one day I will save yours."

The Apache sat his pony for long moments, staring at Dan. Now the sound of gunfire, loud, ragged fusillades, fractured the silence that had held the two men in its freakish spell. There was also an ominous tang of woodsmoke in the air.

Taklishim ended the standoff. He raised his rifle above his head, let loose with the hair-raising, undulating Apache war cry, and swung his horse around. He turned at the corner of the house and vanished from sight.

CHAPTER EIGHTEEN

Unarmed, his horse gone, Dan Caine knew he was in a heap of trouble.

The gunfight seemed to be centered on a main door of the mansion, away from his hiding place, but the Apaches could find him anytime and . . . he didn't dare think about that. The shooting was intense, and it seemed that the white men, whoremasters though they be, were giving a good account of themselves. But the smoke smell was stronger, the stench of ancient wood flaming. Fire arrows? The Apaches were known to use them against wood structures and could be trying to burn High Time down around Misty Maguire's ears. The threatening dark sky had cleared and with it the rain that could have saved her.

To try to make a run for it into open ground would mean certain death, and Dan dismissed that thought from his mind. The kitchen was seemingly deserted and the window was still open, but it was a good fifteen feet above the ground, and the wall of the house was smooth timber with no handholds. Then it came to Dan that the rope meant to kill him could save him. The end cut by the bullet still dangled from the block and tackle. He grabbed it, and the pulley rocked but held. High above his head on the second floor, the twin loading doors of the storeroom were closed . . . and locked? That was a mind-jarring possibility, but there was only one way to find out. Dan grabbed the rope, jerked on it a couple of times, and then hauled himself up and braced his feet against the wall. It occurred to him then that if an Apache without a sense of humor came up on him, he'd be shot down like a possum off a tree branch. That thought gave him strength, and he redoubled his efforts to climb higher, hand over aching hand, booted feet slamming, then skidding on the wall. It seemed to take an eternity to reach the storehouse loading entrance but finally he made it. A hinge-splintering kick, and the doors crashed inward, followed by Dan's right leg. For a moment he hung precariously from the rope and then managed to swing both legs into the opening. Then a heart-stopping shock! My God, he was falling backward!

Frantically, Dan grabbed the top of the door to his left, and his stomach muscles took the strain as he pulled himself forward. For a split second out of the corner of his eye he caught a cartwheeling glimpse of the ground. Damn, it was a long way down, and scattered rocks and gravel promised a back-breaking landing. But then the weight of Dan's upper body asserted itself and he toppled forward and ended up on his hands and knees in a puddle of molasses leaking from a barrel.

Dan rose to his feet, his hands a sticky mess. He found a piece of sacking and cleaned himself up as best he could. The sound of gunfire reached the storeroom and so did the acrid smell of smoke, and neither boded well. He looked around him, his eyes searching. The storeroom was small but stacked from floor to ceiling with sacks of coffee, pinto beans, spices, oatmeal, flour, sugar, canned meat and fruit, eggs, milk, butter in pottery crocks, sacks of potatoes, apples, and vegetables, smoked hams and whiskey, cigars and tobacco. To Dan's chagrin, what was missing were the essentials . . . namely pistols, rifles, and the ammunition to feed them. He tossed the piece of sacking into a corner, muttered a heartfelt "Damn it," and stepped to the door . . . into a hellish nightmare of smoke and fire.

Dan Caine stood on the broad balcony that ran the length of the mansion's interior and looked down on the foyer. The storeroom, the next-door kitchen, and the adjoining staff dining room had been hidden behind a heavy ruby red velvet curtain that was now burning and scorched cloth hanging from the curtain rail in charred shards. The house, tinder dry from decades of Texas sun and wind, was burning from the inside, like a gigantic roman candle, flames, sparks, and glowing cinders shooting upward toward the rafters. A flaming arrow crashed through a window, faltered in flight and landed harmlessly on the floor. But the damage was already done by many others, and the mansion was in its death throes.

As Dan watched from the balcony, the next to last act of the High Time drama played out in the foyer where the five surviving white men seemed resolved to die like gentlemen. Only four of the whores were still alive, the rest having succumbed to Apache bullets and arrows. Violetta Bullen was not among the living. The men, armed only with revolvers, formed a circle around the terrified women and awaited the final Apache onslaught. Warriors assembled outside the main door and loudly encouraged one another to make a final attack. Their numbers had been badly depleted by the white man's gunfire and only twenty-three of them remained. But the big house was burning and a few wiser heads argued that it would be better to guard the doors and windows and let their enemies burn to death. But the young bucks wanted to end this battle with a great victory, and they coveted women, horses, and guns. In the end, their wishes prevailed, and the Apaches launched the attack, bursting through the door into the smoke-filled foyer.

The distance the Indians charged was about forty feet, a space they covered in a moment of time with only one young warrior wounded by gunfire. Several years later, Dan Caine told *The Illustrated London News* that the five white men, one of them ninety years old, were killed very quickly. "The massacre was probably over in a matter of two or three seconds and all of the deaths were caused by knives and stone war clubs. It was very bloody, and there was much screaming." Asked why he didn't intervene, Dan said, "An unarmed man doesn't meddle in an Apache fight . . . not if he wants to keep his hair." The ultimate fate of the four women is unknown. All Dan told the magazine was that "they were taken."

He did not describe the final act in the tragedy . . . the terrible deaths of Misty Maguire and her two musicians.

"No! For God's sake no!" Dan Caine yelled.

Misty Maguire and the musicians, who'd played no part in the fight, emerged from the thickening smoke and staggered across the foyer each carrying a water bucket in each hand. Blood-and-brain-splashed dead men lay sprawled on the floor, naked, stripped of their clothes and possessions.

"Get up! Get up, damn you!" Misty Maguire screamed at the still corpses. "Don't lie there sleeping. Help us put out the fire so the gentlemen and their ladies can dress for dinner."

"They're dead," the piano player, a pale, longhaired man who looked scared, said. "All of them are dead."

"No, they'll wake up soon," Misty said. "Soon, soon, soon, when the fire is out. Oh, and we must tell Lucretia and

Gwendolyn that Artemus has repaired the furnace." She laid down the water buckets, smiled, and clapped her hands. "Look, see how well it burns."

Dan sprinted along the balcony through smoke and fire and stopped when he overlooked the grand staircase. "Miss Maguire!" he yelled. "Get the hell out of there."

The woman turned to the sound of Dan's voice and called out, "Why, Mr. Caine. You naughty boy, I thought I'd hanged you."

"I'm coming down," Dan said. He choked on smoke and then wheezed, "Stay right there."

He had no great regard for Misty Maguire, a woman who'd ordered his neck stretched, but he couldn't just stand by and see her burn to death. He hurried to the narrow flight of stairs that ran down from the balcony to a shadowed area to the left of the grand staircase that was now blazing in several places. But a bullet crashed into the wall inches above his head and stopped him in midstride. A young Apache stood in the foyer and slowly lowered a Winchester from his shoulder. He now ignored Dan, all his attention on Misty. The woman's hair was hanging unbound over her shoulders, her dress was torn and bloodstained, and her eyes were wild and crazy. The Apache attitude toward insanity was as notional as everything else about them. Some believed the gods used the mentally ill to carry messages to medicine men and women. Others that mad people were possessed by demons and were to be feared, and a few couldn't care less. But the young brave who'd taken a pot at Dan wasn't one of them. He took one last look at the crazy woman who was now climbing the blazing grand staircase with a water bucket in each hand and jogged out the door.

Dan Caine watched helplessly as Misty Maguire met her terrifying end.

A fire-weakened step collapsed and she dropped straight down as though a trapdoor had opened under her feet. A column of white fire jetted upward and turned to scarlet as the woman screamed in pain and terror. Then rose a greasy column of black smoke accompanied by silence . . . the only sound the crackling of the inferno and thud, thud, thud of tumbling charred beams from the upper stories of the mansion, flames fluttering along their lengths like blood-red butterflies.

It was time for Dan to get the hell out of there.

He took the flight of stairs to the foyer and ran for the door, then pulled up in midstride as the toe of his boot hit something heavy that skittered across the blackened floor, a self-cocking Colt revolver that an Apache had dropped in his haste to leave the building. Dan stopped long enough to shove the gun into his waistband and then sprinted out the door, expecting to run into a bunch of angry Indians eager for his scalp.

But the Apaches were gone.

They'd set the hated house on fire, a white man's folly that for too long had stuck out like a rotten tooth on prairie they considered their own. And they'd taken guns, fine horses from the stable, and beautiful women that would not remain that way for long, but long enough. They also carried their dead with them and would return to the San Carlos, lick their wounds, and bide their time.

The High Time mansion was a sorry skeleton of charred timbers and spars, and only part of one wall still stood, black and ugly, too stubborn to fall, when Clint Cooley rode in leading Dan Caine's mustang. He drew rein where Dan squatted on the grass and said, "I found your horse, Dan. I reckoned you wouldn't want to lose such a fine ten-dollar animal." Dan stared at him, said nothing, and Cooley looked over the still-smoking ruin and said, "Looks like the place was hit by the hammer of God."

"Not God. Apaches and fire," Dan said. "It's a tomb, a lot of dead. One of them dead for a thousand years, maybe longer."

"I'm not catching your drift," Cooley said.

"Look among the wreckage, Clint. See what you can see."

Cooley swung out of the saddle, dropped the reins, and stepped to the smoking ruin. It didn't take long before he said, "What the hell is that thing? It looks like a coffin of some kind?"

"It is a coffin," Dan said. "Hundreds and hundreds of years ago it was made for Lady Teshet, a chantress of the temple of Amun Ra in Ancient Egypt, or so I was told. She's what they call a mummy."

"Where is she?" Cooley said. "Hell, the coffin is barely scorched."

"I saw that," Dan said. "But I don't know where she is. I think she fell out of the coffin and burned up. Just as well, because she could put a curse on people." Cooley was silent and Dan said, "You don't believe that, huh?"

Cooley took a seat on the grass beside Dan and said, "Yeah, I believe it."

"Talk to me, Clint," Dan said. "Tell me things that will keep my mind busy. I want to see other pictures in my head that will get rid of all the dying men and women. Tell me why you believe in curses."

Cooley, seeing the haunt in Dan's eyes, said, "Well, back in New Orleans, before she died, my mother was friends with Marie Laveau, the Voodoo Witch Queen. Marie Laveau could put a hex on a man that could kill him quicker'n scat. His heart would just stop beating."

"Hell, Clint, I didn't know you had a mother," Dan said, trying his best to smile and failing woefully.

"Well, I did, at least for a spell. My mother was a beautiful lady, but she died of consumption when I was just a younker. They tried, but neither the doctors nor Marie Laveau could save her. Two years later my father died, of a broken heart they said, and Marie took me in and raised me until I was almost man grown. Then she consulted the Tarot and told me my future was to be a gambling man like my father, but that I should steer clear of the Mississippi steamboats for that way was my death. Marie gave me fifty dollars in gold, the British Bulldog revolvers I wear, and this . . ."

Cooley reached into the pocket of his breeches and produced a silver cigar case. He snapped open the case and took out a card that showed a drawing of a naked woman by a pool, a star above her head. "It's called the Star Upright, one of the luckiest of all the Tarot cards. Marie said it will safely guide me toward my destiny."

Dan Caine was unimpressed. "Hell. It's got a hole right through it."

Cooley nodded. "That happened at a poker game in George DeMoore's saloon in Wichita three, four years back. A sore loser by the name of Hunt Gates put the hole there with a ball from a Dragoon Colt. The cigar case in my inside pocket stopped the ball at a time when I carried the Tarot card inside it. See, there's the bullet hole in the case."

Dan was in a mean mood and said, "I hope you drilled him."

"Gates? Well, let us just say he did not live long enough to boast of his marksmanship." Cooley smiled. "And now to a much more pleasant subject. Did you run into Clay Kyle's boy? That is, if he was Kyle's boy?"

"His name was Shadow Beck, and I killed him with a lot of help from a whore."

"Tell it," Cooley said.

Dan told him how the shooting in Room 32 had gone down, and then Cooley said, "You sure this Beck feller was one of Kyle's boys?"

Dan took the ring that was miraculously still in his shirt pocket and passed it to Cooley. "Beck had given this to his whore. It's Nancy Calthrop's wedding ring."

Cooley saw a sudden drain of emotion from Dan's face and said, "Your first kill?"

Dan nodded.

"You'll get used to it," Cooley said.

"No, I'll never get used to it," Dan said. "Maybe I'm just not cut out for it."

"Hell, soldiers do it all the time, but I guess it's easier to kill to the sound of bugles," Cooley said.

Dan looked up at the gambler with bleak eyes. "They tried to hang me for killing Beck."

It was Cooley's turn to be taken aback. "Hang you? String you up for gunning that sorry piece of trash? Hell, Dan, you've got a story to tell."

"Yeah, I do," Dan said. "I'll tell you all about it on our way back to the vigilantes."

Cooley smiled. "You still call that ragtag, and bobtail bunch vigilantes?"

"Why not?" Dan Caine said. "That's sure as hell what they are."

CHAPTER NINETEEN

Brothers Zack and Arlo Palmer and their sidekick Boon Shanks stank up the East Texas hill country. Wolfers by trade, the three also dabbled in murder, rape, and robbery.

Clay Kyle greeted them like long lost brothers, ignored their gagging stench, and leaned from the saddle to embrace each in turn. Boon Shanks, a shaggily bearded brute in filthy buckskins, opened his arms, grinned toothlessly at Susan Stanton, and said, "And what do I get from you, little darlin'?"

"What you always get from me, Boon," Susan said. "A kick in the teeth."

"Bitch, one day I'll cut you down to size," Shanks said, still smiling.

"Try it, and that's the day I'll kill you," Susan said.

"Enough!" Kyle said. "We're all friends here and well met. Light and set, boys. We got whiskey to drink and now I'm in the mind for it, a proposition to discuss."

Zack Palmer, older and little more intelligent than his brother Arlo, stared at Shanks and his black eyes glittered a warning. "Like Clay says, we're friends here, Boon. Leave the woman alone. She has no interest in you."

Shanks spat over the side of his saddle and said, "I don't care." He jutted his chin, using it as a pointer. "I see something better. Younger and fresher. Clay, how much for the farmer's daughter? I got a double eagle in my pocket waiting to be spent."

"We'll talk about her later," Kyle said. "Now let's have a drink." He glanced at the sky. "Be dark soon."

The men dismounted, old acquaintances were renewed and handshakes exchanged with Loco Garrett, one-eyed Morris Bennett and Charlie Bates. But not with Doug Avila. The former vaquero was fastidious in the extreme and did not clasp hands with wolfers who smelled like gut piles. Neither the Palmer brothers nor Boon Shanks took offense, or at least they didn't show any. Such was the power of the breed's rep as a draw and shoot fighter.

The whiskey bottle made the rounds, men relaxed, and tongues loosened. Stands of mesquite, rare in most of the Texas hill country, provided wood for a fire and a meal of salt pork and pan bread was eaten just as the day faded into night.

Zack Palmer shoved the last of his pork and bread into his mouth, chewed noisily, burped, and said, "You got a proposition, Clay?"

"Yeah, and I reckon it's one you'll like," Kyle said.

"Well, let's hear it," Palmer said. He scratched under his filthy buckskin shirt, stared at something embedded in his fingernail, and said, "Then I'll tell you if I cotton to it or not."

Aware of Palmer's lack of intelligence and short attention span, in as few words as possible, Clay Kyle told the story of Sheik Bandar al-Salam and his gold-crammed fortress in the Sierra del Carmen.

"There's a fortune just waiting to be took," Kyle said. "By God, Zack, we'll leave Old Mexico as mighty rich men."

Palmer listened in silence and then turned his head and

said to his brother, "Arlo, do you mind that time when you and me and Boon was talked into robbing a Southern Pacific payroll train at Dennison cut over in the Arizona Territory?"

Boon Shanks's eyes were hot on Jenny Calthrop, and his reptilian gaze didn't slither from her body as he said, "Sure I mind. We lost three men on that holdup. Big Jim McKay, remember? We lost him. Best dark alley man as ever lived."

"I agree with you there. He was good with a dirk, was Jim," Zack said. "None better."

"Them Arizona lawmen hung him from a bridge trestle," Arlo said. "And him with both legs shot through and through an' bleeding like a stuck pig."

Kyle's irritation showed. "What the hell has all this to do with what I was talking about?" he said.

"Just this," Zack Palmer said. "We was told we'd get rich, and instead we got shot up by a bunch of lawmen. Skinny-assed Sam Bass misinformed us on that one, the Hoosier."

"Zack, we grab the Sheik's—"

The wolfer shook his head. "Damn it all, Clay, what the hell is a sheik? You never did say."

"He's a big auger, lives in the desert with a hundred wives, and has so much money he never has time to count it," Kyle said.

"Man with a hundred wives don't have much time for anything," Arlo said.

"That's why they'll be no gunplay," Kyle said. "We grab the kid and hold him until his pa pays his ransom. It will be done quick and over quicker on account of how the Sheik is a busy man and by all account dotes on his son."

That made Boon Shanks laugh, and he put his arm around Jenny's waist and pulled her close. "I'm gonna be real busy real soon," he said. The girl looked uneasy, pale, and scared.

Shrouded by pale moonlight, Zack Palmer drew up his knees, hunched over, and sat in silence, studying on things. Finally, he said, "It's thin, Clay." He pointed. "Thin as yonder prairie mist." Then, his voice rising, "Hell . . . wait . . . did I just see something move out there?"

"You saw a coyote, maybe," Kyle said.

"Something . . ." Palmer said.

Susan Stanton smiled. "You scared of coyotes, Zack?"

"It wasn't a coyote," Palmer said. He rose to his feet. "And I ain't scared of nothing." He angled an angry look at Susan. "An' that includes a black-eyed woman."

"It was a wolf then," Kyle said. "A gray wolf won't come near the fire, so sit down, Zack. We still got a business proposition to cuss and discuss."

Palmer shook his head and pulled his gun. "There's something out there, I tell ya, and it ain't a wolf. Hell, I can smell a wolf a mile off."

He stepped out of the circle of firelight and into the surrounding darkness.

Boon Shanks grinned and said, "I never knowed ol' Zack to be so spooked of the dark."

"If Zack said he seen something, then he seen something," Arlo said. "An' if it is a wolf, he won't be back here until it's skun."

"Hell on lobos is ol' Zack," Shanks said.

Arlo nodded. "Yeah, he's put the fear of God into every wolf in Texas."

"And he's hell on women," Shanks said, grinning. "Just like me."

The wolfer pulled Jenny Calthrop close, his hand busy on her breasts. The girl sobbed, tried to pull away, but

Shanks jammed his hairy mouth on hers, bestial growls deep in his throat.

"Leave her the hell alone."

Susan Stanton was on her feet, standing tall and slender like a column of spectral fire, her right hand behind her back.

Shanks pulled his face away from the girl and snarled, "You go to hell."

The speed of Susan's throw mocked credibility. Her right arm described an arc and she cast the bowie at waist level. The blade buried itself between Shanks's thighs a quarter inch . . . less . . . a hairsbreadth . . . from the V of Shanks's crotch. The man looked down at the knife, horrified.

The woman held her Colt steady and level. "I won't miss with this," she said. "I can geld you from here, Boon."

By any measure, Boon Shanks was an idiot and a coward, and his reaction was that of a wounded animal. He shrieked in terror and then, uttering a series of panicked yips, he crawled on all fours and threw himself against Arlo Palmer, seeking his protection.

"Leave him the hell alone," Palmer said. He remembered the knife and saw the unwavering Colt and added, "Miss Stanton." Then to the cowering Shanks, "They're all set on selling that girl to a Mexican brothel."

"And she'll get there a virgin," Susan Stanton said.

Loco Garrett, Charlie Bates, and Morris Bennett looked on Shanks with a mix of contempt and amusement. Doug Avila watched, his face expressionless, waiting to see what happened next.

Clay Kyle provided it.

"You heard the lady," Kyle said. "Boon, try anything like that with the girl again and I'll kill you myself."

Boon whimpered and Arlo said, "He was only having some fun, Clay."

"He almost lost his balls," Kyle said. "You boys ain't here for fun, you're here to talk business." He looked into the darkness and said, "And talking about business, where the hell is Zack?"

"Taking a piss, more like," Garrett said.

But Kyle's question was answered a few moments later when the wolfer slowly emerged from the gloom.

Kyle smiled. "What did you see, Zack?"

Palmer looked distracted, confused, like a man with a disintegrating mind.

"What did you see?" Kyle said again.

"Nothing," Zack said.

"Not even a gray wolf?"

"Nothing. I told you, I saw nothing."

"Good. Are you ready to consider my proposition again?" Kyle said.

"Yeah . . . I'll talk."

"Hell, Zack, you feeling all right?" Kyle said.

Palmer was immediately defensive. "What do you mean?"

"All at once you don't seem to be yourself," Kyle said.

"I'm fine," Palmer said. "And don't ask me what I seen out there. Don't ask me never again. You hear?"

"Anything you say, Zack," Kyle said. "Not another word from me."

"Where's the whiskey?" Palmer said.

"Yeah, good idea. Set yourself down and have a drink," Kyle said. "Then we'll talk business."

Palmer nodded. "Business. Yeah, we'll talk business and nothing else." He sat by the fire, took a slug from the whiskey bottle, and then hugged it close. "It's good to talk business," he said. "Sets a man's brain to rights."

* * *

After a time, while the men talked, Susan Stanton strolled unnoticed to the edge of the prairie darkness. She saw nothing. Jenny Calthrop joined her on silent feet. The girl said, "I wanted to thank—"

"No need to thank me," Susan said. "As a virgin you're worth twice as much to us in Mexico." She smiled slightly. "It's just business. You understand?"

"I want to thank you anyway, Miss Stanton," Jenny said.

"You think I'm a nice lady, huh?"

"Yes, I think I do."

"I'm not. If you were a whore, I'd have let Boon Shanks have you. Little girl, you mean nothing to me. Does that shock you?"

"I don't think so," Jenny said.

"Do you even know what a whore is?"

The girl was silent.

"Get away from me," Susan said. "No, wait. Do you smell something in the air?"

"Perfume," Jenny said. "Like my ma wore."

"It's nothing like your ma wore," Susan said. "It's called incense and it's ancient." She put a hand on Jenny's shoulder. "What did Zack Palmer see out here?"

"I don't know," Jenny said.

"I don't know either," Susan Stanton said. "But he saw something. Or smelled it."

NOTE: *What did wolfer Zack Palmer see that night in the Texas Hill Country? We'll never know. In the mid-1920s, an Austrian archaeologist hunting dinosaur bones did a brief excavation at the ruins of the old High Times mansion. He later reported that he'd uncovered human, skeletal remains, including a female pelvic girdle of great age, probably dating to Indians that lived in the area from 6000 B.C. to 500 A.D. The pelvis was later destroyed during WW2. Was it the pelvis from the mummy of the temple chantress Lady Teshet . . . and did her restless spirit, at least for a while, haunt the living? Zack Palmer might have been able to answer that question.*

CHAPTER TWENTY

"Three more joined them here," the Kiowa said. "They camped for the night, drank whiskey, emptied the bottle, and all headed south, eight men and two women."

"Bad news for us," Clint Cooley said. He moved the smoking coffeepot off a handful of fire and didn't look up. "Dan, you were almost hung, an Apache had some dolorous plans for your scalp, Shadow Beck could've killed you in a gunfight, and then you almost burned to death. Don't you think you've had enough misadventures without trying to take on eight hard cases?"

"Nothing's changed. I still have it to do," Dan Caine said. "The women must be Jenny Calthrop and Susan Stanton. Thank God the girl is still alive and we can rescue her."

"For God's sake, Dan, there's too many of them," Cooley said. "If Clay Kyle signed on more riders, you can bet they're the same stripe as himself . . . gun-handy border trash."

Fish Lee looked doubtful. "Eight gunmen and if everything I've heard is true, Black-Eyed Susan Stanton makes it nine. Call it, Dan. Where do we go from here?" He looked at the Kiowa. "What about you, Injun?"

"I'll scout. I won't fight for white men."

"What about the rest of you?" Dan said. "You heard Fish, and now you know what we're up against."

Cornelius Massey, already trail worn, straight up and down skinny, tired, his dusty frockcoat hanging on him like an overcoat on a scarecrow, said, "I'll stick so long as my whiskey holds out. There's got to be a newspaper story in this debacle somewhere. Hell, I already come up with a headline, *The Vigilante Trail.* How does that set with you, folks?"

"It sounds just fine, Mr. Massey," Estella Sweet said. She was young, strong, and was holding up well, a slight tan from the prairie sun flattering her.

Clint Cooley smiled and said, "Well, newspaperman, it isn't *The Iliad,* but I guess it will do."

"What the hell kind of newspaper story is that?" Fish Lee said.

"It isn't. It's a book, a long poem really, written by a feller by the name of Homer. I have a copy back in Thunder Creek," Massey said. "Some time when you got a few months to spare, I'll let you read it, Fish."

"Hell, I don't cotton to a book that takes months to read," Fish Lee said. "You got any of them dime novels?"

Massey let Fish down easy. "I don't know," he said. "I'll take a look once we get back."

Estella said, "I read one of those once, about a girl working in a cotton mill who bravely defended her virtue when the owner tried to seduce her. It was very exciting."

Cooley smiled. "I bet it was."

"I read one in the Doan store," young Holt Peters said. "It was about pirates."

"Was it exciting?" Estella said.

"Oh yeah, about walking the plank and firing cannons and buried treasure," Holt said.

"Were there women in it?" Estella said.

"Oh yes, even a lady pirate," Holt said.

"Then I'd like to read it," Estella said.

"It's called *Tip Top Tales of Bloodthirsty Buccaneers,* and I'm sure it's still there," Holt said. "But Mr. Doan will charge you fifty cents for it."

"What does that there walking the plank mean, sonny?" Fish Lee said.

Even the Kiowa seemed interested, a little less stone-faced.

Holt said, "Well, after pirates capture a merchant ship . . ."

Dan Caine let the others talk.

When they discussed dime novels, their minds were not on the dangers that lay ahead of them. But Clint Cooley was silent, a thinking man who'd been up the trail a few times and knew exactly how weak they were. Dan figured that Cooley would quit and head back to Thunder Creek and play the penny-ante gaming tables until his luck turned.

By its very nature, a dime novel discussion was a limited subject. There was only so much talk could be wrung from tales of piracy and the struggles of a mill girl to protect her maidenhood. After the others were talked out and Fish Lee determined that he'd one day walk a plank over a stream, or better still a dry wash, the talk fell silent and the thinking began.

Young Holt Peters was the first to speak. "Deputy Caine, I'll stick with you. I don't aim to spend the rest of my life shelving beans and canned peaches."

"I'm not a deputy any longer," Dan said. "And there's one thing to be said about setting cans on a shelf . . . it's safe."

"Oh, I don't know about that," Cooley said. "Stacking cans can be a mighty dangerous profession. Hey, grocery boy, suppose a can of tomatoes fell on your foot and broke a toe? I mean, that would hurt, wouldn't it?"

"And suppose a grown man discovers that it's dangerous to sass a boy with a Winchester under his knee?" Holt said. "I mean, a bullet would hurt, wouldn't it?"

Clint Cooley was taken aback, so was Dan Caine, and the others looked from the gambler to the boy and back again in slack-jawed amazement. Finally, Estella Sweet broke the spell. "Huzzah for the man from Doan's store!" she cried, clapping her hands.

To Dan's relief, Cooley smiled. "You're growing up, youngster. Hell, you're almost talking like a man."

"I'm not grown up yet," Holt said. "That's why I'm sticking with this posse. If I show yellow and turn back to Thunder Creek with my tail between my legs, I'll always be a boy."

"And truer words was never spoke," Fish Lee said. "I'm proud of you, son. You ride along of me an' we'll drag that gang of murderers to the reckoning they deserve."

Dan smiled. "And what about you, Estella?"

"Jenny Calthrop is my friend," the girl said. "I'm like the girl in the dime novel. I'll fight for what I believe in, and like Holt, I admit I've got some growing up to do. Deputy Caine, I'm not just an empty-headed girly." She smiled. "Yes, I know that's what most of the cowboys think of me, but when I must, I'll draw a line in the sand and I won't cross it. I'll sum it up for you . . . you can count on me. I'm not turning tail and running." She looked hard at Cooley, her eyes hidden behind her dark glasses. "What about you, gambling man? What do you think?"

Cooley poured coffee into a sooty tin cup, took a sip, and said, "Ow . . . hot, hot, hot . . ." He laid the cup gingerly on the grass and said, "What do I think? Well, I think we got ourselves a posse and I'm right damned proud to ride with you." Cooley picked up his cup again and motioned with it. "And Miss Estella, words of wisdom . . . there's a certain breed of men that say ugly things about women they know they can never have. Best to ignore them."

"Or shoot them," Fish Lee said.

"All right, let's finish the coffee and hit the trail," Dan Caine said. He seemed immensely pleased by his go-to-the-wall posse. And then a stray thought made him smile . . . they were a credit to vigilantes everywhere.

But Dan's smile was not to last.

After the dregs of the coffee had been thrown on the fire and cinches tightened, disaster struck . . . an event that Dan and the others neither expected nor were prepared for . . . Apaches blocked their road . . . and they were looking for a brawl.

CHAPTER TWENTY-ONE

Before he got into a fight, an Apache always figured the odds, and that meant the numbers were in his favor. There were seven of them, all young bucks. They'd lost warriors in the High Time scrap and the older men had headed back to the San Carlos with the captured women and horses. Apart from some rifle cartridges, a ship's telescope, and a few shiny trinkets, the six youngest had seen little of the spoils and had decided to strike out on their own for one last stab at plunder and glory.

The Apaches sat their horses just out of rifle range and one of them scanned Dan Caine and the others with the telescope. What he saw encouraged him. Two old men, a boy, and three adult males, one of them a Kiowa judging by his braids, and a golden-haired woman who would bring many nights of pleasure to any young man's wickiup.

The Apaches discussed whether or not an attack would be a fitting end to the raid. They would return to the San Carlos with horses and a woman and the older men would nod and smile and say they did well, and they would surely tell them that they were mighty warriors, brave of heart and strong of limb.

But the Kiowa gave them pause, a member of a tribe that produced first-rate fighting men who did not know the meaning of fear. But then the youngest of them spoke up, a sixteen-year-old named Bodaway, who had already taken three scalps in Mexico. He said that the Kiowa wore white man's clothing and had no doubt inherited their weaknesses and womanish fears.

"The wolf is gone," Bodaway said. "Only the sheep is left."

The others listened, then praised the young man's wisdom. Then all agreed they should attack, kill the men, and then tarry for a while to enjoy the woman before riding north again.

But they'd very soon realize that they'd made a devastating, gut-wrenching mistake.

The Apaches were correct in their assessment of the Kiowa . . . but their opinion of the fighting prowess of the white man was way wide of the mark. The young warriors had never met a top ranked Texas drawfighter before . . . they were about to meet one now.

Dan Caine watched the Apaches shake out line-abreast, each armed with a Winchester. "Get ready. They're coming right at us," he said.

"Fools, damned fools," Clint Cooley said. He stepped forward and waved a hand at the Indians. "Get the hell away from here."

The young braves were puzzled by that and heads turned as they discussed the white man's strange behavior. But they showed no inclination to leave.

Cooley said, "They won't listen. At that age, white or red, they never do." Then, "Dan, here with me. Holt, on my right, step wide. Fish, do the same on my left." After the men deployed, he said, "Kiowa, will you fight?" The Indian shook his head. "Then step clear, damn you," Cooley said.

After a quick glance at the Apaches he said, "Miss Sweet you stand back there with Massey. You'll be our last line of defense."

"Wait," the newspaperman said. He reached into his pocket and produced a stub of pencil. "Now I'll find out if the pen really is mightier than the sword."

"Sharpen it good, Cornelius," Dan said, managing a grin.

"They're coming," Cooley said. "The rest of you stay where you are. Holt, Fish, you'll have time for one shot, maybe two. Make them count. Dan, back my play." The gambler stepped forward a couple of yards just as the Apaches charged.

Behind him the inexperienced Holt fired and missed. Fish held his fire and Dan drew his fire-scorched Colt from the waistband and waited.

Even riding tired horses, the Apaches could cover the hundred yards between them and the vigilantes in about eight seconds. But most of them were destined never to make it.

Thirty yards . . . Cooley drew his revolvers.

Twenty yards . . . he waited.

Ten yards . . . he opened fire with amazing speed and accuracy, displaying a gun-handling dexterity possessed by perhaps one man in a thousand. The British Bulldogs barked and bucked in his fists and his .44 bullets tore the center out of the Apache charge. In the space of a few terrifying moments, Cooley killed three Apaches, wounded another, and dropped two horses. Still at the gallop, the surviving Indians instinctively swung away from Cooley's murderous fire and immediately ran into a barrage of bullets from Dan, Fish Lee, and Holt Peters. After the battle it could not be determined which of the three scored hits, but two more young Apaches were shot and tasted dust. Five of the warriors were now dead and a sixth was badly wounded and out of the fight, slumped over the neck of his frightened horse carrying him north.

It was enough.

The two surviving Apaches galloped through the camp and one of them, unharmed and with his rifle held out like a pistol, took a spite shot at Massey. There was a *dong!* sound and the old newspaperman fell like a puppet that just had its strings cut. Estella Sweet fired at the fleeing Indian and missed. She tried a second shot when the brave wheeled his pinto around, raised his rifle over his head, and yipped his defiance. She missed again, but the bullet cracked the air close enough to the Apache to scare him because he turned tail and fled.

Estella took a knee beside Massey. The man was ashen, and he had difficulty breathing. She raised his head to her lap and whispered, "Cornelius, where are you hit?"

"Chest, I . . . I think," Massey said. "I can't catch my breath." Then, "I guess the sword is mightier than the pen, huh?"

Estella spread the lapels of the old man's frockcoat. She was puzzled. "I don't see any blood."

"There must be blood." Massey gasped. "I'm shot through and through."

The others stood around Estella, and a circle of solemn faces watched the girl put her hands under Massey's coat.

"Be brave, old fellow," Fish Lee said. "Die game." He wiped his eyes with a huge yellow bandana.

"I'm trying, Fish," Massey said. "But it ain't easy."

"You're not dying, Cornelius," Estella said. "At least not today. Now sit up and take a few deep breaths."

"How the hell can I take deep breaths when I'm breathing my last?" Massey said.

"Dan, Fish, help him sit," the girl said. "Is the Kiowa looking out for Apaches?"

"Those two won't be back," Dan said. "I reckon they're already lighting a shuck for the San Carlos."

After much groaning and grim warnings from Massey about his imminent demise, Dan and Fish Lee eased the man into a sitting position.

Immediately, Estella brandished a silver coin under the newspaperman's nose. "You're not dying," she said. "The bullet hit this . . . whatever it is."

"Let me see that," Dan said.

He examined the coin, silver, with each side milled off and then engraved. On one side were the letters DG with a rude cross underneath and on the reverse, *Sabine Pass/ Sept 8th/1862.*

Clint Cooley fed stubby .44 cartridges into one of his revolvers as he looked over Dan's shoulder and said, "What kind of coin is that, newspaperman?"

"It was a peso coin, but it isn't any longer. It's a medal given to me by General Braxton Bragg's own hand for helping keep the Yankees out of the Sabine Pass. That's down Jefferson County way for those of you who don't know."

"It saved your life, Cornelius," Dan said.

"Yeah, it did, that and an underpowered cartridge," Cooley said. "Seems the Apaches got their hands on some pretty inferior ammunition."

Massey took the medal from Dan and said, "It's got a dent in it."

"The bullet hit hard enough to take your wind," Cooley said. "One time I had a cigar case save my life like that, stopped a ball from a Dragoon Colt."

"Then we're two of a kind," Massey said.

"No, we're not," Cooley said.

"How come you never told us you were a Johnny Reb?" Dan said.

"Because I don't tell folks my story; I tell folks other people's stories," Massey said. "Estella, there's three pints of whiskey in my saddlebags. Bring me the one that's already opened. I've been all shot to pieces and I need a drink."

"We all need a drink," Dan said.

"Then help yourselves," Massey said. "You deserve it, every damn one of you."

Clint Cooley drew rein and stared down at the scattered Apache bodies. He shook his head and said to Dan Cainc, "I killed boys, Dan, half-grown boys."

"An Apache boy can kill you just as dead as any man," Dan said. He dismounted, equipped himself with a better Colt and a gunbelt and holster.

"I know that, but it sure doesn't make it any easier," the gambler said.

Massey, half drunk, his lined face ashen, overheard Cooley and said, "Among the Apache there are no boys, Cooley. Their childhood is both brief and endangered. Yes, they die like children but they fight like warriors. It's the Indian way, a wrong way maybe, but it's their way." He managed a wan smile. "Just don't notch your guns, huh?"

"Massey, only a tinhorn or a wannabe notches his gun," Cooley said. "And I wouldn't notch my gun to remind myself that I'd killed boys."

"I know that," the old newspaperman said. "Please forgive my poor attempt at a joke."

The Kiowa was gone most of the remainder of the day, and he returned when the sun's lemon glare gave way to the lilac shades of evening. A rising wind ruffled the prairie grass and bore the scent of evening primrose and marigold.

"Still due south," the Kiowa said without any kind of greeting. "They will be in Mexico before us."

"How long before us?" Dan said.

"Three days, maybe four," the Kiowa said.

Clint Cooley stood in his stirrups and for a long time stared at the vast rolling country ahead of him.

"What do you see, Clint?" Dan Caine said.

"A whole lot of nothing," the gambler said.

Then, surprising everybody, Estella Sweet said, "Clay Kyle, damn you. Damn you to hell."

CHAPTER TWENTY-TWO

Just as the sun came up, Clay Kyle and his band splashed across the shallows of the Rio Bravo into the desert country of the Mexican state of Coahuila. They rode south in the shadow of the northern finger of the nine-thousand-foot-high peaks of the Sierra del Carmen, the higher slopes green with sky islands of mixed oak and pine and, growing at a higher elevation, forests of Engelmann spruce and Douglas and Durango fir. This was a vast, empty land, called by some the most remote region on earth. Part of the Chihuahuan Desert, it was the haunt of antelope, black bear, a small species of white-tailed deer, beaver, and cougar. Its rugged vistas of sand, rock, and shrub were relieved only here and there by cactus and stands of ponderosa pine and wild oak. The foothills were cut through by rugged canyons and arroyos, and in one of those, Clay Kyle hoped to find the golden fortress of Sheik Bandar al-Salam.

Clay Kyle drew rein, and the others followed his lead. They sat their horses on a low shelf of rise and stared intensely at the wilderness ahead of them, each busy with his own thoughts, appalled by the sight of endless mountains with thick islands of trees and steep limestone escarpments that rose vertically from the flat like castle walls. There was no sound, and nothing moved.

Where to find al-Salam's hideaway in this wasteland?

Susan Stanton saw humor in the situation and called, "Little rich boy, come out, come out wherever you are."

Zack Palmer scowled. "Damned wild goose chase," he said. "There ain't nothing here but rocks and cactus."

"I say we sell the girl at the nearest village and at least make a few dollars' profit," Boon Shanks said. He leered at Jenny. "And she don't need to be a virgin."

"The price we'd get for a downright homely gal split eight ways would hardly buy us a cup of coffee," Morris Bennett said. His one eye glittered. "Zack, how much will you pay us for the girl?"

Angry now, Kyle said, "Forget the girl for now. I told you, a dying man doesn't lie. The Sheik's place has got to be around here somewhere. All we have to do is find it."

"Find it how?" Bennett said.

"By looking, damn it," Kyle said.

Susan Stanton glanced at the sun-scorched sky. "It's going to be hot in those canyons," she said.

Kyle smiled. "Think of the money, Suzie."

"Sure, I'll think of the money," the woman said. "And that all we have to do is find the brat and become rich. Suppose he isn't the outdoors sort."

"Then we'll find another way," Kyle said.

"Water, Clay," Charlie Bates said. "We'll need water."

"Yeah, well I don't think the Sheik would've built his fortress in a place without water," Kyle said. "My guess he's using streams coming off them treed mountains. If the worse comes to the worst, we can refill our canteens from the Rio Bravo. It's close enough."

"So what now?" Bates said.

"Now? Why we start searching the canyons and arroyos for something that looks like a palace," Kyle said. "The Sheik's riders may be about, so be careful and keep your eyes peeled for trouble. Above all, no gunfire. If you have to make a killing, use your knife." He smiled. "Or a rock."

"Hey, Zack," Arlo said. "Are we gonna stick?"

"For a while," Zack Palmer said.

"I don't like these mountains," Arlo said. "So how long is a while?"

"Until I tell you we're leaving, Arlo," Zack said. "Not until then."

Three hours later, after fruitless searching under a burning sun, Kyle spotted two Mexican peons walking out of a narrow arroyo leading a burro loaded with picks, shovels, a pair of canvas sacks, and a shotgun in a canvas scabbard.

Probably the presence of two women made a difference, and that's why the Mexicans showed no signs of obvious alarm as Kyle and his riders approached. The younger man was a ringer for the older one and Clay Kyle pegged them as father and son . . . fools prospecting for gold in a mountain range that didn't have any.

The peons were small, undernourished, thin, dressed in white cotton pants and shirts, straw and rope sandals. Both wore faded green bandanas around their skinny brown necks.

Kyle drew rein, smiled, and said, "Howdy."

The older Mexican returned the smile and said, "I speak English." He made a space between his thumb and the tip of his forefinger and said, "Un poco."

"He means a little," Loco Garrett said. The man was sweating heavily, as the rest of them were, except for Susan Stanton who never seemed to feel heat or cold.

Kyle nodded. "I had that figured out for my ownself."

"Are you hunting?" the old peon said.

Kyle shook his head. "No, we're looking for a man they call the Sheik. You heard of him?"

"I don't think so," the old man said.

The younger peon stood off a ways, his face shut down, listening, thinking, his eyes now and then darting to the shotgun on the burro's back. It seemed the mention of the Sheik had scared the hell out of him.

"Big chief," Kyle said. "He lives in a castle and has many wives."

"I don't understand," the man said.

"Try castillo," Doug Avila said. The muscles of the half-breed's face were bound hard. He'd grown up with peons, just like those two.

Susan Stanton leaned forward in the saddle. "Castillo," she said. "Is there a castillo in one of the canyons?"

The peon grinned. "Ah, si, castillo." He shook his head. "No, there is no castillo."

"Hacienda," Susan said. "Is there a hacienda around here?"

The younger peon hissed words that sounded like a warning, and the older man quickly said, "No hacienda." Suddenly, his gaze was furtive, and he was obviously scared. "Now we must go home," he said. "We found is no gold in these mountains."

"Where is the hacienda?" Susan Stanton said.

Another muttered warning from the younger man, and the old peon said, "No hacienda here. Now we will leave."

It's already been established that Susan Stanton was a dazzling beauty, a woman that every man wanted to possess. But her loveliness was so flawless, so without equal that even the most ardent suitor hesitated to approach her, knowing he'd be a man competing for a prize beyond value that could never be his. What men didn't realize, though a few women did, was behind that exquisite façade seethed a moldering mass of corruption and a soul as black as mortal sin. Western men later puzzled over the question . . . how could a woman so beautiful be so ugly and evil, such a vicious monster, the bastard child of Medusa? Susan Stanton's childhood and early life is unknown, and there's no evidence to suggest why she turned to the dark side, her violence surprising everyone who saw it . . . a sudden, killing flash of black lightning.

Clay Kyle and the others saw it now.

Susan Stanton stood in the stirrups and threw her knife. An instant later the blade buried itself in the chest of the young peon. His mouth agape, eyes wild, the man looked down at the bowie's staghorn handle, horror-struck at the manner of his death. He sank to the ground as his father rushed to his side and wailed over the body of his dead son.

Susan Stanton dismounted and walked in the direction of the peons. Clay Kyle was fascinated, a slight smile on his lips, but the others shrank from her as she passed, and Boon Shanks even pulled his restless horse aside when the woman stepped past him.

The old Mexican threw himself over the body of his dead son and sobbed uncontrollably until Susan Stanton's shadow fell over him like a dark cloak. He looked up at the woman, his eyes full of grief and hate, and spat, *"Bruja!"*

"Witch," Avila said. "He just called you a witch, Miss Stanton."

The woman ignored that and said to the peon, "Where is the hacienda?"

The old man's only answer was the burn of detestation in his eyes.

Susan pulled the knife from his son's chest, wiped the blade on the old man's shoulder, leaving a streak of red, and said, "Where is the hacienda?"

He said nothing.

Susan Stanton pressed the tip of the bowie into the old man's neck, drawing a bead of blood. She said, "Where is the hacienda?"

"Curse you to the inferno," the peon said. He was old, he was wise, and he knew the moment of death was near. This woman with the black eyes was an evil spirit that would not let him live.

"Where is the hacienda?" Susan Stanton said.

The old man made no reply and the woman shoved the knife to the hilt into his neck, and he made a choking sound and died.

Susan turned and said to Kyle, "Well, we know the fortress is here, so all we have to do now is find it." She nodded in the direction of the dead men. "I had to silence them."

"With a knife," Kyle said. "That was good work."

Susan Stanton shrugged. "I couldn't use a gun."

Kyle grinned. "The Mexicans knew where the Sheik's place is all right, and I have the notion that it's close to where they were prospecting."

"I guess we'll find out," Susan said.

Arlo Palmer let out a whoop, and he and Boon Shanks leaped from their horses and ran to the burro. Shanks got there first and claimed the shotgun while Palmer ransacked the rest of the pack, and came up with some tortillas, jerky, and a bottle of mescal. Shanks stepped to the dead peons and picked up the younger man's sombrero. For a few moments he compared it to his own battered, sweat-stained hat that he finally tossed away before donning the sombrero.

"Hey, Doug, now I look like you!" Shanks yelled.

"You look nothing like me," Avila said. "And it's bad luck to wear a dead man's hat."

Shanks grinned. "Like I care. It's just another of your cowboy big windies."

"You'll see," Avila said. "Wear the sombrero, and you'll never have a day's luck in your life."

"Boon, get the sombrero the hell off your head," Clay Kyle said. As a sixteen-year-old he'd cowboyed for Captain Richard King in south Texas, and the punchers' superstitions survived strong inside him. "We don't need bad luck on this job."

"Aw, Clay . . ." Shanks said.

Even drawing from high, horseman's leather Kyle was lightning fast with the iron. His Colt pointed at Shanks, he said, "Boon, get rid of the hat or I'll shoot it right off'n your head."

Boon didn't hesitate. He grabbed the sombrero and sailed it away from him. He found his own hat and jammed it on his head. He managed a wan smile. "We don't want any bad luck, Clay."

"No, we don't," Kyle said, holstering his gun. "Especially since yours was just about to start. Now you and Arlo get mounted. We got some scouting to do."

"And a rich man to rob," Susan said. "First you men strip the burro and turn him loose. Poor little thing." She stepping into the saddle beside Jenny Calthrop, who was trembling and sobbing softly. "What's the matter, little girl, did I scare you?"

Jenny said nothing, tears staining her cheeks.

"A cutting is never a joy to watch, too much screaming, too much blood," Susan said. "There, there, don't cry, you'll get over it." She leaned over in the saddle and tried to put her arm around the girl's shoulder, but Jenny jerked away from her. Immediately Susan shifted the direction of her hand and clamped Jenny's jaw in her strong fingers. She squeezed hard, and the girl's eyes fluttered tight shut in pain. "Life is tough, my little darling, but I'm tougher, and

I don't give a damn how my actions look to others . . . they feel just fine to me. I'm a cold-hearted bitch who long ago discovered all her inner demons and now wears them proudly like bat wings." She shoved Jenny away from her. "You're a woman and you're stronger than any man. Remember that, you little slut, and you'll survive."

"I don't want to be like you," Jenny said, wiping away tears with the back of her hand. "I don't ever want to be like you."

"So be it," Susan said. "Men will use and abuse you, and in the end they'll kill you." She looked straight ahead at where Arlo Palmer and Shanks had released the burro, her beautiful face hard. "Don't talk to me for the rest of the day."

"I won't talk to you ever," Jenny said. "You were with those others who murdered my family, and I hate you."

"Clay," Susan Stanton said, "time's a-wasting. We should begin the search."

Kyle, a man branded with his own evil and a born killer, nonetheless had sand, but after listening to Susan Stanton he said, "Sure thing, Suzie. Sure thing."

An hour later, and after some fruitless searching, Doug Avila was riding point when two events happened simultaneously . . . a light flashed on the nearest mountain slope and Avila threw up his arm, ordering a halt.

"What the hell?" Clay Kyle said.

"Boss, it's a signal mirror," one-eyed Charlie Bates said, a note of alarm in his voice.

"It's got to be the Sheik's boys," Loco Garrett said, just as troubled as Bates.

The light winked again, on and off, on and off, in some kind of sinister code, and a suddenly uneasy Kyle didn't like it one bit. To his right, there was a deep recess at the base of the mountain, a rock-walled amphitheater strewn with boulders that had fallen from the surrounding slopes during some ancient earthshake. Here and there grew some stunted pines and wild oak and, around the base of some of the rock, clumps of bunchgrass. Because of the angle of the retreating sun, the place was deep in shadow, in contrast to the surrounding brightness.

Kyle, blowing through his nose, snorting, made a decision and ordered everyone into the alcove. "Take cover," he said. "Let them come to us, whoever they are. Loco, keep an eye on the girl."

"With pleasure, boss," Garrett said, grinning.

Normally Kyle would've told the man to behave himself, but as he and the others took cover behind the scattered boulders, he had other things on his mind. Apaches? Unlikely. No, it had to be the Sheik's men. The place was guarded like a gold deposit in Leavenworth. He looked around him. Knowing that a gunfight would call for rifle work, everybody, including the six-gun-handy Susan Stanton, held a Winchester. The horses were at the rear of the recess under the shelter of a narrow rock shelf, protected from stray bullets by brush and a few wild oaks.

The day slowly shaded into evening as Kyle studied the sky . . . it would be dark soon.

CHAPTER TWENTY-THREE

The day was shading into evening and Dan Caine had ordered a halt to make camp when the sharp young eyes of Holt Peters spotted the dot of scarlet in the darkening sky.

"What the hell is that?" Dan said. He used the ship's telescope he'd taken from a dead Apache and studied the phenomenon. He shook his head and said to Clint Cooley, "What do you make of that?"

Cooley took the glass, studied the sky for a few moments, then shook his head and said, "Beats me."

"It's getting bigger," Holt said.

"Maybe's it's a firebird," the Kiowa said. For the first time ever, he looked worried.

"I know what it is," Cornelius Massey said, surprising everybody. "It's Professor Lazarus Latchford and Miss Prunella in their balloon."

"Crazy Professor Latchford?" Holt Peters said.

"I don't know of any other," Massey said.

"He's dropping," Holt said. "Coming down fast."

"Dropping with the north wind," Massey said. "Holla, what's this?"

The red balloon was now close enough that Latchford could be seen leaning over the side of the basket, a cylindrical object in his hands. Latchford waved to Dan and the others and then tossed the barrel-shaped cylinder over the side. The vigilantes watched the thing fall until it hit the ground. A couple of seconds passed and then an ear-shattering explosion accompanied by a V-shaped gout of flame, smoke, and shrapnel about twenty feet high erupted into the air. Dan Caine and the others hugged the ground as the blast wave hit the balloon, and the gondola swung wildly like a censer swung by a drunk altar boy. Horrified, Dan watched the basket hit the ground hard and violently tumble on its side, and then the rapidly deflating silk envelope slowly sank and settled over it. In the aftermath of the explosion, an eerie silence ensued, eventually broken by Fish Lee who said with great solemnity, "Well, that's it. Latchford's done broke his damn fool neck this time." Then waxing philosophical, "If the good Lord had wanted us to fly through the air, he'd have given us wings."

Dan Caine and the others got to their feet. Caine stepped toward the downed balloon, only to stop as the envelope bulged and a tiny woman, no more than four feet tall, crawled out from under the silk. She wore a specially tai-lored safari suit consisting of a belted tan jacket, long skirt of the same color, and brown, lace-up boots. She scouted around, found a pith helmet that she jammed on her short, blonde curls and then got to her knees and quickly bur-rowed like a gopher under the collapsed envelope again. The silk then bulged in several places like a crimson snake that had just swallowed a litter of pigs, and moments later the tiny woman crawled out from under, followed by a man in a black suit, white shirt, and black four-in-hand tie. The man was tall, impossibly skinny, with an unruly shock of white hair, and he stood and grinned when he saw Dan Caine and the others. Then he dived back under the enve-lope again and pulled out an iron ship's anchor that he spiked into the ground.

"There, that will hold *Icarus* in place. What do you think?" Professor Lazarus Latchford said.

"About what?" Cornelius Massey said, looking testy. "The anchor, the landing, or you?"

Latchford's grin widened. "My descent was a bit rough, wasn't it? The north wind dropped suddenly and for a moment there, I declare that Miss Prunella was quite shaken. No, I'm talking about the bomb. Went off splendidly, didn't it? Oh, yes!"

"You could've killed us all," Massey said. "Latchford, you're a raving lunatic."

"No!" Miss Prunella said, and stomped across the grass and landed a kick on Massey's shin.

"Ow!" the newspaperman yelled, hopping on his good leg. "What the hell did you do that for?"

"Don't say bad things about Professor Latchford," she said, her voice high and squeaky, her cheeks rose pink with anger. "He's a great man who will take us all to the moon one day."

Latchford grinned again and poked the air with a skeletal forefinger. "Someday. Oh, yes."

As Estella Sweet first commiserated with Massey and then told a defiant and unrepentant Miss Prunella that she was "very naughty," Dan said, "Latchford, come over to our camp and have a cup of coffee. You, too, Miss Prunella. And then tell me why the hell you're here."

After he was settled with his coffee, Latchford said, "The reason Miss Prunella and I are here is to help you catch the vicious Kyle gang, as I promised," the professor said. "That is, if I can catch a north wind again. I have two more splendid bombs ready to go." He saw the perplexed expression on Dan's face and said, "A metal case packed with powder and lead balls that uses a contact fuse to explode on impact.

A couple of those on Clay Kyle's gang, and they won't murder another rancher and his family."

"Latchford, you don't expect us to fly in that thing?" Massey said, scowling, rubbing his shin.

"Oh, dear no," the professor said. "I'm sure come morning, you'll wish to get back on the heels of the murderous fugitives, but myself and Miss Prunella must wait for another north wind. Until then, we're earthbound with broken wings, and I fear the balloon's burner is also damaged and must be repaired." Latchford shrugged. "Besides, there's no room for all of you."

"When will you get a north wind, Professor?" young Holt Peters said.

"Ah, good question, my boy," Latchford said. "Back in Thunder Creek, I constructed a machine that forecasts the weather and it assured me the prevailing wind will blow from the north for the next week or so." He smiled. "But since it's accurate less than half the time, Miss Prunella and I must wait and see, oh yes."

Suddenly, Clint Cooley peered into the gathering darkness and said, "What the hell is that crazy Indian doing?"

Vaguely visible in the gloom the Kiowa danced beside the collapsed balloon, hoppy little steps combined with a "Hi . . . hi . . . hi . . . hi . . ." chant.

"I've seen that before," Professor Latchford said. "Our red brethren always treat a balloon as a sacred object. I think they believe it carries the Great Spirit from the heavens or something like that." He sighed, shook his head, and said, "You know, I never did blame that Indian boy for killing the vile Lem Jones, and neither did Miss Prunella." He smiled and dug his sharp elbow into Dan Caine's side. "And speaking of Miss Prunella, I believe she could be persuaded to entertain us with a song or two before sleep, couldn't you, my dear?"

"Anything you'd particularly like to hear?" the little woman said.

Dan didn't really want to hear anything, but he went along, smiled, and said, "Your choice."

Miss Prunella was a dwarf, but her voice was big, bold, and tuneful. She removed her pith helmet, laid it aside, and sang "Mrs. O'Farrell's Cow" and the plaintive "The Fishmonger's Daughter." And then, her head on Latchford's bony shoulder, "He's Just Like a Father to Me."

After everyone complimented Miss Prunella on her singing, Dan decided it was time to dig into his dwindling supplies and prepare supper. But Latchford dived under the balloon envelope and emerged with a loaf of not-yet-stale bread, slices of ham, and canned peaches.

"A veritable feast," Latchford said, holding high his provisions. "The best that Pete Doan's store has to offer."

"You've redeemed yourself, Latchford," Massey said, eagerly eyeing the ham. "I forgive you for bombing us."

Later Dan lay on his back, courting sleep that was long in coming. The nearer they got to Clay Kyle and his gang, the more he feared for his people. Only two of them, Clint Cooley and Fish Lee, were fighting men. The rest, Estella Sweet, Cornelius Massey, and Holt Peters, would be sheep among wolves. He'd told them to go back to Thunder Creek, but they'd refused. Well, he'd try again tomorrow. Maybe they'd see sense.

A shooting star blazed across the night sky in a southerly direction.

Dan Caine frowned. That meant bad luck . . . for somebody.

CHAPTER TWENTY-FOUR

Clay Kyle watched a shooting star flash across the sky, and around him the silence of the towering mountain was as deep as death. Behind him Broken Nose Charlie Bates coughed, a man whose weak lungs always seemed to get worse after sundown. As it turned out, he was also a false prophet. "Clay," he whispered, breathing hard, "them fellers ain't coming."

Kyle said nothing. There was something out there all right. He could feel it, his outlaw instincts as finally honed as a razor's edge. A few moments later his hunch was proved right. A man called from the darkness, his voice strangely hollow in the quiet.

"Hey, you, in the rocks!"

"What do you want?" Kyle said.

"A better question is what do you want?" the hidden man said. "Are you Texas Rangers bringing your womenfolk with you for protection?"

"Go to hell," Kyle said.

"Are you Rangers? Answer the question, man."

"No, we ain't Rangers. We ain't in the law business."

"Then what the hell are you?"

"Traders."

"What kind of traders?"

"We got a woman to sell."

A pause, then, "We ain't in the market for a woman."

"She ain't for you. She's for the Sheik."

A longer pause, this one stretching for a few seconds, then, "What the hell is a cheek?"

"Sheik, an Arab," Kyle said. "S-h-e-i-k. Don't tell me you don't know."

"My name is Shannon, Dave Shannon," the man said. "Maybe you're lookin' for me?"

Morris Bennett called out, "Dave Shannon out of Abilene?"

"And other places. Who are you?"

"Morris Bennett."

"Yeah, I know you. You rode with Jesse and them and killed Banjo Art Benson that time up Wichita way. Lost an eye in that scrape, as I recollect."

"I never did get that eye back, Dave," Bennett said.

"Then why the hell are you here trying to sell a woman?" Shannon said. "There's plenty of women in Old Mexico going for free."

"Well, you could say that ain't exactly why we're here, Dave," Bennett said. "Like Kyle said, we're looking for the Sheik."

Shannon said, "Is that Clay Kyle?"

"None other," Bennett said.

"Is Black-Eyed Suzie Stanton with him?"

"She sure is," Bennett said.

"Hell, this is like old home week," Shannon said. "Kyle, I thought you'd been hung years ago and Suzie long since wedded and bedded."

"We're still around, Dave," Kyle said. "You working for the Sheik?"

"Like I asked you before, who the hell is the Sheik?"

"You know who he is."

"Hell if I do," Shannon said. "You tell me."

"All right, I will," Kyle said. "He's an Arab, and his name is Bandar al-Salam, and he has a palace hereabouts that's crammed to the rafters with gold. I aim to relieve him of some of that."

Harsh laughter from a dozen throats sounded like a flourish of trumpets in the gloom. After a while, his voice sobbing from his recent merriment, Shannon said, "Who told you that?"

"I heard it from an old Chinaman when I was doing a turn in Leavenworth," Kyle said. "He says the Sheik is so fat he's lowered on top of his women with ropes of solid gold."

More laughter, then Shannon said, "That old Chinaman told you a big windy, Kyle. There's no gold in the Sierra del Carmen, and the only women for miles around are the two you brung."

"You're a damned liar, Shannon," Kyle yelled. "You want all the gold for yourself or you're working for the Sheik. Come now, tell the truth. Maybe we can get together on this thing."

"Damn you, Kyle, there's no *thing* because there is no sheik," Shannon yelled. "There's only a robber's roost where me and a dozen other boys are holed up until our next job. Now come first light, you get the hell out of here. The likes of you attracts the attention of the Texas Rangers and the local Rurales. The women can stay. We got no objection to that."

Doubt and disappointment tugged at Kyle. Had the Chinaman lied to him? Dying men don't lie. Or do they? He tried the question out on Shannon.

"Shannon, the Chinaman was dying, and dying men don't lie," he said. "Everybody knows that."

"Kyle, I thought you were smarter than that," Shannon

said. "Now you sound like a damned rube. I seen men on the gallows with nooses around the neck swear blind that they didn't do such and such a crime when all present knew they damn-well did. I mind before the trap sprung on Red River Tom Salt, he swore he hadn't killed a Kansas parson and raped his new bride. Hell, he was caught in the act and still swore he was as innocent as a newborn puppy. Kyle, dying Chinamen lie just like dying white men."

"It's hard to take, Shannon," Kyle said. Somewhere a night bird called, and the shadows of the moon-silvered boulders were long and deep.

"Well, take it or leave it, Kyle, but I want you out of here come first light."

"Dave, can we talk?" Kyle said.

"My talking's done," Shannon said.

A few moments passed. The suddenly a fusillade of rifle fire opened up from Shannon's position, muzzle flashes like fireflies in the darkness. Bullets crashed into the alcove, *spaaanged* off stone walls and ricocheted wildly among the boulders. A horse, stung by a flying fragment of rock screamed and reared, and Loco Garrett cried out in pain and surprise as a bullet creased his shoulder. Susan Stanton and the others cursed and hit the ground as the barrage continued for a few more seconds, then stopped as suddenly as it had begun.

Shannon's mocking voice echoed in the ringing silence.

"Hey, Kyle, you wanted to talk! How did you enjoy that conversation?"

"Shannon, you're crazy!" Kyle yelled.

He threw his Winchester to his shoulder and levered round after round into the gloom and when he ceased firing was rewarded by roars of laughter, and again Dave Shannon called out. "Kyle, come sunup don't let me see your face around here or you're a dead man. Y'heah me?"

"Go to hell!" Kyle said, and on the far side of the darkness, men hooted and hollered.

"What's driving you, Clay?" Susan Stanton said. She'd torn a strip from Jenny Calthrop's petticoat and now used it to bandage Loco Garrett's bleeding shoulder. "Is it greed, stupidity, or are you just being bullheaded?"

"The Sheik's palace and the gold is close, I tell you," Kyle said. "Why else would Dave Shannon be here in this damned wasteland? I don't believe what he said about a robber's roost. Plenty of them in Texas and closer to banks and trains. He knows the Sheik is here in the Sierra del Carmen, and he and his boys are being paid to protect him."

Susan tied off the knot of Loco Garrett's bandage, slapped him on the back, and said, "You'll live." And then to Kyle, "Shannon sounded pretty convincing to me."

"That's because you never met the Chinaman. Suzie, the little runt wasn't lying. You just don't make up a story like that, especially when you know you're breathing your last."

"You heard Shannon, dying men can lie."

"Not the Chinaman. He wanted to get even with the Sheik for abandoning him."

Susan Stanton sighed. "I got a feeling . . ."

"What kind of feeling?"

"The feeling that hard times are in store for everybody."

"Tell me you still got that feeling when you're driving down the Champs-Élysées in Paris in your own coach with a pretty little girl at your side."

Susan smiled. "Try Bourbon Street in New Orleans and I'll bite."

"Whatever your little heart desires," Kyle said. "You'll have money enough." Then, "You in?"

"Yes, I'll stick until it's time to leave."

"Good enough for me," Kyle said. "Saddle your horse. We'll pull out in an hour when Dave Shannon and his boys are rolled in their blankets."

"It's a cinch he's got somebody standing guard," Loco Garrett said. He had a bloodstained bandage on his upper arm and shoulder.

"And that's why we have to be quiet," Kyle said. "When Dave Shannon looks for us in the morning, we'll be long gone."

"Gone where, boss?" Garrett said.

"Deeper into the mountains, I reckon," Kyle said. "We just got to keep our eyes peeled."

"And watch our backtrail," Garrett said.

"I can handle Dave Shannon," Kyle said. "He surprised me once. He won't do it a second time."

Susan Stanton and Loco Garrett exchanged glances, and the woman said, "Clay, remind me later to ask you to tell me about how rich I'm goin' to be and how pretty will be the little French girl."

CHAPTER TWENTY-FIVE

"A day's ride to the Rio Bravo," the Kiowa said. "I believe that Clay Kyle and his gunmen have already crossed."

"Taking Jenny Calthrop with them," Dan Caine said. The Kiowa answered with a shrug, and Dan said, "Where the hell are they headed?"

Clint Cooley replied to that question. "Somewhere deeper into Old Mexico where they can sell the girl, would be my guess."

"Why such a long ride, way out of Kyle's home range, to sell a young girl?" Dan said. "I've been thinking about it, and it doesn't make sense."

"Hey, newspaperman, what's the going rate for a white girl in Mexico?" Cooley said.

Cornelius Massey shook his head. "That question is nothing my experience can answer," he said. "I didn't even know there was such a market for white women in Mexico."

Estella Sweet said, "Holt, if I was for sale in Pete Doan's store, how much would he ask for me?"

"Miss Estella, that's a hell of a question to ask a man," Holt Peters said. It was the first time he'd called himself a man, another sign that in his own mind he'd left his boyhood behind. The others noted it, Cooley smiled slightly, but no one commented on his new status.

"Take a guess," Estella said. "Come on, don't be shy, how much?"

"You won't like my answer," Holt said.

"Try me," Estella said.

"All right, then. You know Steel Wagner?"

"Yes, I know him. He's a top hand on the Rafter-T."

"The very same," Holt said. "One day I overheard him say to another cowboy in the store that if Pete Doan sold brides, he'd pay top dollar for Estella Sweet, four months' wages for each tit and another four months' pay for the rest." Holt blushed. "Well, that's what he said."

Estella was unperturbed. Her face showed only slight amusement as she said, "Dan, how much does a top hand like Steel Wagner make a month?"

Dan Caine, wary of saying the wrong thing, managed, "I'd say forty a month."

Estella said, "So let me count that up. Two tits . . . the rest . . . adds up to four hundred and eighty dollars." She smiled. "Let's call a spade a spade. Jenny is my friend, but she's not near as pretty as me, so I'd say her going price in Old Mexico would be three hundred dollars. In pesos."

Dan said, "Clint, what do you think?"

"Sounds about right," Cooley said.

"Damn it all, why does nobody ever ask me stuff like that?" Fish Lee said. "I've spent some time in Old Mexico, you know."

"Well, Fish, what do you think?" Dan said.

"Yeah, it sounds about right," Fish Lee said. "So why would ol' Clay cross hundreds of miles of wilderness and risk being jumped by Rangers and Apaches for three hundred lousy dollars? He could've headed back across the Brazos and sold the girl there."

"He's got something else in mind, that's for sure,"

Cooley said. "I've racked my brain, but I can't even begin to figure what it is."

"Seems like there's something, all right," Dan said. "But it doesn't matter a damn. I'm still going after Kyle, and when I find him, I'll hang him."

"You mean when we find him, Deputy Caine," Holt Peters said.

Dan nodded, smiling. "Yes, that's exactly what I mean."

He and the others stood around the fire, finishing the last of the morning's coffee. The new-aborning day was coming in clean and bright, and the air smelled of long grass and sage.

Lanky Lazarus Latchford left his stranded balloon and stepped beside Dan. "Good news," he said. "The burner wasn't as badly damaged as I thought. Me and Miss Prunella will have it fixed by dark."

"And then what?" Dan said.

"Then we wait for a north wind and follow your trail. I'll have my bombs ready and nice and handy."

"We don't know where Kyle is going," Dan said. "You may have a time finding us."

"Ah, I consulted Miss Prunella on that . . . oh wait, here she comes. I'll let her speak for herself. Miss Prunella is as smart as a tree full of owls and I always say that she stores more facts in her head than a Montgomery Ward mail-order catalogue." Latchford smiled. "She can recite Mr. Jules Verne's *Twenty Thousand Leagues Under the Sea,* in French, from memory, and that's the truth, not just a little professorial humor there."

Miss Prunella, a blue wildflower bloom in the brim of her pith helmet, a tin cup in her hand, stepped to the fire, hefted the pot, and then poured herself coffee. "Fine morning, isn't it?" she said.

"Indeed, it is, my dear," Latchford said. "Now think carefully . . . where would Clay Kyle go in Mexico?"

"Not just to sell a girl," Miss Prunella said. "I doubted that from the git-go since they could kidnap pretty girls in Mexico and sell them. No, he's after something else, something much more valuable, is Mr. Kyle."

"Have you any idea what?" Latchford prompted. "Anything in all those newspapers and magazines you read?"

For a while, Miss Prunella screwed up her pretty little face in thought and then recited, "*The Houston Post,* January seventh, 1879, Page one, anchor story. Headline, uppercase, IS THERE GOLD IN THEM THAR HILLS? Lowercase, italic, *We hear that local prospector Ives Brentwood is once again off to the Sierra del Carmen in Old Mexico in search of the Lost Chinaman gold mine. This will be his fourth attempt to find the elusive pot of gold, said to have been first mined by Chinese railroad workers and then abandoned. Mr. Brentwood said that he's convinced there is a fortune in fist-sized nuggets just lying around waiting to be found. So all we can do is admire his perseverance and pluck and wish him a hearty good luck!*"

Miss Prunella said, "I never read any mention of Ives Brentwood and his quest again, and I can only surmise he perished in the mountains. My guess is that Kyle is in search of the Lost Chinaman."

Cornelius Massey was stunned. "You memorized that from the paper."

"Everything I read, I memorize," Miss Prunella said. "I don't know why this is so, but I do, so there it is."

Massey searched his brain for obscurity and then said, "Have you read Mr. Edgar Allan Poe's *Masque of the Red Death*?"

"Of course, she has," Professor Latchford said, irritated. "Miss Prunella is very well read."

The little woman smiled and said, *"The Red Death had long devastated the country. No pestilence had ever been so fatal, or so hideous. Blood was its Avatar and its seal—the redness and the horror of blood. There were sharp pains and sudden dizziness, and then profuse bleeding at the pores, with dissolution. The scarlet stains upon the body and especially upon the face of the victim were the pest ban that shut him out from the aid and from the sympathy of his fellowmen. And the whole seizure, progress and termination of the disease, were the incidents of half an hour . . ."*

Massey clapped his hands and yelled, "That snapped my girdle! Miss Prunella, you have a rare gift."

"That's not what the nuns at the orphanage told me," the little woman said. "They said dwarves are obstinate children and have magical powers like great strength, memorizing what they read, wearing cloaks of invisibility, and foretelling the future. And they said it all comes from the devil and they beat me. Not every day, just on most days."

"I wish I'd been there. I'd have given those nuns a piece of my mind," Massey said.

"I'm sure you would have, Cornelius," Dan said. "Now it's time to mount up. We got a river to cross." He studied the Kiowa's impassive face and said, "What about you, Indian. Will you stick?"

The Kiowa nodded. "Until the job is done, or you're dead. Whatever comes first."

"Well, if I turn up my toes any time soon, you can have all the money in my pockets," Dan said. "You deserve it."

"Ah, it is good. You will give up your life to pay me my due," the Kiowa said.

"No, that ain't exactly what I meant," Dan said. "But I guess for now, it's close enough."

* * *

The Kiowa took point and soon lost himself in the distance. As Dan Caine and the others rode out, Clint Cooley looked behind him where Professor Latchford and Miss Prunella stood on either side of the balloon basket like mismatched bookends. He said to Dan, "You think we'll see those two again this side of Thunder Creek?"

Dan smiled. "Who knows? They'd have to catch a north wind and steer straight for the mountains. Somehow I kinda doubt it."

"Would you go up on one of those things?" Cooley said.

"You couldn't pay me enough," Dan said.

"I'd do it," Holt Peters said. "I'd like to fly right over Thunder Creek and drop a pail of molasses on Sheriff Hurd's head."

"You don't like him very much, kid, huh?" Cooley said.

"Mr. Doan said Chance Hurd was an outlaw and is still an outlaw. He takes stuff out of the store and never pays for it."

"What kind of stuff?" Cooley said.

"Anything he wants," Holt said. "Once he took a brand new Greener hammerless from the gunrack and told Mr. Doan he'd pay him later. He never did."

"I always wondered where he got the money to buy himself a new, eighty-dollar scattergun," Dan said.

"Well now you know," Holt said.

"Damned villain," Dan said.

CHAPTER TWENTY-SIX

The search had not gone well. Clay Kyle and his band rode under a blistering sun and a sky as transparent as blue glass. The heat was unrelieved by still, hot air that was thick and hard to breathe. Ahead of them, dust devils danced like hunting rattlesnakes and by noon, when the talking mirror again flashed on a mountainside, tempers frayed. One-eyed Morris Bennett and Loco Garrett got into it about Robert E. Lee's role in the defeat of the South until Susan Stanton told them to shut the hell up. Doug Avila, busy with his own dark thoughts, grew very silent and when he did, the men around him sensed the tension and danger in him and gave him room.

Just before noon, Kyle spotted shade under a massive shelf of rock and ordered a halt for an hour. He and the others drank a little water, ate some jerky, and nobody spoke until Susan Stanton lit a slim cheroot, slowly exhaled a curling ribbon of blue smoke, and said, "Clay, so far we've passed a couple of arroyos too narrow to hold a palace and we've found nothing else. Maybe the Sheik's place is on a shelf higher up the mountain."

"Maybe," Kyle said. He sounded almost disinterested, as though heat and exhaustion had gotten to him.

Doug Avila spoke for the first time that morning.

"Woman, the sky islands you speak of are at least five thousand feet above the flat, impossible for men and horses. And I know it's a good day's ride, maybe two, through these badlands until we reach the foothills at the end of the Sierra del Carmen. And all that time we'll have Dave Shannon's gunmen on our backtrail."

Susan Stanton had an elegant way of holding her cigar, her right elbow resting on her left arm, which she held across her waist, the cheroot near her cheek.

"What are you telling us, Doug?" she said.

"I've laid it out for you," Avila said. "Make of it what you will."

"Shannon's men are the Sheik's bodyguards, I know it," Kyle said. "Dave Shannon is lying through his teeth, but I'll deal with him when the times comes."

"You'll do it without me, Clay," Avila said. "I'm done." He nodded in the direction of Jenny Calthrop. "You can keep my share of the girl, just look me up sometime and buy me a drink."

Kyle shook his head. "You're going nowhere, Doug. I need all the men I got."

"Clay, I'm leaving. This is a ride from hell into nowhere," Avila said. "I advise you to call it quits and in the future don't listen to tall stories told by Chinamen." He looked around him at men with hard, exhausted faces. Only the distant mountains and Susan Stanton looked cool, and everyone stank of sweat but her. "Anyone coming with me?" he said.

Clay Kyle rose to his feet, sunlight harsh on his face, the rest of his body in shade deep enough that it could cover up his draw. He'd also positioned his gun so that it was handy, the butt between his elbow and wrist. He was angry now and that made him unpredictable and dangerous. "Doug, no one is riding with you, because you ain't leaving. You'll stick this out with the rest of us, and at the end of it, you'll be a rich man."

"Or a dead man," Avila said. "I'm saddling up, Clay. It's been nice knowing you."

The breed half turned in the direction of his horse. Then one word from Kyle, low, dark, and ominous, like a whisper in a sepulcher, stopped him.

"Avila."

The man's back stiffened. He turned slowly. His hand was close to his Colt. "Clay, don't try to stop me," he said.

"Nobody walks out on me," Kyle said. "Nobody. Seems like you've got a decision to make."

"I can shade you, Kyle," Avila said. "Any day of the week." His voice was calm, evenly paced, but his whiplike body was tense. "I'm pulling out of here without water and grub, but I'd rather do that than stay in this hellhole a minute longer."

"I said you ain't going, Doug," Kyle said. "You'll stick, by God."

"Go to hell," Avila said.

Clay Kyle didn't telegraph his draw. An amateur will raise his gun hand shoulder as he makes his play, but only Kyle's arm moved and since it was in in deep shadow and difficult to see, Avila lost a full half second before he clawed for his Colt. It was all the time Kyle needed. His gun hammered, shot after shot roaring among the surrounding rock faces like the sound of a titanic boulder bouncing along a marble corridor.

Avila staggered back, a bullet in his belly, another two in his chest. A dying man, the death darkness closing in on him. But he fired back, missed, fired again, missed. Suddenly his revolver seemed too heavy for him, and it fell from his hand onto the rocky ground. Avila fell a moment later, dead when he hit the ground.

In later years there was talk that Clay Kyle was not fast on the draw and shoot and that he got lucky the day he killed Doug Avila. But most agreed, and still do to this day, that after Kyle's gun was in his hand, he got his work in very quickly. They compared him to the shootist Wyatt Earp who thumbed off shots at extraordinary speed once his firearm was drawn. What's sure is that light and shade played a part in the Kyle/Avila gun battle and for now, that's where the matter must rest.

Susan Stanton walked to the dead man and looked down at his shot-up body. She turned to Kyle and said, "You sure ventilated him, Clay. It's a pity. I kind of liked him. He was a sharp dresser."

"I didn't want to lose him," Kyle said. "But he pushed it. What about you, Suzie? If he'd bested me, would you have shot him?"

"Probably not," Susan said. "It wasn't my fight."

Arlo Palmer and Boon Shanks scuttled across the rocks like grounded vultures and studied the dead man. Shanks grinned and said, "Mr. Kyle, can we have his gun and boots?"

"Sure, go ahead," Kyle said. "His *madre* probably wanted him buried with his boots off anyhow."

Palmer and Shanks stripped the man bare and then shared out his gun, boots, pocketknife, a few dollars, a silver ring, and from around his neck a small gold cross and chain.

Kyle watched this happen and then said, "You two shared the spoils, now you two bury him. There's plenty of rocks around, so pile them high to keep animals away."

Shanks looked stricken. "Boss, is that necessary? Avila was only half a white man."

"I told you to bury him," Kyle said. "Boon, he may have been a breed, but he was ten times better a man than a piece of white trash like you. Now get it done or as God is my witness, you'll join him under a pile of rocks."

Jenny Calthrop sat with her head on her knees quietly sobbing. Susan Stanton stepped beside her and said, "What ails you, sweetie? Sight of a dead man trouble you?"

The girl raised her tearstained face. "I saw a dead man before. I saw my father, the man you killed."

"I didn't kill him," Susan said. "Clay Kyle did that."

"You were part of it. You helped kill my entire family and as long as I live, I'll never forgive you."

Susan Stanton smiled. "Well, don't worry about it, you won't live long. Bought-and-paid-for whores seldom do."

"Unlike you, I'm not a whore," Jenny said. "And I'll live long enough to see you in hell."

Susan backhanded the girl across the face, the sharp crack of knuckles meeting flesh turned the heads of the men around her. "You have an impertinent tongue," the woman said. "Someday I may silence it for you permanently."

Kyle said, "What just happened? I don't want that girl damaged."

"Just a little disagreement about who's the whore in this outfit," Susan said.

"Ain't any question about that," Kyle said.

Susan Stanton watched him walk away, the sound of his mocking laugh loud in the silence.

It crossed the woman's mind right there and then that someday she might have to put a bullet into Clay Kyle.

CHAPTER TWENTY-SEVEN

"I wish I was close enough to put a rifle bullet into Clay Kyle," Fish Lee said. "Then we could all turn and go home with a clear conscience."

"There are others, and they're just as guilty as he is," Dan Caine said. "And what about Black-Eyed Susan?"

"What about her?" Fish said. His horse shook its head at a fly, the bit chiming in the late morning silence.

"You gonna put a bullet in her?" Dan said.

"She's a problem, ain't she?" Fish said.

"What kind of problem?" Clint Cooley said. "Apart from her being a woman, that is."

"Apart from her being a woman, he says." Fish looked serious. "That's exactly the dang problem, gambling man. You ever shot a woman?"

Cooley smiled. "I don't think so, but I'm sure I'd remember if I had."

"Well, I ain't never shot a member of the female sex afore, and I never will," Fish said. "So put that in your pipe and smoke it."

"Hear that, Estella?" Cooley said. "You're safe around ol' Fish. He don't hold with gunning ladies."

"Mr. Lee is a gentleman," Estella said. "That's more

than can be said for some around here." And then, "Put that in your pipe and smoke it, Clint Cooley."

"The Kiowa's coming in," Dan Caine said, smiling, his gaze reaching into the distance.

"The river is close, and there's a shallow crossing," the Kiowa said. "Kyle and his men forded there maybe two days ago." He glanced at the menacing sky. "Thunderstorm coming. Lightning among those peaks will not be pleasant."

"We'll chance it," Dan said. "I don't want to lose Clay Kyle in the mountains."

"Wiser if you'd said that you don't want to meet Clay Kyle in the mountains," the Kiowa said. "He has many gunmen with him."

"Indian, answer my question with something wise," Cooley said. "If we meet up with Kyle what are our chances?"

"None," the Kiowa said. "I could give you advice, but the white man never listens."

"I'm listening," Dan Caine said.

"Then wash the warpaint from your faces and go home quietly, like beaten warriors," the Kiowa said.

"That is not my intention," Dan said.

The Kiowa nodded. "I know I waste my breath. White men are deaf to good advice from an Indian."

To the north, still at a distance, angry thunder growled like a hibernating bear roused from sleep, and a rising wind rushed across the long grass. The air smelled strange, of ozone and far-off rain, and the horses grew restless, sensing what their riders could not . . . the violence to come.

"What about you, Kiowa?" Fish Lee said. "Come now, state your own intentions. Will you tuck your tail between your legs and run?"

"I told deputy Caine that I will lead him to Clay Kyle,"

the Kiowa answered. "As I've said before, my job is not yet done." He again glanced at the threatening sky. "When Kyle is within rifle shot, I will leave. I have no quarrel with the man."

It was growing darker as though the too-heavy black thunderclouds were falling to earth, and a few dismal drops of rain rode the wind and cooled the scorching heat of the day.

Dan saw Estella Sweet stare at the sky, her pretty face anxious, anticipating the coming tempest.

"Kiowa," Dan said. "we'll flap our chaps to the Rio Bravo and cross before the storm hits. It's going to be a big 'un, and we need to find shelter."

"Anybody here raised a Catholic like me?" Clint Cooley said. No one answered, and he said, "Then I'll say it for all of us . . . Jesus, Mary, and Joseph help us."

"Amen, brother," Cornelius Massey said. "We're going to need all the heavenly help we can get."

The storm hit with clangorous venom as the vigilantes were halfway across the Rio Bravo. Illuminated by lightning, the rain fell in flashing sheets as thunder bellowed and the surface of the river turned choppy and treacherous. Everyone was soaked to the skin within moments, and the horses changed color to glistening black.

Dan Caine dropped back and urged his riders to quicken their pace. "Get out of this damn water!" he yelled. But the gusting wind took his words and tossed them away, unheard, and the rain hammered relentlessly and blurred the surrounding terrain like a waterlogged Monet masterpiece.

Fish Lee gained the far bank first and went back to help a floundering Cornelius Massey keep his seat in the saddle. For a newspaperman, he had a fine vocabulary of cuss words, but his tirade was lost in the tumult, though Fish managed to get the gist of it. As Dan pushed his horse closer to Massey's mule, thunder blasted and lightning cracked close. Dan's spooked mount suddenly reared and threw him into the river. As he staggered to his feet in waist-high water, Clint Cooley's horse breasted the current and, showing considerable strength, the gambler reached down and pulled Dan by the back of his shirt onto his saddle. "Damn you, Dan, this is no time to go swimming," he yelled.

"I just took the notion," Dan said. "Where's my hat?"

"Right beside you, snagged on your gun," Cooley shouted in Dan's ear. "Keep that Colt, it's a fine hat-snatcher, since you can't use it for anything else."

Dan jammed the hat on his head and tried to come up with a sharp retort . . . but he couldn't think of anything.

Everybody reached the riverbank without further mishap and found the Kiowa waiting for them. He held the reins of Dan's horse, and, a rare sight, a smile played around his lips. Soaking wet, his dignity bruised, Dan climbed into the saddle, and the Indian cupped his hand to his mouth and yelled above the rage of a sky being torn apart, "Arroyo." He waved a hand behind him. "Shelter."

Dan nodded, and he and the others fell in behind the Indian. The Kiowa silently led the way to a narrow gulch that gouged the base of a mountain like a knife cut and rode at a walk inside. The rest followed and were suddenly cut off from the wind and the worst of the rain. The rock-walled passage was so narrow, they rode in single file for about fifty yards before the arroyo opened up into a grassy area about two acres in extent, surrounded by high walls. Here the rail fell, coming straight down, but there was little wind. But what surprised Dan and the others was a small stone cabin, coarsely built, with a sagging timber and shingle roof. To the front it had a rough wood door and one small window with four dirty panes that looked like cataract eyes trying to catch a glimpse of the world. The cabin crouched low behind a slight rise, as though trying to hide, but from its iron chimney a black string of smoke rose and gave it away. It was a rundown, dreary place, but what caught Dan Caine's attention was the man who pushed out of the cabin door, a Winchester in his hands.

He did not look friendly. In fact, he looked downright hostile.

"This," said Fish Lee, "looks like trouble."

"Just what we need," Dan Caine said.

CHAPTER TWENTY-EIGHT

"What are you doing here?" the man at the cabin door yelled. Then, his voice rising even louder, "If you're robbers, the gold is all gone. They already took it, cleaned me out."

"Who took your gold?" Dan Caine said. Clint Cooley had split to his left, giving himself gun room. "Was it Kyle?" Dan said. "Was it the outlaw Clay Kyle?"

"Never heard of him," the man said. "I had five thousand gold coins and the Rurales took them. They carried them out of here on a pack mule, those sons of dogs."

The man with the rifle was tall and thin and slightly stooped and he wore a ragged version of the Mexican peon's shirt, pants, and sandals. Black eyes glittered in a long, wrinkled face, saved from the unremarkable by a great hook of a nose.

"We did not come here to find gold, we came to arrest the outlaw, Clay Kyle," Dan said. "We have no ill intentions toward you."

Thunder crashed above the arroyo and lightning flashed on its soaked walls and for brief moments turned them into sheets of glimmering steel.

"I do not know this man," the rifleman said.

"Then we will trouble you no longer," Dan said.

"Wait!" came the desperate cry of a lonely man desperate for human contact. "I have coffee and a fire and there is graze for your horses. You are welcome." He lowered his Winchester. "Peace be upon you. You will be safe under my roof."

Dan Caine and the others unsaddled their horses and let them graze behind the cabin on a patch of surprisingly good grass. Nearby, a thin fall of water from higher up the mountain cascaded into a flat boulder that over centuries had worn away into a holding tank that was filled almost to the brim. Dan figured that the man, whoever he was, had chosen the site of his hideaway well.

The Kiowa, as drenched as the rest, was reluctant to enter the cabin, a distrust of strangers strong in him. But Dan convinced him to at least stay long enough to dry off a little and drink a cup of coffee and the man finally agreed, though reluctantly.

Inside, the cabin was small and cramped and crudely furnished, but it boasted a rather beautiful stone fireplace that some amateur Mexican artist had decorated with well-painted scenes of deserts and palm trees and a few rather iffy camels. A door opened into a bedroom where the man told Estella Sweet she could remove her clothes, and he gave her a blanket to wrap herself in. The men removed as much of their sopping clothing as they could and laid them out in front of the fire, but Estella made room for her corset and underwear by pushing aside the male garments with a bare foot. Young Holt Peters thought she might blush, but she didn't, so he did.

After they had all been settled in with small cups of

bitter, spicy coffee, Dan introduced himself and the others and then said to their host, "And you are?"

With great dignity the man said, "My name is Sheik Bandar al-Salam."

Cornelius Massey brightened. "Ah, you are from the Arabian lands."

"That is correct."

"How did you come to reside here?" Massey said.

"That was not my intention. I did not build this cabin. It was already here. I was very sick with a war wound, and the Mexicans led me to this place. They said it was safer than any village. I had two servants then who guarded my gold, but they were killed by the Rurales." The Sheik's face changed, closing down all expression. "With me was my young son, and Lihua, the beloved concubine. Her name means one who is elegant and beautiful, and that's what she was."

"Mr. Sheik, what happened to them?" Holt Peters said.

"The Rurales took them. I never saw Lihua and my son again. I begged the Rurales captain to take me with my family, but I was very sick and he thought it a good joke to leave me here to die."

The newspaperman in him coming to the fore, Massey said, "Where did you get the gold?"

"I was a mercenary during the Second Opium War with Britain and under the orders of the Chinese Grand High Admiral, I commanded a war junk in the South China Sea with orders to stop and sink British opium ships."

"Mr. Sheik, what's a war junk?" Holt Peters interrupted, his face alight, suddenly a boy again, enjoying an adventure story.

"It's a Chinese ship built to carry cannon," the Sheik said. "My ship was the *Shen Yang*. She carried twenty guns and sailed across the ocean like a swan in flight."

Massey tried his coffee, liked it, smiled, and said, "Good coffee, Sheik. Now, about the gold?"

"The day China surrendered to the British, I boarded a British merchantman carrying opium," the Sheik said. "I also found six thousand gold sovereigns, profit from that vile trade. I hanged the captain from his own yardarm and then sank his ship with his crew locked up in the hold with the opium. From that moment on, the British wanted me dead. Another mercenary captain, an Irishman named O'Rourke, was tied to the mast and flogged to death on the deck of HMS *Warrior,* moored in Shantou harbor for that very purpose. I knew the British government wouldn't rest until I joined him and would send assassins after me. I fled to Texas, but after a few years, though I posed as a poor man, word of my gold spread and I then, by night, escaped to Mexico where I thought I would be safer. But I was betrayed by a Chinaman I had befriended, and the British, may Allah take their souls, found me. The Britishers did not wish to soil their hands with the blood of a dirty Arab, so they paid the Rurales to kill me and recover their gold. But their Mexican captain thought I was already dying and saved his bullet."

"How have you managed to live since?" Dan Caine said.

"The Mexicans feed me," the Sheik said. "A father and son who live in a village about three miles to the east of here bring me beans and tortillas." The Arab managed a weak smile. "They believe I'm favored by Santa Muerte, the holy lady of the dead."

"Well, Sheik, I don't want to alarm you," Dan Caine said. "But I think your life is in great danger. I believe Clay Kyle, the outlaw I mentioned earlier, may be here in the Sierra del Carmen in search of your gold."

"Then it will be the last of his sorrows," the Sheik said. He waited until a peal of thunder crashed and then said,

"Mr. Caine, the gold was cursed. I never spent a peaceful night as long as I possessed it. Six thousand golden sovereigns cost me the lives of my son, Lihua the beloved, and two faithful manservants. In my nightmares, I still hear the screams of the British sailors drowning in the hold of their ship and when I wake up in fright, their dreadful curses still ring in my ears. I am now dying of a cancer deep in my bowels, and thus it would seem that this man Clay Kyle can do no worse to me than I've already done to myself." The Sheik smiled. "More coffee?"

"Right here in my cup," Fish Lee said, grinning. "You make good coffee fer a heathen."

A few minutes later, while the persistent storm still raged, keen-eared Holt Peters said, "What was that?"

"I hear it too," Estella said, tugging up the blanket that had just slipped from her naked shoulder. "Was it thunder?"

"Hell no, it was gunfire," Holt said.

"The boy is correct," the Kiowa said.

"Everyone held their breath and listened. There it was again . . . a drumroll rattle cutting through the sound of the storm.

"It's gunfire all right," Dan Caine said. "And mighty close."

Chapter Twenty-nine

"Shannon! Only a damned fool starts a gunfight in a thunderstorm!" Clay Kyle yelled.

The rain was torrential, falling from cataclysmic clouds as black as foam-swept rocks.

"I do, Kyle," Dave Shannon called back. "And I'll keep it up until I drive you out of here. You're a disgrace to the neighborhood."

Kyle and the rest were still sheltered under the rock overhang that kept off the worst of the rain but offered little by way of cover. Everyone had hit the ground when Shannon and his men started shooting, and suddenly even a fist-sized pebble became a prized barricade.

Bullets hammered into the underside of the shelf and whanged away, kicking up startled Vs of sand and gravel on the floor. Loco Garrett, a man born under a dark star, had been hit again, this time in the groin. The gunman bled a bucketful of scarlet gore and his kicking heels chawed up the ground as he shrieked in mortal agony. Loco was as stupid as a stump, but even he knew he'd received a death wound and was on a straight path to hell.

As rifles slammed on either side, Kyle cursed the storm and his exposed position. He took a quick pot with his Winchester and nailed a visible leg of one of Shannon's men.

When the gunman carelessly leaned forward to grab his shattered knee, his hat brim and then the right side of his head appeared beyond the protecting boulder. It was all the target Kyle needed. Another quick shot, and the .44-40 bullet crashed into the gunman's temple, traversed the man's skull and exited just above his left ear, taking brain and bone with it. It was a devastating wound, and the gunman, a man named Farrell, who'd briefly ridden with young Bill Bonney and his Regulators, died instantly.

There was a lull in the fire, and Kyle looked around him. Loco Garrett was silent now, gasping his last, his face turned to the rain. One-eyed Morris Bennett was wounded, but still in the fight. Broken Nose Charlie Bates, a former bareknuckle pugilist, a man with weak lungs, was never the steadiest of hands in a gunfight and he looked scared, breathing hard. Susan Stanton and the Calthrop girl were still unharmed and Zack and Arlo Palmer and Boon Shanks held to their positions, rifles at the ready. The vilest of the vile frontier trash, the three nonetheless had a brand of coyote courage and would fight well when cornered.

And right now, Clay Kyle was cornered.

Thunder rolled and banged, and lightning scratched across the sky like a skeletal hand. Kyle and his remaining fighting men, with the exception of Bates who seemed to be out of the fight, poured fire into Shannon's boulder-strewn position in the middle of a stand of stunted wild oak and heavy brush. In the exchange of shots, Bennett was hit a second time and Arlo Palmer lost a left earlobe.

In later years, two of Shannon's surviving gunmen credited Susan Stanton with an incredible kill at more than fifty yards . . . a revolver shot that hit the Missouri gunman Zebulon Hopperton right in the middle of his forehead. In 1905, Bat Masterson credited Zack Palmer with the shot, but since the Suffragette movement was at its height, like many others, Bat may have been unwilling to give a woman the credit. But Shannon's men swore that they saw a beautiful woman shoot Hopperton with a Colt Peacemaker at fifty or sixty yards. One of them claimed to have later paced off the distance and said, "It was kinda like how Wild Bill shot Dave Tutt that time."

Whatever the case, the killing of Zeb Hopperton ended the engagement . . . at least for that day. Under the cover of the storm, carrying their dead with them, Dave Shannon withdrew his soaked and sulky gunmen and stopped only to yell at Kyle. "Damn you, Kyle, we'll be back!"

"I know you will," Kyle said, but only to himself.

Loco Garrett was dead and so was Charlie Bates, shot through the top of his head and also the biggest loss of all, the skilled drawfighter Morris Bennett had taken two bullets to his upper chest and died.

Zack and Arlo Palmer . . . Boon Shanks . . . only the trash was left.

"Why did Dave Shannon quit?" Susan Stanton said.

"Two reasons . . . his men didn't like fighting in a thunderstorm any more than we did, and he'd lost two of them," Kyle said. "He'll be back. He wants us out of these mountains."

"A man shouldn't be able to own a mountain," Boon Shanks said.

"Shannon doesn't want to own a mountain," Kyle said. "He wants a place where he and others like him can hide out after a job without worrying about lawmen. Seems like just by being here I spoiled his plan."

"What about the gold?" Zack Palmer said. Bearded and

shaggy, he looked like a satyr in the firelight. "Is there gold?"

Susan Stanton said, "If there's a rich Arabian sheik in the Sierra del Carmen with tons of gold, a harem of beautiful women, and a much-loved son who now and then comes out to play, Dave Shannon and other outlaws would own it all already. Don't you think?"

Kyle was silent for long moments, then said, "Hell, maybe I figured it wrong. The Chinaman . . ."

"Took a legend he'd overheard in a whorehouse or on a railroad gang, embroidered the truth, and sold it to you as a natural fact," Susan said.

"But why would he do that?" Kyle said.

"What did you give him in return?" Susan said.

"He was only a little runt, the Chinaman. I gave him protection from the other cons, and I made sure he got his fair share of whatever grub was going around," Kyle said.

"And he spun you a yarn to keep you doing those things," Susan Stanton said.

"He lied to me," Kyle said. "The Chinaman was dying, but he lied to me. Don't that beat all."

"You helped him survive, Clay, but he hated your guts for it," Susan said. "I knew a Chinese whore once on the Barbary Coast in California. She called her white clients, *Gwai,* meaning ghost men, and she hated them. Dying or not, the Chinaman had no love for you."

Kyle shook his head. "I should have wrung that Chinaman's scrawny neck."

"Yes, you should have," Susan said. "But it's too late now."

"Listen up, Clay," Boon Shanks said. His hot eyes went to Jenny Caltrop. "I'll take the girl off your hands right now. Can we make a deal?" He reached in a pocket and said, "Look. It's Morris Bennett's gold watch and fifty dollars and a silver gambler's ring I took from Charlie Bates's finger. Hell, that's a lot more than the girl is worth."

"Boon, you're a filthy, slimy, slithering lizard of a man," Susan Stanton said. "I can't stand the sight of you."

Boon's smile was sly. "Does that mean you want the girl for yourself, man-woman?"

Susan Stanton's backhanded slap across Shanks's hairy face sounded like the crack of a pistol shot. The man had been squatting by the fire and he fell backward and his shoulders thumped on rock. His eyes slitted, Shanks screamed an obscenity, and his hand flashed for his gun. Susan was now in a kneeling position, her Colt unhandy. She skinned it but was slower than Shanks, a man fast and sure on the draw and shoot.

But Clay Kyle was also a man born with quick reactions.

As Shanks drew and started to pull himself up, Kyle had already grabbed the handle of the coffeepot. He threw the contents into Shank's chest just as the man's Colt came level. Boiling hot coffee splashed all over the sitting gunman, and he howled in sudden pain and dropped his gun to pull his blackened shirt away from his scalded skin.

If it had been anyone else but Susan Stanton it might have ended right there.

But the woman was not one to let a despised enemy off the hook.

She laughed and put two bullets into Shanks, and he fell back and lay still, steaming like a manure pile.

Kyle was on his feet, furious. He glared at the woman and said, "Damn you, you didn't need to kill him."

"Yes, I did," Susan said. "He was a pig."

Zack Palmer said, "Hell, Clay, keep this up and there'll be none of us left."

"I didn't want Boon dead," Kyle said.

"Oh dear, I'm as silly as a goose," Susan Stanton said. "I thought you did."

Zack rose to his feet, his brother Arlo flanking him. He pointed. "That woman will be the death of us all. First Arch Pitman and now Boon Shanks. Two good men gone."

"They were not good men, they were inbred scum, as welcome at a campfire as a pair of wet dogs at a square dance," Susan said.

"I say we get out of here," Arlo said. "Head south until we find a place to sell the girl."

"Arlo, how much is she worth?" Zack Palmer said.

"Depends on the brothel," Arlo said. "Maybe five hundred. Maybe more."

"We might do better back in Texas," Zack said. He looked at Boon Shanks's body. "Are we going to bury that?"

Kyle made no answer, and his shoulders slumped as he said, "Five hundred dollars. It ain't even decent whiskey money." He exhaled a long-suffering sigh and said, "Suzie, take the girl behind a boulder someplace and strip her down. See what you think she'll bring in a Fort Worth brothel."

Susan Stanton smiled. "Not much." She stepped to Jenny. "Come on you. Let's take a look at what you have to offer a man."

The girl looked horrified. She bent over and picked up a rock and backed away, ready to throw. "I'm not taking my clothes off for you or anybody else. Take another step and I'll chunk this rock right at your head. My brothers taught me how."

Susan Stanton was a little taken aback. She smiled. "So little miss goody two-shoes shows some spunk."

"Just try me," Jenny said. Her dress was getting ragged, and she had a smear of dirt on her cheek.

"All right, sister, let's see what's faster," Susan said. "Your rock or my gun."

"Suzie, no! Leave the girl be," Kyle said. "I just thought up a better plan for her."

Susan Stanton relaxed, uncoiling slowly like a sleek serpent. "Whatever you say, Mr. Kyle." Then to Jenny, in a thin hiss, "Sass or backtalk me again and I'll cut your tits off, you little slut." She turned and stepped to Kyle. "So what's your plan, Clay?"

"She's to be a gift . . . call her a peace offering," Kyle said. "I got a hunch that little gal will get us out of these mountains alive."

CHAPTER THIRTY

The storm passed, grumbling its way south, and Dan Caine didn't wish to impose on the Sheik's hospitality any longer. The man invited them to stay the night, but there were at least six more hours of daylight, and in any case the cabin was too small to sleep so many people.

"You won't see me again," Sheik Bandar al-Salam said. "Tonight or tomorrow night, I'll end it. I'm very sick, much in pain, and all that's left to me is the privilege of choosing the time of my own death, may Allah forgive me."

The others were mounted outside the Sheik's cabin, but Dan Caine stood at the door, holding his horse. "I'm sorry," he said. He had no other words.

The Arab shrugged. "*Ma sha Allah*. God has willed it." He held out a bulging sack. "This is for you, tortillas and coffee for your journey. I no longer have need of them. And this . . ." He dropped a coin into Dan's hand. "It's a gold sovereign, one the Rurales missed."

"I can't . . ."

"I say again, I have no need for it," the Sheik said. "Carry it in good health."

"Thank you," Dan said. And since he could find nothing else to add, "You make good coffee."

The Sheik smiled and bowed from the waist. "May Allah protect you," he said.

The sun rode high and bright in a blue sky as though nature apologized for the thunderstorm's boorish behavior. A profound silence lay on the land, and the soaring, tree-covered mountains that stretched into the distance were remote, aloof, uncaring of the tiny humans so far below and their petty affairs.

The Kiowa again rode point, but, because of the broken terrain, most of the time he stayed out of sight of the others.

Clint Cooley kneed his horse alongside Dan and said, "I reckon Clay Kyle is chasing a pot of gold at the end of the rainbow . . . only there ain't no rainbow."

"Seems about right," Dan said. "He didn't ride all this way to sell Jenny Calthrop into slavery. There are no brothels in the Sierra del Carmen."

"There's no nothing in the Sierra del Carmen," Cooley said. "Give me a big city, or even a cow town full of flies and the stink of the stockyards and I'm as happy as a pig in slop."

"And that's why you headed for Thunder Creek, huh?" Dan said, grinning.

"Now that was a kick in the teeth, Deputy Caine," Cooley said. "I'd nowhere else to run."

"I'd say that goes for me too," Dan said. "I'd pretty much used up all my options by the time I rode into Thunder Creek, and I couldn't see anything beyond it."

"Grass," Cooley said. "Like me, you saw unending grass and figured you'd reached the end of the line."

"You going back there, Clint?" Dan said.

"Maybe. I don't know. I'll wait and see how this thing plays out."

"Not me. After we do right by Tom Calthrop and his family, I'll ride," Dan said.

"Where?"

"Hell, I don't know."

"They say Kansas City is a sight to see, and Denver."

"Maybe New Orleans," Dan said.

"I got kissin' kinfolk there," Cooley said. "I'll write you a letter of introduction."

"It sounds like a possible plan," Dan said.

The gambler nodded. "Now all we have to do is arrest Clay Kyle and his gang of gunmen and hang them."

"That's the reason we're here," Dan said.

"And God only knows why," Cooley said. "Look ahead. The Kiowa is coming in and he seems kind of unhappy, though you can never tell with an Indian."

As usual, the Kiowa's face was without expression. "Three riders," he said. As was his habit he held up that many fingers. "They come this way."

"Kyle's men?" Dan said.

The Indian shrugged. "I don't know."

"It could be Kyle and a couple of his boys," Cooley said.

"Vigilantes, get ready," Dan said to the others. "But no gunplay until I order it."

"No fear of that," Fish Lee said. "I ain't drawing down on Clay Kyle."

The Kiowa split to the side as the others shook out into a line, rifles at the ready. The day had not yet run its course, and the sun was still bright, the air steamy.

Clint Cooley tried to stifle his tongue, but in the end, he had to say it. "My, but ain't we a fearsome bunch."

Dan made no answer.

Now the chips were down, he was keenly aware how vulnerable they were.

CHAPTER THIRTY-ONE

The three riders came on at a walk, tough, capable, well-mounted men with the flint-faced stamp of the outlaw about them. All three wore belt guns, but to Dan Caine's relief their rifles were still in the scabbards. They drew rein at revolver distance, and a man who wore a back frockcoat and pants, frilled white shirt, and black hat, rivaling even Cooley's gambler finery, was the first to speak. And what he said surprised everybody.

"Howdy, Cooley," he said. "You on the scout?"

"Not hardly, Duran," Cooley said. "I'm riding for the law."

James Duran smiled. "I don't believe it."

"Believe it," Cooley said. "I'm what they call in these parts a vigilante."

Duran's gray eyes moved from Cooley to Dan and then the others, lingering on Estella for a few moments before dismissing the rest.

"Cooley, there was a time you rode in better company," Duran said.

"They'll do," Cooley said, knowing he lied through his teeth. The sun was warm on his shoulders and he sweated a little, aware of the tightness in his belly. James Duran was a named pistolero and demanded, and got, five thousand dollars for a contracted kill. He'd fought in a dozen range wars, great and small, and in victory he was the wrath of God, in defeat as fierce and dangerous as a wounded bear.

Duran said, "Did you know that Five Ace Phil Coates died?"

"No, I didn't," Cooley said. "Sorry to hear it."

"Are you?"

"Not really."

Duran said, "Took him a six-month, but he finally turned up his toes. Your bullet was still in him all that time." He smiled. "He died cursing you, Cooley. Maybe that's when your luck turned bad."

"Could be," Cooley said. "I've been through it ever since."

"Still," Duran said, "you get credit for the kill."

"Coates was notified. You know that, Duran. Hell, you were there," Cooley said. "His cheating was too obvious. Marking the cards with his thumbnail was a greenhorn's trick."

"He didn't listen that day, as I recollect," Duran said.

"He should have," Cooley said. "What do you want from us?"

"First you tell me why you're here. This is a robber's roost, and if you'd been on the scout, you'd have been welcome. But your welcome ran out when you mentioned vigilantes. That's a bad word around these parts."

Dan Caine said, "To sum it up, we aim to arrest a man by the name of Clay Kyle for murder and then hang him. And his cohorts."

Amid laughter from his two companions, Duran pointedly ignored Dan and said, "Tell me why you're here, Cooley."

"You heard the deputy," Cooley said.

"Sure, I heard what the rube said, but I can scarce believe it."

"Believe it," Cooley said.

Duran shook his head and grinned. "Well, maybe you'll get lucky and Kyle will laugh himself to death."

"He won't laugh at me," Cooley said.

"No, I guess he won't," Duran said. "As for the rest of you . . . what's the saying? Ah, yes, lambs to the slaughter."

"Right, you've had your say, now will you give us the road?" Dan said.

"No . . . deputy . . . I won't. but I'll give you some advice . . . turn around and head back to where you came from. Lawmen, even your kind, ain't welcome in the Sierra del Carmen."

Cooley could've done it of course, maybe Fish Lee, but it was young Holt Peters who pushed it. He kneed his horse forward, pointed his Winchester at James Duran and said, "Mister, give us the road or I'll blow you right out of that saddle."

The youngster's muzzle didn't waver and his jaw was set. He obviously experienced a whole range of emotions in that moment, but fear wasn't one of them.

James Duran was as surprised as the rest. "Hell, Cooley, what are you feeding this kid? Gunpowder?"

"Duran," Dan Caine said, "like the rest of us he's been eating fire and brimstone since we saw what Kyle and his vermin did to the Calthrop ranching family up Concho County way."

Duran grinned. "Steal a maverick or two from them Calthrops?"

"Murder, torture, rape and kidnapping . . . a whole family wiped out. Try that on for size," Dan said. "And take the grin off your face or this rube will blow it off with a bullet." Suddenly his Colt was in his hand. "Maybe I'm two shades meaner than you think, mister."

The time for grinning was past, and Duran knew it. "You heard of Dave Shannon?" he said.

"Can't say as I have," Dan said.

"I work for him. And he's pushing Kyle out of these mountains because his kind attracts lawmen. If he hasn't found a grave here, and I'd say that seems mighty unlikely, wait across the Rio Bravo until he leaves and grab him then."

"If you want rid of Kyle so bad, why don't you assist us?" Dan said.

He holstered his gun, a thing Cooley noted. He moved his own hands closer to his Bulldogs.

"Is there a reward?" Duran said.

"Not that I know of," Dan said.

"Well, it doesn't matter a damn. Dave Shannon won't hand one of his own kind over to the law," Duran said. "If he did, news of his treachery would get around, and he'd never be trusted again by the outlaw fraternity. That word means brotherhood, if you don't know. Sure, he'll probably kill Clay Kyle, but that's just good business, a whole different matter than selling him out to a bunch of tinhorn vigilantes."

Dan said, "All right, Duran, you presented your case. Now let us pass."

"I'll ask you one more time . . . will you leave?" Duran said. "Come now, state your intentions."

"I intend for you to give us the road," Dan said.

Duran's eyes shifted to Estella. "You look like a smart young lady. Can you talk sense into him?"

Estella shook her head. "Jenny Calthrop is my friend, and Clay Kyle took her captive. I want her back, and I want to see Kyle hang."

"Then it's done and done," Duran said. "The next time we meet, hot lead will do my talking."

James Duran pulled his horse aside and made a show of

a sweeping bow from the saddle. "The road is now yours," he said.

As Cooley rode past, Duran said, "Clint Cooley, I'm glad your onetime mistress, the beautiful and charming Countess Celeste de la Cour, isn't here to see how far you've fallen since the gaming tables of New Orleans. I'd say I'm sorry to see you sunk so low, but I'm not. You were always arrogant and lucky."

"Now all that sounds just like you, James," Cooley said. "You made a habit of mistaking skill for luck and that's why you were such a rotten poker player. When, or perhaps I should say if, you see Celeste again, give her my love."

CHAPTER THIRTY-TWO

"I knew one of them," James Duran said. "His name is Clint Cooley and he's a gun. The rest, a rube lawman, a half-grown boy, a couple of old men, and a girl, won't give us any trouble. There was an Indian with them, but he didn't seem interested."

"And they say they're vigilantes here to hang Clay Kyle?" Dave Shannon said.

"That's what they say."

Seven of Shannon's surviving gunmen were present, and all laughed heartily, Duran himself joining in the mirth.

Finally, Shannon said, "Come again, who is the ranny you knew?"

"Clint Cooley," Duran said.

That drained the laughter from Shannon mighty fast. "Could that be the New Orleans Clint Cooley, made a name for himself on the steamboats and fought all those duels?"

"Not many duels, maybe three or four, but he always killed his man," Shannon said. "What the hell game is he playing, running with a hick lawman and a bunch of rubes?"

"It seems he's had a long spell of bad luck, ever since

he shot Five Ace Phil Coates in New Orleans that time," Duran said.

"I remember that name. Phil Coates had a gun rep, killed more than his share."

"Yeah, he was good with a gun was Phil, but Cooley was better." Duran shrugged. "It's no concern of ours. Kyle will take care of Clint Cooley. The lawman doesn't even figure. He's a nobody."

"So Kyle takes care of Cooley and then we take care of Kyle," Shannon said. "Is that it?"

"Seems about right," Duran said. "What about the woman with him?"

Shannon winked. "We'll take care of her too."

"Are we still scouting Kyle?" Duran said.

"Yeah, Reb Walker and Ezra Flint are keeping an eye on him," Shannon said. "The last I heard, he still hasn't moved from his position under the rock shelf, damn his eyes. Well, I'll give him another day to take care of the vigilantes, and then we'll dig him out of there."

"How many men does Kyle have left?" Duran said.

"I don't know, the woman and maybe a couple more, but that's a guess," Shannon said. "The way they were holed up, all of them flat on their bellies, it was hard to say." He nodded. "Yeah, I'd guess he lost two, maybe three."

"Kyle still has enough to take care of the vigilantes, as they call themselves," Duran said. "But if I was him, I'd be a tad worried about Cooley. He's fast and he hits what he aims at."

"I don't care how fast he is, he ain't faster than Clay Kyle," Shannon said.

"I don't know about that because I never saw Kyle shoot," Duran said. "But I saw Cooley kill Phil Coates across a card table in New Orleans. I reckon my heart beat

once, and it was all over . . . and that was two shots . . .
Bang! Bang! Hell, I can't even say it as fast as it happened."

"Kyle can take him," Shannon said. "I got no doubts
about that."

"We'll soon find out," Duran said. "Cooley and them
rubes are about due to ride right into him."

CHAPTER THIRTY-THREE

The Kiowa glanced up at the blue sky and the brassy ball of the dropping sun. Two hours of daylight, he figured, and he smelled coffee and saw the column of smoke from a white man's fire that tied bows in the still air.

He left his horse and advanced on foot, using every weather-worn boulder or patch of brush as cover. He was sure Clay Kyle was near. He sensed the man, smelled his danger like the odor of death.

On cat feet, the Kiowa scouted another hundred yards across broken terrain, and then he saw it . . . an overhanging shelf of rock, an obvious camping space sheltered from the sun. A man wearing rough range clothes, chosen with no particular care, stood talking with a tall woman, and even at a distance, her slender beauty was obvious.

The Kiowa took cover behind a large rock, annoying a panting lizard that scuttled away in panic. The Indian nodded to himself. Clay Kyle and the one they called Black-Eyed Susan. It had to be. Because of the contour of the mountain, he could see no others, nor the Calthrop girl. But he'd seen enough. The Kiowa worked his way back to his horse and wary of raising dust, slowly walked his mount back to Caine.

* * *

"Then we have him," Dan Caine said after talking with the Kiowa.

"Or he has us," Clint Cooley said. "Best to wait and catch him out in the open."

"No, there's an hour of daylight left and I want Kyle in irons and ready for a noose by nightfall," Dan said, his chin set. He looked as stubborn as a government mule.

"We don't have any irons," Cooley said.

"Then I'll truss him up with rope," Dan said.

Cooley's sigh was long on exasperation. "How do you want to play this, Deputy Sheriff Caine?"

"We'll ride up to his camp, and I'll order him to surrender in the name of the law," Dan said.

"And then he'll laugh and shoot you right off the back of your horse," Cornelius Massey said.

Young Holt Peters said nothing and neither did Fish Lee. Estella Sweet looked nervous, and the Kiowa stood listening, his face like stone.

"I have my duty, Clint," Dan said. "Not a legal duty, but a duty toward the Calthrop family and young Jenny still in their clutches. God knows what's happened to her by now."

"Then wait until tomorrow and do your duty," Cooley said. "Stand off a hundred yards and kill him with a rifle shot and save a rope."

"That would be an assassination. I want Kyle to face a legal hanging, him and the other guilty parties."

"So we just walk up to his camp and arrest him?" Cooley said.

"Yes, that's my intention. But not all of us, just you and Fish Lee," Dan said. He looked around him, his gaze lingering on a fairly steep talus slope that rose from the flat and reached the lower level of the mountain. "This is a fair place to make camp," Dan said. "Plenty of rock and brush to give us cover if we need it."

"We'll need it," Fish Lee said.

"Perhaps not, if Kyle comes quietly."

"He won't," Fish said.

"We don't know that until we try, do we?" Dan said, irritated.

"Clay Kyle and his kind don't surrender to anybody," Fish Lee said.

"Then if the worst comes to the worst, I'll shoot him," Dan said.

"If he don't shoot you first," Fish said.

"A very likely occurrence," Cooley said.

"I rode all this distance, was nearly hung, nearly shot to death, and damn near burned alive and now you expect me to just walk away from it," Dan said.

"Nobody's saying that," Fish Lee said. "Use the Kiowa to spy on ol' Clay, and when he moves, we ambush him and plug him."

"From a safe distance," Cooley said.

"I want him to hang," Dan said.

"Dead is dead," Cooley said. "Hanging is just another way of getting there."

"But hanging is legal," Dan said.

"So is a .44-40 bullet," Cooley said.

Estella Sweet said, "Dan, you're a brave man, but you're no match for a shootist like Clay Kyle and probably not for any of the others who ride with him. Listen to Clint. Yes, execute Kyle the Calthrop murderer, but do it on your own terms. Don't go toe to toe with a skilled gunman . . ."

"And expect to come out of it alive," Fish Lee said.

"Cornelius, what do you think?" Dan said.

"My advice?" Massey said. "Listen to Cooley. I have a feeling he's been up this road before."

Cooley smiled and touched his hat. "Very perceptive of you, newspaperman. But trying to talk down a slowpoke who plans to brace a notoriously fast gun is a first." His smile swung on Dan. "I saw the draw you made on James Duran. If he'd been serious, you'd be dead."

"Damn it all, I can stand on my own two feet, take my hits, and shoot back," Dan said.

"Yes, Deputy Caine, you can do that, but there's no future in it," Cooley said. "Is there?"

Dan's shoulders slumped in defeat. He could circle around and around about this and never get anywhere, like a blind mule in a grain mill. He knew all along that bringing Clay Kyle to justice would not be easy. Now it was shaping up to be a herculean task, like moving a mountain. He called to the Kiowa, and the man led his beautiful appaloosa to Dan's mount. The Indian stood at Dan's stirrup and looked up at him, his face like lead.

"Can you keep an eye on Clay Kyle and tell me when he moves out?" Dan said.

"I can do that," the Kiowa said.

Dan managed a smile. "Thank you. I owe you."

"You owe me nothing but wages," the Kiowa said.

He turned, mounted his horse, and left at a walk, parting the gathering gloom.

After the Kiowa was gone from sight, Fish Lee said, "Someday, somebody is gonna put a bullet into that uppity Injun."

"Don't ever try it, Fish," Cooley said. "If Clay Kyle is a demon, then the Kiowa is the devil himself. I look into his eyes, and all I see is a hundred different kinds of hell."

CHAPTER THIRTY-FOUR

"Don't worry, Dave Shannon will find you before you find him," Clay Kyle said.

"Suppose he just hauls off and shoots me," Arlo Palmer said.

"He won't," Kyle said. "Even Shannon respects a white flag."

Arlo looked helplessly at his brother. "Zack, tell me again what I have to do," he said.

"It's simple, Arlo," Zack said. "You just speak your piece. You tell Shannon that Clay wants to meet and pow-wow. Tell him we want free passage out of the mountains and tell him Clay has a gift for him, a fresh young gal who hasn't even been broken in yet." Zack slapped his brother on the shoulder. "That's what you tell him."

"He'll kill me, Zack, I know he will," Arlo said. He stood in morning sunlight, dirty and unkempt, the heat making him smell even worse.

Susan Stanton, after slapping the girl into near unconsciousness, had pulled off what remained of Jenny Calthrop's petticoat and tied it to the barrel of Arlo's rifle. "Here, you'll carry this," she said. "Hold it upright so it can be seen."

"Why don't you do it?" Arlo said. "Shannon won't shoot a woman."

"Because if he kills a sorry piece of rat crap like you, it's no great loss," Susan said. "It's a question of priorities, understand?"

"Then I ain't doing it," Arlo said.

"Arlo," Kyle said, "you got a choice to make . . . you either make big talk with Dave Shannon"—his Colt flashed from the holster—"or I'll shoot you in the belly right now and then we'll all sit around and drink whiskey and listen to you die." Kyle smiled. "It may take hours, maybe a whole day and a night."

"Why does this always happen to me?" Arlo said. "And never to any of you?"

Susan Stanton smiled. "I told you why, Arlo," she said. "In a word, you're expendable. That means disposable."

"Suzie, don't tease him," Kyle said. "Go now, and get the job done, Arlo. I'll see you get a big reward later."

"I'll do it," Arlo said. He turned a menacing glance on Susan. "Lady, if I was you, I wouldn't sleep easy at nights. One time, you're gonna wake up and I'll be there at your bedside, your worst nightmare."

"I look forward to it," the woman said. "Killing a man always makes me sleep better."

The Kiowa watched the man leave Clay Kyle's camp under a flag of truce.

For a moment, he thought the rider was headed for Dan Caine and the others, but he swung his horse around and headed south. That puzzled the Indian, but then it occurred to him that Kyle's man was probably looking for a peace parley with the outlaw called Dave Shannon. Kyle and Shannon now shared a common enemy, the vigilantes, and it made sense for them to act together. At least, as far as the Kiowa was concerned, that was the answer to the white flag.

In the meantime, he would watch and wait and earn his wages.

The hot day wore on, and the sun dropped lower in the sky. Once a small, whitetail deer, seldom encountered on the flat, tiptoed to within twenty feet of the well-hidden Kiowa. A slight change in the direction of the breeze and the little animal scampered away, its bobbing tail signaling the alarm. A pair of buzzards lazily quartered the sky on the scout for dying things. And then there were two more . . . and three more . . . and then too many to count . . . and that made the Kiowa anxious . . .

There were dead men in the Sierra del Carmen.

CHAPTER THIRTY-FIVE

The day had not yet melted into evening when the Kiowa spotted two riders coming from the south. One of the men sat stiff and awkward in the saddle, like a ranny with an injured back, the other was James Duran, the dying sun glinting on the silver conchos that adorned his saddle. As the riders got closer, the Indian saw that Duran was leading the horse of the stiff man by the reins.

But the man didn't have an injured back . . . he was dead.

Now the Kiowa could make out details and wondered, as he often did, how savage white men could be toward one another. The white rag that Kyle's man had used as a flag had been stuffed into his mouth and the remainder hung over his chest and since his throat was cut, that part of the rag was soaked, glistening with blood. The dead man had been tied to his saddle, his back braced with a couple of wild oak branches bound into the shape of a T. His eyes were wide open, fixed, staring at nothing.

Then Duran made his presence known. Keeping his distance, he yelled, "Hey, Kyle."

The Kiowa reckoned that the outlaw saw his dead emissary, but his voice was steady as he returned, "What the hell do you want?"

"Only this," Duran said, "if you want to talk with Dave

Shannon, don't send a pig to stand among men. Now show me the girl."

Kyle stepped to Jenny, grabbed her roughly by the arm, and pushed her ahead of him, making sure she was between him and the gun of Shannon's man.

"Here she is," he yelled. "A rancher's daughter and never been kissed."

"I can understand why," Duran said. "She ain't much. And kinda sulky."

Kyle drew back his hand. "I'll soon wipe that sulkiness off her face."

"No"—a long pause then—"don't. Dave won't want her marked."

"Will he talk with me?" Kyle said, shoving Jenny away from him.

Duran didn't answer that directly. "There's vigilantes in the mountains, Kyle, or at least, that's what they call themselves."

"What's that to me?" Kyle said. "Sounds like it's a problem for Shannon."

"Not for him. For you, Kyle. They aim to hang you, something about the murder of the girl's family," Duran said.

That hit Kyle like a punch to the gut. "How many?"

"It don't really matter. One of them is Clint Cooley."

"Never heard of him."

"He's hell on wheels with a gun," Duran said. "A bad man to have on your backtrail."

"What does Shannon say about this?" Kyle said.

"He don't want vigilantes in the Sierra del Carmen. That's way too close to home."

"If he helps me get rid of the vigilantes, I'll leave the mountains and never come back," Kyle said.

"That's a better bargaining chip than the girl," Duran

said. "I'll tell him what you said, and if he's all right with it, he'll be in touch."

Zack Palmer had walked closer to his brother, a blue-faced corpse on a horse. Now, like a bolt from the blue, his words sounded loud and clear in the silent land. To Duran, he said, "Why did you kill him?"

"He stank up our camp, and he offered to buy the girl after Dave was finished with her, said he was willing to wait until the girl was available," Duran said. "Dave said he was trash and told him to go to hell and your man . . . what was he called?"

"Arlo. Arlo Palmer," Zack said.

"Well, Arlo was so annoyed about not getting the girl he gave Dave sass and backtalk," Duran said.

"And then you cut his throat," Zack said.

Duran shook his head. "I didn't, not my style. We had a blade man ride in a few days ago, goes by the name of John Smith. Seems he cut a man in a saloon in Austin and has been on the dodge since." Duran sighed as though the story bored him and then said, "Anyway Smith cut . . . what was him name again?"

"Arlo," Palmer said.

"Yeah, Arlo. Well, Smith was tired of listening to him and cut his throat," Duran said. "As Dave Shannon said, it saved us a twelve-cent cartridge."

"That's how much my brother meant to you, twelve lousy cents?" Zack said.

"I didn't put a price on him, Dave Shannon did," Duran said. "But by the way he looked and smelled, a lot like you, in fact, I guess twelve cents was just about right."

"Zack . . . no," Kyle said.

Too late. A split second too late.

Zack Palmer cursed and went for his gun. He didn't even come close. James Duran was a named gambler/shootist, and he was fast. Palmer was still clearing leather when Duran's first shot hit him in the middle of the chest. The follow-up shot, too hurried, missed. But by then Zack Palmer was dead on his feet. His legs went from under him, and he hit the ground in a heap, his open eyes staring glazed and empty at his crucified brother.

Duran's Colt, hammer back, swung on Clay Kyle. But the man raised his hands and yelled, "I'm not making a play."

Duran's eyes moved to Susan Stanton, who stood motionless, and then searched beyond her for more of Kyle's men. There were none.

"Kyle, what did you see?" Duran said.

"He called it."

"You?" That to the woman.

"He drew first, and you killed him," Susan said. "Cost you twenty-four cents, two shots of whiskey. Was he worth it?"

"I didn't want to kill him," Duran said.

"You could've fooled me," Susan Stanton said.

"He drew down on me," Duran said.

"Yeah, like Clay said, he called the play," Susan said. She glanced at Zack Palmer's body. "Who the hell cares?"

Duran looked at Kyle. "Holler for the rest of your boys," he said.

The outlaw shook his head. "I have no boys, not any longer. Me, Suzie, and the Calthrop girl are all that's left."

"What happened to your men?" Duran said.

"One way or another, they each took a bullet, and Arlo got his throat cut," Kyle said. "That's the way it goes sometimes. Hell, it even happened to Jesse and Frank at Northfield."

"There's still vigilantes in the mountains and because of Clint Cooley they could be too much for you to handle," Duran said. "Dave wants them out of here before the Rurales and Texas Rangers take an interest. Men on the scout pay Dave Shannon big money to lie low here, so you can consider him a businessman looking out for his own interests."

"So where does that leave me?" Kyle said.

Duran thought that through for a few moments and then said, "Saddle up, Kyle, you're coming with me. It's time you spoke to Dave again. Maybe you and him can team up against the vigilantes, and then you leave the Sierra del Carmen and never come back."

Then, putting words to a random thought, "There's no gold here anyway," Kyle said.

"And there never was," Duran said. "Now mount up."

"What about me and the girl?" Susan Stanton said. Her beauty was unsullied, her legs and breasts magnificent, but there were tired shadows under her eyes.

"I'll come back for you," Duran said. "No point in complicating matters with women. Some of those hunted outlaws ain't to be trusted."

The Kiowa waited until two men rode together into the gathering dusk before he left his position among the rocks and slipped away, keeping to the shadows. He recognized one of the riders as James Duran. The other was probably Clay Kyle, a big man on a fine, blood horse that would cost a Texas cowboy a year's wages. This could only be bad tidings for Deputy Caine, the Kiowa decided. It looked like the vigilantes were headed for the fight of their lives.

CHAPTER THIRTY-SIX

"If Kyle throws in with Dave Shannon, it's a fight we can't win," Clint Cooley said.

"We don't know that it was Kyle the Kiowa saw with Duran," Dan Caine said.

Cooley said, "A big man on a two-hundred-dollar horse? Who else could it be? And wasn't he riding with James Duran, not the most sociable of gents at the best of times?"

"Clint, all you give me are questions and no answers," Dan said.

"Then ask me a question and I'll answer it," Cooley said.

"How do we get at Kyle?"

"We don't."

"What does that mean?"

"It means we pull out of here at sunup, and don't look back until we reach Thunder Creek."

"You mean, just let him go?"

"I mean try for him again . . . when you've got a dozen well-armed and determined men at your back."

"I'd never catch up with him again," Dan said. "If he gets back across the Brazos, I'll lose him. An outlaw like him is a will-o'-the-wisp, here today, gone tomorrow."

"If you wait here much longer, you'll see him again right soon . . . coming up this hill with Dave Shannon and his outlaw gunmen. Depend on it, they'll be a bunch of hard cases not to be trifled with."

"Anyone else want to say something?" Dan said.

"I'm with Cooley," Fish Lee said. "I say we skedaddle."

"Massey?" Dan said.

"I want no part of Caine's Last Stand," the newspaperman said. "I guess that answers your question."

"Holt?"

The boy's young face bore a worried expression, but he was still game. "I'll stick with you, Deputy Caine."

"And what about you, Estella?"

A rising breeze tugged at the girl's hat, her dark glasses now resting on the wide brim. She placed her hand on top of the crown to prevent the hat from flying away and said, "I've done some growing up since we started out, and I'm now much more at ease around grown men. In other words, I've learned a great deal. But, Dan, I won't throw my life away in a hopeless cause. We did our best, but the odds were stacked against us from the beginning. I say we leave Kyle for another day and another lawman."

"What about Jenny Calthrop?" Holt said. "Are we forgetting about her?"

"No, we're not forgetting about Jenny," Estella said. "My heart is broken, and it will never mend."

Holt put his arm around Estella's shoulders and said, "Jenny will be all right. I know she will."

The young man's words were sympathetic but empty. He knew it, and Estella knew it, but hollow as they were, they brought her a measure of comfort.

"I didn't mean to put go or stay up for a vote," Dan said. "I still think we should brace Kyle and do what we came to do."

"Dan, do what you have to do, but I won't see you throw away the lives of the people around you," Cooley said.

"Sure, go after Clay Kyle, face-to-face like a man, and die in the attempt. But include me out. I draw the line at suicide."

"I reckon what Cooley said goes for all of us," Cornelius Massey said. "You're trying to hold onto a cause that was lost the day we rode into these mountains."

"I won't be here to watch you die, Dan," Estella said.

"None of us will, and that includes you, Holt," Cooley said.

The young man's face was miserable. "We can't win, can we, Mr. Cooley?" he said.

Cooley shook his head. "No. If we try bucking the odds facing us, all we can do is die."

"Wait, I've got something to say," Dan said. "I'm not much of a one for speechifying, but it's been a rare privilege to ride with all of you, and, as much as I hate to admit it, I reckon you're right. I won't put your lives at risk any longer. That's it, all the words I have. Tomorrow at first light, we ride out of these mountains, and as Clint says, we won't look back."

"I'll look back," Estella said. "I'll look back and hope and pray that I'll see Jenny waving to me."

Later, as the day shadowed into evening, the Kiowa started a small fire and filled the coffeepot with water from the canteens. After a while he stepped to the others and said, "Tortillas and coffee for supper."

Fish Lee laughed and slapped his thigh. "Damn it all, Injun, I knew there was white man in you somewhere."

CHAPTER THIRTY-SEVEN

"Put yourself in my position, Kyle," Dave Shannon said, firelight flickering on his stubbled face. "Tell me why I shouldn't put a bullet into you right now and have it done?"

Kyle said, "Well, for one thing there's honor among thieves."

"No, there ain't," Shannon said.

"And for another, kill me and you don't get the girl," Kyle said. "I told Suzie Stanton to gun her if I don't leave this camp alive."

Shannon nodded. "Well, there's always that. I need a woman around here, keep me entertained at night, that's for damned sure."

"So, can we . . ."

"Shut the hell up, Kyle," Shannon said. "Get yourself coffee and let me study on this for a spell." He waved a hand in the direction of a row of weathered canvas pup tents. "And while you're at it, find a place to sleep."

After ten minutes staring into the guttering fire, Shannon spoke again. He called Kyle over and said, "Kyle, here's how I see it. Vigilantes have no legal authority, but their very presence here is annoying the hell out of me. The first order of business is to get rid of them. Once they're dead, you give me the girl and you get out of the Sierra del

Carmen and never again show your ugly face around here. If you ever do, I'll shoot you down on sight like a dog. Do you comprende?"

Kyle nodded. "I understand, Dave. You're true blue."

"What about the Stanton woman?" Shannon said. "I hear she's a real beauty."

"Yeah, she's a beauty all right, but her inclination don't exactly run to men," Kyle said. "Take Suzie to bed and you'll wake up with a knife in your chest."

"I could tame her," Shannon said, "but I'll settle for the other girl." A look of momentary doubt crossed his face. "Here, she ain't dangerous, is she?"

Kyle smiled. "She won't bite, Dave. Hell, she'll probably fall head over heels in love with you. She's that kind of girl, all blonde hair, brown eyes, and innocence."

A wind gust swept across the fire and sent up a fan-shaped torrent of sparks.

"The wind is rising," Shannon said. "It can blow hard through these mountains. Sometimes if you listen hard enough, it sounds like the pines are whispering to one another up on the slopes. I remember hearing that sound when I was a boy in Tennessee, lying in bed all affeered that my pa would come home drunk again and beat my ma."

"Bad way for a boy to be raised, Dave," Kyle said.

Shannon shrugged. "As soon as I could lift it, I shot him with his own Kentucky rifle. After that me and Ma did just fine."

"Is your ma still in Tennessee?" Kyle said, anxious to be sociable.

"No. She died of a summer cold the year before I saddled up the mule and left for Texas," Shannon said. "I was thirteen then, and I'd already killed my first man." He smiled. "Funny that, me being so young an' all." He rose to his feet and said to the dozen men in camp that night,

"Listen up, all of you. Gabe Glass took a scout for me and he says the vigilantes are camped on a rise about thirty minutes from here. So it's me for my blankets and you boys should do the same. We got a busy day ahead of us tomorrow."

"Vigilantes to kill," Kyle said, grinning.

"Saddle your horse, we're getting out of here," Susan Stanton said.

"Why?" Jenny Calthrop said.

"Because I have a bad feeling . . . a feeling that something terrible is coming down," Susan said. "I fell asleep and just before I woke saw fire fall from the sky like rose petals and there was a noise like thunder and there were dead men without heads lying on the ground, and it scared me."

"I thought nothing scared you," Jenny said.

"My dream scared me. My God, where did this wind come from?"

"It's a north wind," Jenny said. "Our pastor once told me that God appointed the north wind to remind us that we live in hell of our own making. You're in hell, Susan Stanton."

"Saddle your horse, you little slut, you're talking nonsense," Susan yelled. The slashing wind tossed strands of hair across her face, and her eyes were wild.

"I'm not going anywhere with you," Jenny called back. "You're evil. You're a devil woman."

Susan Stanton smiled. "You know what will happen to you when Clay gives you to Dave Shannon and his hard cases? You'll be passed from man to man, every single day and night of your miserable life, and then, when you can't bear it any longer, you'll kill yourself. Is that what you want, you stupid, backwoods hick?" The woman pulled

Jenny toward her by the front of her dress and when they were nose-to-nose, she said, "You're better off with me."

Jenny Calthrop was not particularly intelligent, but she was savvy enough to realize that the picture Susan Stanton painted for her was a horrific one and probably true. Her choices limited, she whispered, her head bowed, "I'll go with you."

"That's the first smart thing I've heard you say since we took you from that two-by-twice chicken farm your father called a ranch," Susan said. "Turn around." Then when the girl hesitated, "Now!"

With sudden aggression, Susan roughly gagged the girl with a bandana she'd earlier taken from the body of Loco Garrett and knotted it tight at the back of her head. Jenny's eyes were wide with anger and terror and she tried to talk, but the gag bit so cruelly into her mouth, she couldn't utter a word.

"We can't have you crying out for help, girlie, can we?" Susan said. "Get used to it, because I plan to rope you to your saddle horn." Tears starting in her eyes, Jenny again tried to talk . . . an outburst of muffled sounds. The woman's smile was thin and mean. "Life's tough all over, innit?"

Thirty minutes later, riding their horses through a vast and impenetrable darkness, heads bent against a wailing wind, Susan Stanton and Jenny Calthrop passed the hill where Dan Caine and his vigilantes were holed up.

They were neither seen nor heard.

CHAPTER THIRTY-EIGHT

Clay Kyle and Dave Shannon were awake before first light, surrounded by coughing, cursing men struggling to keep the windblown fire alight enough to boil coffee. Kyle was not a talking man in the morning, and he and Shannon checked their guns in silence as their fellow outlaws bustled around them. None seemed concerned about the fight to come. James Duran had made it clear what they faced and they agreed that clearing out the nest of vigilante rubes would be as easy as shooting fish in a barrel. Duran had mentioned Clint Cooley as their most dangerous gun, but at least half of Shannon's men had fought in bloody range wars and had multiple kills to their credit. One man with a vague duelist's rep didn't trouble them in the least.

After coffee and several cigarettes, Shannon glanced at the dawning sky and gave the order to saddle up. The mountains were still deeply shadowed, and the timbered sky islands were dark, waiting for the sun. The north wind was relentless, wild, and blustery, and Shannon commented that he'd never known such a gale in the five years he'd spent in the Sierra del Carmen.

"I've faced hot desert winds that blistered my lips and chafed my skin," he told his men. "But never anything like this. Damn strange if you ask me." Then after a few moments, he said to Kyle, "What time does the Stanton woman expect you back?"

"I told her noon," Kyle said.

"I don't want to lose that girl, Kyle," Shannon said. "If she dies, you die."

"I'll be back in plenty of time," Kyle said. "You heard Duran. We're facing a bunch of rubes. It will be all over in ten minutes, maybe less."

"Duran says there's a woman with the vigilantes," Shannon said. "Be nice to add two ladies to my camp."

"Then tell your boys not to shoot at the woman," Kyle said.

Shannon turned his head, grinning, and said, "You hear that, boys. There's a woman with the vigilantes, so don't shoot her unless it's very necessary."

"She got big tits?" a man asked to a chorus of ribald laughter.

"Hey, Duran, does the vigilante woman have big tits?" Shannon said.

"Of course she does," Duran said.

"Then we'll be sure to recognize her," Shannon said to more laughter.

Kyle smiled. "I got a feeling this is going to be a crackerjack morning."

Shannon nodded. "It's sure shaping up that way."

The north wind blew even stronger, and up on the mountain slopes the green pines tossed their heads and whispered secrets to the new aborning day.

Dave Shannon's first attack fared badly, even though it caught the vigilantes by surprise. They were breaking camp and saddling their horses when Shannon's mounted men appeared at the bottom of the hill. The outlaws, Shannon and Clay Kyle in the lead, came on at a trot and then spread out into line-abreast. The horsemen drew rein and stared up at the scampering vigilantes with undisguised contempt.

"They're lighting a shuck," a man cried out. "Look at them scoot!"

"All right, boys, let 'em have it," Shannon yelled. He grinned, showing his bared teeth. "Get them!"

His men charged, a few of them howling the rebel yell.

But Shannon's initial maneuvering had taken time . . . time enough for Dan Caine and the others to take cover behind scattered boulders and thick brush. To Dan's surprise, the Kiowa kneeled beside him, his Colt up and ready.

"The white men aiming to kill you will sure as hell kill an Indian," he said.

The charge was uphill across ground muddy from the recent heavy rains, and that made the going heavy and slowed the horses. Worse for the attackers, Shannon's grasp of cavalry tactics extended only as far as using horses to expedite his escape from angry townsmen who'd just seen their bank robbed. He ignored the lesson so painfully learned during the War Between the States that it's folly to attack entrenched infantry with light cavalry . . . he and Kyle learned that lesson now.

Stonewall Jackson once said that a cavalry horse must be a bit mad, its rider completely so, but Shannon's horses and men were the direct opposite. Outlaws with a strong instinct for self-preservation, they ran into a hail of lead that shocked the hell out of them. Clint Cooley and the Kiowa laid down the heaviest and most accurate fire, but Dan, Fish Lee, and Holt Peters scored hits and Estella worked her rifle well. Cornelius Massey, aware of his deficiencies as a marksman, sprayed puny rounds from a small, pearl-handled revolver.

The fire from the defenders was devastating.

Wounded, screaming horses and men went down, cartwheeling into the mud as the charge staggered, and then broke like an ocean wave on a rock.

James Duran and a couple of others drew rein and managed to return fire, but Shannon stood in the stirrups and waved his revolver. "Back!" he yelled. "Back!"

Clay Kyle was stunned and hadn't fired a shot. He sat his horse, staring in horror at the carnage around him.

James Duran rode up to Kyle and yelled, "Wake up, you damned fool!" He grabbed the man's reins and pulled him away, forcing him back down the hill as bullets split the air around them.

In a few moments of hell-firing fury, Shannon had lost about half his men. He joined the survivors at the base of the rise and yelled, "Dismount! Damn their eyes, we'll take them on foot. Kill them all, boys. Kill them all!"

"It ain't gonna be easy," one man said.

"Hell, starve them out," said another.

"Do as you're told or by God, I'll kill you myself," Shannon said.

In the middle of the carnage on the slope, a man screamed in pain, probably gut shot, and a horse limped down the incline, favoring a shattered foreleg.

Some grumbling followed, and Clay Kyle's face was stiff with shock. "Wait until dark, Dave," he said. "We can injun up there unseen and then rush them."

"Go to hell," Dave Shannon said.

When he saw the attackers break and run, Dan's inclination was to cheer, but the sight of Fish Lee down and bleeding sobered him. He took a knee beside the old man and said, "Fish, are you hit bad?"

"Shot all to pieces," Fish Lee said. His face was gray, his entire chest covered in blood. "Dan . . . listen," he said.

"I'm listening, Fish," Dan said.

Estella kneeled and laid the old prospector's head on her lap.

"Deputy Caine," Fish said, "take care of Sophie. When you can afford it, give her oats now and then. She loves oats but never got them too often." He smiled. "Helluva fight, huh?" He then closed his eyes and died.

Dan looked into Estella's tearstained face. "Who's Sophie?"

"His burro," the young woman said. "When we get back to Thunder Creek, I'll make sure she gets all the oats she wants."

Clint Cooley said, "Looks like they're arguing down there."

Dan laid a hand on Fish Lee's forehead and then got to his feet. He stared downhill and said, "Now they're trying to figure out the best way to kill us."

"Wait long enough and we'll all die of thirst or starvation, whatever comes first," Cooley said. "If I was Kyle, that's what I'd do."

Harried by random bullets from Shannon's men, they buried Fish Lee under a tomb of rocks, a long, arduous task that took several hours. Estella Sweet's father read to her from the Bible every night of her life, and she said good words over the grave. The rest said, "Amen," and then it was done.

* * *

It's strange that Fish Lee's last resting place can no longer be found in the Sierra del Carmen. Only the mountains know what happened to the rock grave . . . and they keep their secrets.

CHAPTER THIRTY-NINE

"Damn it all, Dave, if we try walking up that hill again, we'll step into the same mess," Clay Kyle said. "They got a couple of shootists up there."

James Duran said, "Yeah, Clint Cooley and the Indian. I saw them cut loose, and those boys can unravel a bullet with the best I've seen." He shook his head. "Damn it to hell, I knew Cooley would be a problem."

"What do you suggest, Kyle?" Shannon said, his voice hoarse with a seething anger, staring at the other man through tightened eyelids.

"Wait until dark," Kyle said. "Injun up on them and then do some throat cutting."

"Duran?" Shannon said.

"I reckon Kyle is right. We'd have a better chance at night," Duran said. "Get close and then charge right into them. Hell, Cooley and the Indian have got to doze off sometime."

"It's thin," Shannon said. "Way too thin." Then, irritably, "Will this damned wind never stop?"

One of the outlaws, a train robber named McMurray whose participation in the El Paso Salt War gave him a measure of respect, said, "Dave, I sure as hell ain't charging up that damned hill in daylight in the teeth of this big blow."

"Dave, it can be done," Duran said. "The darkness will cover us until we're almost on top of them and the three dead horses will help our cover and so will the wind."

Shannon thought that through and then said, "All right, then that's how we'll play it. We go come sundown. But in the meantime, we'll hunker down and take pots at them all day, keep their heads down, and give them no rest. Shake 'em up, like. Hell, we might even wing a few."

That last won a chorus of agreement from the relieved gunmen. Events had not gone how they'd hoped . . . a quick victory over a bunch of rubes and maybe a pretty woman as a spoil of war. Instead, all they'd found was hot lead and death.

Clay Kyle grinned. "Hey, lookee there, Dave. I bet ten dollars that he doesn't make it to the bottom of the hill."

Shannon looked and saw what Kyle had seen, a wounded towhead on all fours making his painful way down the slope. The man looked like he'd been gut-shot because blood and black bile hung in thin strands from his mouth.

"Duran, who is that?" Shannon said.

For a few moments, Duran studied the man and then said, "His name's John Shivers. He murdered his wife and the man in bed with her and then lit a shuck. The Rangers were only a day behind him when he rode into the Sierra del Carmen. He's neighborly enough, I guess, but he don't talk much."

"Right now, I reckon he's never gonna talk again," Shannon said.

"Good boy," Kyle said. "Another ten yards and you'll be home free."

"Free to clutch at his belly and scream for hours," Duran said. "After what happened, we don't need to hear that all damned day." He pulled his gun, drew a bead, and shot Shivers in the head. The man collapsed and didn't move.

"Good shot, Duran," Kyle said.

"Bad for him," Duran said.

Shannon said, "Kyle, we got time, so head back to the Stanton woman and tell her I want the girl," Shannon said. "I don't want her harmed, understand?"

"Sure thing, Dave," Kyle said.

"Just make tracks back here before dark," Shannon said. He drew, fired off a few shots at the top of the hill, and then said, "We'll keep them busy until then."

"I'll return very soon," Kyle said, his eyes fixed on the sky. At that moment, he didn't know that he stared into the agent of his own death.

Tossed around by the gusting wind, the red balloon was in difficulty.

No one saw it until it rounded the north slope of the mountain and scraped along a projecting rock outcrop. The wicker basket swung wildly, and Professor Lazarus Latchford and Miss Prunella struggled to keep their feet and at the same time reduce the burner flame.

The balloon came closer, dropped height rapidly, and the basket now careened back and forth like a pendulum as it soared over the vigilante position on the hilltop. Dan Caine and the others, conscious of the nonstop fire from Dave Shannon's gunmen, frantically tried to wave Latchford away. But Miss Prunella, mistaking their warning for a greeting, leaned over the rim of the basket, held onto a rope cable with one hand, and waved with the other.

The balloon seemed badly out of control as Dan Caine cupped his hands around his mouth and yelled, "GET THE HELL OUT OF HERE!"

It seemed that Miss Prunella still didn't hear him be-cause she continued to smile and wave as the balloon soared over them like a runaway freight train. Professor Latchford joined Miss Prunella and waved, grinning. His mouth opened in a shout, but Dan couldn't hear him. If anything, the wind had gained in intensity, and the red balloon bounced crazily in turbulent air at a height of about fifty feet.

And then the death and the carnage began.

Witnesses, including Dan Caine, would later say that the entire incident that claimed the lives of so many men was over in less than a couple of minutes.

Someone, most sources say it was Dave Shannon, raised his rifle and shot into the basket. Agreeing that this was fine sport, others joined in and soon bullets rattled through the wicker. It's quite possible that Miss Prunella was mortally wounded at this stage but that's never been verified. Latch-ford was as mad as a hatter, but he was smart . . . smart enough to realize that the shooters were the enemy. As he hurtled over them, he leaned over the side of the basket and dropped two of his contact-fuse bombs into the middle of the clustered gunmen. Both exploded with a terrible crash and a blinding flash of light. Lead balls tore into human flesh like volleys of canister from a battery of cannon, killing and maiming . . . tearing bodies apart. Most of the outlaws died instantly, a couple lingered for a few shriek-ing, agony-filled minutes.

The balloon, made lighter by the weight of the bombs, suddenly rode an upward current of wind and, the canopy flaming from flying burner coals, skyrocketed up the side of the mountain and then lost height rapidly, crashing head-long into a pine-covered sky island before it vanished from sight. A thin column of smoke, quickly shredded by the wind, marked the balloon's last resting place.

* * *

It was reported that in 1926 rock climbers discovered what they described as the scattered bones of a child and an adult male on the mountaintop. If that is the case, the remains were never recovered.

CHAPTER FORTY

A man screamed and continued to scream, splintering the silence of the morning. Dan Caine retrieved something from his saddlebags and then he and Clint Cooley warily walked down the hill to witness the effect of the balloon's attack. Seven men, among them Dave Shannon and Clay Kyle, lay sprawled on the ground. Shannon was dead, Kyle mortally wounded. Nearby lay the headless body of James Duran, recognizable only by his expertly tooled gun rig.

The screaming man's belly had been ripped open, purple intestines coiling on the ground beside him, and Clint Cooley shot him in the head, ending his agony.

All the others except Kyle were dead. The effect of Professor Latchford's fragmentation bombs, bursting in the middle of the gathered outlaws, had been horrific. Behind Dan and Cooley, Estella Sweet was violently sick, and Holt Peters looked stunned, his young face ashen. Only the Kiowa seemed unmoved.

Cornelius Massey, conjuring up vivid memories in his mind, talked more to himself than the others. "On the last day of Gettysburg, I saw the bodies of Pickett's men who'd walked into the mouths of cannons loaded with double canister. Until today, I thought I'd never see the like again."

"It's a sight to see, newspaperman," Cooley said. Then to Dan, "Kyle is still kicking, but only barely."

Dan's shadow fell over the wounded man as he stepped beside him. Kyle had a massive chest wound and was dying fast. He looked up at Dan and said, "So you're the vigilante? You ain't much."

"Clay Kyle," Dan said, "I arrest you for the murders of Tom Calthrop, his wife Nancy, his sons Jacob and Esau and his daughters Rose and Grace. And for the unlawful transportation and confinement of a person against their will. That person is Jenny Calthrop, daughter of the deceased Tom and Nancy."

Dan kneeled and shackled Kyle's hands with cuffs he'd taken from his saddlebags. "You will now be taken to Thunder Creek to face trial and execution, at the judge's convenience."

"You damned rube," Kyle said. "The only place I'm going is hell."

"Make it easier on yourself, Kyle," Dan said. "Tell me the whereabouts of Jenny Calthrop and your accomplice Susan Stanton."

"I looked for them and couldn't find them," Kyle said. "And neither will you. Now go away, let me die in peace."

He closed his eyes, opened them again, and tried to spit at Dan, but succeeded only in drooling bloody saliva over his bearded chin. "You damned fool," he said, "you won't hang anyone in Thunder Creek. It was your sheriff who planned the whole thing."

Dan Caine felt like he'd been punched. "Kyle, you're a liar," he said.

Kyle grimaced a smile. "Except for Chinamen, dying men don't lie. Chance Hurd told us that Tom Calthrop had a big stash of money hidden in his ranch house. He said if we found it, the split would be fifty-fifty. We toasted

Calthrop's toes at the fire, but he swore he was broke, that there was no money." Now Kyle struggled to speak. "Well, Suzie Stanton got angry. She shot Tom Calthrop and then the shooting became general. See, we was all riled up. It was Suzie's idea to take the girl as . . . as insurance and she said later we could sell her in Old Mexico."

"I was there with Hurd," Dan said. "You never came near Thunder Creek."

"Me and Chance Hurd rode together a time back," Kyle said. "He knew he could write to my brother in Waco and I'd get the letter. It . . . it took months to plan." He smiled. "And you never guessed what was happening right under your nose." Blood filled Kyle's mouth and he said, "You . . . stupid . . . ignorant . . . rube . . ."

Cooley looked down at the outlaw and said, "He's gone, Dan."

Dan Caine nodded. Said nothing.

"Looks like Chance Hurd is as guilty as Kyle was, huh?" Cooley said.

"Seems like." Dan rose to his feet. "When we get back to Thunder Creek, I aim to lock Hurd up in his own jail and see him hang."

"We all heard what Kyle said, Dan," Massey said. "We'll be your witnesses."

"Deputy Caine, we're vigilantes," Holt Peters said. "We'll still be vigilantes when we return to Thunder Creek."

"Holt is right," Estella said. "We'll make Sheriff Hurd pay for his crimes."

"I appreciate that," Dan said. "But let me deal with Hurd."

"I'll back you, Dan," Clint Cooley said. "Chance Hurd is good with a gun."

"And I'm learning," Dan Caine said. "I'm learning fast." He looked at Kyle. "Let him lie there and rot with the cuffs on his wrists. And as for the rest of them, outlaws neither expect nor deserve to be buried decent with words said over them. We can't dig holes in solid rock." His gaze moved to the timbered sky-island high on the mountain slope. "Can we get up there?" he said.

Cooley shook his head. "A mountain goat could, but not a human. Dan, they're dead. They couldn't survive a crash like that."

"No, I guess they couldn't," Dan said. "It's a pity. Now Professor Latchford and Miss Prunella will never go to the moon."

Estella said, "My guess is that those two are there already, looking around hand in hand and making friends with the moon folk."

"It's comforting to think that way," Massey said.

"Damn right it is," Dan said.

"Black-Eyed Suzie Stanton isn't among the dead," Cooley said. "Like Kyle said, she must be with Jenny."

"We'll spend the rest of the day searching for them," Dan said. "If we don't find them, then come first light tomorrow, we'll head for Thunder Creek. Maybe Chance Hurd will know where they are."

Cooley sloshed the contents of his half-empty canteen. "Water is low, Dan. And all we got left to eat are a few stale tortillas."

"Dave Shannon must have a permanent camp around here somewhere with supplies," Dan said. "We'll search for that too."

The search for Susan Stanton and Jenny Calthrop lasted most of the day but turned up nothing. The stench of decaying bodies led to a camp under a rock shelf, the rocky ground strewn with empty rifle cartridge cases, but Susan and the girl were long gone.

"Looks like Kyle had a standoff here with Dave Shannon, but later they became allies," Clint Cooley said. "I guess they figured that we were the common enemy."

"Seems like," Dan said. He looked around him. "Kyle lost men here."

"And I bet Shannon did too," Cooley said. "That's when they decided that it was better to kill us than each other."

"And we won," Holt Peters said, smiling.

"In a manner of speaking, yeah, I guess we did," Dan said. "Kyle and Shannon are dead, and we're still alive. But we don't have Jenny Calthrop, so to sum things up . . . we won and lost."

The day was beginning its slow shade into night when the Kiowa found Dave Shannon's camp. A search of the tents uncovered a good supply of flour, beans, salt pork, and vegetables and peaches in cans. There was also a sack of coffee, sugar to go along with it, and to Dan Caine's joy a plentiful supply of Bull Durham and cigarette papers.

In the end, all agreed that they wouldn't go hungry on the trail back to Thunder Creek.

CHAPTER FORTY-ONE

"Hungry, girlie? Feeling gant?" Susan Stanton said. "Well, get used to it. You'll be a sight hungrier before we reach a settlement." She had removed Jenny Calthrop's restraints and handed her a canteen. "Here, chew on some water. That'll help."

A sparse stand of blackjack oak and mesquite provided enough wood for a small fire that took all of Susan's lucifers to light. She'd complained bitterly, cursed Jenny for a Jonah, and prophesied that they would not have another fire.

"Seems like our luck is already running muddy, huh?" she said.

"I could've lit the fire with one match," Jenny said. "You lack patience."

"Right now, I lack a lot of things, a good meal, a soft bed and, above all, money," Susan said. She stretched out her long, booted legs and tapped her toes together. "Look at my thighs," she said. "All bruised and scratched from scrambling around that damned mountain and my skirt is torn."

"That's because you dress like a fallen woman," Jenny said.

Susan raised an eyebrow. "How would you know how a fallen woman dresses, you little prig?"

"I imagine they wear a lace-up corset like you that shows off the tops of their . . . bubbies."

"Bubbies? You mean tits?"

"I don't want to talk to you anymore," Jenny said.

Susan Stanton lay back on her elbows and tilted her head to the night sky where the stars looked like scattered diamonds on black velvet. The moon rode high, surrounded by a red and blue halo. The prairie was silent, apart from insects that made their small sounds in the grass.

Susan Stanton talked, uncaring if Jenny listened or not.

"I was raised in a brothel in Austin because my mother still had to work as a whore to keep us both alive. She was a mulatto and I was told she was beautiful, at least for the first few years she worked in the Lucky Star. Do you know what a mulatto is, you ignorant little whelp?"

Jenny made no answer.

"A mulatto means she was half black, half white, kind of coffee colored. She died when I was six and the brothel madame raised me, a woman by the name of Henriette Melancon. She was all right, kind of rough and ready, and when I was sixteen, I took my mother's place. Well, girlie, that didn't last long. There are men whose idea of a good time is to beat a woman. The first one who tried that with me ended up with a bullet in his belly from my derringer. Of course, the law would've hung me since the man I killed was a respected businessman in Austin. Henriette got me out of town thanks to a stagecoach driver who was a client of hers. She gave me fifty dollars and a word of advice. Want to know what that advice was?"

Jenny Calthrop was silent.

"Well, I'll tell you anyway," Susan said. "She told me I'd never make it as a whore because I hated men too much. She said I should become a nun where I'd never be around the male gender." The woman laughed, the laugh of a fallen angel. "I didn't become a nun. I followed the outlaw's path, rolling drunks, later killing men for money, and then I fell in with Clay Kyle and the rest, as they say, is history."

She turned her head and stared at Jenny. "Does it surprise you that a woman raised in a brothel dresses like a whore?"

Jenny's mouth was tight. "How many men have you killed?"

"Hold up your hands and spread your fingers. Now count."

"Ten."

"That's how many men I killed for profit. Count the fingers on one hand, and that's the number I killed for fun. Susan Stanton laughed again. "Girlie, I'm your worst nightmare, a creature straight out of the lower pits of hell. Am I not?"

"Stop!" Jenny said. "You scare me when you talk like that."

"I love scaring little girls," Susan said. "Especially strait-laced little bitches like you." She shook her head. "I don't know, I may shoot you before this trip is over. I'll have to think about that."

"I'd rather die than work in a place like the Lucky Star," Jenny said.

"Hmm, is that fact? We'll just have to wait and hear what you decide when you have to choose between a bullet and a brothel, won't we?"

Jenny didn't answer, her eyes staring into the darkness. A light bobbed in the gloom and then came a clanking, rattling, metallic sound like the clattering of a stack of cheap tin trays.

* * *

Susan Stanton rose to her feet, buckled on her gunbelt, and stood, legs apart, ready. "You stay right where you're at," she told Jenny. "If there's shooting, get down on your belly and stay there."

A moment later, a man's voice called from the darkness. "Hello, the camp!"

"Who's out there?" Susan answered.

"Out here?" the man's voice said. "Who would it be but Jacob the peddler?"

"State your intentions," Susan said.

"And what would my intentions be? Do I want to sit at your fire and warm my old bones and drink coffee?"

"We have no coffee and no food either," Susan said.

"And don't I have both?"

"Then come on in," Susan Stanton said. "If I see a gun in your hand, I'll shoot you."

"A gun? What does a peddler need with a gun?"

A bobbing lantern parted the night and a horse-drawn wagon, both animal and conveyance small, emerged from the gloom. The peddler drew rein on his horse and, with surprising alacrity, hopped down from the driver's seat. He was a small man, thin, dressed in shirt, pants, and a vest, and he removed the cloth cap from his head, revealing an unruly mop of gray hair, and bowed. He then straightened and addressed Susan Stanton. "Is this not Jacob Birkin, the peddler? And, you ask, what do I peddle? Do I not sell, all at cost mind you, coffee beans, spices, baking powder, oatmeal, flour, sugar, hard candy, eggs when available, honey, molasses, crackers, cheese, syrup, dried beans, ammunition, and cigars and tobacco? And what do I have for the ladies? Do I not carry cloth, pins and needles, thread, silk, buttons, collars, undergarments, hats and shoes, soaps, toiletries, and elixirs? And don't I always have in stock, lanterns, lamps, ropes, crockery, pots and pans, tin trays, cooking utensils, and dishes? And does Jacob Birkin not always carry an adequate supply of Dr. Jenkin's Ladies' Remedy, guaranteed to cure female hysteria, put a shine on hair, banish the rheumatisms, and restore a wandering womb?"

"And you get all that stuff in your peckerwood-sized wagon?" Susan said.

"Ah, is that not one of the peddler's secret skills?" Jacob said. He smiled. "Now, shall we tap my water barrel and put the coffee on to boil while I take care of my horse? Do I not have coffee already ground and crackers and good cheese? Do you like cheese?"

"Mister, right now I'm hungry enough to eat a longhorn steer, hide, horn, hooves, and beller," Susan said.

"And what about you, young lady?" the peddler said to Jenny. "Are you hungry?"

The girl nodded.

Jacob smiled and reached into his wagon. A glass jar opened and he came up with a pink and white candy stick that he handed to the girl. "Do you like peppermint?"

"Yes, thank you," Jenny said.

"Now, is it not time to put the coffeepot on the fire?" the peddler said.

As the coffee boiled, Susan Stanton found it difficult to carry on a conversation with a man who answered a question with one of his own. But she gathered that Jacob Birkin was one of an estimated twenty thousand peddlers, most of them Jews, who traveled all over the frontier selling their goods at isolated ranches, farms, and settlements. He was now headed for a booming town named McLaren's Landing that lay to the southwest where there was a brisk cowboy trade.

The coffee was drunk, a goodly amount of cheese and

crackers eaten, then Birkin, a perceptive man with shrewd blue eyes, turned them on Jenny and said, "Why are you so quiet, young lady? Is something troubling you?"

Jenny's gaze darted to Susan Stanton. As of that instant, she knew the peddler's life hung in the balance.

"I took her from a house where she was being abused by her drunken stepfather," Susan said. "I plan to take her to live with my parents in Thunder Creek, that's a small town north of here." She looked hard at the girl and then said, "She's very mentally disturbed and doesn't talk much."

"Is that not heartbreaking?" Birkin said, shaking his head.

"Yes. Yes, it is," Susan Stanton said. "Heartbreaking." Her eyes glittered in the firelight.

"Do you know why I was concerned about the girl?" Birkin said.

"No, tell me," Susan Stanton said.

"Two days ago, on my way south, did I not meet up with a Texas Ranger who stopped me to buy coffee and tobacco? And did he not tell me to keep my eyes skinned for a young girl kidnapped from a ranch north of here?"

"It's not this girl," Susan said. Her voice was strangely flat, emotionless, almost menacing.

"No, not this girl, is she?" Birkin said. "But what did the Ranger tell me? Did he not say that the Concho County Cattleman Association has posted a five-thousand-dollar reward for the girl's safe return?"

Susan raised an eyebrow at that. "Five thousand?"

"Is that not what the Ranger said?"

"Posted by the cattleman's association?"

Birkin nodded, the closest he'd come all night to a direct answer.

"Then we'll keep our eyes open," Susan Stanton said.

The peddler glanced at Jenny Calthrop but said nothing.

* * *

At first light, Jacob Birkin made more coffee and shared a breakfast of beef jerky and hardtack. Susan Stanton dug into her saddlebags and came up with money enough to buy more dried beef and biscuit and a handful of black cheroots. The peddler threw in a few candy canes for Jenny and a box of lucifers.

After he put his nag in the traces he climbed into the wagon's driver's seat and said to Jenny, "Have a safe journey, young lady." He tipped a perfunctory nod to Susan Stanton but said nothing more.

CHAPTER FORTY-TWO

Despite his heroics in the Sierra del Carmen, the Kiowa didn't consider his job finished until he returned the vigilantes to Thunder Creek, and he took his usual position at point. Dan Caine and the others were in the saddle at dawn, anxious to get back to their everyday lives. A sullen air of defeat hung over all of them. Clay Kyle was dead and the Calthrop family avenged, but they'd failed to free young Jenny, and that was a bitter pill to swallow.

The morning sun was still low in the sky when the Kiowa trotted back and raised a hand. "Wagon ahead," he said. "Looks like a peddler man."

"He may have seen Jenny," Estella Sweet said, excitement spiking in her young voice.

"Maybe," Dan said, but he held out little hope. If the girl was with Susan Stanton the woman could've taken her in any direction.

He met the peddler thirty minutes later, a smallish man driving a wagon that clattered and clanged like a steam locomotive. Jacob Birkin drew rein, looked over the riders, and felt none of the air of menace he'd sensed from Susan Stanton . . . more poised cobra than woman.

"Are you a welcoming committee or new customers?" the peddler said.

"Welcome to this corner of the prairie," Dan Caine said. "Have you been here before?"

"Have I been here before?" Birkin said. "And have I not traveled over this same ground many times?"

"We're looking for a girl, young, may be traveling with an older woman," Dan said. "Have you seen such?"

"Would this young lady be right partial to stick candy?" Birkin said.

"I don't know," Dan said.

"Yes, she is!" Estella Sweet said. "When we were younger, I often saw her buy candy sticks at Pete Doan's store. She liked peppermint."

"Then could that be the young lady I met last night?" Birkin said. "Was she with a very beautiful woman who wears a corset and skirt and boots, a costume so immodest it surely makes the angels weep?"

"That's her," Dan said. "Her name is Susan Stanton and she helped kidnap the girl. Her name is Jenny Calthrop, from a ranch north of here."

"And didn't a Texas Ranger tell me, not three days ago, that there is a five-thousand-dollar reward for the girl's safe return?" the peddler said. "And wasn't the money put up by a cattleman's association?"

Clint Cooley said, "Now Black-Eyed Susan has a girl worth five thousand, but she can't cash in. Young Jenny would spill enough beans to put Suzie's beautiful neck in a noose."

"As a peddler who travels the frontier, have I not met females of all kinds from schoolmarms to laundresses, housemaids to dance hall girls, but as soon as I saw the woman you call Susan Stanton, didn't I know what she was? Will you permit two words in Yiddish . . . *fakhman retsyeckh*? Does that not mean 'professional killer'?" The peddler shook his head. "Did I ever in my life think I'd use those words to describe a lady? No, I did not. But God forgive me, now I have."

"Don't blame yourself for that, peddler man," Dan said. "That's exactly what Susan Stanton is, a killer."

"How long before she decides that Jenny Calthrop is a burden and gets rid of her?" Cornelius Massey said.

"I was thinking the same thing," Dan said. Then to Jacob Birkin, "When you left her this morning, did Susan Stanton say where she was headed?"

"North," Birkin said. "Am I a mind reader?"

Dan said to the Kiowa, "Can we get on her trail and track her?"

"Two horses across long grass. It should not be difficult," the Kiowa said.

"Then we're going after her," Dan said.

"Count me out," Massey said. "I'm an old man, and I'm tired. I'd just slow you down."

"That's no matter," Dan said. "This is a job for me and the Kiowa. I want the rest of you to head for Thunder Creek and wait for me there. Let me deal with Sheriff Chance Hurd."

"Deputy Caine, I'd like to go with you," Holt Peters said.

"No, this is my job," Dan said. "And even if it wasn't, I'd make it mine. Hurd took back my star, but he's a criminal, so what he did doesn't count. As far as I'm concerned, I'm a deputy sheriff and probably the only lawman within a hundred miles."

Cooley said, "If it's all right with you, Deputy, I'd admire to put a bullet in Hurd as soon as I get back."

"Me too," Holt said.

Dan shook his head. "Leave the sheriff to me. He wronged me, and he played me for a fool. And worse than that, he was the brains behind the massacre of the Calthrop family. Clint, a bullet is too easy. I want to see him hang."

"As you say, you're the lawman," Cooley said. "But if Hurd tries to make a run for it, I'll gun him down like the dog he is, and that's a promise."

"All right, I can understand that," Dan said. "Just don't miss, huh?" Then to Jacob Birkin, "Hey, peddler man, want to do some peddling?"

"Am I not a peddler, and am I not open for business? Is not everything I carry in this wagon for sale?" Birkin raised a forefinger and pointed at the sky. "All merchandise at cost, mind."

Since Dan was leaving, he was served first, spending his couple of dollars on beef jerky and hardtack, enough to last several days, and a box of cartridges for his Colt. The rest of the vigilantes were not immune to the lure of the peddler, and, as Dan Caine and the Kiowa rode out, they surrounded the wagon, munched on crackers and cheese, and bought stuff they needed and even more stuff they didn't need, Clint Cooley standing good for young Holt Peter's lack of funds.

Estella Sweet delicately used the tip of a pinkie finger to remove a cracker crumb from the corner of her mouth and then said, "Clint, do you think Deputy Caine will be all right. I mean, when he meets up with Susan Stanton?"

Cooley thought for a moment and said, "If you'd asked me that question the day we left Thunder Creek, I'd have told you he had about as much of a chance with Black-Eyed Susan as a steer in a packing plant."

"And now?" Estella said.

"And now?" Cooley said. He smiled. "And now Deputy Sheriff Dan Caine is all growed up."

CHAPTER FORTY-THREE

As Susan Stanton and Jenny Calthrop rode due east under an endless blue sky, their horses cut deep swathes through the buffalo grass. The two rode in silence, once startling a jackrabbit that bounded ahead of them like a rubber ball, and then a small herd of pronghorns watched them closely for several minutes before dismissing them as harmless.

Susan broke her silence. "If I shot an antelope, could you gut it, skin it, and butcher it for supper?" she said.

"No, I couldn't," Jenny said.

"I could," Susan Stanton said. She sighed. "Your hide is worth five thousand dollars, you useless little tramp, but I can't take you to the cattleman's association and collect my reward."

"I wouldn't tell them anything," Jenny said.

"You're a damned liar. You'd sell me out the first chance you got."

"Let me go and I'll have the association send you the money."

"You blushed, you pathetic little trollop. You can't even lie well," Susan said. "I know what I can do, I'll sell you for fifty dollars first chance I get. At least that's something."

"You can't sell a person," Jenny said. "Slavery ended with the war."

"Is that a fact? Girlie, there are wolfers and outlaws all over this neck of the woods who don't give a damn about slavery ending. They'll buy you for fifty dollars and I assure you, they'll make damn sure they get their money's worth."

Susan Stanton turned in the saddle and smiled. "Of course, if you become too much of a burden to me, I'll just shoot you." Her eyes were as hard as flint. "And, little lady, you're fast becoming a burden."

"You won't shoot me," Jenny said. "Even you aren't that evil."

Suddenly, the woman's revolver was in her hand, pointed at Jenny's head. "Try me. Say, 'Go ahead, shoot me,' and see what happens."

Tears started in the girl's eyes. "Why do you torment me like this? What have I ever done to you?"

"I torment you because I hate you," Susan said. "I hate your kind. Little pink and white princesses who have everything handed to them on a silver platter. When you become wives, you expect to be treated in exactly the same way. But what do you give your men in return? You open your legs and stare at the ceiling and figure that your matrimonial duty is done. Spend some time in a brothel, see what men really want. They're wild animals. They want whores, not princesses. But when the time comes, who do they marry? They marry you."

Susan Stanton holstered her gun. "Don't ever tempt me again. I came close to putting a bullet into you."

* * *

"They're close," the Kiowa said. "We could catch up tonight."

"No, we'll wait until morning," Dan Caine said. "If it comes to shooting, I don't want Jenny Calthrop to catch a stray bullet. I want to see what I'm shooting at."

"You're shooting at Susan Stanton," the Kiowa said.

"Maybe not. She might see sense and surrender."

"Maybe," the Kiowa said without conviction.

Dan Caine and the Kiowa made a cold camp and had a meal of jerky and hard biscuit.

"What will you do to Chance Hurd?" the Indian said.

Dan chewed on a piece of tough beef slowly, thinking, and then he said, "I don't know. Lock him in his own cell for sure."

"And then hang him?"

"That will be up to the citizens of Thunder Creek."

"Nobody lives in Thunder Creek."

Dan smiled. "There are a few. One way or another, he'll pay for his crime."

"Why not shoot him?"

"Because I'm an officer of the law. I'll hang him, but I'll do it legally."

"You stopped being a law officer when you became a vigilante," the Kiowa said.

"And now I've taken up the star again," Dan said.

"Those few people you talk about in Thunder Creek may not see it that way."

Dan shrugged. "Who knows how folks will react. First thing I'll do is pin my star on again, and the second will be to arrest Chance Hurd. I reckon when I tell them how he planned the Calthrop robbery, they'll see it my way. I have witnesses, remember."

"I won't be a witness," the Kiowa said. "Nobody believes an Indian."

"I think they'll believe you."

"Why do you think that?"

"You have an honest face."

"Of the wrong color," the Kiowa said.

Dan smiled. "We'll wait and see."

"It doesn't matter. I won't wait for Hurd's trial," the Kiowa said.

"Why not?" Dan said. "You have nothing to fear."

"I must find my wife," the Kiowa said. "She is Chiricahua Apache. Two years ago, while I scouted for the army in the Arizona Territory, she and five hundred other Apache men, women, and children were sent to Florida. I haven't seen her since."

"You'll go to Florida?" Dan said.

"I grieved and got drunk for two years, but now is the time to find her. Yes, I will go to Florida."

"I'll help you any way I can, Kio . . . hell, what's your given name?" Dan said.

"My people named me Gomda. It means Wind."

"Gomda, when we get back to Thunder Creek, I'll make some enquiries," Dan said. "At least we may find something for you to go on."

"Why would a white man help me?" the Kiowa said.

"I can only speak for this white man," Dan said. "You helped me in the Sierra del Carmen, and now I want to help you." He looked down at the cigarette he was building. "And there was another Apache, a man who did not kill me when he could have. I can't do anything for him, but I can do something for you and perhaps that's enough."

"Then I am grateful . . . for both of us."

"You're a good man, Gomda."

"Since we first rode together, I have tried to remember who I am and to forget what white men forced me to be," the Indian said. "It took a while but I think I succeeded, mainly because of my time in the Sierra del Carmen." He shook his head. "So many dead men. And then as I watched Professor Latchford and Miss Prunella die so bravely it took away much of my hate." He put out his hand. "Friends."

Surprised, Dan took the Indian's hand and said, "Friends."

"Now we should sleep," the Kiowa said. "You will face a test tomorrow, Deputy Sheriff Caine."

"I'm ready for it," Dan said. "Or as ready as I'll ever be."

"Black-Eyed Susan is a woman like no other," the Kiowa said.

"Seems like," Dan said. "But this is my arrest, my fight, Gomda. Leave her to me."

"And if she kills you?"

"Then do all you can to save Jenny Calthrop, no matter what it takes."

"Then, maybe we should've brought the vigilantes," the Kiowa said.

Dan shook his head. "I won't risk their lives any longer. It's my job, and I'll do it."

Later, Dan lay on his back and stared at the stars, willing himself to sleep.

But he was scared . . . scared that he'd dream of Susan Stanton and her lightning-fast gun . . . and scared that young Jenny Calthrop could be one of her targets.

CHAPTER FORTY-FOUR

"They're just ahead of us," the Kiowa said.

"I see them," Dan Caine said.

"Black-Eyed Susan just scouted her backtrail. Wait . . . she's stopped."

"She's waiting for us," Dan said. "She thinks she has nothing to fear." A word clogged in his throat, and he finally managed, "God knows, but she's a beautiful woman."

"Beauty and the beast, two women in one skin," the Kiowa said.

"I know it," Dan said. "But it sure doesn't make this arrest any easier."

"She won't be arrested," the Kiowa said.

Dan nodded but said nothing.

He and the Kiowa rode closer through a bright, clear West Texas morning that late summer of 1888, and across the prairie, mistflowers were in bloom and lark buntings sang.

When he and the Kiowa were fifty yards from Susan Stanton and the girl, they dismounted and closed the distance on foot. They stopped at pistol-fighting range and Dan said, "Susan Stanton?"

The woman smiled. "You're aware of who I am."

Susan had pulled her hair back and tied it at the nape of

her neck with a rawhide string. Dan had once heard that it was a precaution longhaired gunmen took to avoid their hair flying across their faces during a fight. He'd never expected to see a woman do it. Her twin gunbelts were crossed over her hips, pistol butts slightly forward for the draw. Her left hand strayed to the oval medallion around her neck that bore an image of Macha, the man-slaughterer, the Celtic goddess of war and death.

"I'm Deputy Sheriff Dan Caine. Do you know why I'm here?" Dan said.

"Sure, you're a rube lawman come to arrest me for kidnapping"—she took her hand from the medallion and waved in Jenny's direction—"this little slut."

"And for taking part in the massacre of the girl's family," Dan said. He swallowed hard and said, "Now unbuckle your gunbelts and let them fall to the ground."

Susan shook her head. Her slim, elegant hand was near the pearl handle of her Colt. "That is not my intention." She turned her head slightly and said to Jenny, "Get over there beside the lawman. I want you where I can see you."

Jenny walked toward Dan but had the good sense to stand well apart from him.

"Miss Stanton, please don't make me use force," Dan said. "Surrender now and I promise you'll get a fair trial."

"Don't be stupid, little man," Susan said. "You're arresting nobody."

Her eyes moved to the Kiowa, and Dan said, "He's not a part of this. You're dealing with me."

Dan didn't anticipate what happened next. It was so blindingly fast, so ruthless, it took him completely by surprise.

Susan Stanton drew and shot the Kiowa. Dan saw the Indian stagger back a couple of steps, sudden blood on his shirt, then crumple to his knees before pitching over onto his face.

"Now he's not a part of this," Susan Stanton said. She smiled, enjoying the situation. Her mouth drew tight and small. "Now get on your horse and ride away. Don't look back or I'll gun the Calthrop tramp."

Anger slashed at Dan Caine like the serrated edge of a red-hot knife.

"You damned . . ." he drew and a split second later the realization hit him that he was slow . . . way too slow. Susan Stanton's bullet hit him on his left side and she took time over her second shot, right arm straight out using the sights like a duelist. Dan, faint from the hit, tried to bring up his gun. Too late.

BAMM!

The shot tore through the still morning like a great shard of glass.

Dan Caine watched in horrified surprise as the bullet slammed into Susan Stanton's corset, just between her breasts. The woman screamed, not in anger, nor in fear, but in an unholy, screeching rage that came from the black recesses of her soul. Dan Caine forgotten, dying on her feet, the urge to kill was still strong in her. Susan Stanton swung her gun in the direction of Jenny Calthrop, who stood holding the Kiowa's smoking Colt in both hands.

Dan had a fraction of a second to make the shot. There could be no hesitation. He fired and instantly a small red rose blossomed between Susan Stanton's eyes. For a moment, the woman stared at Dan Caine with fading eyes, and then she dropped to the ground.

Gun in hand, Dan stepped to the body. It was strange that in death all her spectacular, animated beauty fled her and all that remained was an empty, soulless shell.

Revulsion strong in him, Dan turned away. A glistening

fan of blood spread upward from just above his gunbelt to midway up his left side. The wound pained him considerably, and he felt weak and sick as he walked to where Jenny Calthrop kneeled beside the Kiowa.

Jenny rose and rushed to Dan. "How bad are you hit?" she said.

"I don't know. How is Gomda?" Dan said. Then, by way of explanation, "The Indian."

"The bullet went all the way through his shoulder," Jenny said. "It's a bad wound." She studied Dan's face and said, "I think you'd better sit down."

"Let me see Gomda first," Dan said.

Dan half kneeled, half collapsed beside the Kiowa. The man's eyes were open, but he seemed to be in considerable pain. "How are you feeling?" Dan said.

The Indian managed a small smile. "A white man's question deserves a white man's answer. I'm doing just fine."

"What's a Kiowa answer?" Dan said.

"I'm in great pain, but it tells me I'm not dead yet." The Kiowa touched Dan's chest. "For a while I was out like a dead cat. You killed Susan Stanton?"

"Jenny Calthrop killed Susan Stanton. I just finished her off."

The Kiowa nodded. "The woman was truly evil, and I rejoice at her death." He took his hand from Dan's chest and saw blood on his fingers. "You're wounded," he said.

"Black-Eyed Susan put a bullet into me," Dan said.

"And it's still inside you," Jenny said. "Dan, I must get you to a doctor."

"It's a fair piece to Thunder Creek, and there is no doctor," Dan said.

"There's a doctor in Paint Rock," Jenny said. "I'll wire the sheriff and tell him we need help."

"Hell, I'll be dead by then," Dan said.

"No, you won't," Jenny said, her face stubborn. "I won't let you die, so there."

"I don't think I can get up again," Dan said. "How do I get on my horse?"

"With great difficulty and a lot of pain," Jenny said.

Dan shook his head. "I hope you never become a nurse."

"Until we reach Thunder Creek, I am your nurse," the girl said. "Don't worry, I had brothers, and I know how to set a broken bone and treat cuts and bruises."

"How are you with gunshot wounds?" Dan said.

"I've seen a lot of those recently, but I've never treated one," Jenny said.

The girl sacrificed the tattered remainder of her chemise to tightly bind up Dan's side and the Kiowa's shoulder. "That may stop the blood," she said. "But I don't know."

Dan wasn't feeling too good, and he couldn't muster the strength to make a comment.

Jenny stripped saddle and bridle from her horse, slapped its rump and watched it trot away, tossing its head. She then caught up Susan Stanton's big American stud, a harder mount to handle, but a much better horse.

To her surprise, the Kiowa was back on his feet, but blood already stained the fat bandage at his shoulder. "I'll help you get Deputy Caine into the saddle," he said.

Dan weighed a hundred and seventy pounds that summer, but for a wounded man and a young girl he was a dead-weight, and they struggled mightily to get him onto his horse, and when he finally got seated, his feet in the stirrups, he apologized profusely for all the trouble he'd caused.

"You're wounded, Deputy Caine," Jenny said. "So none of that was your fault."

"Except come tomorrow morning, when we have to do

it all over again," the Kiowa said. But despite his own pain, he smiled.

Before they headed north, Jenny took one last look at Susan Stanton's body.

"Doesn't . . . doesn't seem right leaving her there . . . huh?" Dan said. He was slumped in the saddle and barely able to talk.

"I think she'd have killed me today or tomorrow," Jenny said. "And she would've left my body where it fell." She shook her head. "I think early in her life Susan Stanton discovered that doing evil was easy, and I have no sympathy for her. As she would have done to me, let her lie where she fell."

"Not one to hold a grudge, are you, little lady?" Dan said, gasping the last few words of that question.

"I hated her because I was afraid of her," Jenny said. "Tonight, I'll pray for God's forgiveness."

CHAPTER FORTY-FIVE

First Lieutenant Owen Wallace of K Company, 8th Cavalry lowered his field glasses, then said to the officer beside him, "They're white people, not Apaches. I see a woman with yellow hair, the others lying on the ground I can't make out." He shook his head. "They may be dead."

"The work of the hostiles sir?" Second Lieutenant John Anderson said.

"Maybe. They could've been caught out in the open," Wallace said. He raised his glasses and again scanned the surrounding terrain. "But I see no sign of Apaches." Then, "Give Captain Watts my compliments and ask him to join me at the head of the column."

Gray-haired army surgeon Captain Steven Watts drew rein alongside his commander and said, "Trouble?"

"I don't know yet," Wallace said. "Come with me, doctor. You too, Mister Anderson."

The three soldiers cantered toward Jenny and the others, and the girl watched them come. This was her third day on the trail, and she was exhausted. The Kiowa seemed strong enough, but Dan Caine was drifting in and out of consciousness, and his breathing was labored.

The officers dismounted and Jenny said in a rush,

"They've both been shot. But Deputy Sheriff Caine is very ill. He still has a pistol bullet in his side."

Wallace gestured to the doctor, and Watts immediately took a knee beside Dan.

"Apaches?" the lieutenant said.

"No," Jenny said. "An outlaw." She didn't feel the need to explain further.

Watts sniffed Dan's wound and said, "There's no gangrene. But I have to operate on this man as soon as possible. The pistol ball has to be removed."

"Will he . . . Doctor, will he be all right?" Jenny said.

"It's too early to tell," Watts said. "I won't know the prognosis until I operate."

"How long will that take, Doctor?" Wallace said.

"The bullet is deep," Watts said. He shook his head. "I can't say. And the other man needs treatment."

First Lieutenant Wallace looked hard at the Kiowa and said, "Apache?"

"No, Kiowa. And I was once an army scout."

The officer took a moment to think that through, decided the Kiowa was an unnecessary complication best ignored and said, "Doctor, my orders are to press the hostiles closely. Take what you need from the supply wagon and catch up as soon as you can." He read the question on Watts's face and said, "Yes, and you can have your assistant."

"Private Evans is a good man," Watts said. "He'll make a fine physician one day."

"Yes, I'm sure he will," Wallace said. "Pity he'll never make a fine soldier one day."

Before First Lieutenant Wallace and his sixty troopers and two Navajo scouts left in pursuit of the handful of lobo

Apaches that had so far eluded death or capture, he unloaded Watts's medical supplies from the wagon. He also provided a small tent, to be discarded after use, blankets, a bundle of firewood, taken from a supply packed under the wagon, a loaf of sourdough bread, bacon and coffee, and, vitally, an oil lamp.

Captain Watts and his assistant Private John Evans, an earnest young man whose brown eyes blinked constantly from behind his round glasses like an intelligent owl, wasted no time in getting Dan Caine ready for surgery. The tent was erected, a blanket spread inside as a makeshift operating table, and the oil lamp was lit.

Earlier, Watts had examined the Kiowa's wound and again detected no gangrene.

"Through and through wounds are less of an infection risk and he's not losing blood," Watts told Jenny. "He can wait for a while yet." The doctor glanced at a scarlet sky bannered by ribbons of gold and purple, and said, "It will be dark soon. I'd better get started."

"I'll pray for him, Doctor," Jenny said.

"That can't hurt. And while you're at it, say one for yourself, young lady," Watts said. "If I was your doctor, I'd recommend a week's bed rest and plenty of beef tea."

"I'll sleep after I know Dan Caine is recovering," Jenny said.

Captain Watts patted her on the cheek. "Good girl," he said.

When the doctor and his assistant went into the tent, Private Evans carrying the oil lamp with its halo of yellowish light, the Kiowa immediately kneeled and turned his copper face to the copper sky. He chanted softly, repetitive incantations that Jenny realized were prayers to his god.

* * *

Only thirty minutes passed before Watts ducked out from under the tent opening, wiping bloody hands on a white towel. Jenny considered it a good omen. Didn't surgeries take hours and hours?

The captain saw the girl's concerned face and said, "He's still under from the ether, and he'll sleep for a while. I found the bullet quite easily since it didn't lodge in any major organs."

Jenny said, "Will he be . . . well again?"

"Mr. Caine is young and strong, and I'm sure he'll recover nicely," Watts said.

"And the captain is a fine surgeon," Private Evans said.

"Thank you, Evans," Watts said. "I blush at your completely unbiased opinion."

He held up a bullet. "Forty-five caliber. Mr. Caine may wish to keep it, have it bronzed perhaps. It came within an inch of killing him." He handed the bullet to Jenny, a bloody cloth to Evans, and said, "After you clean up, Private Evans, perhaps you'll start a fire and fix us a supper of the army's excellent bacon and moldy biscuit. In the meantime, I'll see to the Indian's shoulder."

"I'll cook supper," Jenny said. "I need something to occupy my mind."

CHAPTER FORTY-SIX

At dawn, Captain Watts and Private Evans saddled up, expressing an urgent need to catch up with the column. But before he left, the doctor gave Jenny Calthrop a small brown bottle that he told her was tincture of iodine.

"Apply to the wounds several times a day to prevent infection," he said. He smiled. "The good, clean prairie air will help with their recovery. I found tobacco in Mr. Caine's shirt pocket, so encourage him to smoke. It's very good for the lungs."

"I will, doctor," Jenny said.

"And take care of yourself," Watts said. "You look as though you've been through it."

"Yes, I have," Jenny said.

"Maybe one day you will tell me all about it," Captain Watts said.

The girl said, "My family was killed by some evil people and I was kidnapped. Deputy Sheriff Caine and his vigilantes saved me."

Watts managed a smile. "And now you're going home."

"I have no home," Jenny said.

"Then maybe I can remedy that," Watts said. "I'm a widower and I have a daughter about your age. Her name is Clara, and she has a paint horse she calls Geronimo. Perhaps you'd like to come live with us at the officers' quarters in Fort Concho."

Jenny smiled. "I think I'd like that."

"Where can you be reached?"

"Thunder Creek, I guess."

"Then stay there. As soon as this campaign is over, my daughter and I will come for you," Watts said.

"I'll take care of her until then."

All heads turned to Dan Caine who'd stepped from the tent and now stood shirtless, a thick white bandage around his middle. He was pale and drawn but seemed steady on his feet.

"Easy, Mr. Caine, easy now," Watts said. "You should spend the rest of this day and at least the next two or three resting. And that also goes for your Indian friend."

"We'll spend the rest of this day in the saddle, Captain," Dan said. "There's something I have to do in Thunder Creek. And just in case I forget, thank you for saving my life."

"You might have lived a long, happy life with a bullet in you, but I doubt it," Watts said. "And you're most welcome."

Before the captain rode out, he drew rein beside Dan and said, "Take good care of Jenny. I see fine qualities in that young lady."

Dan nodded. "So far she's endured a lot in her life," he said. "I think now she deserves a chance at happiness."

"She'll be happy with Clara and I," Watts said. "A frontier army post can be lonely for a girl, and my daughter will welcome her with open arms." The officer extended his hand. "Hopefully I'll see you again very soon, Mr. Caine. Good luck."

"You too, Captain," Dan said. "Good luck."

* * *

They spent another two days and nights on the trail and on the third day around noon Dan and the others rode into Thunder Creek. The ride had weakened Dan and though his wound showed no sign of infection, it had bled profusely, and the massive loss of blood had made him a very sick man. He rode slumped over in the saddle and Jenny Calthrop had to reach out and support him.

Frank Halder, the boy whose mother had dragged him away from the posse, was on the porch outside Doan's store drinking a soda pop and was the first in town to see them.

"Deputy Caine is back!" he yelled.

Sheriff Chance Hurd heard that cry and looked out his office window. He saw Dan, and a jolt of alarm went through him.

CHAPTER FORTY-SEVEN

In recent days, Clint Cooley had broken the habit of a lifetime by rising before noon and stationing himself on a chair, his eyes fixed on the trail into town from the south. He spotted Dan Caine and two others and then as they rode closer, identified the Kiowa and a young woman that he took to be Jenny Calthrop.

A cautious man, Cooley's British Bulldogs were in his shoulder harness, his mistrust of the murderous Chance Hurd running deep.

Cooley rose from his chair and walked toward the riders. Under a high, noon sun they met outside Ma Lester's Guest House for Respectable Christian Gentlemen. Ma herself stood on the front porch, a tall, rangy, and wide-shouldered woman who looked as though she lived on a diet of scripture and prune juice. Her dress was black with white collar and cuffs, her brown hair pulled back in a tight bun, and her steel trap of a mouth was tightly shut in disapproval. Two wounded men, one of them a savage, with a ragged girl could give her place a bad name.

Dan drew rein and, his voice a weak whisper, said, "Howdy, Clint."

Cooley nodded. "I see you lost your shirt. Got into a poker game with Black-Eyed Susan, huh?"

"She's dead," Dan said. He was as pale as bleached bones. "She got a bullet into me."

"You don't say. You have to tell me about it sometime when I've got nothing more pressing to do," Cooley said. "In the meantime, let's get you off that horse and into bed."

Ma Lester's intolerant eyes flew open. "Not one of my beds. He's all bloody."

"Lady, he's your deputy sheriff," Cooley said.

"Not any longer. He resigned his situation and took up with outlaws." She sniffed. "And just look where that's gotten him."

"Who told you Deputy Caine had joined outlaws?" Jenny said. "Was it Sheriff Hurd?"

"You just never mind who told me, missy," Ma Lester said. "Pete Doan keeps a bed for drunk cowboys behind his store. Take him there."

"He needs a proper bed and plenty of rest," Jenny said.

"Not in my house," Ma said. "I run a respectable place here."

Then Jenny Calthrop surprised the hell out of everybody and scared the living daylights out of the stubborn proprietress.

Jenny reached out, jerked Dan's Colt from his holster, pointed the gun at Ma, and thumbed back the hammer. "Lady, I've already shot one woman and another sure as hell won't make any difference."

"I'll pay for the room," Cooley said, smiling. "That way there will be no gunplay."

Visibly shaken, Ma Lester drew her remaining dignity around her like a tattered cloak and said, "I don't have accommodation for the savage. There will be no Hindoos in this house, and I am adamant on that."

"The Hindoo has his own cabin," the Kiowa said. "It's not much, but it's home."

This was a day of surprises for Ma. She'd been threatened violence by a slip of a girl and now she'd met a savage who spoke like a gentleman. The woman shook her head. She didn't know what the world was coming to.

"Bring Deputy Caine inside," Ma said. "No credit, pay in advance . . . no women in the rooms after ten . . . no spurs on the beds . . . meals will be charged whether eaten or not . . . and last but not least, no profanity, singing, or dancing. Now haul him in."

Dan Caine lay on a narrow cot in a small, boxy room with two wall hooks to hang clothes, a washstand with a blue and white porcelain jug and basin, and a chamber pot of the same color. A narrow, six-paned window, dusty and flyspecked, looked out on a brown landscape as drab and boring as staring at a brick wall.

Under the sheets, apart from his bandage, Dan was as naked as a seal, stripped by Clint Cooley and the Kiowa, men who knew no shame. He was aware of how feeble he was, too weak to object to their manhandling, and badly in need of a couple of days' rest. Cooley allowed Estella Sweet, Cornelius Massey, and young Holt Peters a short visit. Holt, conscious of his recently acquired adult status, shook hands, Estella stained Dan's face with her tears, and Massey brought a special issue of his newspaper "hot off the press" and held up the front page with cascading headlines that promised a hair-raising and greatly exaggerated account of their battle with Clay Kyle:

A DESPERATE ENCOUNTER

GREAT SLAUGHTER IN THE SIERRA DEL CARMEN

Dozens of Outlaws Bite the Dust

Gallant Thunder Creek Vigilantes
Destroy the Dreaded Kyle Gang

Deputy Sheriff Dan Caine Badly
Wounded and Lies at Death's Door

Drink Dr. Drake's Bitters
for Serene Slumbers

Dan didn't like the line about his imminent demise, but he felt too worn-out to object.

After everyone left, all of them promising to return the next morning, Ma Lester surprised him when she shook him awake and insisted on spoon-feeding him a bowl of beef broth.

The window rattled in its frame, and a high wind restlessly prowled around the eaves of the building. "The wind is coming from the south, and it's blowing sand," Ma said. "Like you, Mr. Caine, it's going to get worse before it gets better. Well, that will be two-bits for the broth. It's against house rules, but I'll make a bill for Mr. Cooley for services rendered during your convalescence."

The woman was right about the coming sandstorm. As the day drew into evening the wind grew in strength and intensity and cartwheeled through the house, banging doors like a drumbeat.

Dan slept fitfully, then woke with a start. The wind still raged, loud and aggressive, and the old frame boardinghouse creaked and squeaked and groaned with every whipping gust.

Then another noise in the hallway outside.

Slow footsteps and the measured *chink, chink* of spurs. Coming closer. Dan's gunbelt hung from a hook in the wall.

He tried to rise, and a wave of pain and nausea swept over him. Exhausted his head hit the pillow again.

The door handle turned slowly, and little by little the door opened, rasping on the wood floor . . .

CHAPTER FORTY-EIGHT

The hotel room door opened wide and then closed again. Chance Hurd, huge in a sand-covered canvas slicker open at the front to display the buckles of his gunbelts, stood at the bottom of Dan Caine's bed.

"I didn't bring beef broth for the invalid on account of how this ain't what you'd call a friendly visit," Hurd said.

"Then say your piece and get the hell out of here," Dan said.

"You been spreading lies about me, Dan, and I don't like that," Hurd said.

"I speak the truth, Chance, and that truth is going to hang you," Dan said. "Damn you, I'll see that it does."

"Your word against mine, Dan. And yours don't stand for much."

"Clint Cooley and the others will back my story," Dan said. "They all know you planned the massacre of the Calthrop family."

"I didn't mean for them to get killed," Hurd said. "That was all Clay Kyle's doing and not mine. Now I hear both Clay and Black-Eyed Susan are dead. What happened, Dan? Did you shoot them in the back?"

"Get the hell out of here, Hurd," Dan said. "As soon as I leave this bed, I plan to arrest you. And then I'll hang you."

Hurd smiled. "The only way you're gonna get out of the bed is when six guys carry you out by the handles."

"You shoot me, Chance, and within minutes the whole town will come down on you," Dan said.

"Who said anything about shooting?" Hurd said. "I got something better planned for you, Dan."

Moving fast for a big man, Hurd stepped to the bed, jerked the pillow from under Dan's head and then shoved it over his face. In his weakened state, Dan was no match for the big man's strength, and his struggles against the smothering pillow were futile.

"What in the world is going on here?"

Ma Lester had silently entered the room, a candlestick in one hand, a glass of warm milk in the other.

Hurd immediately lifted the pillow from Dan's face and said, "We was just funnin' around, Miss Lester."

Dan was battling for breath, great, heaving gasps, and Ma said, "That didn't look like funnin' to me. Were you trying to kill that man?"

She grabbed the pillow out of Hurd's hands.

"No ma'am, I was just teaching him a lesson, scaring him back to the straight and narrow, you might say. He's been spreading lies about me, and I want them to stop."

"So you thought you'd smother him to death?"

"No, nothing like that, Miss Lester. As I said, all I wanted was to put the fear of God into him and set him on the path of righteousness was all."

Ma backed toward the door. "Sheriff Hurd, I know what I saw," she said. "You tried to murder Mr. Caine, and I plan to ask Mayor Doan to call an emergency town meeting. I'll demand that you be arrested for attempted murder and be held in your own jail cell until a circuit judge gets here."

The woman turned and stepped out the door. Chance Hurd followed. He caught Ma Lester in the hallway and violently pulled her back by her shoulders. She yelled out in fear and the candle fell out of her hands and the milk spilled over the floor. Hurd was a powerful man with huge hands, and Ma had a slender throat. Strangling her to death was easy for him. When Dan Caine staggered groggily into the corridor Hurd was too fast for him. The big man knocked Dan's gun hand aside and hit him flush on the chin. Dan dropped like a poleaxed ox and joined his shadow on the floor. Moving quickly, Hurd dragged Dan closer to the dead woman. He ripped the front of Ma's dress, exposing her breasts, and disarranged her clothing. Smiling now, satisfied, it was the work of a moment to pick up Dan's fallen Colt, shoot Ma in the chest, and then shove the revolver into his former deputy's hand.

Thunder Creek was a small place and despite the roar of the wind, the shot was heard all over town.

Hurd ran downstairs onto the front porch and yelled, "Help! Rape! Murder!"

Those were words that always brought the citizens of a Western cow town running, and after a moment a sizeable crowd braved the sandstorm and gathered to hear their sheriff say, "Dan Caine tried to rape Ma Lester and when she struggled, he shot her. I caught him in the act"—he shook a massive fist—"and put him out of action."

Including Pete Doan and Mike Sweet the blacksmith, Hurd led about a dozen people upstairs and the unvarnished evidence was there to see. Dan Caine, dazed from Hurd's punch, sat on the floor, his back against a wall, and at his feet the body of Ma Lester, the horror that she carried into eternity frozen on her face.

Hurd dragged Dan to his feet and backhanded him across the face. "Not so tough now, are you? Not when there's men to face and not a weak woman."

That last drew a few murmurs of approval, but Clint

Cooley silenced the crowd when he said, "Hurd, leave Deputy Sheriff Caine the hell alone. A couple of you men, Sweet, Doan, help him back into bed."

Doan looked doubtful. "Cooley . . . I . . ."

"Do as I say, Pete," Cooley said. "Dan Caine is no more guilty of murder than I am."

"Not guilty? Hell, I saw him shoot poor Miss Lester and he'd have shot me if I hadn't been too quick for him," Hurd said. "Are you calling me a liar?"

"Yeah, Hurd, I'm calling you a damned liar," Cooley said. He then provided the spark that would later send Chance Hurd into the fires of hell. "You planned the murder of the Calthrop family and Dan Caine knows it. Now to cover your tracks, you're willing to see him hang for a murder he didn't commit. For some reason Ma Lester found out about the Calthrops, and you killed her to keep her quiet."

"Those are serious allegations, Clint," Doan said, his face stiff and hard.

"And a pack of damned lies," Hurd said. "From the git-go, I was suspicious of Caine; especially after he let slip that him and Kyle had ridden together years back. You want to know who really planned the massacre of the Calthrop family? It was Dan Caine. He and the rest of his vigilantes were in cahoots with Clay Kyle up to their necks. Yeah, that's it. Caine said they killed Clay Kyle down in Old Mexico, and maybe that's true. But Kyle had discovered a gold mine, and they murdered him for it."

"Sheriff Hurd, are you saying my daughter was in league with one of the worst outlaws on the frontier?" Sweet said. "That's preposterous."

"No, the only one who knew about the mine was Caine," Hurd said. "He duped the others into following him to provide the extra guns he needed."

Clint Cooley said, "Hurd, you're really reaching, telling lies to cover other lies. Dan never set eyes on Clay Kyle until he saw him over the barrel of his gun in the Sierra del Carmen."

"Cooley, you and Dan Caine are in it together," Hurd said. "You're nothing but a tinhorn gambler and as guilty as he is."

"You're heeled, Hurd," Cooley said, anger in his face. "You want to back up your lies with the iron?"

"Just what I'd expect to hear from a crooked gambler and back shooter," Hurd said.

"Enough!" Pete Doan said. "I've heard enough. The citizens of Thunder Creek will have their voices heard tonight and decide on the right or wrong of this thing." Backed by the muscular presence of Mike Sweet and a few other men, Doan said, "Sheriff, surrender your guns. You too, Mr. Cooley. Both of them."

"Anything you say, Pete," Hurd said. "You're the mayor."

He handed his revolvers to Doan, and Cooley said, "Pete, lock Hurd in his cell, and I'll surrender my guns. There's rifles and shotguns in his gunracks, and he can go on killing."

"Yes, lock me up, that's fine by me, Pete," Hurd said. "Just so long as you bring me three square meals a day and a bottle of bourbon to go with them." He grinned and looked around at the men in the crowd. "Eh, boys?"

Hurd expected laughs, cheers even, but all he got was a tense silence. Suspicions were running deep.

The sheriff tried again. Grinning, he said, "Bring on the chains, Pete."

Word by word, this declaration dropped like rocks into a tin bucket and was once more greeted by a profound quiet.

Angry now, Hurd said, "Right, take me to the damned

jail. You'll let me out quick enough after I've proved my innocence."

"You've done a power of talking, Hurd, and proved nothing but your own guilt," Cooley said. Then, "Take him to his cell, Pete. I'll follow."

Pete Doan looked around and his eyes lighted on Holt Peters. "Holt, can I ask you to get your rifle and stand guard here in Deputy Caine's room."

The young man had quit his job at Doan's store and planned to sign on as a puncher with one of the big cattle outfits east of Thunder Creek, but there was no hesitation in his reply. "Of course, Mr. Doan," he said. He looked Hurd in the eye. "I'll make sure that nothing happens to Deputy Caine."

CHAPTER FORTY-NINE

Clint Cooley, Cornelius Massey, Estella Sweet, and Jenny Calthrop were among those who attended the crowded emergency town meeting in Doan's store at nine o'clock that night. The wind still had not abated and roamed all over town slamming doors and rattling shutters, blowing sand over everything and everybody. The moon and stars were blotted out, and the sky was as black as coal.

People had some time to think, and arguments began to run against Sheriff Chance Hurd. And the point was made again and again by Massey and others that Dan Caine was too badly wounded and weakened by surgery and loss of blood to have attacked Ma Lester, much less strangle her with his bare hands.

"Ma Lester was a strong lady," Massey said. "I once watched her manhandle a fifty-pound sack of flour off the back of a wagon and when I spoke to her, she wasn't even breathing hard. Singlehandedly running a boardinghouse is no job for a weakling. I can assure you, good people, that if Deputy Caine had laid hands on her with ravishment in mind, she would've nailed his hide to the outhouse wall, quicker n' scat."

"But Chance Hurd had the strength to strangle her," Estella Sweet said.

Massey nodded. "That he did. He's a big man and strong."

"Has anyone taken time to examine Deputy Caine since he returned to Thunder Creek?" one plump matron in a poke bonnet asked. "That might tell the tale."

"Lady, we're not doctors," a man said.

"No, we're not," the woman said. "But we can tell how sick a man is. We don't need a medical diploma for that."

"I know how sick Deputy Caine is," Jenny Calthrop said. She was living with the Sweets and wore a blue cotton dress Estella had long since grown out of. "When we rode into town this morning, he was too weak to sit his horse. I had to support him or he would've fallen out of the saddle." She reached into the dress pocket and held up the iodine bottle. "The army surgeon who removed the bullet from Dan's side gave me this to stop infection, but the wound opened and he lost a lot of blood. He was as weak as a two-day-old kitten."

"Jenny's dress was stiff with blood when she arrived in town," Estella said.

Jenny nodded. "Deputy Caine's blood."

"I say we go to the boardinghouse and look for ourselves," a middle-aged man named Tom Roberts said. He was a former locomotive engineer, and he and his wife worked as a team doing odd jobs around town.

"That's an excellent idea," the woman in the poke bonnet said. "Let's settle this thing."

Pete Doan thought about that for a few moments and then said, "I don't want a crowd in Deputy Caine's room. Tom, you, Mike Sweet"—he nodded to the woman in the poke bonnet—"and you, Mrs. Blackwood, will study on the state of Deputy Caine's health and report back to us. Remember, all we want to know is . . . was he strong enough to attack Ma Lester? Come back with a yes or a no."

"I want to go too, Mr. Doan," Jenny said. "By now, Dan's wound needs more iodine."

"Does that set all right by everyone?" Doan said. "No objections?"

There were no protests, and Tom Roberts, Mrs. Blackwood, Jenny Calthrop, and Mike Sweet left the store and walked into the raging night.

"Now we wait," Pete Doan said.

Footsteps on the hallway brought Holt Peters out of his chair, his Winchester at the ready. Showing good sense, Sweet said, "Holt, it's me. Mike. I'm with Tom Roberts, Mrs. Blackwood, and Jenny Calthrop."

"Come on in," Holt said.

The door opened and the four people stepped inside. Taking his guard duties seriously, his rifle still at the ready, the youngster said, "State your intentions, Mr. Sweet."

The blacksmith smiled. "On the authority of Mayor Doan, we've been sent by the citizens committee to make an examination of Deputy Caine."

"Why?" Holt said.

"In a nutshell, to see if he was strong enough to rape Ma Lester," Sweet said. "Or at least make the attempt."

"That's the most ridiculous thing I've ever heard," Holt said. "It wouldn't even enter into Dan Caine's thinking to do such a thing."

"I know it, you know it, but there are some who don't," Sweet said. "We're here on their behalf."

"You have Ma's murderer in your jail cell," Holt said.

"Once again, you're preaching to the converted," Sweet said. "But let's take a look at Deputy Caine and put other minds at rest."

"He's sick and talking in his sleep," Holt said. "But it's hard to figure out what he's saying."

"I'll examine him," Mrs. Blackwood said. She was plump, pretty, and capable and had raised seven young'uns and as a result was familiar with all common ailments and some not so common.

The woman placed the back of her fingers on Dan's forehead and then nodded. "Just as I thought, he's fevered. Let me take a look at his wound." Mrs. Blackwood pulled down the sheet and exposed the blood-stained bandage around Dan's middle. "Oh, sweet Jesus," she said. "That wound is severe." She looked around at her companions. "This man may have had death and Judgment Day on his mind. What he was most certainly not studying on was raping poor Ma Lester."

"Some of the stain is from tincture of iodine," Jenny said.

"I know the difference between blood and iodine stains, missy," Mrs. Blackwood said. "How much iodine did you use?"

Jenny took the bottle from her pocket and showed it to the woman.

"It's half empty," Mrs. Blackwell said. "You used too much, girl. All you needed was a couple of drops in the wounds."

"The army doctor told me to use it," Jenny said. "He didn't tell me how much."

A wind gust threw sand against the window, and the oil lamp's flame guttered and shadows danced on the bare walls.

"It's my opinion that Deputy Caine was incapable of attacking Miss Lester," Mrs. Blackwell said.

Mike Sweet and Tom Roberts nodded, carefully averting their eyes from Dan's wound. One glance had been enough.

"Well, he's young and strong and I think he'll pull through," Mrs. Blackwell said. She pushed up the demure sleeves of her widow's dress. "The first thing to do is get the bandage changed. Miss Calthrop, you stay. Mr. Roberts and Mr. Sweet, you may go and tell the others what I said . . . Dan Caine was in no fit state to assault Miss Lester." She turned and looked at Holt. "Now, young Mr. Peters, run along to the general store and tell Pete Doan I need bandages and gauze pads. And tell him I also need a pint of whiskey for medicinal purposes."

"For Dan?" Holt said.

"No," Mrs. Blackwell said. "For me."

CHAPTER FIFTY

"All right, this has gone far enough," Chance Hurd said. "Now let me out of here."

"Dan Caine is in no fit state to attempt the rape of a woman," Pete Doan said. "To say otherwise is nonsense."

"Damn you, Doan, let me out of here," Hurd said.

"Hurd, you went to the boardinghouse to murder Dan Caine and silence him forever," Doan said. "But Ma Lester caught you in the act and you killed her and then arranged it to look like Dan did it. That's what I think and what everybody else in this town thinks."

"And it's a pack of lies," Hurd said. "You're trying to railroad me to the gallows, Doan, you and every other scurvy lowlife in this damned hick town."

"We'll let a judge decide who is lying and who is not," Doan said.

Clint Cooley had accompanied the storekeeper to the sheriff's office to pick up his guns. Now he said to Hurd, "Still blowing hard out there, Chance, and we got a blowhard in here. Kinda funny, ain't it?"

"You shut your damn trap, Cooley," Hurd said, his voice loud, enraged. "You were in cahoots with Caine all along. You planned the murder of the Calthrop family, and when that didn't work out, you followed Clay Kyle to Old Mexico and killed him for his gold mine."

Cooley smiled and shook his head. "Chance, Chance, Chance, we've been all through that already. Not a word that comes out of your lying mouth is true."

"Damn your eyes, we'll see if the judge thinks I'm lying," Hurd said.

Cooley's smile was still in place.

"Chance, even if a judge was stupid enough not to sentence you to hang, do you really think I'm going to let you ride out of here?"

"What do you mean?"

"You know what I mean."

"Tell me."

"All right then, I'll spell it out. I'll kill you. Is that plain enough?"

Hurd's smile was brutal. "Gambling man, don't bet the farm on your draw. I can shade you."

"Chance, on your best day you couldn't shade me. Not even close."

Hurd's anger grew. "Hey, Doan, give me my guns," he yelled. "Me and Cooley will have it out right now."

Pete Doan said, "Hurd, you're in jail on suspicion of multiple murder, serious charges. Conduct yourself like the prisoner you are."

"Damn you, Doan, I hope you die," Hurd said.

"I suspect that will come soon enough," Doan said, a man being eaten alive by cancer.

"And Caine!" Hurd screamed. "I hope he dies. I hope all of you die."

The roaring wind battered the sheriff's office, and the joints of its wooden frame groaned. Outside in the street, six-foot-tall veils of sand and dust rose and then scattered like birdshot, peppering everything in their path. Somewhere a sheltering dog barked in distress, terrified by a force of nature it could not understand. The night was as black as pitch, shredded into rags by the tempest.

"Sorry I couldn't oblige you, Hurd," Cooley said. "Maybe next time, only there won't be a next time."

"Go to hell!" Hurd raged. "Die! *Die!*"

The lantern held up well and splashed a bobbing circle of yellow light around Clint Cooley's feet as he made his way to the boardinghouse. Dan Caine worried him, and he decided to pay another sick call before he turned in.

Cooley stepped onto the front porch, only to collide at the door with a small man in a long white nightshirt and tasseled cap, a burning candle in his hand.

"Damn it, man!" Cooley said after he'd jumped a foot in the air. "You scared the living hell out of me. I took you for a ghost."

"Don't shoot! It's only me, Timothy Bean, as ever was," the little man said.

Cooley said, "Why in blue blazes are you wandering around in a sandstorm putting the fear of God into folks?"

The little man's face, which had never been exposed to sun, was bookended by frizzy muttonchop whiskers and his nightshirt flapped around his skinny legs. "I couldn't sleep," Bean said.

"Because of the storm?" Cooley said. Now that his fright was over, he was prepared to be amiable. "It's only a big wind."

"No, not the wind," Bean said. "I'm so afraid I might be murdered in my bed." He dropped his voice to a whisper. "I was told that a vicious killer is confined in the room adjoining mine."

Cooley smiled. "The man in the next room is Deputy Sheriff Dan Caine who was badly wounded by outlaws. The man who murdered Ma Lester is now in jail."

"I'm so glad to hear that," Bean said. "I'm of a somewhat timorous nature myself and to be around guns and gunmen causes me the utmost distress."

"You're quite safe, Mr. Bean," Cooley said. "If you run into any problems just knock on the wall and me or another guard will come to your assistance."

The candle in Bean's hand went out, extinguished by the wind. "Oh dear," he said.

"Now go back to bed, Mr. Bean," Cooley said. "As I told you, this place is guarded day and night by armed and resolute men, and you have nothing to fear."

"I'm so glad to hear that," Bean said. "Now I'll be able to sleep knowing that such stalwarts are on duty." He nodded in the direction of the lantern in Cooley's hand. "Perhaps you will lead the way?"

As the two men stepped into the house, Cooley said, "What are you doing in Thunder Creek? I suspect it's a long way off your home range."

"I'm a drummer, traveling in glassware, canning jars, and the like," Bean said, stopping, standing close to Cooley in the lantern-lit gloom as though he sought his protection. "Mr. Doan has been a regular and faithful customer of mine for many a long year."

"The stage only visits once a month," Cooley said. "You must sit around town kicking your heels for weeks at a time."

"And that's the secret of a happy marriage. Mr. ah . . ."

"Cooley. Clint Cooley."

"Yes, Mr. Cooley, it is," Bean said. "You see, Mr. Cooley, my lovely lady wife, despite her two hundred and fifty pounds, is a delicate creature, most fragile, and of a very nervous disposition. By mutual consent, we find it most agreeable that I come home to San Angelo only at longish intervals. My dearest Mrs. Bean finds that the strain on her nerves is thus much diminished. As some author or other once said, 'Absence makes the heart grow fonder.'"

Cooley nodded. "Then my kindest regards to Mrs. Bean the next time you see her."

"Thank you," Timothy Bean said. "Gertrude will be most grateful for such kind words."

Cooley made to mount the stairs, but Bean's voice, sounding strangely low and hesitant, said, "Mr. Cooley, I have something to tell you."

Cooley's frown betrayed his exasperation. "What is it now, Mr. Bean?"

"Should I or shouldn't I, Mr. Cooley?" the little man said, his furtive eyes blinking, trembling hand on Cooley's arm.

"Should you or shouldn't you do what?" Cooley said.

The little drummer was irritating. He'd shot men for less or at least thought about it.

"I mean, should I tell you what I know," Bean said.

"What do you know?"

"I know what I saw when I heard a turmoil in the hallway and opened my door a crack to peep outside. Oh, Mr. Cooley, that was a bad decision."

"What did you see?"

"I saw Sheriff Hurd's hands around Miss Lester's neck."

"Then what?"

"Then I closed the door and later I heard a shot."

Cooley was about to say, "Why didn't you try to save her?" Then he remembered Hurd's muscular size and undoubted strength and said, "Why didn't you tell us about this earlier?"

"Because I was sore affeered," Bean said. "Later I spoke with old Mr. Erikson, the permanent resident, and he told me that Sheriff Hurd was being held in the bedroom next to mine because the town's jail cell had no lock. He told me to keep my mouth'shut and he'd do the same. He's almost ninety years old, is Mr. Erikson, and he's always down with something, poor man."

Cooley thought about frog marching Timothy Bean to the sheriff's office where he could tell Doan what he'd seen. But the little man was already in such a state of fright that he didn't want to add to his distress. "Go to bed and don't forget to lock your room door," he said. "I'll bring Pete Doan to talk with you in the morning."

Bean nodded and said, "Lead the way with your lantern, Mr. Cooley, and then stand at my door until you hear the key turn in the lock. When I tell Mrs. Bean about all this, I do hope her poor heart will stand the strain."

CHAPTER FIFTY-ONE

An oil lamp burned in Dan Caine's room, but since Hurd was in jail, Holt Peters had been told to go home. Clint Cooley stepped to the bed, his lantern held high, and the orange glow fell on Dan's face.

"I'm still alive, Clint," Dan said. "If that puts your mind at rest."

Cooley smiled. "Don't you dare go over the river before I shake your hand and say goodbye. It's the decent thing to do and all that."

"That's true blue of you," Dan said. "Now help me get out of this damned bed. I've spent so much time on my back I counted every crack in the ceiling."

"How many are there?"

"Seventy-six and a half. One was just a small crack."

"Damn, ruined your count, didn't it? Let's get you sitting up, Dan. I've got stuff to tell you," Cooley said. And then by way of a tease: "Hurd is presently languishing in his own jail cell."

"Damn, I'm weak," Dan said as Cooley pulled and pushed him into a sitting position, pillows at his back. "Hand me down my gun from the holster."

"Who are you planning to shoot?"

"Nobody . . . yet. Just give me the Colt."

Cooley did as he was told, and Dan hefted the revolver in his hand and then worked the action a few times. He handed the gun back to Cooley. "It didn't feel heavy. Maybe I'm not as puny as I thought."

"You want to know what happened tonight or not?" Cooley said.

"Don't tell me, I'll tell you," Dan said. "Chance Hurd is locked in his own cell, suspected of taking a part in the murder of the Calthrop family and Ma Lester."

"How do you know all this?" Cooley said.

"I was barely holding on to consciousness but heard most of what you and Doan and Hurd were talking about," Dan said. "Hurd was always a bad liar."

"Doan says he'll hold him until a circuit judge gets here," Cooley said.

"I couldn't save Ma Lester," Dan said. "I tried and Hurd laid me out cold." His breathing was heavy and troubled. "That stays with a man, Clint, gives him no peace."

"You tried, Dan. Nobody can fault you."

"I had a gun in my hand, and I let myself walk right into Hurd's fist."

"You were sick, out of your mind."

"If I had it to do over again, I think I could've saved her."

"Hell, man, you've been gut shot. Don't beat yourself up."

Dan groaned and said, "I've got to get out of this bed. I've had enough of being a damned invalid."

Cooley smiled. "I got a ten says you can't make it to your pants without falling flat on your face."

"Just watch me. And I'll see your ten and raise you ten."

"You've got no money."

"I've got back wages coming."

"Maybe, but I don't trust you, Dan. You've got shifty eyes and you associate with low persons."

"Including gamblers."

"Sir, you speak of the second oldest profession. Or is it the third?"

Dan said, "I think it comes dead last. Now help me out of this bed."

"The Bible says Roman soldiers tossed dice for Jesus's duds at the foot of the cross. I'd say that makes gambling pretty darned old."

"We'll talk about this some other time when I'm really, really bored," Dan said. "Now take hold of me."

He grasped Cooley's hand, and the gambler hauled him to his feet and then grabbed him around the shoulders when Dan swayed and nearly fell.

"Easy, hoss, easy," Cooley said. "You're feeling a little faint, like a girl at her first ball, huh?" He eased Dan into a sitting position at the edge of the bed. "Comfy?"

"Bring me my pants and my shirt and boots," Dan said, breathing hard.

"You don't have a shirt."

"Where did it go?"

"Nowhere. It got all torn to pieces by bullets, blood, and an army surgeon." Cooley looked penitent. "And I'm sorry to tell you this, but so did your long johns."

"Clint, bring me one of your shirts and . . . oh, my God . . . where is my hat?"

"You mean this thing?" Cooley said. He grabbed a battered, sweat-stained black hat from its perch on top of the water jug and pushed it onto Dan's head. "There, you look better already," he said.

"Get me a shirt, Clint," Dan said.

"Ah, well there we have a problem," Cooley said. "All my shirts were handmade by Alperstein and Fienberg, my tailors in New Orleans. They're not for the likes of you who dribbles his soup down his front at every meal. But . . ."

"Clint, listen to me . . ."

"But . . . I will brave the storm and venture to Doan's store to obtain a shirt, underwear, and socks to cover your nakedness. Don't worry, I'll write them into Pete's credit ledger." Cooley shook his head. "But I very much doubt you'll be able to stay vertical long enough to wear them."

"I'll wear them, and I'll stand on my own two feet when I do," Dan said.

"Why all this effort to become active again?" Cooley said.

"I don't know," Dan said.

"You don't know?"

"Something is driving me, but I don't know what it is."

"Not Hurd. He's in jail."

"Yeah, but it could be Chance Hurd. I have a feeling about him, a feeling I can't explain or shake. Whatever is coming down, he's at the center of it."

"Dan, I reckon this Hurd thing has you as nervous as a frog in a frying pan and it's making you imagine things," Cooley said.

"My nerves are just fine," Dan said. His face was flushed and sweaty as though he'd just ran a mile in the noonday sun. "Maybe Hurd's got friends who'll try to bust him out of jail . . . or it's something else. But when the trouble comes down, I want to be ready for it."

"I'll go get your duds," Cooley said. He stepped to the window. "The storm isn't easing any. In fact, I think it's getting worse." He picked up his lantern, walked to the door, and then turned and said, "Once more unto the breach . . . Deputy Sheriff Caine, you owe me."

Dan said, "More than you'll ever know, gambling man."

* * *

Clint Cooley emerged from the storm and returned to Dan Caine's room like the Sandman come to sprinkle slumber dust. "Blowing a gale out there," he said. He laid out a shirt, underwear, and socks on the bed.

"I guess Pete Doan considers you a bad credit risk because you weren't in the debt ledger. I had to start a new page, just for you."

Dan examined the nondescript collarless shirt, the fire engine red long johns, and woolen socks and then said, "I can't owe him much for these."

"To a man without money, any amount is too much," Cooley said. "Six dollars ought to cover it, but I didn't bother to check the prices. Look on the sunny side, Dan. When you pay Doan, he'll more than likely give you a ceegar."

"He's never done that before," Dan said.

"You've never gone in the tick book before," Cooley said.

The gambler watched Dan struggle into his clothes, helped him with his pants and boots, and when the other man was fully clothed and sitting, exhausted, on the bed again, he said, "Just where do you think you're going? It's the middle of the night, and the sandstorm is about to blow Thunder Creek fifty miles into the prairie."

"I'm not lying down on this damned bed again," Dan said. "Once my head hits the pillow, I'll never get up."

"So why get dressed? Hell, you're even wearing your gun, not that you can do much with it."

"I plan to be ready . . ."

"I know . . . for when some bad medicine comes down."

"You got it, Clint."

"Dan, you can barely stand. You look like a man who just hard wintered in a hollow log he shared with a bobcat."

"Come the day, I'll be on my feet."

"Suppose the day is tomorrow?"

"I'll be ready," Dan said. Then, more thoughtfully, "I have to be ready."

"Now look what you've done," Cooley said. "You've got blood on your nice new shirt that you bought on tick."

Dan looked down at his side where scarlet blood seeped from his wound. "Yeah, so I have," he said.

CHAPTER FIFTY-TWO

The storm blew itself out around three in the morning, and the stars became visible, the moon as round and bright as a new coin. The dust had settled and the air had been scrubbed clean, and out in the long grass the coyotes rose, shook themselves off, and yipped their hunger.

The sudden silence woke Ernie "Shorty" Key who'd been sleeping in Pete Doan's back room. Shorty rode for the Mustang Ranch and was a top hand, but he kept right poorly, or so he imagined, and had been in town to buy a supply of *Doyle's Dixie Tonic* that always made him feel better. Considering the medicine was 90 percent alcohol, that wasn't too surprising, but Shorty swore by the stuff and would accept no substitute.

Despite complaining about the state of his health to all who would listen, Shorty Key was by nature a happy-go-lucky puncher who had a seemingly inexhaustible supply of dirty stories about whores, brothels, madams, and preachers. But as he began the four-mile ride to the Mustang, he was seething with a fire-hot rage, incensed beyond measure, his fury painfully eating at him like a cancer. Shorty Key had never drawn down on a man in his twenty-three years of life, but that starry morning he was ready to kill.

Chance Hurd.

The name burned into his brain like a cherry-red branding iron.

Chance Hurd.

The two-gun braggart and bully who lorded it over the unarmed cowboys who came into town on Friday nights. The damned monster who'd dabbled his dirty paws in the blood of big Tom Calthrop and his family. The piece of human filth was now locked up in a cell in Thunder Creek and according to the townsfolk boasting that a judge would never convict him for being in cahoots with the outlaw Clay Kyle and having a hand in the Calthrop massacre.

Mike Sweet the blacksmith had told Shorty how Deputy Sheriff Dan Caine, a well-liked and respected young lawman, had turned vigilante and tracked Kyle to the Sierra del Carmen Mountains in Old Mexico where he'd destroyed him and his murderous gang.

"Hurd accused Caine of telling a pack of lies about Kyle," Sweet said. "But my daughter rode with Dan, and she doesn't lie."

Cowboy loyalties went deep, all the way to bedrock, and Tom Calthrop was a highly respected cattleman who had a reputation as a rancher who treated his punchers well and stood by his word. Such a man was worth avenging, and Shorty figured that's how the Mustang punchers would feel.

Shorty Key rode onto the Mustang an hour before sunup, and the hands were still snoring in the bunkhouse. He had no need to wake them. His news could wait until the coffee was saucered and blowed and they were prepared to listen.

Shorty stripped his pony, brushed him down, and then made his way to the cookhouse. The cook's name was

Idaho Barnes and the word around the ranch was that he never slept. An intuitive man, Barnes seldom initiated a conversation with a puncher in the morning when the average hand was as sparing of words as a rich young widow at her ancient husband's funeral.

The cook stepped out of his kitchen, tossed away a basin of soapy water, and saw Shorty coming from the barn. He had a cup of coffee ready when the little puncher stepped inside and said his howdy.

After Shorty worked on his coffee and then built and lit a cigarette, he said, "I got news from town."

Barnes was surprised. He handed Shorty a warm biscuit and said, "I never knowed Thunder Creek to make any news."

Shorty wiped crumbs off his mustache and said, "Big news."

Bacon sputtered in the pan, beans simmered in a cast iron Dutch oven, and coffee biled. The cookhouse was very hot, like an annex of hell.

"It's about Sheriff Hurd," Shorty said.

"What now? Did he shoot somebody?" Barnes said.

"In a manner of speakin' . . . yes," Shorty said.

Barnes used a dishrag to lift the lid of the Dutch oven, stirred his beans with a wooden spoon, and then said, "Spill, Shorty."

"I was gonna wait until the boys have et."

"Then wait."

"Hell, I reckon I can tell you first, Mr. Barnes, you being the cook an' all."

"I reckon you can, me being the cook an' all."

And Shorty told him.

Barnes seemed to take the news in stride, silently fussing over his breakfast vittles, not looking at Shorty. Then he took a deep breath as though he suddenly needed air and said, "One time I worked as a trail cook for Charlie Goodnight and he loaned me out to Tom Calthrop for one drive, repaying a favor. Big Tom was a gentleman, a kind man, always making jokes and laughing, and he'd talk forever about his young'uns, the funny things they done and said and about how proud he was of them, stuff like that. You know that trail cooks like nobody?"

"Yeah, I heard that," Shorty said, being diplomatic.

"Well, I liked Tom Calthrop. I liked him a lot."

Barnes busied himself with his cooking, his talking done for now, but his wide, florid face wrinkled in thought. Shorty took the hint and stepped outside with his coffee, smoking cigarettes, waiting for the hands to stir. The long night slowly brightened into morning, and the sky was aflame, burning away the stars.

As men coughed and stumbled into the bunkhouse Shorty said finally, "Mr. Barnes, every puncher from miles around will be in the courthouse when Hurd goes on trial, depend on that."

The cook's silence finally erupted into noisy anger. "What trial?"

"The Hurd trial," Shorty said.

"And see that damned lowlife walk out the door a free man, arm in arm with a fast-talking lawyer?" Barnes said. Shorty couldn't come up with an answer and the cook said, "There ain't gonna be a trial."

"But . . . but Hurd's in jail," Shorty said.

"I know where he is," Barnes said.

"But a circuit judge will . . ."

"I said there won't be a trial. If what you've told me is right, Hurd is as guilty as hell. And that don't surprise me none. I always took him for a snake."

"I said it how it is," Shorty said. Then it slowly dawned on him. "Mr. Barnes . . . no trial. Are you talking vigilantes?"

Barnes said, "I'm talking justice . . . justice for Tom Calthrop and his family. Yeah, we'll become vigilantes if that's what it takes."

Eight Mustang hands with their foreman, a hard-eyed, dour man named Burt Wells who numbered among his friends the equally morose Frank James, gathered in the cookhouse to eat breakfast. It was there that Shorty Key lit the fire and Idaho Barnes fanned the flames of cowboy wrath.

Wells slammed his fist on the dining table so hard the salt and pepper shakers jumped, and said, "I always knew there was something crooked about Chance Hurd. He was always a damned bully who talked big until he faced somebody a sight meaner than himself. Then he backed down pretty damn fast."

"Burt, remember that night at Doan's when Hurd got drunk and waved a revolver around and said he planned on killing a cowboy for breakfast?" a young puncher said. "You put the crawl on him."

"Yeah, I recollect," Wells said.

"You told him to get to using the Colt or put it back in the scabbard, pronto!" the puncher said. "He said he was only funning and holstered that gun mighty quick."

"All gurgle and no guts. He's yellow," Wells said.

Idaho Barnes wanted the hands to stay focused on the Calthrop killings. He needed a hanging mob, not just a bunch of riled-up cowboys.

"Hurd said if he's charged with having a hand in the Calthrop family massacre, he'll walk free from the court,"

Barnes said. "He's telling everybody in Thunder Creek that they can't convict him because they don't have a shred of proof. He says Deputy Caine is spreading lies about him."

As Cornelius Massey later wrote in his newspaper, two things conspired to seal Chance Hurd's fate that morning: Dan Caine was liked by both ranchers and punchers while Hurd was universally detested. And secondly, there's a thin, fragile line between an angry crowd and a mob.

It was Friday, pay day. The night punchers from the surrounding ranches crowded into Doan's store to drink their wages. Idaho Barnes had experienced out-of-control mobs before and he knew they were easily led. Raw whiskey was kerosene thrown on a fire of cowboy resentment of Chance Hurd . . . and the resulting blaze of hatred and madness would consume them.

CHAPTER FIFTY-THREE

Dan Caine rested on top of his bed most of the night and come morning got up and rubbed his stubbled chin, wishful for a razor. He looked in the mirror, didn't like what he saw, and moved to the window. Thunder Creek was busy with the dawn. Three matrons with shopping baskets over their arms headed toward Doan's store, and Estella Sweet and Jenny Calthrop, the Estella-adoring Holt Peters in tow, were just leaving on a morning ride. Timothy Bean, dressed in a gray ditto suit and plug hat, left the boardinghouse and stepped rapidly in the direction of the general store, no doubt hunting coffee and breakfast. He was the only man in town who looked nervous just walking.

Someone rapped sharply on the hotel room door.

Dan drew his gun and then said, "Come in. Slow."

"I can't. My hands are full."

Clint Cooley's voice.

"Full of what?" Dan said.

"Hell, man, I brought you breakfast," Cooley said. "Open up before it all gets cold."

Dan opened the door and Cooley stepped inside. "Bacon, eggs, sourdough bread, and coffee," he said. "I've been slaving all morning in the kitchen. Where do you want the tray?"

"On the bed. What kitchen?"

"Ma's boardinghouse kitchen. She ain't around to cook breakfast anymore, remember?"

Dan eyed the tray. "I'm hungry."

"Three fried eggs and about a pound of bacon. Dig in. How are you feeling?"

"Death warmed over and in some pain."

"Good. I'm glad you're feeling better," Cooley said. "Now eat. I always took you for an over easy man. I hope you really do like your eggs that way."

"Where did you learn to cook?" Dan said, picking up his fork.

"At my first mistress's naked knee," Cooley said.

Dan Caine sopped up egg yolk with the last of his bread and said, chewing, "You cook good, Clint." Then, "How is Hurd?"

Cooley shrugged. "I don't know. Still in the hoosegow, I guess."

"I've got to ask Pete Doan how we get a circuit judge here," Dan said.

Cooley said, "In the meantime I don't suppose Hurd is going anywhere."

"Not if I can help it."

"You look like hell," Cooley said.

"Thank you."

"When I come back, I'll bring you a razor and maybe some lavender water. You'll still feel bad but you'll smell better."

"What day is this?" Dan said.

"Friday."

"The cowboys come into Doan's tonight."

"You stay away from there," Cooley said. "You're not fit to handle a bunch of punchers if things get rowdy."

"Pete Doan can manage," Dan said. "He always has."

"Tonight, I'll bring my checkerboard over," Cooley said. "A few games will keep you from being bored."

"I don't play checkers," Dan said. "Bring a pack of cards and we'll play poker."

"Do you know how to play poker?"

"Of course."

Cooley shook his head. "It will be like taking candy from a baby."

Chance Hurd sat on the uncomfortable iron cot in his cell, an untouched plate of bacon and beans on the floor at his feet. He scowled as he searched his brain, trying to remember if any of the outlaws with whom he'd done business in the past were still in the area . . . men who'd shoot up this hick town and bust him out.

Lucas Sunday . . . no, he'd been running with Tom Warner and them east of the Colorado for the past couple of years.

John Lorne . . . hung.

Ben Koch . . . hung.

Eli Chaney . . . shot by Texas Rangers.

Benny Home . . . doing twenty in Huntsville.

John Shivers . . . present location unknown, maybe hung.

Hurd gave it up. Even if any of them were still around, how could he get word to them? And there was the time factor, depending on when the circuit judge got to Thunder Creek.

Angry, frustrated, Hurd rose from the cot and grabbed the bars of his cell. "Let me out of here!" he yelled. "You hicks have locked up an innocent man." He paused for breath and shouted, "Put Dan Caine in here! He murdered Ma Lester, not me."

No one in Thunder Creek heard Chance Hurd that morning, and if they had they would've ignored him. In people's minds, the big, blustering sheriff was as guilty as hell, and there was an end to it.

CHAPTER FIFTY-FOUR

The coming dark had thinned the daylight to the color of tin, and Cooley lit the oil lamp in Dan Caine's room. He smiled. "Eighteen games of five card stud and you only won two. You're surely a disgrace to the gambling profession, Deputy Caine."

"I think you cheated," Dan said.

"And you're a sore loser," Cooley said. "You know I always play fair when I've got a winning hand."

Dan tossed his cards onto the bed. "I don't want to play anymore. Looking at all those damned kings and queens and knaves gave me a headache."

"Next time I'll deal you a sight fewer of those," Cooley said. Then, after studying Dan's ashen face, "Not feeling so good, are you?"

"The pain in my side gives me no rest, like a hungry gopher is gnawing at me," Dan said. "Susan Stanton sure knew where to put a bullet."

"You look tired," Cooley said.

"Tired? I feel like I've been run down, run over, and wrung out," Dan said.

"And here I am beating you like a drum at poker when you should be in bed."

"I'm staying awake, Clint," Dan said. "I still feel something mighty bad is coming down . . . soon . . . like it's just over the horizon and headed my way."

"Well, whatever it is, I'll side you, just like I did in the mountains," Cooley said.

Dan shook his head. "Not this time, Clint. Hurd is in jail, and now I'm the only law in Thunder Creek. I'll handle it."

"Not when your misery has you feeling so poorly," Cooley said.

"Let me rest this damned aching head for a spell and I'll be fine," Dan said. "Whatever it is coming at me, I got it to do. And I mean alone."

"As you say, Deputy Sheriff Caine," Cooley said. "But if you need me . . ."

"Don't worry, I'll squeal like a piglet caught under a gate," Dan said.

After Clint Cooley left, Dan lay back on his pillows, closed his eyes, and dozed.

He'd been asleep for two hours when the cowboys came to town.

Doan tried to calm things down, even giving the twenty punchers a round on the house, something he did only once a year on Independence Day.

But he bucked a stacked deck.

Idaho Barnes and Shorty Key worked the crowd, whipping them into a frenzy of loathing for Chance Hurd and all he stood for. Barnes played up the murders of the Calthrop family and the sheriff's hand in it.

"Hurd and Clay Kyle planned the whole thing," Barnes said. "Hurd was convinced Tom Calthrop had a large sum of money in the house, and Kyle damn near burned his toes off trying to get Tom to tell where it was. But the Calthrops was broke, there was no money, and Tom died for it."

"Deputy Caine made Kyle pay for his crime when he killed him in the Sierra del Carmen Mountains," Shorty Key said. "But now Hurd thinks he'll walk free once the circuit judge gets here."

"I'm damned if he will," a cowboy said, a statement that was met with growls of approval.

"Shorty, where is the drummer?" Barnes said.

The little puncher smiled. "He's waiting outside under guard. He's afraid to come inside."

"No harm will come to him in Doan's," Barnes said. "Bring him in."

"He'll piss his pants for sure," Shorty said. "But I'll go get him."

A cowboy pushed a frightened little man into the store who was uneasily aware that he stood among mighty salty men with huge mustaches and angry faces.

"State your name and occupation," Barnes said.

"Timothy Bean. I'm a . . ."

"LOUDER!" Barnes roared.

"Tim . . . Tim . . . Timothy Bean. I'm . . . I'm . . . a traveling salesman," the little man said, no louder than before, but even more scared.

"And you were in Ma Lester's boardinghouse the day she was murdered," Barnes said, now that he'd well and truly intimidated his witness.

"Yes . . . yes, I was," Bean said, his face a picture of misery. "Oh, I do wish my lady wife was here."

"Pete, give Timothy a drink," a grinning puncher said.

"I don't drink," Bean said. "My lady wife always says, 'There's a serpent in every bottle and he biteth like the viper.'"

"She sounds like a woman with horse sense," Barnes said.

"Oh, she has," Bean said. "But she says I have none. Horse sense, I mean."

"A fine lady, no doubt," Barnes said. "Now tell these gentlemen what you saw and heard in the hallway when Ma Lester was murdered. Spread the gospel, Mr. Bean."

What Timothy Bean had to say came out in a rush, as though he wanted to get this ordeal over. "I saw Sheriff Hurd with his . . ."

"Slow down, Mr. Bean," Barnes said. "Damn it, man, take a deep breath and try again."

"Sorry, I'm of a most nervous disposition," Bean said.

Pete Doan, standing behind his counter that also served as a bar, intervened. "Just tell what you saw, Timothy. And take a chair."

Bean nodded and sat. "Well, I opened my hotel door a crack and saw Sheriff Hurd with his hands around Ma Lester's throat. I closed my door, and then I heard a shot."

"And that shot came after Deputy Caine tried to intervene but collapsed unconscious in the hallway from an earlier wound," Barnes said. "Hurd fired into Ma Lester, pressed Dan Caine's own revolver into his hand and then ran into the street to spread the word that the deputy had tried to rape the woman and had then shot her."

That last was greeted with a profound, stunned silence that slowly grew into savage growls of anger . . . the roar of the mob.

"Wait, just wait!" Doan yelled with great urgency. He froze, a bottle of whiskey in his hand and a bar towel draped over his left shoulder. "Mr. Bean, are you willing to testify at Hurd's trial? Will you tell the court what you saw?"

Bean swallowed hard several times and his fingers tied themselves in knots in his lap. He tried to talk, but all that came out was a squeak, a fearful rodent noise from a mousy little man.

Idaho Barnes said nothing, but his actions attracted the attention of every man present. Shorty Key would say later that it was a moment of truth that tested the resolve of the cowboys and dictated their future deeds. The cook stepped to the back of the store where ranch and farm supplies were displayed and took a coil of hemp rope from a hook on the wall. He ran about fifty feet of rope through his hands and then skillfully made a hangman's noose at one end. As a man who'd ridden with Captain William Clarke Quantrill during the late war, it was a thing he'd done before.

Barnes dangled the noose for all to see. "I say Chance Hurd has had his trial, right here in this room," he said. "Now let me hear the verdict."

To a man, the cowboys yelled, "Guilty!"

"Then let's hang the murderer," Burt Wells said, a man with darkness in him.

"No!" Doan said. "We must do this legally."

A cowboy said, "It is legal, Pete." He pushed the storekeeper aside. "Now get out of the way."

The cowboys spilled from the store and noisily headed for the sheriff's office. Barnes carried the noose as the moon cast a fragile, beautiful opalescent light on the scene . . . uncaring of the dark, violent doings of men.

CHAPTER FIFTY-FIVE

A fist pounded on Dan Caine's door, loud, demanding, panicked.

"Deputy Caine!"

Dan swung his legs off the bed and stood and swayed alarmingly before he found his footing. Gun in hand, he stepped to the door and said, "What's happened?"

"The cowboys!"

Dan recognized Pete Doan's voice and opened the door. "What about the cowboys?" he said.

"They're going to lynch Chance Hurd," Doan said. His gray face showed pain. "Vigilantes."

Dan brushed past Doan, walked down the stairs with the hesitancy of a wounded man and out onto the street. In the dark of night, with only a few street lanterns here and there to dispel the gloom, he heard the lynch mob first, a low roar seasoned with the laughter of raging men.

Running was beyond Dan Caine but he adopted a fast shuffle as he headed toward the crowd.

Surrounded by cowboys, Hurd was being dragged to a dead cottonwood on the bank of the dry creek that gave the town its name. Hurd, cursing his tormentors, struggled every step of the way. Blows rained down on him, and then the boots went in . . . vicious kicks to his legs and butt that bruised and hurt.

Dan angled across open ground to cut off the vigilantes, elbowing his way through the townspeople who gathered to watch the fun.

Dan drew his gun and fired a shot in the air that momentarily brought a halt to the festivities. For a moment, the punchers were distracted and a little uncertain at Deputy Sheriff Dan Caine's sudden appearance.

Then came an event so unexpected, so mindlessly violent, that no one could've anticipated it.

There are several versions of what happened that night, but the newspaper account by Cornelius Massey was probably the most accurate:

A LYNCHING SPOILED

The Cowboys Lament

Hurd Foils the Vigilantes

Deputy Sheriff Dan Caine's Cool Head Saves the Day

As a general rule, the *Gazette* does not wholeheartedly approve of vigilante justice, yet there are times when desperate times need desperate measures. We are referring, of course, to the recent attempted lynching by the cowboy element of former Sheriff Chance Hurd, a man who richly deserved such an ignominious fate.

This reporter, if I dare rise to that lofty aspiration, was present in situ when Hurd was dragged, with many a curse from his loathsome mouth, to the dreadful hanging tree where justice would be served.

But oh, sweet Jesu!

With one bound, Hurd, a tall and powerful man, broke free from his captors who were momentarily distracted by the sudden appearance of Deputy Caine. Hurd, that ravening wolf in law officer's clothing, drew a murderous knife from his boot and dashed at Deputy Caine and with many a vile oath, threatened to gut him like a fish.

Taking into consideration that Mr. Caine had earlier been grievously wounded by Hurd's cohorts and was feeling very poorly indeed, this eyewitness and many others were sure that that the young officer was a dead man, so ferocious and determined was Hurd's unexpected attack.

But Deputy Caine stood his ground, like a young David facing a dread Goliath. Displaying amazing speed and dexterity, that stalwart drew his pistol and commenced to firing. His first shot hit Goliath . . . er . . . Hurd and stopped him in his tracks. His second bullet staggered him and his third dropped him. Chance Hurd ate dirt for a few moments and then died.

Deputy Sheriff Caine then addressed the crowd thusly, "And so perishes any who would stoop so low as to kill their fellow men for monetary gain."

This speech brought forth a cheer from townspeople and vigilantes alike, and all that remains is the *Gazette* to now tip its hat and give Deputy Sheriff Caine a heartfelt Huzzah!

And a sincere, "Well done, sir."

Dan Caine watched Chance Hurd fall and then stood over him in the orange glow of lantern light provided by one of the onlookers.

Hurd's dying eyes looked up at him, and the man said, "I didn't know you could shoot like that."

"I'm learning," Dan said.

Then Hurd managed to utter his last, gasping words, "You're a son of a—"

"Damn right," Dan Caine said.

CHAPTER FIFTY-SIX

"Pete Doan said the town paid for Chance Hurd's burial," Dan Caine said. "Apart from the two chicken thieves who planted him, I was the only mourner."

"You mourned him?" Clint Cooley said.

"No. But I was there," Dan said. "For a spell it looked like rain."

"It didn't rain," Cooley said.

"No, it didn't."

The day was far gone, and the two men sat in the sheriff's office. Dan wore his deputy's star.

"I'm heading out tomorrow," Cooley said. "Going back to New Orleans. After all that's happened, I figure my luck has changed."

"I appreciate what you did for me, Clint," Dan said. "You and the others. Fish Lee and Professor Latchford and Miss Prunella . . . I'll never forget their sacrifice."

Cooley waved a negligent hand. "I was glad to be of help, and like you I'll always remember our dead." He smiled. "On a happier note, Jenny Calthrop got a letter by the Patterson stage. The army surgeon who saved your life is coming with his daughter to Thunder Creek to take her back to Fort Concho. Estella Sweet told me Jenny is very excited about starting her new life. And talking about Estella, she and Holt Peters are walking out together and talking marriage. Young Holt gave up on his plan to become a drover and signed on with Mike Sweet as an apprentice blacksmith." He smiled. "Estella and Holt make a handsome couple."

"Yes, they do," Dan said. "I'm happy for them and for Jenny. She went through it. By the way, the Kiowa left early this morning. He rode up to the window, gave me a wave, and then was gone. I didn't get a chance to thank him. Or pay him, either."

"The Kiowa will do all right," Cooley said.

"I sure hope so," Dan said. "Pete Doan has kinfolk all over the country, including Florida, and he gave the Kiowa the name of a businessman cousin of his in Pensacola. Doan gave the Kiowa a letter of introduction and he says his kin will help him find his wife."

"Then let's hope he does," Cooley said, "The Indian played a man's part in the Sierra del Carmen. I set store by him."

Dan got busy with the makings of a smoke and said, "I hope you're a big success in New Orleans, Clint. I really mean that," Dan said.

"Well, first I aim to get reacquainted with a certain countess I loved and left, and secondly pay homage to a voodoo priestess named Elena Maria Brussette and ask her to cast a spell on me."

"What kind of spell?" Dan said, lighting his cigarette. "And I've no idea what a voodoo priestess is."

"Elena Maria Brussette is a kind of witch," Cooley said. "She'll cast a spell on me for gambling luck, that is if she's forgiven and forgotten that I shot one of her lovers in the Silver Hat Club on Christmas Eve about four or five years back. I didn't kill him, but I put him on his back for a while."

Dan shook his head and smiled. "Clint, sometimes you have some mighty strange notions."

"New Orleans is a mighty strange place," Cooley said. "Maybe that's why I love her so much." He rose to his feet and said, "I'm not one for long goodbyes, so I'll quit right here." He stuck out his hand and Dan took it.

Cooley stepped to the door and then stopped and said, "What about you, Dan, will you stay on as the law in Thunder Creek? Hey, did they ever give you your back pay?"

"No. Apparently Doan gave it to Hurd and he spent it. Didn't do him much good, did it?" Dan said. "Like you, I'm moving on, Clint. There's nothing to keep me here but bad memories. I'll ride out just as soon as the town finds another sheriff." He patted the head of the calico cat that intently studied him with its golden gaze. "Well, me and the Calthrop cat," he said.

Cooley said, "If you need a grubstake . . ."

Dan reached into his pocket and produced a gold coin. "This is the British sovereign the Sheik gave me. It will see me through."

"Where will you go?" Cooley said.

Dan Caine waved a vague hand to the east.

"Yonder," he said.

TURN THE PAGE FOR AN EXCITING PREVIEW!

MONTANA

**Two Families. Six Generations.
One Stretch of Land.
A Bold New Saga Centuries in the Making.**

An exciting new series from the bestselling Johnstones celebrates the hardworking residents of Cutthroat County: the ranchers who staked their claims, the lawmen who risked their lives, and the descendants who carried their dreams into the twenty-first century.

Bordered by the Blackfeet Reservation to the north and mountain ranges to the east and west, Cutthroat County is seven hundred glorious square miles of Big Sky grandeur. For generations, the Maddox and Drew families have ruled the county—often at odds with each other. Today, Ashton Maddox runs the biggest Black Angus ranch in the country, while County Sheriff John T. Drew upholds the law like his forefathers did more than a century ago. A lot has changed since the county was established in 1891. But some things feel straight out of the 1800s. Especially when cows start disappearing from the ranches . . .

Intrigued, a local newsman digs up the gun-blazing tale of the land-grabbing battles fought by Maddox's and Drew's ancestors. Meanwhile, their present-day descendants face a new kind of war that's every bit as bloody. When a rival rancher's foreman is found shot to death, Ashton Maddox is the prime suspect. Sheriff Drew is pressured into arresting him, in spite of a lack of evidence. So the two families decide to do what their forefathers did so many years ago: join forces against a common enemy. Risk their skins against all odds. And keep the dream of Montana alive for generations to come . . .

National Bestselling Authors
William W. Johnstone and J.A. Johnstone

MONTANA

On sale wherever Pinnacle Books are sold.
Live Free. Read Hard.
www.williamjohnstone.net
Visit us at www.kensingtonbooks.com

PROLOGUE

*From the May issue of Big Sky Monthly Magazine
By Paula Schraeder*

The bestselling T-shirt for tourists at Wantlands Mercantile in Basin Creek has an image of a colorful trout in the center circle and these words on the front.

WELCOME TO CUTTHROAT COUNTY

*We're Named After Montana's
State Fish*

But on the back is the image of a tough-looking, bearded cowboy wearing an eyepatch and biting down on a large knife blade, with these words below.

But WATCH Your Back

Yes, this is Cutthroat County, all 1,197 square miles, according to the US Geological Survey's National Geospatial Program, with 31.2 of those square miles water. According to the 2020 US Census Bureau, the county's population is a healthy 397, though the sunbaked, silver-headed lady working the counter at Wantlands Mercantile when I dropped in on a windy but wonderfully sunny June afternoon told me differently. "Oh, 'em guvment volunteers mighta missed a coupla dozen or so. Folks live here 'cause they've lived here all their lives. Or they come because—"

I waited. Finally, I had to ask, "Why do folks come here?"

"To hide," she said.

Having been in Cutthroat County for three days, I know there must be roughly 1,130 square miles (not including the 31.2 miles of water) for anyone to hide.

It seemed like a good place to hide.

And getting to Basin Creek wasn't easy.

I left Billings early in the morning in my Toyota Camry, winding through plenty of Big Sky country, and after hitting the turnoff north at Augusta, I drove and drove and drove, with nothing to see but pastures and open country.

Aside: A truck driver at a Great Falls coffee shop on my way back home laughed when he heard my story.

"Was it at night?" he asked.

"No, sir," I told him.

"You should drive through there at night. It's like you're in a [expletive] bowl." He sipped his latte. "Liked to've sent me to the looney bin a time or two."

Back to my trip: Finally, reaching a crossroads store, I stopped for coffee and confirmation. "Is this the right way to Basin Creek?" I asked the young Native man who rang me up.

"Yes." He took my money.

He must have read the skepticism on my face. Then he smiled, titled his head north, and confirmed it. "Just keep going that way, and drive till you reach the end of the earth."

Cutthroat County is bordered by the Blackfeet Indian Reservation on the north, the Ponoká (Elk) Mountains to the east, the Always Winter mountain range on the west, and US Highway 103 on the south. If you are driving to Glacier National Park or the Canadian entry point at Milk River City, it's a good idea to take your potty break at Basin Creek. Maybe top off the gas tank as well. (That crossroads station I stopped at on the drive north has no gasoline for sale, and I did not have courage enough to use the outhouse.) There are only two gas stations in Cutthroat County, and both are in Basin Creek.

"That's not exactly true," I was later told.

"Roscoe Moss has a pump at Crimson Feather [a community of four trailers and a ranch far to the east of where owner Garland Foster has brought in wind turbines]. At least when the Conoco truck driver—there's a refinery in Billings, you know—remembers to stop on the first of the month. 'Course, old Roscoe's prices are higher than a loan shark's interest rates, and his pump is slower than spring getting here."

The speaker, a handsome man of slightly above average height, dark hair flecked with gray, and the darkest eyes I've ever seen, paused to sip coffee—black (his third cup since I'd been interviewing him)—and appeared to be counting the other gas pumps.

"And most ranchers and mining companies have their own pumps," he continued. "Though some stopped after they had to dig up their old pumps and haul them away. EPA thing, if I remember right." His smile was disarming. "But you're too young to remember leaded gasoline."

He did not appear to be flirting. But he sure was charming.

"If you run out of gas, there's a pretty good chance someone will top you off with enough to get you to East Glacier. Maybe as far as Cut Bank." The disarming man was John T. Drew, Cutthroat County sheriff, one of those fellows *"who's lived here all their lives."*

"Well," he politely corrected, "if you don't count four-and-a-half years in Bozeman." He points to the Montana State University diploma—criminal justice—on the wall to the right of the window overlooking the county courthouse grounds.

Those four and a half years might be the only period of time when any Drew male had not dined, slept, and worked in Cutthroat County since long before Cutthroat County was carved out of Choteau County in 1891. I pointed out the first Maddox to set foot in Cutthroat County was a mountain man—perhaps *seven, eight, nine generations ago.*

Drew smiled and shrugged—"I've never figured the math"—then nodded at the diploma. "Math's why it took me an extra semester to get that sheepskin on the wall."

"Do people hide here?" I asked.

"People escape here," he said, the smile still warm. "Tourists come here to fly-fish for cutthroat trout or to pick up one of those T-shirts Maudie sells by the scores during peak season. The three hundred and ninety-seven folks who call this patch of heaven home live here because they love it. Because this country's in their blood. The air's clean. The water's pure. And if you don't mind a whole lot of winter most years, it's a good place to call home."

Sixty years ago, Cutthroat County made national headlines for being the last of the Old West towns. The sprawling Maddox Ranch, now headed by Ashton Maddox, was likened to the Ponderosa of TV's *Bonanza*. The county

sheriff then—John Drew's grandfather—was called a real
Matt Dillon, the character played by James Arness in the
long-running western series *Gunsmoke*.

Tourists from across the world flocked to Cutthroat
County not just to go trout fishing in America but to see
the wildest Wild West. A Montana state tourism guide
raved about four guest ranches—three of which boasted to
be real, working ranches—and a restored historic hotel.
Two stables offered guided horseback rides along the
county's myriad peaks, valleys, and creeks. A plan was to
turn part of the long abandoned railroad tracks, originally
laid in the 1890s, into an Old West tourism train complete
with a coal-powered locomotive and mock gunfights and
train robberies.

That boom lasted slightly less than a decade.

A few years later, Cutthroat County, and especially
Basin Creek, got statewide attention and a joke on *The
Tonight Show* [though I have been unable to confirm it
since there's no video on YouTube] as a speed trap.

Drew laughed at that memory. "Well, the town speed
limit was thirty-five, and my daddy did not like speeders.
Maybe because his daddy preferred riding a horse than
driving that Ford Galaxy. We have Ford Police Interceptor
SUVs now, by the way. But we're getting some pressure
from the state to move to hybrids. If we get another electric
charging unit, we might go for that. But that's up to the
county. And the annual budget."

Today, no 1890s train runs through Basin Creek. There
aren't even any iron rails anymore. The only electric-
charging station in the county is at my motel, though the
Wantlands Mercantile is investigating the costs and reli-
ability of adding one in the next two years. The restored
historic hotel burned down twenty-five years ago. The site
is home to the cinder block Wild Bunch Casino, where

cowboys, sheepherders, townspeople, and a few passing tourists drink beer and play video poker, video keno, video blackjack, video slots, while Chuckie Corvallis serves up food. The day's special was $7.99 for Tater-Tot Casserole.

I opted for coffee and the soup of the day, cream of mushroom, probably straight from a can.

There's a NO SMOKING sign on the outside door, but Chuckie Corvallis was lighting a new filterless Pall Mall with the one he'd just burned down to almost nothing.

"It's my place," he said when he noticed my questioning, healthy-lung face. "I own this place. I can smoke if I wanna. Nobody else can. Ain't my law. It's the [expletive] feds."

Aside: By the time our interview was over, I had to race back to my motel room, shower twice, and find a laundromat to rid my clothes of tobacco stink.

"What happened to Basin Creek?" I asked Corvallis.

"The [expletive] government. [Expletive] feds. [Expletive expletives]. Folks stopped carin' 'bout their country. Hippies. Freaks. Now it's the [expletive expletives] and their [expletive] ignoramus politics. [Expletive] 'em." He pulled hard on his cigarette and blew smoke. "Pardon my [expletive] French."

Both town stables have been paved over. On one site sits my quaint motel.

Things, however, are changing in Basin Creek.

A month before my arrival, newcomer Elison Dempsey announced his candidacy for Cutthroat County sheriff—a position that has been held almost exclusively by Drews since the county's founding. Dempsey heads the Citizens Action Network, a quasi-military vigilante group, which MSNBC said nothing is "quasi" about it. Dempsey has been getting plenty of press, statewide, regionally, and nationally.

Tan, clean-shaven, his dark hair buzzed in crew-cut fashion, and white teeth, he looks like he might have been an Olympic track star or boxer. Smiling after I told him that, he corrected me.

"I might have done well in the biathlon. I'm a great skier, downhill or cross-country. Out here, it's good to be able to ski. Winters can be long, and skiing sure beats snow-shoeing when it's forty below zero. But I am an excellent marksman. Rifle. Shotgun. 45. automatic."

A Colt .45 was holstered on his hip. The rack behind him in his massive four-wheel-drive Ford carries a lever-action Winchester, a twelve-gauge pump shotgun, and a lethal-looking assault rifle, perhaps an AK-47. I don't know. And I don't want to ask.

"I do have a concealed carry permit," he assures me when he notices my focus on the automatic pistol. "You can ask our soon-to-be ousted sheriff." He chuckles. "All the members of C.A.N. have concealed carry permits, too. But as you can see, we *conceal* nothing."

Dempsey volunteered to take me on a tour of Cutthroat County. His truck gets eight miles a gallon, he said, but told me not to worry.

The gas container in the bed of the Ford looks like it could refill an aircraft carrier.

"The problem here," he said as he slowed down and pulled off the road, "is that two men run this county." He nods at a gate on the left. The arched sign above the dirt road reads *Maddox Cattle Company*. An encircled *M*—a brand well recognized across Montana—hangs just below the company's name.

"There's one of them. Ashton thinks he's God," Dempsey said. "Maddoxes have been gods here for too long. Maddoxes and Drews. It's time for someone to put both of those gods in their place."

Dempsey wore a camouflage T-shirt that appeared painted to his chest and upper arms. It was not a tourist

T-shirt from Wantlands Mercantile, but a red, white, and blue Citizens Action Network T-shirt.

CUTTHROAT COUNTY

C.A.N.!

WE WILL!

Citizens Action Network

He flexed his muscles and grinned, showing those white teeth. "And I happen to be Zeus, Hercules, and Apollo rolled into one."

For the record, Ashton Maddox declined my multiple interview requests.

"Who's the other god?" I asked.

He snorted. "You just spent a couple hours with him in the sheriff's office. You know that. For more than a century—two centuries really—this county has been all Drew and all Maddox. I'm here to change that. And I will. For the better."

Several miles up the road, we turned onto another two-track. An hour later, I was thinking *No one's going to find my body. Ever!*

Dempsey finally stopped, rolled down his window, and nodded at a ramshackle building. "Here's another problem nobody seems to want to fix."

Figuring it was abandoned, I stared at the *house*, if that's the right word. One wall was made of straw bales. The rest that I could see appeared to be made of anything and everything someone could throw together. Wooden crates. Driftwood. Broken two-by-fours. Cans. Cinder-blocks. Dirt. The window—singular—was apparently made of Coke bottles and Mason jars.

"Someone lives there?" I finally asked.

"If you call that living," Dempsey answered.

I was about to ask what someone who lived there does. Maybe it was a line camp for Ashton Maddox. Then I remembered the lady at Wantlands Mercantile.

They hide.

"You've heard of folks wanting to live off the grid?" Dempsey asked.

"Sure, but—"

"You can't get farther off the grid than Cutthroat County and fifteen miles off the highway." Dempsey shifted the gear into first and we pulled away.

"He's not so bad. I mean, he likely paid money for four or five acres. Land's cheap here. This ain't Livingston or Missoula. If he's registered to vote, I like him. He can vote for me come November. I don't care what party he belongs to. See, I'm running as an independent. I like all folks, those who don't break the law, I mean. Maybe he grows a little grass. Does some illegal trapping. There's a good crick four miles northeast. Poaches a pronghorn or takes an elk out of season. I don't know. Maybe he's like you. Wants to be a real writer. A real Louis L'Amour."

I let him know. "I am a *real* writer."

A half hour later, he stopped again. "Here's another problem," he said, pointing at another rundown trailer home. "The dude that lives here is a poacher. See, that good-looking deputy that Drew got himself, she was pulling off the road a deer that got hit by a tourist on the way back from Glacier. This dude comes by in that Jap rig and asked if he could take the deer carcass. Deputy Mary Broadbent let him. That's illegal.

"This isn't deer season. She broke the law. Broadbent, I mean. When I heard of it, I told Drew. He didn't do a thing. So I called Trent, the local game warden here. He didn't do a thing. Because if Ashton Maddox isn't ruling Cutthroat County, John T. Drew is."

We drove back to the main highway, and headed back to Basin Creek. When we saw two hitchhikers, Dempsey swore, blew the horn, and floored the rig, sending the lean man and tall woman jumping over the ditch and almost falling against the barbed-wire fence.

"That's another problem," Dempsey said after he stopped laughing. "Blackfeet Indians keep coming down here, taking jobs away from folks who live here and want to work."

I didn't bring up the fact that Cutthroat County covers what once was Blackfeet country and that anyone has the right to work anyplace in America.

He had to slow down when we found ourselves behind a semi hauling cattle.

"And there's the final biggest problem in Cutthroat County. I aim to fix it once I send John T. Drew to pasture," Dempsey said.

I smelled cattle manure over diesel.

"You won't believe this, lady, but this spring, we had a report of rustling here. Cattle rustling. Just like you'd see in an old movie on Channel 16."

"Rustling?"

He nodded, then named his suspects, but I left them out of this article. My editor and publisher have a policy that they don't want to be sued for libel.

Elison Dempsey said he had reached out to George Grimes, a noted Texas Ranger recently retired, and the subject of last year's action movie titled *Beretta Law*. He asked him to join C.A.N. as a stock detective, but fears the fee George Grimes demands is far more than C.A.N. can afford.

Grimes could not be reached for comment.

"Is rustling why Garland Foster put up wind turbines on his ranch?" I asked.

"Foster is a fool" was all Dempsey would say. "He won't vote for me. But he'll be the only one."

When I reach Garland Foster by telephone, he laughed when I asked for a response to being called a fool. "Been called worse, little lady." He still reaps millions from his Florida condos and myriad business interests in Texas, many Great Plains states, and in Mexico, Central and South America. He moved from southern Texas after the death of his wife four years ago.

Dempsey isn't the only person who has criticized Foster.

"Ashton Maddox hates my guts," Foster said with another chuckle. "But it's not my fault his granddaddy had to sell off part of that big ol' Circle M spread during the Great Depression. I just happened to have a few million bucks to spend and thought Montana would sure beat the heat in Florida, Texas, and Mexico. I didn't know a blasted thing about Sacagawea Pasture when I paid cash for eleven sections [7,040 acres] of real estate."

Sacagawea Pasture, according to legend once the property of Maddoxes and Drews, has a name that dates to the 1840s, but the Maddox and Drew names go back even further in Montana lore and legend and actual history.

So why, I asked, is a longtime cattle rancher turning to wind turbines?

"More sheep than cattle," he corrected. "Least for the past coupla years. Wind turbines don't smell like cattle or sheep, and while beef and wool prices fluctuate, the wind always blows in this country."

"What about rustling?" I ask.

Foster laughed. "Nobody's rustled one of my turbines yet."

Back in town, John T. Drew confirmed there had been one report of rustling on a small ranch. He and both deputies were investigating. "Not to sound like a fellow running for public office, but I cannot comment further because this is an active investigation." He smiled that disarming smile again.

"Elison Dempsey says he has offered his Citizens Action Network volunteers to help with your investigation," I told him.

The sheriff nodded. "Elison Dempsey says lots of things. Offers a lot of things. Most of them I ignore. No, I reckon I ignore anything Dempsey says. But I did tell him and some of his C.A.N. folks they are welcome to volunteer for the county's search and rescue team.

"There's a lot of country for hikers, hunters, and anglers to get lost in," he explained, "and a lot of my time as county sheriff is spent searching and rescuing, not citing speeders who think all Montana highways are autobahns."

I asked about the controversy with Mary Broadbent, game warden Ferguson C. Trent, and the deer given to a so-called squatter.

"Deputy Broadbent told that man he could have the deer as long as he told the game warden about it the next morning, which he did." Drew smiled. "No sense in letting good deer meat rot when it could feed a family for a week. I'm partial to backstrap myself."

That was confirmed by Trent of the state Department of Fish, Wildlife and Parks. Not the backstrap part. But that the taker of the deer did call Warden Trent about taking the roadkill for many suppers.

Drew stared at me. "This place can still be the frontier."

I asked about Mary Broadbent, who, like Ashton Maddox, declined to talk to me for this article.

The sheriff's smile was gone, and the eyes again hardened. "She's a good deputy."

I looked around the office and kept looking.

"You look confused, Miss Schraeder," he said politely.

I was. "Do you have a dispatcher? I mean, where do calls come in? If you're patrolling how do you—"

"Nine-one-one calls go to Cut Bank in Glacier County. Those are relayed here." The smile returned. "We're small. But we are efficient."

"Do you think you'll win reelection?"

"That's up to the voters."

"Are things changing in Cutthroat County?" I asked.

"Nothing ever stays the same." The look on his face tells me he's okay with change . . . unlike some Westerners I've interviewed over the years. "We've never been on CNN or *Face the Nation* or NPR till recently. That takes some getting used to. But if that brings us some tourist dollars that won't hurt us. We thank *Big Sky Monthly Magazine* for sending you here.

"Just remind your readers we indeed have speed limits. If you speed here, you'll get pulled over. And fined. And if you commit a major crime, there's one thing you need to know."

"What's that?"

There was that smile again. "The judge might not be in town for some time. Our jail holds ten comfortably. But it's like any jail anywhere. It loses its uniqueness after a few hours."

The jail is in the basement of the combination county courthouse and town hall, a rectangular two-story building of limestone that is dwarfed by Basin Creek's biggest structure, a leaning wooden granary next to the old depot in what is called Killone Memorial Park.

Abe Killone was a rancher who paid out of his own pocket for the construction of the county courthouse. He was murdered on the streets of Basin Creek in 1917.

Except for the bathrooms, the entire eastern wing of the first floor holds the county library. Several rooms labeled storage, and town-related government offices (or desks) are also on the first floor.

Mayor Sabrina Richey, tax assessor Henry Richey, and constable Derrick Taylor, though he likes to call himself the town marshal. His hours are the same as the county's justice of the peace, 9:00 a.m.–noon Mondays, and 1:00–4:00 p.m. Thursdays.

Other kiosks are scattered across the western side of the dark building for the school superintendent, clerk, and recorder, while the county's road department, treasurer, and assessor have their own offices.

"They keep the important stuff downstairs," librarian Phyllis Lynne told me. "So people don't have to walk up those stairs."

Don't worry. The building is ADA compliant. An elevator at the far corner was completed in 1992. County Manager Dan O'Riley told me, "It runs like it was put in in 1492."

His offices are upstairs, along with Sheriff Drew's and the three elected county commissioners, chairwoman Grace Gallagher, Sid Pritchard, and Mack "Yes, it's my real name. Wanna see my birth certificate?" McDonald. They are responsible for the hiring of all nonelected county officers, including the county coroner and county attorney. Cutthroat County went to a county commissioner management style in 1948.

Most of the second floor covers what's officially called the Cutthroat County Courthouse Basin Creek Municipal Building, even if the court is hardly used . . . for trials, anyway. Town hall meetings are sometimes held there, and the public school put on a presentation of *Inherit the Wind* three years ago.

The clerk, James Alder, says the last criminal case tried was six months ago. "Connie Good Stabbing stole a truck to get back to the rez. Well, she said she borrowed it. Dom Purcell pressed charges. But they reached a plea deal while the jury was deliberating. So everybody was happy. The jurors got paid for their time, Connie had to paint the Catholic church here in town and pay Malone a 'rental fee' and reimburse him for gas."

I stared at him, and expected to wake up in front of an *Andy Griffith* rerun on MeTV.

"It's not always this tame," John T. Drew said when I found my way back to his office. "And it's a long way from Mayberry."

There have been four deaths over the past eighteen months, two in traffic accidents (neither involving alcohol), one hiker who met up with a bear in the Ponoká range, and this past December, a cowboy on Garland Foster's ranch was killed while working alone. Apparently he was killed in what the coroner called "a horse wreck."

The coroner, George J. White, by the way, does not live in Cutthroat County. He resides in Havre, Hill County seat and "a bit of a haul" from Basin Creek. The county attorney lives in Choteau, Teton County seat and "not as far away as Havre," attorney Murdoch Robeson tells me over the phone, "but it sure ain't close."

"Does that work?" I asked Dan O'Riley, who was standing in the doorway to the sheriff's office.

"It has to. Lawyers can't make a living in Cutthroat County. Coroners don't have much to do here, either."

I asked O'Riley why Elison Dempsey was talking about the need for his Citizens Action Network in a town and county like this. "He told me Cutthroat County needs a change and a lot of illegal activity goes unreported."

O'Riley laughed. "Most illegal activity goes unreported everywhere, miss. But how much illegal activity do you think you can find in a county of fewer than four hundred people?"

Dempsey also said he would reopen the investigation into the death of one of those traffic accidents. A single-car accident that claimed the life of forty-nine-year-old Cathy Drew, wife of Sheriff John T. Drew.

Disgusted as this makes me, I have to bring that up to the charming sheriff because those charges have been flying around the state–and on some cable news networks–since Mrs. Drew was found in her overturned Nissan Rogue on US Highway 103 between 12:30 and 4:15 a.m. on Friday, December 3, 2021. She was rushed to a Missoula hospital and pronounced dead on arrival.

Drew sighed. "US Highway, so Montana State Police troopers were the primary on that. They handled the investigation. Best guess is that she swerved, overcorrected. I'm a cop. I don't like best guesses. I'd like to know for sure what happened. But I have gotten mighty sick of Elison Dempsey and one of these days, he's going to wish he kept his mouth shut."

Dan O'Riley quickly changed the subject. "You read enough history books on Montana and you'll come across lots of names you'll still find on the list of registered voters."

"Like Drew and Maddox?" I asked.

"More than that," O'Riley said. "My ancestors came here in 1881. But I'm a newcomer. You don't read anything about Dempseys."

"There you have it," Elison Dempsey yelled when I met him at the Busted Stirrup Bar in Basin Creek. "If your roots don't go back to fur trappers and cattle rustlers and Indian killers, you got no right to live in Cutthroat County. That's what I'm fighting. That's why I'm running for sheriff. And that's why the truth will come out and I will be elected."

Yet, when I left my motel, and drove down Main Street,

I saw Sheriff John T. Drew getting out his Interceptor in front of the county-town courthouse. I stopped, rolled down the window, and thanked him for all his help.

His eyes were mellow again, and he leaned against the passenger door. "You're welcome back anytime, Miss Schraeder."

"You haven't read my story yet."

His grin widened and his eyes twinkled. "Most likely, I won't. No offense. I just don't like reading about me or Drews or Maddoxes. Got enough of those yarns growing up."

Well, we heard the stories, too, read the novels, some so-called histories, and heard the schoolground rhymes even when I was a child.

> *Pew Pew*
>
> *Marshal Drew*
>
> *Killed a Maddox*
>
> *Times Thirty-two*
>
> *Pew Pew*
>
> *Marshal Drew*

"Drive safe," the sheriff said, tipped his hat, and stepped back. "And watch your speed. Remember what I told you. A person can wait a long time before the judge comes to town."

As I headed out of Basin Creek to return to Billings I made sure I didn't go a hair over thirty-five miles per hour and just to be safe, kept my Camry at sixty-five as I headed out of Cutthroat County, the last frontier in Montana.

But a frontier that is rapidly changing.

CHAPTER 1

After opening the back door, Ashton Maddox stepped inside his ranch home in the foothills of the Always Winter Mountains. His boots echoed hollowly on the hardwood floors as he walked from the garage through the utility room, then the kitchen, and into the living room.

Someone had left the downstairs lights on for him, thank God, because he was exhausted after spending four days in Helena, mingling with a congressman and two lobbyists—even though the legislature wouldn't meet till the first Monday in January—plus lobbyists and business associates, then leaving at the end of business this afternoon and driving to Great Falls for another worthless but costly meeting with a private investigator. After crawling back into his Ford SUV, he'd spent two more hours driving only twelve miles on the interstate, then a little more than a hundred winding, rough, wind-buffeted miles with hardly any headlights or taillights to break up the darkness, which meant having to pay constant attention to avoid colliding with elk, deer, bear, Blackfoot Indian, buffalo, and even an occasional moose.

Somehow, the drive from Basin Creek to the ranch road always seemed the worst stretch of the haul. Because he knew what he would find when he got home.

An empty house.

He was nothing short of complete exhaustion.

But, since he was a Maddox, he found enough stamina to switch on more lights and climb the staircase, *clomp, clomp, clomp* to the second floor, where his right hand found another switch, pushed it up, and let the wagon wheel chandelier and wall sconces bathe the upper story in unnatural radiance.

Still running, the grandfather clock said it was a quarter past midnight.

His father would have scolded him for leaving all those lights on downstairs, wasting electricity—not cheap in this part of Montana. His grandfather would have reminded both of them about how life was before electricity and television and gas-guzzling pickup trucks.

Reaching his office, Ashton flicked on another switch, hung his gray Stetson on the elk horn on the wall, and pulled a heavy Waterford crystal tumbler off the bookshelf before making a beeline toward the closet. He opened the door and stared at the mini–ice maker.

His father and grandfather had also rebuked him for years about building a house on the top of the hill. "This is Montana, boy," Grandpa had scolded time and again. "The wind up that high'll blow you clear down to Coloradie."

Per his nature, Ashton's father had put it bluntly. "Putting on airs, boy. Just putting on airs."

What, Ashton wondered, would Grandpa and Daddy say about having an ice maker in his closet? "Waste of water *and* electricity!"

Not that he cared a fig about what either of those hard rocks might have thought. They were six feet under. Had been for years. But no matter how long he lived, no matter how many millions of dollars he earned, he would always hear their voices.

Grandpa: *The Maddoxes might as well just start birthin' girls.*

Daddy: *If you'd gone through Vietnam like I did, you might know a thing or two.*

Ashton opened the ice maker's lid, scooped up the right number of cubes, and left the closet door open as he walked back to the desk, his boot heels pounding on the hardwood floor. Once he set the tumbler on last week's Sunday *Denver Post*, which he still had never gotten around to reading, he found the bottle of Blanton's Single Barrel, and poured until bourbon and iced reached the rim.

Grandpa would have suffered an apoplexy had he known a Maddox paid close to two hundred bucks, including tax, for seven hundred and fifty milliliters of Kentucky bourbon. Both his grandpa and father would have given him grief about drinking bourbon anyway. As far back as anyone could recollect, Maddox men had been rye drinkers.

The cheaper the better.

"If it burns," his father had often said, "I yearns."

Ashton sipped. *Good whiskey is worth every penny*, he thought.

Glass still in his hand, he crossed the room till he reached the large window. The heavy drapes had already been pulled open—not that he could remember, but he probably had left them that way before driving down to the state capital.

They used to have a cleaning lady who would have closed them. One of the hired men's wife, sweetheart, concubine, whatever. But that man had gotten a job in Wyoming, and she had followed him. And with Patricia gone, Ashton didn't see any need to have floors swept and furniture dusted.

He debated closing the drapes, but what was the point?

He could step outside on the balcony. Get some fresh air. Close his eyes and just feel the coolness, the sereneness of a summer night in Montana. Years ago, he had loved that— even when the wind come a-sweepin' 'cross the high plains. Grandpa had not been fooling about that wind, but Ashton Maddox knew what he was doing and what the weather was like when he told the man at M.R. Russell Construction Company exactly what he wanted and exactly where he wanted his house.

Well, rather, where Patricia had wanted it.

Wherever she was now.

He stood there, sipping good bourbon and feeling rotten, making himself look into the night that never was night. Not like it used to be.

"You can see forever," Patricia had told him on their first night, before Russell's subcontractor had even gotten the electricity installed.

He could still see forever. *Forever*. Hades stretching on from here north to the Pole and east toward the Dakotas, forever and ever and ever, amen.

The door opened. Boots sounded heavy on the floor, coming close, then a grunt, the hitching of jeans, and the sound of a hat dropping on Ashton's desk. "How was Helena?" foreman Colter Norris asked in his gruff monotone.

"Waste of time." Ashton did not turn around. He lifted his tumbler and sipped more bourbon.

"You read that gal's hatchet job in that rag folks call the *Big Sky Monthly*?"

"Skimmed it. Heard some coffee rats talking about it at the Stirrup."

"Well, that gal sure made a hero out of our sheriff."

Ashton saw Colter's reflection in the plate glass window.

"And made Garland Foster sound like some homespun hick hero, cacklin' out flapdoodle about cattle and sheep prices and how wind's gonna save us all." Holding a longneck beer in his left hand, Colter lifted his dark beer bottle and took a long pull.

Ashton started to raise his tumbler, but lowered it, shook his head, and whispered, "'While beef and wool prices fluctuate, the wind always blows in this country.'"

The bottle Colter held lowered rapidly. "What's that?"

"Nothing." Ashton took a good pull of bourbon, let some ice fall into his mouth, and crunched it, grinding it down, down, down.

The foreman frowned. "Thought you said you just skimmed that gal's exposé." Colter never missed a thing—a sign, a clear shot with a .30-.30, a trout's strike, or a half-baked sentence someone mumbled.

Raising the tumbler again, Ashton held the Waterford toward the window. "He didn't put up those wind turbines," he said caustically, "because of any market concerns." He shook his head, and cursed his neighboring rancher softly. "He put those up to torment me. All day. All night."

A man couldn't see the spinning blades at that time of night. But no one could escape the flashing red warning lights. Blinking on. Blinking off. On and off. Red light. No light. Red light. No light. Red light. Red . . . red . . . red . . . red . . . all night long. All night long till dawn finally broke. There had to be more wind turbines on Foster's land than that skinflint had ever run cattle or sheep.

Ashton turned away and stared across the room. Colter held the longneck, his face showing a few days growth of white and black stubble and that bushy mustache with the ends twisted into a thin curl. The face, like his neck and wrists and the forearms as far as he could roll up the sleeves of his work shirts, were bronzed from wind and sun and scarred from horse wrecks and bar fights. The nose had been busted so many times, Ashton often wondered how his foreman even managed to breathe.

"You didn't come up here to get some gossip about a college girl's story in some slick magazine," Ashton told him. "Certainly not after I've spent three hours driving in a night as dark as pitch from Helena to here by way of Great Falls."

"No, sir." The man set his beer next to the bottle of fine bourbon.

"Couldn't wait till breakfast, I take it." Ashton started to bring the crystal tumbler up again, but saw it contained nothing but melting ice and his own saliva. "I figured not."

Few people could read Colter's face. Ashton had given up years ago. But he didn't have to read the cowboy's face. The voice told him everything he needed to know.

Colter wasn't here because some hired hand had wrecked a truck or ruined a good horse and had been paid off, then kicked off the ranch. Colter wasn't here because someone got his innards gored by a steer's horn or kicked to pieces by a bull or widow-making horse.

Frowning, Ashton set the glass on a side table, walked to the window, found the pull, and closed the drapes. At least he couldn't see those flashing red lights on wind turbines any longer.

Walking back, his cold blue eyes met Colter's hard greens. "Let's have it," Ashton said.

The foreman obeyed. "We're short."

Ashton's head cocked just a fraction. No punch line came. But he had not expected one. Most cowboys Ashton knew had wickedly acerbic senses of humor—or thought they did—but Colter had never cracked a joke. Hardly even let a smile crack the grizzled façade of his face. Still, the rancher could not believe what he had heard.

"We're . . . *short*?"

Colter's rugged head barely moved up and down once.

Ashton reached down, pulled the fancy cork out of the bottle, and splashed two fingers of amber beauty into the tumbler. He didn't care about ice. He drank half of it down and looked again at his foreman.

No question was needed.

"Sixteen head. Section Fifty-four at Dead Indian Pony Crick." His pronunciation of *creek* was same as many Westerners.

Ashton took his glass and rising anger to the modern map hanging on the north-facing wall, underneath the bearskin. Colter left his empty longneck on the desk and followed, but the foreman knew better than to point.

Ashton knew his ranch, leased and owned, better than anyone living. He found section fifty-four quickly, pointed a finger wet from the tumbler, and then began circling around, slowly, reading the topography and the roads. "You see any truck tracks?"

"No, sir. Even hard-pressed, a body'd never get a truck into that country 'cept on our roads. What passes for roads, I mean. Our boys don't even take ATVs into that section. Shucks, we're even careful about what horses we ride when working up there."

Ashton nodded in agreement. "Steers? Bull or . . . ?"

"Heifers."

"Who discovered they were missing?"

"Dante Crump."

Ashton's head bobbed again. Crump had been working for the Circle M for seven years. He was the only cowboy Ashton had ever known who went to church regularly on Sundays. Most of the others were sleeping off hangovers till Mondays. A rancher might question the honesty of many cowboys, but no one ever accused Dante Crump of anything except having a conscience and a soul.

Ashton kept studying the map. He even forgot he was holding a glass of expensive bourbon.

Colter cleared his throat. "No bear tracks. No carcasses. The cattle just vanished."

"Horse tracks?" Ashton turned away from the big wall map.

The cowboy's head shook. "Some. But Dante had rode 'cross that country—me and Homer Cooper, too—before we even considered them cattle got stoled. So we couldn't tell if the tracks were ours or their'uns."

"Do we have any more cattle up that way?" Ashton asked.

"Not now. We'd left fifty in the section in September. Dante went there to take them to the higher summer pasture. Found bones and carcasses of three. About normal, but he took only thirty-one up. So best I can figure is that sixteen got rustled."

"Rustled." Ashton chuckled without mirth. The word sounded like something straight out of an old Western movie or TV show.

"Yeah," the foreman said. "I don't never recollect your daddy sayin' nothin' 'bout rustlers."

"Because it never happened." Ashton let out another mirthless chuckle. "I don't even think my grandpa had to cope with rustlers, unless some starving Blackfoot cut out a calf or half-starved steer for his family. Grandpa had his faults, but he wasn't one to begrudge any man with a hungry wife and kids." He sighed, shook his head, and stared at Colter. "You're sure those heifers aren't just hiding in that rough country?"

The man's eyes glared. "I said so" was all he said.

That was good enough for Ashton, just as it had been good enough for his father.

"Could they have just wandered to another pasture?"

"Homer Cooper rode the lines," the foreman said. "He said no fence was down. Sure ain't goin' 'cross no cattle guards, and the gates was all shut and locked."

They studied each other, thinking the same thought. An inside job. A Circle M cowboy taking a few Black Angus for himself. But even that made no sense. No one could sneak sixteen head all the way from that pasture to the main road without being seen or leaving sign.

"How?" Ashton shook his head again. "How in heaven's name . . . ?"

Colter shrugged. "Those hippies livin' 'cross the highway on Bonner Flats will say it was extraterrestrials." Said without a smile, it probably wasn't a joke.

In fact, Ashton had to agree with the weathered cowboy.

The *Basin River Weekly Item* had reported cattle turning up missing at smaller ranches in the county, but Ashton had figured those animals had probably just wandered off. The ranchers weren't really ranchers. Just folks wealthy enough to buy land and lease a pasture from the feds for grazing and have themselves a quiet place to come to and get a good tax break on top of it. Like that TV director or producer or company executive who ran buffalo on his place and had his own private helicopter. There were only two real ranchers left in Cutthroat County, though Ashton would never publicly admit that Garland Foster was a real rancher. He'd been mostly a sheepman since arriving in Cutthroat County, and he was hardly even that anymore.

Ashton looked at the curtains that kept him from seeing those flashing red lights all across Foster's spread. "How did someone manage to get sixteen Black Angus of our herd out of there? Without a truck or trucks. Without being seen? That's what perplexes me." He moved back to the map, reached his left hand up to the crooked line marked in blue *type*—*Dead Indian Pony Creek*—and traced it down to the nearest two-track, then followed that to the ranch road, then down the eleven miles to the main highway.

Colter moved closer to the map. Those hard eyes narrowed as he memorized the topography, the roads, paths, streams, canyons, everything. Then he seemed to dismiss the map and remember the country from personal experience, riding a half-broke cowpony in that rough, hard, impenetrable country in the spring, the summer, the fall. Probably not the winter, though. Not in northern Montana. Not unless a man was desperate or suicidal.

His head shook after thirty seconds. "I can take some boys up, see if we can find a trail."

Ashton shook his head. He had forgotten about a wife who had left him, had dismissed a fruitless trip to the state capital, and then an even more unproductive meeting in a Great Falls coffee shop with a high-priced private dick. "No point in that," he said. "They stole sixteen head of prime Black Angus because we were sleeping. Anyone who has lived in Montana for a month knows you might catch Ashton Maddox asleep once, and only once. I'll never make that mistake again. They won't be back there. Any missing head elsewhere?"

"Nothin' yet," Colter replied. "But I ain't got all the tallies yet."

Ashton remembered the bourbon and raised the tumbler as he gave his foreman that look that needed no interpretation. "I want those tallies done right quick. There's one thing in my book that sure hasn't changed since the eighteen hundreds. *Nobody* steals Circle M beef and gets away with it."

Visit our website at
KensingtonBooks.com
to sign up for our newsletters, read
more from your favorite authors, see
books by series, view reading group
guides, and more!

BOOK **CLUB**
BETWEEN THE CHAPTERS

Become a Part of Our
Between the Chapters Book Club
Community and Join the Conversation

Betweenthechapters.net